Murder
Most
Foul

Murder
Most
Foul

Octopus Books

First published 1984 by

Octopus Books Limited
59 Grosvenor Street
London W1

Copyright © 1984 selection, illustration and arrangement
Octopus Books Limited

Illustration by Angela Barrett

ISBN 0 7064 2051 9

Printed in Czechoslovakia

50 557

Contents

The Fruit at the Bottom of the Bowl

RAY BRADBURY

WILLIAM ACTON ROSE to his feet. The clock on the mantel ticked midnight.

He looked at his fingers and he looked at the large room around him and he looked at the man lying on the floor who was dead and would say no more sayings nor brutalize more brutalities. William Acton, whose fingers had stroked typewriter keys and made love and fried ham and eggs for early breakfasts, had now accomplished a murder with those same ten, whorled fingers.

He had never thought of himself as a sculptor and yet, in this moment, looking down between his hands at the body upon the polished hardwood floor he realized that by some sculptural, clenching and remodelling and twisting of human clay he had taken hold of this man named Arthur Huxley and changed his physiognomy, the very frame of his body.

With a twist of his fingers he had wiped away the exacting glitter of Huxley's grey eyes; replaced it with an airless dullness of eye cold in socket. The lips, always pink and sensuous, were gaped to show the equine teeth, the yellow incisors, the nicotined canines, the gold-inlayed molars. The nose, pink also, was now mottled, pale, discoloured, as were the ears. Huxley's hands, upon the floor, were open, pleading for the first time in their lives instead of demanding.

Yes, it was an artistic conception. On the whole, the change had done Huxley a share of good. Death made him a handsomer man to deal with. You could talk to him now and he'd have to listen.

William Acton looked at his own fingers.

It was done. He could not change it back. Had anybody heard? He listened. The normal late sounds of street traffic outside continued. There was no banging of the house door, no shoulders wrecking the portal into kindling, no voices demanding entrance. The murder, the sculpturing of clay from warmth into cold was done, and nobody knew.

Now what? The clock ticked midnight. His every impulse exploded him in a hysteria toward the door. Get out, get away, run, never come back, board a train, get a taxi, get, go, run, walk, saunter, but get the

9

blazes *out* of here!

His hands hovered before his eyes, floating, turning.

He turned them in slow deliberation; they felt airy and featherlight. Why was he staring at them this way, he inquired of himself. Was there something in them of immense interest that he should pause now, after a successful throttling, and examine them micrometer by micrometer?

They were ordinary hands. Not thick, not thin, not long, not short, not hairy, not naked, not manicured and yet not dirty, not soft and yet not calloused, not wrinkled and yet not smooth; not murdering hands at all – and yet not innocent. He found them miracles to look upon.

It was not the hands as hands he was interested in, nor the fingers as fingers. In the numb timelessness after an accomplished violence he found interest only in the *tips* of his fingers.

The clock ticked on the mantel.

He knelt by Huxley's body, took a handkerchief from Huxley's pocket and began methodically to swab Huxley's throat with it. He brushed and massaged the throat, and wiped the face and the back of the neck with a fierce energy. Then he stood up.

He looked at the throat. He looked at the polished floor. He bent slowly and gave the floor a few dabs with the handkerchief, then he scowled and swabbed the floor; first, near the head of the corpse, secondly, near the arms. Then he polished the floor all around the body. He polished the floor one yard from the body on all sides. Then he polished the floor *two* yards from the body on all sides. Then he polished the floor *three* yards from the body in all directions. Then he——

He stopped . . .

There was a moment when he saw the entire house, the halls, the doors, the furniture; and as clearly as if it were being repeated word for word he heard Huxley talking and himself talking just the way they had talked only an hour ago.

Finger on the doorbell. Door opening.

'Oh. It's *you*, Acton.'

'I want to see you, Huxley. It's important.'

'I don't see – Well, all right. Come in.'

He had gone in.

'Go on into the library,' said Huxley.

He had *touched* the library door.

'Drink?'

'I need one.'

'There's a bottle there of burgundy, Acton. Mind getting it, I'm terribly tired.'

Surely. Get it. *Handle* it. *Touch* it. He did.

'Some interesting first editions there, Acton. Look at the binding. *Look* at it.'

He had *touched* the books and the library table and *touched* the burgundy glasses.

Now, squatting on the floor beside Huxley's cold body with the polishing handkerchief in his fingers, motionless, he stared at the house, the walls, the furniture about him, his eyes widening, his mouth dropping, stunned by what he realized and what he saw. He shut his eyes, dropped his head, crushed the handkerchief between his hands, wadding it, biting his lips with his teeth, pulling it on himself.

The fingerprints were everywhere, *everywhere!*

'Mind getting the burgundy, Acton, eh? The burgundy bottle, eh? With your fingers, eh? I'm terribly tired. You understand?'

A pair of gloves.

Before he did one more thing, before he polished another area, he must have a pair of gloves, or he might unintentionally, after cleaning a surface, redistribute his identity.

He put his hands in his pockets. He walked through the house to the hall umbrella stand, the hat-rack. Huxley's overcoat. He pulled out the overcoat pockets.

No gloves.

His hands in his pockets again, he walked upstairs, moving with a controlled swiftness, allowing himself nothing frantic, nothing wild. He had made the initial error of not wearing gloves (but, after all, he hadn't *planned* a murder, and his subconscious, which may have known of the crime before its commitment, had not even hinted he might need gloves before the night was finished), so now he had to sweat for his sin of omission. Somewhere in the house there must be at least one pair of gloves. He would have to hurry; there was every chance that someone might visit Huxley, even at this hour. Rich friends drinking themselves in and out the door, laughing, shouting, coming and going without so much as hello-good-bye. He would have until six in the morning, at the outside, when Huxley's friends were to pick Huxley up for the trip to the airport and Mexico City. . . .

Acton hurried about upstairs opening drawers, using the handkerchief as blotter. He untidied seventy or eighty drawers in six rooms, left them with their tongues, so to speak, hanging out, ran on to new ones. He felt naked, unable to do anything until he found gloves. He might scour the entire house with the handkerchief, buffing every possible surface where fingerprints might lie, then accidentally bump a wall here or there, thus sealing his own fate with one microscopic, whorling symbol! It would be putting his stamp of approval on the murder, that's what it would be! Like those waxen seals in the old days when they rattled papyrus, flourished ink, dusted all with sand

11

to dry the ink, and pressed their signet rings in hot crimson tallow at the bottom. So it would be if he left one, mind you, *one* fingerprint upon the scene! His approval of the murder did not extend as far as affixing said seal.

More drawers! Be quiet, be curious, be careful, he told himself.

At the bottom of the eighty-fifth drawer he found gloves.

'Oh, my Lord, my Lord!' He slumped against the bureau, sighing. He tried the gloves on, held them up, proudly flexed them, buttoned them. They were soft, grey, thick, impregnable. He could do all sorts of tricks with hands now and leave no trace. He thumbed his nose in the bedroom mirror, sucking his teeth.

'NO!' cried Huxley.

What a wicked plan it had been.

Huxley had fallen to the floor, *purposely!* Oh, what a wickedly clever man! Down onto the hardwood floor had dropped Huxley, with Acton after him. They had rolled and tussled and clawed at the floor, printing and printing it with their frantic fingertips! Huxley had slipped away a few feet, Acton crawling after to lay hands on his neck and squeeze until the life came out like paste from a tube!

Gloved, William Acton returned to the room and knelt down upon the floor and laboriously began the task of swabbing every wildly infested inch of it. Inch by inch, inch by inch, he polished and polished until he could almost see his intent, sweating face in it. Then he came to a table and polished the leg of it, on up its solid body and along the knobs and over the top. He came to a bowl of wax fruit, burnished the filigree silver, plucked out the wax fruit and wiped them clean, leaving the fruit at the bottom unpolished.

'I'm *sure* I didn't touch *them*,' he said.

After rubbing the table he came to a picture frame hung over it.

'I'm certain I didn't touch *that*,' he said.

He stood looking at it.

He glanced at all the doors in the room. Which doors had he used tonight? He couldn't remember. Polish all of them, then. He started on the doorknobs, shined them all up, and then he curried the doors from head to foot, taking no chances. Then he went to all the furniture in the room and wiped the chair arms and rubbed the material fabric itself.

'That chair you're sitting in, Acton, is an old Louis XIV piece. Feel that material,' said Huxley.

'I didn't come here to talk furniture, Huxley! I came about Lily.'

'Lily, eh? Oh, come off it, you're not that serious about her. She doesn't love you, you know. She's told me she'll go with me to Mexico City next month.'

'You and your money and your damned furniture!'

'It's nice furniture, Acton; be a good guest and feel of it.'

Fingerprints can be found on fabric.

'Huxley!' William Acton stared at the body. 'Did you *know* I was going to kill you! Did your subconscious know, just as my subconscious knew? And did your subconscious have you make me go about the house handling, touching, *fondling* books, dishes, doors, chairs? Were you *that* clever and *that* mean?'

He washed the chairs drily with the clenched kerchief. Then he remembered the body – he hadn't dry-washed *it*. He went to it and turned it now this way, now that, and burnished every surface of it. He even shined the shoes.

While shining the shoes his face took on a little tremor of worry and after a moment he got up and walked over to that table.

He took out and polished the wax fruit at the *bottom* of the bowl.

'Better,' he whispered, and went back to the body.

But as he crouched over the body his eyelids twitched and his jaw moved from side to side and he debated, then he got up and turned and walked once more to the table.

He polished the picture frame.

While polishing the picture frame he discovered——

The wall.

'That,' he said, 'is silly.'

'Oh!' Huxley had cried, fending him off. He had given Acton a shove as they struggled. Acton had fallen against one wall, had got up, *touching* the wall, and had run toward Huxley again. He had strangled Huxley. Huxley had died. . . .

Acton turned steadfastly from the wall, with equilibrium and decision. The harsh words and the action faded in his mind. He glanced at the four walls.

'Ridiculous,' he said.

From the corners of his eyes he saw something on one wall.

'I refuse to pay attention,' he said to distract himself. 'The next room, now. I'll be methodical. Let's see, altogether we were in the hall, the library, *this* room, and the dining room and the kitchen.'

There was a spot on the wall behind him.

Well, *wasn't* there?

Oh, a *little* one, yes, right – *there*. He dabbed it. It wasn't a fingerprint anyhow. He finished with it and his gloved hand leaned against the wall and he looked at the wall and the way it went over to his right and over to his left and how it went down to his feet and up over his head and he said softly, 'No.' He looked up and down and over and across and he said, quietly, 'That would be too much.' How many square feet? 'I don't give a damn,' he said. But unknown to his eyes his gloved fingers moved in a little rubbing rhythm on the wall.

He peered at his hand and the wallpaper. He looked over his shoulder at the other room. 'I must go in there and polish the essentials,' he told himself, but his hand remained, as if to hold the wall, or himself, up. His face hardened.

Without a word he began to scrub the wall, up and down, back and forth, up and down, as high as he could stretch and as low as he could bend.

Once he stopped and put his hands on his hips.

'Ridiculous, oh my Lord. Ridiculous.'

But you must be certain, his thought said to him.

'Yes, one must be certain,' he replied. 'One *must* be certain.'

And again he rubbed and polished.

He got one wall finished, and then . . .

He came to another wall.

'What time *is* it?' he wondered, drily.

He looked at the mantel clock. An hour gone. It was five after one.

He looked at this new fresh wall. 'Silly,' he said. 'It's flawless. I won't touch it.' He turned away.

From the corners of his eyes he saw the little webs. When his back was turned the little spiders came out of the woodwork and delicately spun their fragile little half-invisible webs. Not upon the wall at his left – that was already washed fresh; but upon the three walls as yet untouched. Each time he stared directly at them the spiders popped back into the woodwork only to spindle out as he retreated. 'Those walls are all right,' he insisted, in a half-shout. 'I won't touch them!'

He went to a writing desk at which Huxley had been seated earlier. He opened a drawer and took out what he was looking for. A little magnifying glass Huxley sometimes used for reading. He took the magnifier and approached the wall uneasily.

Fingerprints.

'But those aren't *mine*!' He laughed, unsteadily. 'I *didn't* put them there! I'm *sure* I didn't! A servant, a butler, or a maid, perhaps.'

The wall was full of them.

'Look at this one here,' he said. 'Long and tapered, like a woman's – I'd bet money on it.'

'Would you?'

'I would!'

'Are you certain?'

'Yes!'

'Positive?'

'Well – yes.'

'Absolutely?'

'Yes, damn it, yes!'

14

'Wipe it out, anyway.'

'There, by gad!'

'Out damned spot, eh, Acton?'

'And this one, over here,' scoffed Acton. 'That's the print of a fat man.'

'Are you sure?'

'Don't start that again!' he snapped, and rubbed it out. He pulled off a glove and held his hand up in the glary light.

'Look at it, you idiot! See how the whorls go? See!'

'That proves nothing!'

'Oh, all right!' In rage he began to sweep the wall up and down and back and forth with his gloved hands, sweating, grunting and swearing, bending and rising.

He took off his coat, put it on a chair.

'Two o'clock,' he said, finishing the wall and looking at the clock.

He walked over to the bowl and took out the waxed fruit and polished the ones at the bottom and put them back and polished the picture frame.

He looked up at the chandelier.

His fingers twitched at his sides. His mouth slipped open and the tongue moved along his lips and he looked at the chandelier and looked away and looked back at the chandelier, and looked at Huxley's body and then at the crystal chandelier with its long pearls of rainbow glass.

He got a chair and brought it over under the chandelier and put one foot up on it and took it down and threw the chair violently into a corner. Then he ran out of the room, leaving one wall as yet unwashed.

In the dining room he came to a table.

'I want to show you my Georgian cutlery, Acton,' Huxley had said.

'I haven't time,' Acton said.

'Nonsense, look at this silver, this exquisite craftsmanship, look at it.'

Acton paused over the table where the boxes of cutlery were laid out, hearing once more Huxley's voice, remembering all the touchings and gesturings.

Now Acton wiped the forks and spoons and took down all the plates and special ceramic dishes from the wall shelf. . . .

'Here's a lovely bit of ceramics by Gertrude and Otto Natzler, Acton, are you familiar with their work?'

'It *is* lovely.'

'Pick it up. Turn it over. See the fine thinness of the bowl, handthrown on a turntable, thin as eggshell, incredible. And the amazing volcanic glaze? Handle it, go ahead, I don't mind.'

Handle it. Go ahead. Pick it up!

15

Acton sobbed unevenly. He hurled the pottery against the wall. It shattered and spread, flaking wildly, upon the floor.

An instant later he was on his knees. Every piece, every shard of it, must be regained. Fool, fool, fool, he cried to himself, shaking his head and shutting and opening his eyes and bending under the table. Find every piece, you idiot – not one fragment of it must be left behind. Fool, fool. He gathered them. Are they all here? He looked at them on the table before him. He looked under the table again and under the chairs and the service bureaus and found one more piece by match-light and started to polish each little fragment as if it were a precious stone. He laid them all out neatly upon the shining polished table.

'A lovely bit of ceramics, Acton; go ahead – *handle* it.'

He took out the linen and wiped it, and wiped the chairs and tables and doorknobs and window panes and ledges and drapes, and wiped the floor and found the kitchen, panting, breathing violently, and took off his vest and adjusted his gloves and wiped the glittering chromium. . . . 'I want to show you my house, Acton,' said Huxley. 'Come along. . . .' And he wiped all the utensils and the silver faucets and the mixing bowls, for now he had forgotten what he had touched and what he had not. Huxley and he had lingered here, in the kitchen, Huxley prideful of its array to cover his nervousness at the presence of a potential killer, perhaps wanting to be near the knives if they were needed. They had idled, touched this, that, something else – there was no remembering what or how much or how many – and he finished the kitchen and came through the hall into the room where Huxley lay.

He cried out.

He had forgotten to wash the fourth wall of the room. And while he was gone the little spiders had come out of the fourth unwashed wall and swarmed over the already clean walls, dirtying them again! On the ceiling, from the chandelier, in the corners, on the floor a million little whorled webs hung billowing at his scream! Tiny, tiny little webs, no bigger than, ironically, your – finger!

As he watched the webs were woven over the picture frame, the fruit bowl, the body, the floor. Prints wielded the paper knife, pulled out drawers, touched the table-top, touched, touched, touched everything everywhere.

He polished the floor wildly, wildly. He rolled the body over and cried on it while he washed it and got up and walked over and polished the fruit at the bottom of the bowl. Then he put a chair under the chandelier and got up and polished each little hanging fire of it, shaking it like a crystal tambourine until it tilted bellwise in the air. Then he leaped off the chair and gripped the doorknobs and got up on other chairs and swabbed the walls higher and higher and ran to the kitchen and got a broom and wiped the webs down from the ceiling and polished the bottom fruit of the bowl and washed the body and doorknobs and silverware and found the hall banister and followed the banister upstairs.

Three o'clock! Everywhere, with a fierce, mechanical intensity, clocks ticked! There were twelve rooms downstairs and eight above. He figured the yards and yards of space and time needed. One hundred chairs, six sofas, twenty-seven tables, six radios. And under and on top and behind. He yanked furniture out away from walls and, sobbing, wiped them clean of years-old dust, and staggered and followed the banister up the stairs, handling, erasing, rubbing, polishing, because if he left one little print it would reproduce and make a million more! and the job would have to be done all over again and now it was 4 o'clock! and his arms ached and his eyes were swollen and staring and he moved sluggishly about, on strange legs, his head down, his arms moving, swabbing and rubbing, bedroom by bedroom, closet by closet. . . .

They found him at 6.30 that morning.

In the attic.

The entire house was polished to a brilliance. Vases shone like glass stars. Chairs were burnished. Bronzes, brasses, and coppers were all aglint. Floors sparkled. Banisters gleamed.

Everything glittered. Everything shone, everything was bright!

They found him in the attic, polishing the old trunks and the old frames and the old chairs and the old carriages and toys and music boxes and vases and cutlery and rocking horses and dusty Civil War coins. He was half through the attic when the police officer walked up behind him with a gun.

On the way out of the house Acton polished the front doorknob with his handkerchief, and slammed it in triumph.

17

Murder!

ARNOLD BENNETT

I

MANY GREAT ONES OF the earth have justified murder as a social act, defensible, and even laudable in certain instances. There is something to be said for murder, though perhaps not much. All of us, or nearly all of us, have at one time or another had the desire and the impulse to commit murder. At any rate, murder is not an uncommon affair. On an average, two people are murdered every week in England, and probably about two hundred every week in the United States. And forty per cent of the murderers are not brought to justice. These figures take no account of the undoubtedly numerous cases where murder has been done but never suspected. Murderers and murderesses walk safely abroad among us, and it may happen to us to shake hands with them. A disturbing thought! But such is life, and such is homicide.

II

Two men, named respectively Lomax Harder and John Franting, were walking side by side one autumn afternoon, on the Marine Parade of the seaside resort and port of Quangate (English Channel). Both were well-dressed and had the air of moderate wealth, and both were about thirty-five years of age. At this point the resemblances between them ceased. Lomax Harder had refined features, an enormous forehead, fair hair, and a delicate, almost apologetic manner. John Franting was low-browed, heavy chinned, scowling, defiant, indeed what is called a tough customer. Lomax Harder corresponded in appearance with the popular notion of a poet – save that he was carefully barbered. He was in fact a poet, and not unknown in the tiny, trifling, mad world where poetry is a matter of first-rate interest. John Franting corresponded in appearance with the popular notion of a gambler, an amateur boxer, and, in spare time, a deluder of women. Popular notions sometimes fit the truth.

Lomax Harder, somewhat nervously buttoning his overcoat, said in a quiet but firm and insistent tone:

18

'Haven't you got anything to say?'

John Franting stopped suddenly in front of a shop whose façade bore the sign: 'Gontle. Gunsmith.'

'Not in words,' answered Franting. 'I'm going in here.'

And he brusquely entered the small, shabby shop.

Lomax Harder hesitated half a second, and then followed his companion.

The shopman was a middle-aged gentleman wearing a black velvet coat.

'Good afternoon,' he greeted Franting, with an expression and in a tone of urbane condescension which seemed to indicate that Franting was a wise as well as a fortunate man in that he knew of the excellence of Gontle's and had the wit to come into Gontle's.

For the name of Gontle was favourably and respectfully known wherever triggers are pressed. Not only along the whole length of the Channel coast, but throughout England, was Gontle's renowned. Sportsmen would travel to Quangate from the far north, and even from London, to buy guns. To say: 'I bought it at Gontle's,' or 'Old Gontle recommended it,' was sufficient to silence any dispute concerning the merits of a fire-arm. Experts bowed the head before the unique reputation of Gontle. As for old Gontle, he was extremely and pardonably conceited. His conviction that no other gunsmith in the wide world could compare with him was absolute. He sold guns and rifles with the gesture of a monarch conferring an honour. He never argued; he stated; and the customer who contradicted him was as likely as not to be courteously and icily informed by Gontle of the geographical situation of the shop-door. Such shops exist in the English provinces, and nobody knows how they have achieved their renown. They could exist nowhere else.

' 'd afternoon,' said Franting gruffly, and paused.

'What can I do for you?' asked Mr Gontle, as if saying: 'Now don't be afraid. This shop is tremendous, and I am tremendous; but I shall not eat you.'

'I want a revolver,' Franting snapped.

'Ah! A revolver!' commented Mr Gontle, as if saying: 'A gun or a rifle, yes! But a revolver – an arm without individuality, manufactured wholesale! . . . However, I suppose I must deign to accommodate you.'

'I presume you know something about revolvers?' asked Mr Gontle, as he began to produce the weapons.

'A little.'

'Do you know the Webley Mark III?'

'Can't say that I do.'

'Ah! It is the best for all common purposes.' And Mr Gontle's

19

glance said: 'Have the goodness not to tell me it isn't.'

Franting examined the Webley Mark III.

'You see,' said Mr Gontle. 'The point about it is that until the breach is properly closed it cannot be fired. So that it can't blow open and maim or kill the would-be murderer.' Mr Gontle smiled archly at one of his oldest jokes.

'What about suicides?' Franting grimly demanded.

'Ah!'

'You might show me just how to load it,' said Franting.

Mr Gontle, having found ammunition, complied with this reasonable request.

'The barrel's a bit scratched,' said Franting.

Mr Gontle inspected the scratch with pain. He would have denied the scratch, but could not.

'Here's another one,' said he, 'since you're so particular.' He simply had to put customers in their place.

'You might load it,' said Franting.

Mr Gontle loaded the second revolver.

'I'd like to try it,' said Franting.

'Certainly,' said Mr Gontle, and led Franting out of the shop by the back, and down to a cellar where revolvers could be experimented with.

Lomax Harder was now alone in the shop. He hesitated a long time and then picked up the revolver rejected by Franting, fingered it, put it down, and picked it up again. The back-door of the shop opened suddenly, and, startled, Harder dropped the revolver into his overcoat pocket: a thoughtless, quite unpremeditated act. He dared not remove the revolver. The revolver was as fast in his pocket as though the pocket had been sewn up.

'And cartridges?' asked Mr Gontle of Franting.

'Oh,' said Franting, 'I've only had one shot. Five'll be more than enough for the present. What does it weigh?'

'Let me see. Four inch barrel? Yes. One pound four ounces.'

Franting paid for the revolver, receiving thirteen shillings in change from a five-pound note, and strode out of the shop, weapon in hand. He was gone before Lomax Harder decided upon a course of action.

'And for you, sir?' said Mr Gontle, addressing the poet.

Harder suddenly comprehended that Mr Gontle had mistaken him for a separate customer, who had happened to enter the shop a moment after the first one. Harder and Franting had said not a word to one another during the purchase, and Harder well knew that in the most exclusive shops it is the custom utterly to ignore a second customer until the first one has been dealt with.

'I want to see some foils.' Harder spoke stammeringly the only words that came into his head.

'Foils!' exclaimed Mr Gontle, shocked, as if to say: 'Is it conceivable that you should imagine that I, Gontle, gunsmith, sell such things as foils?'

After a little talk Harder apologized and departed – a thief.

'I'll call later and pay the fellow,' said Harder to his restive conscience. 'No. I can't do that. I'll send him some anonymous postal orders.'

He crossed the Parade and saw Franting, a small left-handed figure all alone far below on the deserted sands, pointing the revolver. He thought that his ear caught the sound of a discharge, but the distance was too great for him to be sure. He continued to watch, and at length Franting walked westward diagonally across the beach.

'He's going back to Bellevue,' thought Harder, the Bellevue being the hotel from which he had met Franting coming out half an hour earlier. He strolled slowly towards the white hotel. But Franting, who had evidently come up the face of the cliff in the penny lift, was before him. Harder, standing outside, saw Franting seated in the lounge. Then Franting rose and vanished down a long passage at the rear of the lounge. Harder entered the hotel rather guiltily. There was no hall-porter at the door, and not a soul in the lounge or in sight of the lounge. Harder went down the long passage.

III

At the end of the passage Lomax Harder found himself in a billiard-room – an apartment built partly of brick and partly of wood on a sort of courtyard behind the main structure of the hotel. The roof, of iron and grimy glass, rose to a point in the middle. On two sides the high walls of the hotel obscured the light. Dusk was already closing in. A small fire burned feebly in the grate. A large radiator under the window was steel-cold, for though summer was finished, winter had not officially begun in the small economically-run hotel: so that the room was chilly; nevertheless, in deference to the English passion for fresh air and discomfort, the window was wide open.

Franting, in his overcoat, and an unlit cigarette between his lips, stood lowering with his back to the bit of fire. At sight of Harder he lifted his chin in a dangerous challenge.

'So you're still following me about,' he said resentfully to Harder.

'Yes,' said the latter, with his curious gentle primness of manner. 'I came down here specially to talk to you. I should have said all I had to say earlier, only you happened to be going out of the hotel just as I was coming in. You didn't seem to want to talk in the street; but there's some talking has to be done. I've a few things I must tell you.'

Harder appeared to be perfectly calm, and he felt perfectly calm. He advanced from the door towards the billiard-table.

Franting raised his hand, displaying his square-ended, brutal fingers in the twilight.

'Now listen to me,' he said with cold, measured ferocity. 'You can't tell me anything I don't know. If there's some talking to be done I'll do it myself, and when I've finished you can get out. I know that my wife has taken a ticket for Copenhagen by the steamer from Harwich, and that she's been seeing to her passport, and packing. And of course I know that you have interests in Copenhagen and spend about half your precious time there. I'm not worrying to connect the two things. All that's got nothing to do with me. Emily has always seen a great deal of you, and I know that the last week or two she's been seeing you more than ever. Not that I mind that. I know that she objects to my treatment of her and my conduct generally. That's all right, but it's a matter that only concerns her and me. I mean that it's no concern of yours, for instance, or anybody else's. If she objects enough she can try and divorce me. I doubt if she'd succeed, but you can never be sure – with these new laws. Anyhow she's my wife till she does divorce me, and so she has the usual duties and responsibilities towards me – even though I was the worst husband in the world. That's how I look at it, in my old-fashioned way. I've just had a letter from her – she knew I was here, and I expect that explains how you knew I was here.'

'It does,' said Lomax Harder quietly.

Franting pulled a letter out of his inner pocket and unfolded it.

'Yes,' he said, glancing at it, and read some sentences aloud: ' "I have absolutely decided to leave you, and I won't hide from you that I know you know who is doing what he can to help me. I can't live with you any longer. You may be very fond of me, as you say, but I find your way of showing your fondness too humiliating and painful. I've said this to you before, and now I'm saying it for the last time." And so on and so on.'

Franting tore the letter in two, dropped one half on the floor, twisted the other half into a spill, turned to the fire, and lit his cigarette.

'That's what I think of her letter,' he proceeded, the cigarette between his teeth. 'You're helping her, are you? Very well. I don't say you're in love with her, or she with you. I'll make no wild statements. But if you aren't in love with her I wonder why you're taking all this trouble over her. Do you go about the world helping ladies who say they're unhappy just for the pure sake of helping? Never mind. Emily isn't going to leave me. Get that into your head. I shan't let her leave me. She has money, and I haven't. I've been living on her, and it would be infernally awkward for me if she left me for good. That's a reason for keeping her, isn't it? But you may believe me or not – it isn't my reason. She's right enough when she says I'm very fond of her. That's a reason for keeping her too. But it isn't my reason. My reason is that a wife's a wife, and she can't break her word just because everything isn't lovely in the garden. I've heard it said I'm unmoral. I'm not all unmoral. And I feel particularly strongly about what's called the marriage tie.' He drew the revolver from his overcoat pocket, and held it up to view. 'You see this thing. You saw me buy it. Now you needn't be afraid. I'm not threatening you; and it's no part of my game to shoot you. I've nothing to do with your goings-on. What I have to do with is the goings-on of my wife. If she deserts me – for you or for anybody or for nobody – I shall follow her, whether it's to Copenhagen or Bangkok or the North Pole, and I shall kill her – with just this very revolver that you saw me buy. And now you can get out.'

Franting replaced the revolver, and began to consume the cigarette with fierce and larger puffs.

Lomax Harder looked at the grim, set, brutal, scowling bitter face, and knew that Franting meant what he had said. Nothing would stop him from carrying out his threat. The fellow was not an argufier; he could not reason; but he had unmistakable grit and would never recoil from the fear of consequences. If Emily left him, Emily was a dead woman; nothing in the end could protect her from the execution of her husband's menace. On the other hand, nothing would persuade her to remain with her husband. She had decided to go, and she would go. And indeed the mere thought of this lady to whom he, Harder, was utterly devoted, staying with her husband and continuing to suffer the tortures and humiliations which she had been suffering for years – this thought revolted him. He could not think of it.

He stepped forward along the side of the billiard-table, and simultaneously Franting stepped forward to meet him. Lomax Harder snatched the revolver which was in his pocket, aimed, and pulled the trigger.

Franting collapsed, with the upper half of his body somehow balanced on the edge of the billiard-table. He was dead. The sound of the report echoed in Harder's ear like the sound of a violin string loudly twanged by a finger. He saw a little reddish hole in Franting's bronzed right temple.

'Well,' he thought, 'somebody had to die. And it's better him than Emily.' He felt that he had performed a righteous act. Also he felt a little sorry for Franting.

Then he was afraid. He was afraid for himself, because he wanted not to die, especially on the scaffold; but also for Emily Franting who

23

would be friendless and helpless without him; he could not bear to think of her alone in the world – the central point of a terrific scandal. He must get away instantly. . . .

Not down the corridor back into the hotel-lounge! No! That would be fatal! The window. He glanced at the corpse. It was more odd, curious, than affrighting. He had made the corpse. Strange! He could not unmake it. He had accomplished the irrevocable. Impressive! He saw Franting's cigarette glowing on the linoleum in the deepening dusk, and picked it up and threw it into the fender.

Lace curtains hung across the whole width of the window. He drew one aside, and looked forth. The light was much stronger in the courtyard than within the room. He put his gloves on. He gave a last look at the corpse, straddled the window-sill, and was on the brick pavement of the courtyard. He saw that the curtain had fallen back into the perpendicular.

He gazed around. Nobody! Not a light in any window! He saw a green wooden gate, pushed it; it yielded; then a sort of entry-passage. . . . In a moment, after two half-turns, he was on the Marine Parade again. He was a fugitive. Should he fly to the right, to the left? Then he had an inspiration. An idea of genius for baffling pursuers. He would go into the hotel by the main entrance. He went slowly and deliberately into the portico, where a middle-aged hall porter was standing in the gloom.

'Good evening, sir.'

'Good evening. Have you got any rooms?'

'I think so, sir. The housekeeper is out, but she'll be back in a moment – if you'd like a seat. The manager's away in London.'

The hall porter suddenly illuminated the lounge, and Lomax Harder, blinking, entered and sat down.

'I might have a cocktail while I'm waiting,' the murderer suggested with a bright and friendly smile. 'A Bronx.'

'Certainly, sir. The page is off duty. He sees to orders in the lounge, but I'll attend to you myself.'

'What a hotel!' thought the murderer, solitary in the chilly lounge, and gave a glance down the long passage. 'Is the whole place run by the hall porter? But of course it's the dead season.'

Was it conceivable that nobody had heard the sound of the shot?

Harder had a strong impulse to run away. But no! To do so would be highly dangerous. He restrained himself.

'How much?' he asked of the hall porter, who had arrived with surprising quickness, tray in hand and glass on tray.

'A shilling, sir.'

The murderer gave him eighteen pence, and drank off the cocktail.

'Thank you very much, sir.' The hall porter took the glass.

24

'See here!' said the murderer. 'I'll look in again. I've got one or two little errands to do.'

And he went, slowly, into the obscurity of the Marine Parade.

IV

Lomax Harder leant over the left arm of the sea wall of the man-made port of Quangate. Not another soul was there. Night had fallen. The lighthouse at the extremity of the right arm was occulting. The lights – some red, some green, many white – of ships at sea passed in both directions in endless processions. Waves plashed gently against the vast masonry of the wall. The wind, blowing steadily from the north-west, was not cold. Harder, looking about – though he knew he was absolutely alone, took his revolver from his overcoat pocket and stealthily dropped it into the sea. Then he turned round and gazed across the small harbour at the mysterious amphitheatre of the lighted town, and heard public clocks and religious clocks striking the hour.

He was a murderer, but why should he not successfully escape detection? Other murderers had done so. He had all his wits. He was not excited. He was not morbid. His perspective of things was not askew. The hall porter had not seen his first entrance into the hotel, nor his exit after the crime. Nobody had seen them. He had left nothing behind in the billiard-room. No finger marks on the window-sill. (The putting on of his gloves was in itself a clear demonstration that he had fully kept his presence of mind.) No footmarks on the hard, dry pavement of the courtyard.

Of course there was the possibility that some person unseen had seen him getting out of the window. Slight: but still a possibility! And there was also the possibility that someone who knew Franting by sight had noted him walking by Franting's side in the streets. If such a person informed the police and gave a description of him, inquiries might be made. . . . No! Nothing in it. His appearance offered nothing remarkable to the eye of a casual observer – except his forehead, of which he was rather proud, but which was hidden by his hat.

It was generally believed that criminals always did something silly. But so far he had done nothing silly, and he was convinced that, in regard to the crime, he never would do anything silly. He had none of the desire, supposed to be common among murderers, to revisit the scene of the crime or to look upon the corpse once more. Although he regretted the necessity for his act, he felt no slightest twinge of conscience. Somebody had to die, and surely it was better that a brute should die than the heavenly, enchanting, martyrized creature whom his act had rescued for ever from the brute! He was aware within himself of an ecstasy of devotion to Emily Franting – now a widow and free. She was a unique woman. Strange that a woman of such gifts should have come under the sway of so obvious a scoundrel as Franting. But she was very young at the time, and such freaks of sex had happened before and would happen again; they were a widespread phenomenon in the history of the relations of men and women. He would have killed a hundred men if a hundred men had threatened her felicity. His heart was pure; he wanted nothing from Emily in exchange for what he had done in her defence. He was passionate in her defence. When he reflected upon the coarseness and cruelty of the gesture by which Franting had used Emily's letter to light his cigarette, Harder's cheeks grew hot with burning resentment.

A clock struck the quarter. Harder walked quickly to the harbour front, where was a taxi-rank, and drove to the station. . . . A sudden apprehension! The crime might have been discovered! Police might already be watching for suspicious-looking travellers! Absurd! Still, the apprehension remained despite its absurdity. The taxi-driver looked at him queerly. No! Imagination! He hesitated on the threshold of the station, then walked boldly in, and showed his return ticket to the ticket inspector. No sign of a policeman. He got into the Pullman car, where five other passengers were sitting. The train started.

V

He nearly missed the boat-train at Liverpool Street because according to its custom the Quangate flyer arrived twenty minutes late at Victoria. And at Victoria the foolish part of him, as distinguished from the common-sense part, suffered another spasm of fear. Would detectives, instructed by telegraph, be waiting for the train? No! An absurd idea! The boat-train from Liverpool Street was crowded with travellers, and the platform crowded with senders-off. He gathered from scraps of talk overheard that an international conference was about to take place at Copenhagen. And he had known nothing of it – not seen a word of it in the papers! Excusable perhaps; graver matters had held his attention.

Useless to look for Emily in the vast bustle of the compartments! She had her through ticket (which she had taken herself, in order to avoid possible complications), and she happened to be the only woman in the world who was never late and never in a hurry. She was certain to be in the train. But was she in the train? Something sinister might have to come to pass. For instance, a telephone message to the flat that her husband had been found dead with a bullet in his brain.

The swift two-hour journey to Harwich was terrible for Lomax Harder. He remembered that he had left the unburnt part of the letter lying under the billiard-table. Forgetful! Silly! One of the silly things that criminals did! And on Parkeston Quay the confusion was enormous. He did not walk, he was swept, on to the great shaking steamer whose dark funnels rose amid wisps of steam into the starry sky. One advantage: detectives would have no chance in that multitudinous scene, unless indeed they held up the ship.

The ship roared a warning, and slid away from the quay, groped down the tortuous channel to the harbour mouth, and was in the North Sea; and England dwindled to naught but a string of lights. He searched every deck from stem to stern, and could not find Emily. She had not caught the train, or, if she had caught the train, she had not boarded the steamer because he had failed to appear. His misery was intense. Everything was going wrong. And on the arrival at Esbjerg would not detectives be lying in wait for the Copenhagen train? . . .

Then he descried her, and she him. She too had been searching. Only chance had kept them apart. Her joy at finding him was ecstatic; tears came into his eyes at sight of it. He was everything to her, absolutely everything. He clasped her right hand in both his hands and gazed at her in the dim, diffused light blended of stars, moon and electricity. No woman was ever like her: mature, innocent, wise, trustful, honest. And the touching beauty of her appealing, sad, happy face, and the pride of her carriage! A unique jewel – snatched from the brutal grasp of that fellow – who had ripped her solemn letter in two and used it as a spill for his cigarette! She related her movements; and he his. Then she said:

'Well?'

'I didn't go,' he answered. 'Thought it best not to. I'm convinced it wouldn't have been any use.'

He had not intended to tell her this lie. Yet when it came to the point, what else could he say? He told one lie instead of twenty. He was deceiving her, but for her sake. Even if the worst occurred, she was for ever safe from that brutal grasp. And he had saved her. As for the conceivable complications of the future, he refused to front them; he could live in the marvellous present. He felt suddenly the amazing beauty of the night at sea, and beneath all his other sensations was the obscure sensation of a weight at his heart.

'I expect you were right,' she angelically acquiesced.

VI

The Superintendent of Police (Quangate was the county town of the western half of the county), and a detective-sergeant were in the billiard-room of the Bellevue. Both wore mufti. The powerful green-shaded lamps usual in billiard-rooms shone down ruthlessly on the green table, and on the reclining body of John Franting, which had not moved and had not been moved.

A charwoman was just leaving these officers when a stout gentleman, who had successfully beguiled a policeman guarding the other end of the long corridor, squeezed past her, greeted the two officers, and shut the door.

The Superintendent, a thin man, with lips to match, and a moustache, stared hard at the arrival.

'I am staying with my friend Dr Furnival,' said the arrival cheerfully. 'You telephoned for him, and as he had to go out to one of those cases in which nature will not wait, I offered to come in his place. I've met you before, Superintendent, at Scotland Yard.'

'Dr Austin Bond!' exclaimed the Superintendent.

'He,' said the other.

They shook hands, Dr Bond genially, the Superintendent half-consequential, half-deferential, as one who has dignity to think about; also as one who resented an intrusion, but dared not show resentment.

The detective-sergeant recoiled at the dazzling name of the great amateur detective, a genius who had solved the famous mysteries of 'The Yellow Hat,' 'The Three Towns,' 'The Three Feathers,' 'The Gold Spoon,' etc., etc., etc., whose devilish perspicacity had again and again made professional detectives both look and feel foolish, and whose notorious friendship with the loftiest heads of Scotland Yard compelled all police forces to treat him very politely indeed.

'Yes,' said Dr Austin Bond, after detailed examination. 'Been shot about ninety minutes, poor fellow! Who found him?'

'That woman who's just gone out. Some servant here. Came in to look after the fire.'

'How long since?'

'Oh! About an hour ago.'

'Found the bullet? I see it hit the brass on that cue-rack there.'

The detective-sergeant glanced at the Superintendent, who, however, resolutely remained unastonished.

'Here's the bullet,' said the Superintendent.

'Ah!' commented Dr Austin Bond, glinting through his spectacles at the bullet as it lay in the Superintendent's hand. 'Decimal 38, I see. Flattened. It would be.'

'Sergeant,' said the Superintendent. 'You can get help and have the body moved, now Dr Bond has made his examination. Eh, Doctor?'

'Certainly,' answered Dr Bond, at the fireplace. 'He was smoking a cigarette, I see.'

'Either he or his murderer.'

'You've got a clue?'

'Oh yes,' the Superintendent answered, not without pride. 'Look here. Your torch, sergeant.'

The detective-sergeant produced a pocket electric-lamp, and the Superintendent turned to the window-sill.

'I've got a stronger one than that,' said Dr Austin Bond, producing another torch.

The Superintendent displayed finger-prints on the window-frame, footmarks on the sill, and a few strands of inferior blue cloth. Dr Austin Bond next produced a magnifying glass, and inspected the evidence at very short range.

'The murderer must have been a tall man – you can judge that from the angle of fire; he wore a blue suit, which he tore slightly on this splintered wood of the window-frame; one of his boots had a hole in the middle of the sole, and he'd only three fingers on his left hand. He must have come in by the window and gone out by the window, because the hall porter is sure that nobody except the dead man entered the lounge by any door within an hour of the time when the murder must have been committed.' The Superintendent proudly gave many more details, and ended by saying that he had already given instructions to circulate a description.

'Curious,' said Dr Austin Bond, 'that a man like John Franting should let anyone enter the room by the window! Especially a shabby-looking man!'

'You knew the deceased personally then?'

'No! But I know he was John Franting.'

'How, Doctor?'

'Luck.'

'Sergeant,' said the Superintendent, piqued. 'Tell the constable to fetch the hall porter.'

Dr Austin Bond walked to and fro, peering everywhere, and picked up a piece of paper that had lodged against the step of the platform which ran round two sides of the room for the raising of the spectators' benches. He glanced at the paper casually, and dropped it again.

'My man,' the Superintendent addressed the hall porter. 'How can you be sure that nobody came in here this afternoon?'

'Because I was in my cubicle all the time, sir.'

The hall porter was lying. But he had to think of his own welfare. On the previous day he had been reprimanded for quitting his post against the rule. Taking advantage of the absence of the manager, he had sinned once again, and he lived in fear of dismissal if found out.

'With a full view of the lounge?'

'Yes, sir.'

'Might have been in there beforehand,' Dr Austin Bond suggested.

'No,' said the Superintendent. 'The charwoman came in twice. Once just before Franting came in. She saw the fire wanted making up

29

and she went for some coal, and then returned later with some coal. But the look of Franting frightened her, and she went back with her coal.'

'Yes,' said the hall porter. 'I saw that.'

Another lie.

At a sign from the Superintendent he withdrew.

'I should like to have a word with that charwoman,' said Dr Austin Bond.

The Superintendent hesitated. Why should the great amateur meddle with what did not concern him? Nobody had asked his help. But the Superintendent thought of the amateur's relations with Scotland Yard, and sent for the charwoman.

'Did you clean the window here today?' Dr Austin Bond interrogated her.

'Yes, please, sir.'

'Show me your left hand.' The slattern obeyed. 'How did you lose your little finger?'

'In a mangle accident, sir.'

'Just come to the window, will you, and put your hands on it. But take off your left boot first.'

The slattern began to weep.

'It's quite all right, my good creature.' Dr Austin Bond reassured her. 'Your skirt is torn at the hem, isn't it?'

When the slattern was released from her ordeal and had gone, carrying one boot in her grimy hand, Dr Austin Bond said genially to the Superintendent:

'Just a fluke. I happened to notice she'd only three fingers on her left hand when she passed me in the corridor. Sorry I've destroyed your evidence. But I felt sure almost from the first that the murderer hadn't either entered or decamped by the window.'

'How?'

'Because I think he's still here in the room.'

The two police officers gazed about them as if exploring the room for the murderer.

'I think he's there.'

Dr Austin Bond pointed to the corpse.

'And where did he hide the revolver after he'd killed himself?' demanded the thin-lipped Superintendent icily, when he had somewhat recovered his aplomb.

'I'd thought of that, too,' said Dr Austin Bond, beaming. 'It is always a very wise course to leave a dead body absolutely untouched until a professional man has seen it. But *looking* at the body can do no harm. You see the left-hand pocket of the overcoat. Notice how it bulges. Something unusual in it. Something that has the shape of a –

Just feel inside it, will you?'

The Superintendent, obeying, drew a revolver from the overcoat pocket of the dead man.

'Ah! Yes!' said Dr Austin Bond. 'A Webley Mark III. Quite new. You might take out the ammunition.' The Superintendent dismantled the weapon. 'Yes, yes! Three chambers empty. Wonder how he used the other two! Now, where's that bullet? You see? He fired. His arm dropped, and the revolver happened to fall into the pocket.'

'Fired with his left hand, did he?' asked the Superintendent, foolishly ironic.

'Certainly. A dozen years ago Franting was perhaps the finest amateur light-weight boxer in England. And one reason for it was that he bewildered his opponents by being left-handed. His lefts were much more fatal than his rights. I saw him box several times.'

Whereupon Dr Austin Bond strolled to the step of the platform near the door and picked up the fragment of very thin paper that was lying there.

'This,' said he, 'must have blown from the hearth to here by the draught from the window when the door was opened. It's part of a letter. You can see the burnt remains of the other part in the corner of the fender. He probably lighted the cigarette with it. Out of bravado! His last bravado! Read this.'

The Superintendent read:

'. . . repeat that I realize how fond you are of me, but you have killed my affection for you, and I shall leave our home tomorrow. This is absolutely final. E.'

Dr Austin Bond, having for the ninth time satisfactorily demonstrated in his own unique, rapid way, that police-officers were a set of numskulls, bade the Superintendent a most courteous good evening, nodded amicably to the detective-sergeant, and left in triumph.

VII

'I must get some mourning and go back to the flat,' said Emily Franting.

She was sitting one morning in the lobby of the Palads Hotel, Copenhagen. Lomax Harder had just called on her with an English newspaper containing an account of the inquest at which the jury had returned a verdict of suicide upon the body of her late husband. Her eyes filled with tears.

'Time will put her right,' thought Lomax Harder, tenderly watching her. 'I was bound to do what I did. And I can keep a secret for ever.'

31

The Kennel

MAURICE LEVEL

AS TEN O'CLOCK STRUCK, M. de Hartevel emptied a last tankard of beer, folded his newspaper, stretched himself, yawned, and slowly rose.

The hanging lamp cast a bright light on the table-cloth over which were scattered piles of shot and cartridge wads. Near the fireplace, in the shadow, a woman lay back in a deep arm-chair.

Outside, the wind blew violently against the windows, the rain beat noisily on the glass, and from time to time, deep bayings came from the kennel where the hounds had struggled and strained since morning.

There were forty of them, big mastiffs with ugly fangs, stiff-haired griffons of Vendée, powerful beasts that flung themselves with ferocity on the wild boar on hunting days. During the night their sullen bayings disturbed the whole countryside, evoking response from all the dogs in the neighbourhood.

M. de Hartevel lifted a curtain and looked out into the darkness of the park. The wet branches shone like steel blades; the autumn leaves were blown about like whirligigs and flattened against the walls. He grumbled:

'Dirty weather!'

He walked a few steps, his hands in his pockets, stopped before the fireplace and with a kick broke a half-consumed log. Red embers fell on the ashes; a flame rose, straight and pointed.

Madame de Hartevel did not move. The light of the fire played on her face, touching her hair with gold, throwing a rosy glow on her pale cheeks and, dancing about her, cast fugitive shadows on her forehead, her eyelids, her lips.

The hounds, quiet for a moment, began to growl again: and their bayings, the roaring of the wind and the hiss of the rain on the trees, made the quiet room seem warmer, the presence of the woman more intimate.

Subconsciously this influenced M. de Hartevel. Desires stimulated by those of the beasts and by the warmth of the room crept through his veins. He touched his wife's shoulder.

32

'It is ten o'clock. Are you going to bed?'

She said 'yes,' and left her chair, as if regretfully.

He hesitated, his heels against the fender, and without looking at her, asked in a low voice:

'Would you like me to come with you?'

'No . . . thank you. . . .'

Frowning, he bowed:

'As you like.'

His shoulders against the mantelshelf, his legs apart, he watched her go. She walked with a graceful, undulating movement, the train of her dress moving on the carpet like a little flat wave. A surge of anger stiffened his muscles.

In this château where he had her all to himself, he had in bygone days imagined a wife who would like living in seclusion with him, attentive to his wishes, smiling acquiescence to all his desires. She would welcome him with gay words when he came back from a day's hunting, his hands blue with cold, his strong body tired, bringing with him the freshness of the fields and moors, the smell of horses, of game and of hounds, would lift eager lips to meet his own. Then, after the long ride in the wind, the rain, the snow, after the intoxication of the crisp air, the heavy walking in the furrows, or the gallop under branches that almost caught his beard, there would have been long nights of love, orgies of caresses of which the thrill would have been mutual.

The difference between the dream and the reality!

When the door had shut, and the sound of steps died away in the corridor, he went to his room, lay down, took a book and tried to read.

The rain hissed louder than ever. The wind roared in the chimney; out in the park, branches were snapping from the trees; the hounds bayed without ceasing, their howlings sounding through the creaking of the trees, dominating the roar of the storm; the door of the kennel strained under their weight.

He opened the window and shouted:

'Down!'

For some seconds they were quiet. He waited. The wind that drove the rain on his face refreshed him. The barkings began again. He banged his fist against the shutter, threatening:

'Quiet, you devils!'

There was a singing in his ears, a whistling, a ringing: a desire to strike, to ransack, to feel flesh quiver under his fists took possession of him. He roared: 'Wait a moment!' slammed the window, seized a whip, and went out.

He strode along the corridors with no thought of the sleeping house till he got near his wife's room, when he walked slowly and quietly,

33

fearing to disturb her sleep. But a ray of light from under her door caught his lowered eyes, and there was a sound of hurried footsteps that the carpet did not deaden. He listened . . . The noise ceased, the light went out . . . He stood motionless, and suddenly, impelled by a suspicion, he called softly:

'Marie Therèse . . .'

No reply. He called louder. Curiosity, doubt that he dared not formulate, held him breathless. He gave two sharp little taps on the door: a voice inside asked:

'Who is there?'

'I . . . Open the door . . .'

A whiff of warm air laden with various perfumes and a suspicion of ether passed over his face.

The voice asked:

'What is it?'

He walked in without replying. He felt his wife standing close in front of him: her breath was on him, the lace of her dress touched his chest. He felt in his pocket for matches. Not finding any, he ordered:

'Light the lamp!'

She obeyed, and as his eyes ran over the room he saw the curtains drawn closely, a shawl on the carpet, the open bed, white and very large; and in a corner, near the fireplace, a man lying across a long rest-chair, his collar unfastened, his head dropping, his arms hanging loosely, his eyes shut.

He gripped his wife's wrist:

'Ah, you – filth! . . . Then this is why you turn your back on me!' . . .

She did not shrink from him, did not move. No shadow of fear passed over her pallid face. She only raised her head, murmuring:

'You are hurting me . . .'

He let her go, and bending over the inert body, his fist raised, cried:

'A lover in my wife's bedroom! . . . And . . . what a lover! A friend – almost a son – Whore!'

She interrupted him:

'He is not my lover . . .'

He burst into a laugh:

'Ah! Ah! You expect me to believe that!'

He seized the collar of the recumbent man and lifted him up towards him. But when he saw the livid face, the half-opened mouth showing the teeth and gums, when he felt the strange chill of the flesh that touched his hands, he started to let go. The body fell back heavily on the cushions, the forehead beating twice against a chair. His fury turned upon his wife.

'What have you to say? . . . Explain.'

'It is very simple,' she said. 'I was just going to bed when I heard the sound of footsteps in the corridor . . . uncertain steps . . . faltering, and a voice begging, "Open the door . . . open the door . . ." I thought you might be ill. I opened the door. Then he came, or rather, fell into the room . . . I knew he was subject to heart attacks . . . I laid him there . . . I was just going to bring you when you knocked . . . that's all . . .'

Bending over the body, apparently quite calm again, he asked, every word pronounced distinctly:

'And it does not surprise you that no one heard him come in? . . .'

'The hounds bayed . . .'

'And why should he come here at this hour of the night?'

She made a vague gesture:

'It does seem strange . . . But . . . I can only suppose that he felt ill and that . . . quite alone in his own house . . . he was afraid to stay there . . . came here to beg for help . . . In any case, when he is better . . . as soon as he is able to speak . . . he will be able to explain . . .'

M. de Hartevel drew himself up to his full height and looked into his wife's eyes:

'It appears we shall have to accept your supposition, and that we shall never know exactly what underlies his being here tonight . . . He is dead.'

She held out her hands and stammered, her teeth chattering:

'It's not possible . . . He is . . .'

'Yes . . . dead . . .'

He seemed to be lost in thought for a moment, then went on in an easier voice:

'After all, the more I think of it, the more natural it seems. Both his father and uncle died like this, suddenly . . . Heart-disease is hereditary in his family . . . A shock . . . a violent emotion . . . too keen a sensation . . . a great joy . . . We are weak creatures at best . . .'

He drew an armchair to the fire, sat down, and his hands stretched out to the flames, continued:

'But however simple and natural the event in itself may be, nothing can alter the fact that a man has died in your bedroom during the night . . . Is that not so? . . .'

She hid her face in her hands and made no reply.

'And if your explanation satisfies me, I am not able to make others accept it. The servants will have their own ideas, will talk . . . That will be dishonour for you, for me, for my family . . . That is not possible . . . We must find a way out of it . . . and I have already found it . . . With the exception of you and me, no one knows, no one will ever know what has happened in this room . . . No one saw him come in . . . Take the lamp and come with me . . .'

35

He seized the body in his arms and ordered:

'Walk on first . . .'

She hesitated as they went out of the door:

'What are you going to do? . . .'

'Leave it to me . . . Go on . . .'

Slowly and very quietly they went towards the staircase, she holding the lamp, its light flickering on the walls, he carefully placing his feet on stair after stair. When they got to the door that led to the garden, he said:

'Open it without a sound.'

A gust of wind made the light flare up. Beaten on by the rain, the glass burst and fell in pieces on the threshold. She placed the extinguished lamp on the soil. They went into the dark. The gravel crunched under their steps, and the rain beat upon them. He asked:

'Can you see the walk? . . . Yes? . . . Then come close to me . . . hold the legs . . . the body is heavy . . .'

They went forward in silence. M. de Hartevel stopped near a low door, saying:

'Feel my right hand pocket . . . There's a key there . . . That's it . . . Give it to me . . . Now let the legs go . . . It's as dark as a grave . . . Feel about till you find the key-hole . . . Have you got it? . . . Turn . . .'

Excited by the noise, the hounds began to bay. Madame de Hartevel started back.

'You are frightened? . . . Nonsense . . . Another turn . . . That's it . . . Stand out of the way . . .'

With a thrust from his knee, he pushed open the door. Believing themselves free, the hounds bounded against his legs. Pushing them back with a kick, suddenly, with one great effort, he raised the body above his head, balanced it there for a moment, flung it into the kennel, and shut the door violently behind him.

Baying at full voice, the beasts fell on their prey. A frightful death-rattle: 'Help!' pierced their clamour, a terrible cry, inhuman. It was followed by violent growlings.

An unspeakable horror took possession of Madame de Hartevel: a quick flash of understanding dominated her fear, and, her eyes wild, she flung herself on her husband, digging her nails in his face as she shrieked:

'Fiend! . . . He wasn't dead! . . .'

M. de Hartevel pushed her off with the back of his hand, and standing straight up before her jeered:

'Did you think he was!'

'We Know You're Busy Writing . . .'

EDMUND CRISPIN

I

'AFTER ALL, IT'S ONLY US,' they said.

I must introduce myself.

None of this is going to be read, even, let alone printed. Ever.

Nevertheless, there is habit – the habit of putting words together in the most effective order you can think of. There is self-respect, too. That, and habit, make me try to tell this as if it were in fact going to be read.

Which God forbid.

I am forty-seven, unmarried, living alone, a minor crime-fiction writer, earning, on average, rather less than a thousand pounds a year.

I live in Devon.

I live in a small cottage which is isolated, in the sense that there is no one nearer than a quarter of a mile.

I am not, however, at a loss for company.

For one thing, I have a telephone.

I am a hypochondriac, well into the coronary belt. Also, I go in fear of accidents, with broken bones. The telephone is thus a necessity. I can afford only one, so its siting is a matter of great discretion. In the end, it is in the hall, just at the foot of the steep stairs. It is on a shelf only two feet from the floor, so that if I have to crawl to it, it will still be within reach.

If I have my coronoary *up*stairs, too bad.

The telephone is for me to use in an emergency. Other people, however, regard it differently.

Take, for example, my Bank Manager.

'Torhaven 153,' I say.

'Hello? Bradley, is that Mr Bradley?'

'Bradley speaking.'

'This is Wimpole, Wimpole. Mr Bradley, I have to talk to you.'

37

'Speaking.'

'Now, it's like this, Mr Bradley. How soon can we expect some further payments in, Mr Bradley? Payments out, yes, we have plenty of those, but payments in . . .'

'I'm doing everything I can, Mr Wimpole.'

'Everything, yes, everything, but payments in, what is going to be coming in during the next month, Mr Bradley?'

'Quite a lot, I hope.'

'Yes, you hope, Mr Bradley, you hope, you hope. But what am I going to say to my Regional Office, Mr Bradley, how am I going to represent the matter to them, to it? You have this accommodation with us, this matter of five hundred pounds . . .'

'Had it for years, Mr Wimpole.'

'Yes, Mr Bradley, and that is exactly the trouble. You must reduce it, Mr Bradley, reduce it, I say,' this lunatic bawls at me.

I can no more reduce my overdraft than I can fly.

I am adequately industrious. I aim to write two thousand words a day, which would support me in the event that I were ever able to complete them. But if you live alone you are not, contrary to popular supposition, in a state of unbroken placidity.

Quite the contrary.

I have tried night work, a consuming yawn to every tap on the typewriter, I have tried early morning work.

And here H. L. Mencken comes in, suggesting that bad writing is due to bad digestion.

My own digestion is bad at any time, particularly bad during milkmen's hours, and I have never found that I could do much in the dawn. This is a weakness, and I admit it. But apparently it has to be. Work, for me, is thus office hours, nine till five.

I have told everyone about this, begging them, if it isn't a matter of emergency, to get in touch with me in the *evenings*. Office hours, I tell them, same as everyone else. You wouldn't telephone a solicitor about nothing in particular during his office hours, would you? Well, so why ring me?

I am typing a sentence which starts *His crushed hand, paining him less now, nevertheless gave him a sense of.*

I know what is going to happen after 'of': *the appalling frailty of the human body.*

Or rather, I did know, and it wasn't that. It might have been that (feeble though it is) but for the fact that then the door-bell rang. (I hope that it might have been something better.)

The door-bell rang. It was a Mrs Prance morning, but she hadn't yet arrived, so I answered the door myself, clattering down from the upstairs room where I work. It was the meter-reader. The meter being outside the door, I was at a loss to know why I had to sanction its being scrutinised.

'A sense of the dreadful agonies,' I said to the meter-reader, 'of which the human body is capable.'

'Wonderful weather for the time of year.'

'I'll leave you, if you don't mind. I'm a bit busy.'

'Suit yourself,' he said, offended.

Then Mrs Prance came.

Mrs Prance comes three mornings a week. She is slow, and deaf, but she is all I can hope to get, short of winning the Pools.

She answers the door, but is afraid of the telephone, and consequently never answers that, though I've done my utmost to train her to it.

She is very anxious that I should know precisely what she is doing in my tatty little cottage, and approve of it.

'Mr Bradley?'

'Yes, Mrs Prance?'

'It's the Hi-Glow.'

'What about it, Mrs Prance?'

'Pardon?'

'I said, what about it?'

'We did ought to change.'

'Yes, well, let's change, by all means.'

'Pardon?'

'I said, "Yes".'

'Doesn't bring the wood up, not the way it ought to.'

'You're the best judge, Mrs Prance.'

'Pardon?'

'I'm sorry, Mrs Prance, but I'm working now. We'll talk about it some other time.'

'Toffee-nosed,' says Mrs Prance.

Gave him a sense of – a sense of – a sense of burr-burr, burr-burr, burr-burr.

Mrs Prance shouts that it's the telephone.

I stumble downstairs and pick the thing up.

'Darling.'

'Oh, hello, Chris.'

'How are you, darling?'

'A sense of the gross cruelty which filled all history.'

'What, darling? What was that you said?'

'Sorry. I was just trying to keep a glass of water balanced on my head.'

A tinkle of laughter.

'You're a poppet. Listen, I've had a wonderful idea. It's a party. Here in my flat. Today week. You will come, Edward, won't you?'

'Yes, of course, I will, Chris, but may I just remind you about something?'

'What's that, darling?'

'You said you wouldn't ring me up during working hours.'

A short silence then:

'Oh, but *just this once*. It's going to be such a lovely party, darling. You don't mind *just this once*.'

'Chris, are you having a coffee break?'

'Yes, darling, and Oh, God, don't I need it!'

'Well, I'm *not* having a coffee break.'

A rather longer silence; then:

'You don't love me any more.'

'It's just that I'm trying to get a story written. There's a deadline for it.'

'If you don't want to come to the party, all you've got to do is say so.'

'I do want to come to the party, but I also want to get on with earning my living. Seriously, Chris, as it's a week ahead, couldn't you have waited till this evening to ring me?'

A sob.

'I think you're beastly. I think you're utterly, utterly *horrible*.'

'Chris.'

'And I never want to *see* you again.'

A sense of treachery, I typed, sedulously. *The agony still flamed up his arm, but it was now——*

The door-bell rang.

– it was now less than – more than –

'It's the laundry, Mr Bradley,' Mrs Prance shouted up the stairs at me.

'Coming, Mrs Prance.'

I went out on to the small landing. Mrs Prance's great moonface peered up at me from below.

'Coming Thursday next week,' she shouted at me, 'because of Good Friday.'

'Yes, Mrs Prance, but what has that got to do with *me*? I mean, you'll be here on Wednesday as usual, won't you, to change the sheets?'

'Pardon?'

'Thank you for telling me, Mrs Prance.'

One way and another, it was a remarkable Tuesday morning: seven telephone calls, none of them in the least important, eleven people at the door and Mrs Prance anxious that no scintilla of her efforts should lack my personal verbal approval. I had sat down in front of my typewriter at nine-thirty. By twelve noon, I had achieved the following:

His crushed hand, paining him less now, nevertheless gave him a sense of treachery, the appalling frailty of the human body, but it was now less than it had been, more than indifferent to him since, after, because though the pain could be shrugged off the betrayal was a

I make no pretence to be a quick writer, but that really was a very bad morning indeed.

II

Afternoon started better. With some garlic sausage and bread inside me, I ran to another seven paragraphs, unimpeded.

As he clawed his way out, hatred seized him, I tapped out, enthusiastically embarking on the eighth. *No such emotion had ever before –*

The door-bell rang.

– had ever before disturbed his quiet existence. It was as if –

The door-bell rang again, lengthily, someone leaning on it.

– as if a beast had taken charge, a beast inordinate, insatiable.

The door-bell was now ringing for many seconds at a time, uninterruptedly.

Was this a survival factor, or would it blur his mind? He scarcely knew. One thing was abundantly clear, namely that he was going to have to answer the bloody door-bell.

He did so.

On the doorstep, their car standing in the lane beyond, were a couple in early middle age, who could be seen at a glance to be fresh out from The Duke.

The Duke of Devonshire is my local. When I first moved to this quiet part of Devon I had nothing against The Duke: it was a small village pub serving small village drinks, with an occasional commercialized pork pie or sausage roll. But then it changed hands. A Postgate admirer took over. Hams, game patties, quail eggs and other such fanciful foods were introduced to a noise of trumpets; esurient lunatics began rolling up in every sort of car, gobble-mad for exotic ploughman's lunches and suavely served lobster creams, their throats parched for the vinegar of 1964 clarets or the ullage of the abominable home-brewed beer; and there was no longer any peace for anyone.

In particular, there was no longer any peace for me. 'Let's go and see old Ted,' people said to one another as they were shooed out of the bar at closing time. 'He lives near here.'

'Charles,' said this man on the doorstep, extending his hand.

The woman with him tittered. She had fluffy hair, and lips so pale that they stood out disconcertingly, like scars, against her blotched complexion. 'It's Ted, lovey,' she said.

'Ted, of course it's Ted. Known him for years. How are you, Charley boy?'

'*Ted*, angel.'

I recognized them both, slightly, from one or two parties. They were presumably a married couple, but not married for long, if offensive nonsenses like 'Angel' were to be believed.

'We're not interrupting anything,' she said.

Interested by this statement of fact, I found spouting up in my pharynx the reply, 'Yes, you sodding well are.' But this had to be choked back; bourgeois education forbids such replies, other than euphemistically.

'Come on in,' I said.

They came on in.

I took them into the downstairs living-room, which lack of money has left a ghost of its original intention. There are two armchairs, a chesterfield, a coffee table, a corner cupboard for drinks; but all, despite Hi-Glow, dull and tattered on the plain carpet.

I got them settled on the chesterfield.

'Coffee?' I suggested.

But this seemed not to be what was wanted.

'You haven't got a drink, old boy?' the man said.

'*Stanislas*,' the girl said.

'Yes, of course. Whisky? Gin? Sherry?'

'Oh, Stanislas darling, you are *awful*,' said this female. 'Fancy asking.'

I had no recollection of the name of either of them, but surely Stanislas couldn't be right. 'Stanislas?' I asked.

'It's private,' she said, taking one of his hands in one of hers, and wringing it. 'You don't mind? It's sort of a joke. It's private between us.'

'I see. Well, what would you like to drink?'

He chose whisky, she gin and Italian.

'If you'll excuse me I'll have to go upstairs for a minute,' I said, after serving them.

One thing was abundantly clear: Giorgio's map had been wrong, and as a consequence –

'Ooh-hooh!'

I went out on to the landing.

'Yes?'

'We're lonely.'

'Down in just a minute.'

'You're doing that nasty writing.'

'No, just checking something.'

'We heard the typewriter. Do come down, Charles, Edward I mean, we've got something terribly, terribly important to tell you.'

'Coming straight away,' I said, my mind full of Giorgio's map.

I refilled their glasses.

'You're Diana,' I said to her.

'Daphne,' she squeaked.

'Yes, of course, Daphne. Drink all right?'

She took a great swallow of it, and so was unable to speak for fear of vomiting. Stanislas roused himself to fill the conversational gap.

'How's the old writing, then?'

'Going along well.'

'Mad Martians, eh? Don't read that sort of thing myself, I'm afraid, too busy with biography and history. Has Daphne told you?'

'No. Told me what?'

'About Us, old boy, about Us.'

This was the first indication I'd had that they *weren't* a married couple. Fond locutions survive courtship by God knows how many years, fossilising to automatic gabble, and so are no guide to actual relationships. But in 'Us', the capital letter, audible anyway, flag-wags something new.

'Ah-ha!' I said.

With an effort, Stanislas leaned forward. 'Daphne's husband is a beast,' he said, enunciating distinctly.

'Giorgio's map,' I said. 'Defective.'

'A mere brute. So she's going to throw in her lot with me.'

Satisfied, he fell back on to the cushions. 'Darling,' he said.

As a consequence, we were two miles south-west of our expected position. 'So what is the expected position?' I asked.

'We're eloping,' Daphne said.

'This very day. Darling.'

'Angel.'

'Yes, this very day,' said Stanislas, ostentatiously sucking up the last drops from the bottom of his glass. 'This very day as ever is. We've planned it,' he confided.

The plan had gone wrong, had gone rotten. Giorgio had failed.

'Had gone rotten,' I said, hoping I might just possibly remember the phrase when this pair of lunatics had taken themselves off.

'Rotten is the word for that bastard,' said Stanislas. Suddenly his eyes filled with alcoholic tears. 'What Daphne has suffered, no one will ever know,' he gulped. 'There's even been . . . beating.' Daphne lowered her lips demurely, in tacit confirmation. 'So we're off and away together,' said Stanislas, recovering slightly. 'A new life. Abroad. A new humane relationship.'

But was his failure final? Wasn't there still a chance?

'If you'll excuse me,' I said, 'I shall have to go upstairs again.'

But this attempt aborted. Daphne seized me so violently by the wrist, as I was on the move, that I had difficulty in not falling over sideways.

'You're with us, aren't you?' she breathed.

'Oh, yes, of course.'

'My husband would come after us, if he knew.'

'A good thing he doesn't know, then.'

'But he'll guess. He'll guess it's Stanislas.'

'I suppose so.'

'You don't mind us being here, Charles, do you? We have to wait till dark.'

'Well, actually, there is a bit of work I ought to be getting on with.'

'I'm sorry, Ted,' she said, smoothing her skirt. 'We've been inconsiderate. We must go.' She went on picking at her hem-line, but there was no tensing of the leg muscles, preliminary to rising, so I refilled her glass. 'No, don't go,' I said, the British middle class confronting its finest hour. 'Tell me more about it.'

'Stanislas.'

'H'm, h'm.'

'Wake *up*, sweetie-pie. Tell Charles all about it.'

Stanislas got himself approximately upright. 'All about what?'

'About Us, angel.'

But the devil of it was, if Giorgio's map was wrong, our chances had receded to nil.

'To nil,' I said, 'Nil.'

'Not nil at all, old boy,' Stanislas said. 'And as a matter of fact, if you don't mind my saying so, I rather resent that "nil". We may not be special, like writer blokes like you, but we aren't "nil", Daphne and me. We're human, and so forth. Cut us and we bleed, and that. I'm no great cop, I'll grant you that, but Daphne – Daphne –'

'A splendid girl,' I said.

'Yes, you say that now, but what would you have said five minutes ago? Eh? Eh?'

'The same thing, of course.'

'You think you're rather marvellous, don't you? You think you've
. . . got it made. Well, let me tell you one thing, Mr so-called Bradley:
you may think you're very clever, with all this writing of westerns and
so on, but I can tell you, there are more important things in life than
westerns. I don't suppose you'll understand about it, but there's Love.
Daphne and I, we love one another. You can jeer, and you do jeer. All
I can tell you is, you're wrong as can be. Daphne and I, we're going
off together, and to hell with people who . . . jeer.'

'Have another drink.'

'Well, thanks, I don't mind if I do.'

They stayed for four whole hours.

Somewhere in the middle they made a pretence of drinking tea.
Some time after that they expressed concern at the length of time they
had stayed – without, however, giving any sign of leaving. I gathered,
as Giorgio and his map faded inexorably from my mind, that their
elopement plans were dependent on darkness: this, rather than the
charm of my company, was what they were waiting for. Meanwhile,
with my deadline irrevocably lost, I listened to their soul-searching –
he unjustifiably divorced, she tied to a brutish lout who unfortunately
wielded influence over a large range of local and national affairs, and
would pursue her to the ends of the earth unless precautions were
taken to foil him.

I heard a good deal about these precautions, registering them
without, at the time, realizing how useful they were going to be.

'Charles, Edward.'

'Yes?'

'We've been bastards.'

'Of course not.'

'We haven't been letting you get on with your work.'

'Too late now.'

'Not really too late,' lachrymosely. 'You go and write, and we'll just
sit here, and do no harm to a soul.'

'I've rather forgotten what I was saying, and in any case I've
missed the last post.'

'Oh, Charles, Charles, you shame us. We abase ourselves.'

'No need for that.'

'*Naturally* we abase ourselves. We've drunk your liquor, we've sat
on your . . . your sofa, we've stopped you working. Sweetie-pie, isn't
that true? Haven't we stopped him working?'

'If you say so, sweetie-pie.'

'I most certainly do say so. And it's a disgrace.'

'So we're disgraced, Poppet. *Bad*,' she said histrionically. 'But are we so bad? I mean, he's self-employed, he's got all the time in the world, he can work just whenever he likes. Not like you and me. He's got it *made*.'

'Oh, God,' I mumbled.

'Well, that's true,' Stanislas said, with difficulty. 'And it's a nice quiet life.'

'Quiet, that's it.'

'Don't have to do anything if you don't want to. Ah, come the day.'

'He's looking cross.'

'What's that? Old Charles looking cross? Angel, you're mistaken. Don't you believe it. Not cross, Charles, are you?'

'We *have* stayed rather long, darling. Darling, are you awake? I say, we *have* stayed rather long.'

'H'm.'

'But it's special. Edward, it's special. You do see that, don't you? Special. Because of Stanislas and me.'

I said, 'All I know is that I –'

'Just this once,' she said. 'You'll forgive us just this once? After all, you *are* a free agent. And after all, it's only us.'

I stared at them.

I looked at him, nine-tenths asleep. I looked at her, half asleep. I thought what a life they were going to have if they eloped together.

But 'It's only us' had triggered something off.

I remembered that on just that one day, not an extraordinary one, there had been Mrs Prance, the meter-reader, Chris (twice: she had telephoned a second time during working hours to apologize for telephoning the first time during working hours), the laundry man, the grocer (no Chiver Peas this week), my tax accountant, a woman collecting for the Church, a Frenchman wanting to know if he was on the right road to The Duke.

I remembered that a frippet had come from the National Insurance, or whatever the hell it's called now, to ask what I was doing about Mrs Prance, and if not, why not. I remembered a long, inconclusive telephone call from someone's secretary at the BBC – the someone, despite his anxiety to be in touch with me, having vanished without notice into the BBC Club. I remembered that undergraduates at the University of Essex were wanting me to give them a talk, and were going to be so good as to pay second-class rail fare, though no fee.

I remembered that my whole morning's work had been a single, botched, incomplete paragraph, and that my afternoon's work, before this further interruption, had been little more than two hundred words.

46

I remembered that I had missed the post.

I remembered that I had missed the post before, for much the same reasons, and that publishers are unenthusiastic about writers who keep failing to meet deadlines.

I remembered that I was very short of money, and that sitting giving drink to almost total strangers for four hours on end wasn't the best way of improving the situation.

I remembered.

I saw red.

A red mist before his eyes, doing the butterfly stroke.

I picked up the poker from the fireplace, and went round behind them.

Did they – I sometimes ask myself – wonder what I could possibly be doing, edging round the back of the chesterfield with a great lump of iron in my hand?

They were probably too far gone to wonder.

In any case, they weren't left wondering for long.

III

Eighteen months have passed.

At the end of the first week a Detective Constable came to see me. His name was Ellis. He was thin to the point of emaciation, and seemed, despite his youth, permanently depressed. He was in plain clothes.

He told me that their names were Daphne Fiddler and Clarence Oates.

'Now, sir, we've looked into this matter, and we understand that you didn't know this lady and gentleman at all well.'

'I'd just met them once or twice.'

'They came here, though, that Tuesday afternoon.'

'Yes, but they'd been booted out of the pub. People often come here because they've been booted out of the pub.'

Lounging on the chesterfield, ignoring its blotches, Ellis said, 'They were looking for a drink, eh?'

'Yes, they did seem to be doing that.'

'I'm not disturbing your work, sir, I hope.'

'Yes, you are, Officer, as a matter of fact. So did they.'

'If you wouldn't mind, sir, don't call me "Officer". I am one, technically. But as a mode of address it's pointless.'

'Sorry.'

'I'll have to disturb your work a little bit more still, sir, I'm afraid. Now, if I may ask, did this – this *pair* say anything to you about their plans?'

'Did they say anything to anyone else?'

'Yes, Mr Bradley, to about half the population of South Devon.'

'Well, I can tell you what they said to me. They said they were going to get a boat from Torquay to Jersey, and then a plane from Jersey to Guernsey, and then a Hovercraft from Guernsey to France. They were going to go over to France on day passes, but they were going to carry their passports with them, and cash sewn into the linings of their clothes. Then they were going on from France to some other country, where they could get jobs without a *permis de séjour*.'

'Some countries, there's loopholes big as camel's gates,' said Ellis biblically.

I said, 'They'll make a mess of it, you know.'

'Hash-slinging for her,' said Ellis despondently, 'and driving a taxi for him. What was the last you saw of them?'

'They drove off.'

'Yes, but when?'

'Oh, after dark. Perhaps seven. What happened to them after that?'

'The Falls.'

'Sorry?'

'The *Falls*. Their car was found abandoned there.'

'Oh.'

'No luggage in it.'

'Oh.'

'So presumably they got on the Torquay bus.'

'You can't find out?'

Ellis wriggled on the cushions. 'Driver's an idiot. Doesn't see or hear *anything*.'

'I was out at the Falls myself.'

'Pardon?'

'I say, I was out at the Falls myself. I followed them on foot – though of course, I didn't *know* I was doing that.'

'Did you see their car there?' Ellis asked.

'I saw several cars, but they all look alike nowadays. And they all had their lights off. You don't go around peering into cars at the Falls which have their lights off.'

'And then, sir?'

'I just walked back. It's a fairly normal walk for me in the evenings, after I've eaten. I mean, it's a walk I quite often take.'

(And I had, in fact, walked back by the lanes as usual, resisting the temptation to skulk across fields. Good for me to have dumped the car unnoticed near the bus-stop, and good for me to have remembered about the luggage before I set out.)

'Good for me,' I said.

'Pardon?'

'Good for me to be able to do that walk, still.'

Ellis unfolded himself, getting up from the chesterfield. Good for me that he hadn't got a kit with him to test the blotches.

'It's just a routine inquiry, Mr Bradley,' he said faintly, his vitality seemingly at a low ebb. 'Mrs Fiddler's husband, Mr Oates's wife, they felt they should inquire. Missing Persons, you see. But just between ourselves,' he added, his voice livening momentarily, 'they neither of 'em care a button. It's obvious what's happened, and they neither of 'em care a button. Least said, Mr Bradley, soonest mended.'

He went.

I should feel guilty; but in fact, I feel purged.

Catharsis.

Am I purged of pity? I hope not. I feel pity for Daphne and Stanislas, at the same time as irritation at their unconscionable folly.

Purged of fear?

Well, in an odd sort of way, yes.

Things have got worse for me. The strain of reducing my overdraft by £250 has left me with Mrs Prance only two days a week, and rather more importantly, I now have to count the tins of baked beans and the loaves I shall use for toasting.

But I feel better.

The interruptions are no less than before. Wimpole, Chris, my tax accountant all help to fill my working hours, in the same old way.

But now I feel almost indulgent towards them. Towards everyone, even Mrs Prance.

For one thing, I garden a lot.

I get a fair number of flowers, but this is more luck than judgment. Vegetables are my chief thing.

And this autumn the cabbages have done particularly well. Harvest cabbages, they stand up straight and conical, their dark green outer leaves folded close, moisture-globed, protecting firm, crisp hearts.

For harvest cabbages you can't beat nicely rotted organic fertilizer.

Can I ever bring myself to cut my harvest cabbages and eat them?

At the *moment* I don't want to eat my harvest cabbages. But I dare say in the end I shall.

After all, it's only them.

A Thousand Deaths

JACK LONDON

I HAD BEEN IN THE WATER about an hour, and cold, exhausted, with a terrible cramp in my right calf, it seemed as though my hour had come. Fruitlessly struggling against the strong ebb tide, I had beheld the maddening procession of the water-front lights slip by; by now I gave up attempting to breast the stream and contented myself with the bitter thoughts of a wasted career, now drawing to a close.

It had been my luck to come of good, English stock, but of parents whose account with the bankers far exceeded their knowledge of child nature and the rearing of children. While born with a silver spoon in my mouth, the blessed atmosphere of the home circle was to me unknown. My father, a very learned man and a celebrated anti-quarian, gave no thought to his family, being constantly lost in the abstractions of his study; while my mother, noted far more for her good looks than her good sense, sated herself with the adulation of the society in which she was perpetually plunged. I went through the regular school and college routine of a boy of the English bourgeois, and as the years brought me increasing strength and passions, my parents suddenly became aware that I was possessed of an immortal soul, and endeavored to draw the curb. But it was too late; I perpetrated the wildest and most audacious folly, and was disowned by my people, ostracized by the society I had so long outraged, and with the thousand pounds my father gave me, with the declaration that he would neither see me again nor give me more, I took a first-class passage to Australia.

Since then my life had been one long peregrination – from the Orient to the Occident, from the Arctic to the Antarctic – to find myself at last, an able seaman at thirty, in the full vigor of my manhood, drowning in San Francisco Bay because of a disastrously successful attempt to desert my ship.

My right leg was drawn up by the cramp, and I was suffering the keenest agony. A slight breeze stirred up a choppy sea, which washed into my mouth and down my throat, nor could I prevent it. Though I still contrived to keep afloat, it was merely mechanical, for I was rapidly becoming unconscious. I have a dim recollection of drifting

50

past the sea wall, and of catching a glimpse of an up-river steamer's starboard light; then everything became a blank.

I heard the low hum of insect life, and felt the balmy air of a spring morning fanning my cheek. Gradually it assumed a rhythmic flow, to whose soft pulsations my body seemed to respond. I floated on the gentle bosom of a summer's sea, rising and falling with dreamy pleasure on each crooning wave. But the pulsations grew stronger; the humming louder; the waves, larger, fiercer – I was dashed about on a stormy sea. A great agony fastened upon me. Brilliant, intermittent sparks of light flashed athwart my inner consciousness; in my ears there was the sound of many waters; then a sudden snapping of an intangible something, and I awoke.

The scene, of which I was protagonist, was a curious one. A glance sufficed to inform me that I lay on the cabin floor of some gentleman's yacht, in a most uncomfortable posture. On either side, grasping my arms and working them up and down like pump handles, were two peculiarly clad, dark-skinned creatures. Though conversant with most aboriginal types, I could not conjecture their nationality. Some attachment had been fastened about my head, which connected my respiratory organs with the machine I shall next describe. My nostrils, however, had been closed, forcing me to breathe through my mouth. Foreshortened by the obliquity of my line of vision. I beheld two tubes, similar to small hosing but of different composiuon, which emerged from my mouth and went off at an acute angle from each other. The first came to an abrupt termination and lay on the floor beside me; the second traversed the floor in numerous coils, connecting with the apparatus I have promised to describe.

In the days before my life had become tangential, I had dabbled not a little in science, and conversant with the appurtenances and general paraphernalia of the laboratory, I appreciated the machine I now beheld. It was composed chiefly of glass, the construction being of that crude sort which is employed for experimentative purposes. A vessel of water was surrounded by an air chamber, to which was fixed a vertical tube, surmounted by a globe. In the center of this was a vacuum gauge. The water in the tube moved upward and downward, creating alternate inhalations and exhalations, which were in turn communicated to me through the hose. With this, and the aid of the men who pumped my arms so vigorously, had the process of breathing been artificially carried on, my chest rising and falling and my lungs expanding and contracting, till nature could be persuaded to again take up her wonted labour.

As I opened my eyes the appliance about my head, nostrils and mouth was removed. Draining a stiff three fingers of brandy, I

51

staggered to my feet to thank my preserver, and confronted – my father. But long years of fellowship with danger had taught me self-control, and I waited to see if he would recognize me. Not so; he saw in me no more than a runaway sailor and treated me accordingly.

Leaving me to the care of the blackies, he fell to revising the notes he had made on my resuscitation. As I ate of the handsome fare served up to me, confusion began on deck, and from the chanteys of the sailors and the rattling of blocks and tackles I surmised that we were getting under way. What a lark! Off on a cruise with my recluse father into the wide Pacific! Little did I realize, as I laughed to myself, which side the joke was to be on. Aye, had I known, I would have plunged overboard and welcomed the dirty fo'c'sle from which I had just escaped.

I was not allowed on deck till we had sunk the Farallones and the last pilot boat. I appreciated this forethought on the part of my father and made it a point to thank him heartily, in my bluff seaman's manner. I could not suspect that he had his own ends in view, in thus keeping my presence secret to all save the crew. He told me briefly of my rescue by his sailors, assuring me that the obligation was on his side, as my appearance had been most opportune. He had constructed the apparatus for the vindication of a theory concerning certain biological phenomena, and had been waiting for an opportunity to use it.

'You have proved it beyond all doubt,' he said; then added with a sigh, 'But only in the small matter of drowning.'

But, to take a reef in my yarn – he offered me an advance of two pounds on my previous wages to sail with him and this I considered handsome, for he really did not need me. Contrary to my expectations, I did not join the sailors' mess, for'ard, being assigned to a comfortable stateroom and eating at the captain's table. He had perceived that I was no common sailor, and I resolved to take this chance for reinstating myself in his good graces. I wove a fictitious past to account for my education and present position, and did my best to come in touch with him. I was not long in disclosing a predilection for scientific pursuits, nor he in appreciating my aptitude. I became his assistant, with a corresponding increase in wages, and before long, as he grew confidential and expounded his theories, I was as enthusiastic as himself.

The days flew quickly by, for I was deeply interested in my new studies, passing my waking hours in his well-stocked library, or listening to his plans and aiding him in his laboratory work. But we were forced to forgo many enticing experiments, a rolling ship not being exactly the proper place for delicate or intricate work. He promised me, however, many delightful hours in the magnificent laboratory for which we were bound. He had taken possession of an uncharted South Sea island, as he said, and turned it into a scientific paradise.

We had not been on the island long, before I discovered the horrible mare's nest I had fallen into. But before I describe the strange things which came to pass, I must briefly outline the causes which culminated in as startling an experience as ever fell to the lot of man.

Late in life, my father had abandoned the musty charms of antiquity and succumbed to the more fascinating ones embraced under the general head of biology. Having been thoroughly grounded during his youth in the fundamentals, he rapidly explored all the higher branches as far as the scientific world had gone, and found himself on the no man's land of the unknowable. It was his intention to pre-empt some of this unclaimed territory, and it was at this stage of his investigations that we had been thrown together. Having a good brain, though I say it myself, I had mastered his speculations and methods of reasoning, becoming almost as mad as himself. But I should not say this. The marvelous results we afterward obtained can only go to prove his sanity. I can but say that he was the most abnormal specimen of cold-blooded cruelty I have ever seen.

After having penetrated the dual mysteries of physiology and psychology, his thought had led him to the verge of a great field, for which, the better to explore, he began studies in higher organic chemistry, pathology, toxicology and other sciences and sub-sciences rendered kindred as accessories to his speculative hypotheses. Starting from the proposition that the direct cause of the temporary and permanent arrest of vitality was due to the coagulation of certain elements and compounds in the protoplasm, he had isolated and subjected these various substances to innumerable experiments. Since the temporary arrest of vitality in an organism brought coma, and a permanent arrest death, he held that by artificial means that coagulation of the protoplasm could be retarded, prevented, and even overcome in the extreme states of solidification. Or, to do away with the technical nomenclature, he argued that death, when not violent and in which none of the organs had suffered injury, was merely suspended vitality; and that, in such instances, life could be induced to resume its functions by the use of proper methods. This, then, was his idea: To discover the method – and by practical experimentation prove the possibility – of renewing vitality in a structure from which life had seemingly fled. Of course, he recognized the futility of such endeavor after decomposition had set in; he must have organisms which but the moment, the hour, or the day before, had been quick with life. With me, in a crude way, he had proved this theory. I was really drowned, really dead, when picked from the water of San

Francisco Bay – but the vital spark had been renewed by means of his aerotherapeutical apparatus, as he called it.

Now to his dark purpose concerning me. He first showed me how completely I was in his power. He had sent the yacht away for a year, retaining only his two blackies, who were utterly devoted to him. He then made an exhaustive review of his theory and outlined the method of proof he had adopted, concluding with the startling announcement that I was to be his subject.

I had faced death and weighed my chances in many a desperate venture, but never in one of this nature. I can swear I am no coward, yet this proposition of journeying back and forth across the borderline of death put the yellow fear upon me. I asked for time, which he granted, at the same time assuring me that but the one course was open – I must submit. Escape from the island was out of the question; escape by suicide was not to be entertained, though really preferable to what it seemed I must undergo; my only hope was to destroy my captors. But this latter was frustrated through the precautions taken by my father. I was subjected to a constant surveillance, even in my sleep being guarded by one or the other of the blacks.

Having pleaded in vain, I announced and proved that I was his son. It was my last card, and I had placed all my hopes upon it. But he was inexorable; he was not a father but a scientific machine. I wonder yet how it ever came to pass that he married my mother or begat me, for there was not the slightest grain of emotion in his make-up. Reason was all in all to him, nor could he understand such things as love or sympathy in others, except as petty weaknesses which should be overcome. So he informed me that in the beginning he had given me life, and who had better right to take it away than he? Such, he said, was not his desire, however; he merely wished to borrow it occasionally, promising to return it punctually at the appointed time. Of course, there was a liability of mishaps, but I could do no more than take the chances, since the affairs of men were full of such.

The better to insure success, he wished me to be in the best possible condition, so I was dieted and trained like a great athlete before a decisive contest. What could I do? If I had to undergo the peril, it were best to be in good shape. In my intervals of relaxation he allowed me to assist in the arranging of the apparatus and in the various subsidiary experiments. The interest I took in all such operations can be imagined. I mastered the work as thoroughly as he, and often had the pleasure of seeing some of my suggestions or alterations put into effect. After such events I would smile grimly, conscious of officiating at my own funeral.

He began by inaugurating a series of experiments in toxicology. When all was ready, I was killed by a stiff dose of strychnine and allowed to lie dead for some twenty hours. During that period my body was dead, absolutely dead. All respiration and circulation ceased; but the frightful part of it was, that while the protoplasmic coagulation proceeded, I retained consciousness and was enabled to study it in all its ghastly details.

The apparatus to bring me back to life was an air-tight chamber, fitted to receive my body. The mechanism was simple – a few valves, a rotary shaft and crank, and an electric motor. When in operation, the interior atmosphere was alternately condensed and rarefied, thus communicating to my lungs an artificial respiration without the agency of the hosing previously used. Though my body was inert, and, for all I knew, in the first stages of decomposition, I was cognizant of everything that transpired. I knew when they placed me in the chamber, and though all my senses were quiescent, I was aware of the hypodermic injections of a compound to react upon the coagulatory process. Then the chamber was closed and the machinery started. My anxiety was terrible; but the circulation became gradually restored, the different organs began to carry on their respective functions, and in an hour's time I was eating a hearty dinner.

It cannot be said that I participated in this series, nor in the subsequent ones, with much verve; but after two ineffectual attempts at escape, I began to take quite an interest. Besides, I was becoming accustomed. My father was beside himself at his success, and as the months rolled by his speculations took wilder and yet wilder flights. We ranged through the three great classes of poisons, the neurotics, the gaseous and the irritants, but carefully avoided some of the mineral irritants and passed the whole group of corrosives. During the poison regime I became quite accustomed to dying, and had but one mishap to shake my growing confidence. Scarifying a number of lesser blood vessels in my arm, he introduced a minute quantity of that most frightful of poisons, the arrow poison, or curare. I lost consciousness at the start, quickly followed by the cessation of respiration and circulation, and so far had the solidification of the protoplasm advanced, that he gave up all hope. But at the last moment he applied a discovery he had been working upon, receiving such encouragement as to redouble his efforts.

In a glass vacuum, similar but not exactly like a Crookes' tube, was placed a magnetic field. When penetrated by polarized light, it gave no phenomena of phosphorescence nor of rectilinear projection of atoms, but emitted non-luminous rays, similar to the X-ray. While the X-ray could reveal opaque objects hidden in dense mediums, this was possessed of far subtler penetration. By this he photographed my body, and found on the negative an infinite number of blurred

55

shadows, due to the chemical and electric motions still going on. This was an infallible proof that the rigor mortis in which I lay was not genuine; that is, those mysterious forces, those delicate bonds which held my soul to my body, were still in action. The resultants of all other poisons were unapparent, save those of mercurial compounds, which usually left me languid for several days.

Another series of delightful experiments was with electricity. We verified Tesla's assertion that high currents were utterly harmless by passing 100,000 volts through my body. As this did not affect me, the current was reduced to 2,500, and I was quickly electrocuted. This time he ventured so far as to allow me to remain dead, or in a state of suspended vitality, for three days. It took four hours to bring me back.

Once, he superinduced lockjaw, but the agony of dying was so great that I positively refused to undergo similar experiments. The easiest deaths were by asphyxiation, such as drowning, strangling, and suffocation by gas; while those by morphine, opium, cocaine and chloroform, were not at all hard.

Another time, after being suffocated, he kept me in cold storage for three months, not permitting me to freeze or decay. This was without my knowledge, and I was in a great fright on discovering the lapse of time. I became afraid of what he might do when I lay dead, my alarm being increased by the predilection he was beginning to betray toward vivisection. The last time I was resurrected, I discovered that he had been tampering with my breast. Though he had carefully dressed and sewed the incisions up, they were so severe that I had to take to my bed for some time. It was during this convalescence that I evolved the plan by which I ultimately escaped.

While feigning unbounded enthusiasm in the work, I asked and received a vacation from my moribund occupation. During this period I devoted myself to laboratory work, while he was too deep in the vivisection of the many animals captured by the blacks to take notice of my work.

It was on these two propositions that I constructed my theory: First, electrolysis, or the decomposition of water into its constituent gases by means of electricity; and, second, by the hypothetical existence of a force, the converse of gravitation, which Astor has named 'apergy'. Terrestrial attraction, for instance, merely draws objects together but does not combine them; hence, apergy is merely repulsion. Now, atomic or molecular attraction not only draws objects together but integrates them; and it was the converse of this, or a disintegrative force, which I wished to not only discover and produce, but to direct at will. Thus the molecules of hydrogen and oxygen reacting on each other, separate and create new molecules, containing both elements and forming water. Electrolysis causes these molecules to split up and resume their original condition, producing the two gases separately. The force I wished to find must not only do this with two, but with all elements, no matter in what compounds they exist. If I could then entice my father within its radius, he would be instantly disintegrated and sent flying to the four quarters, a mass of isolated elements.

It must not be understood that this force, which I finally came to control, annihilated matter, it merely annihilated form. Nor, as I soon discovered, had it any effect on inorganic structure; but to all organic form it was absolutely fatal. This partiality puzzled me at first, though had I stopped to think deeper I would have seen through it. Since the number of atoms in organic molecules is far greater than in the most complex mineral molecules, organic compounds are characterized by their instability and the ease with which they are split up by physical forces and chemical reagents.

By two powerful batteries, connected with magnets constructed specially for this purpose, two tremendous forces were projected. Considered apart from each other, they were perfectly harmless; but they accomplished their purpose by focusing at an invisible point in mid-air. After practically demonstrating its success, besides narrowly escaping being blown into nothingness, I laid my trap. Concealing the magnets, so that their force made the whole space of my chamber doorway a field of death, and placing by my couch a button by which I could throw on the current from the storage batteries, I climbed into bed.

The blackies still guarded my sleeping quarters, one relieving the other at midnight. I turned on the current as soon as the first man arrived. Hardly had I begun to doze, when I was aroused by a sharp, metallic tinkle. There, on the mid-threshold, lay the collar of Dan, my father's St Bernard. My keeper ran to pick it up. He disappeared like a gust of wind, his clothes falling to the floor in a heap. There was a slight whiff of ozone in the air, but since the principal gaseous components of his body were hydrogen, oxygen and nitrogen, which are equally colourless and odourless, there was no other manifestation of his departure. Yet when I shut off the current and removed the garments, I found a deposit of carbon in the form of animal charcoal; also other powders, the isolated, solid elements of his organism, such as sulphur, potassium and iron. Resetting the trap, I crawled back to bed. At midnight I got up and removed the remains of the second blacky, and then slept peacefully till morning.

I was awakened by the strident voice of my father, who was calling me from across the laboratory. I laughed to myself. There had been no one to call him and he had overslept. I could hear him as he approached my room with the intention of rousing me, and so I sat up in bed, the better to observe his translation – perhaps apotheosis were a better term. He paused a moment at the threshold, then took the fatal step. Puff! It was like the wind sighing among the pines. He was gone. His clothes fell in a fantastic heap on the floor. Besides ozone, I noticed the faint, garlic-like odor of phosphorus. A little pile of elementary solids lay among his garments. That was all. The wide world lay before me. My captors were not.

Back for Christmas
JOHN COLLIER

'DOCTOR,' SAID MAJOR SINCLAIR, 'we certainly must have you with us for Christmas.' It was afternoon and the Carpenters' living-room was filled with friends who had come to say last-minute farewells to the Doctor and his wife.

'He shall be back,' said Mrs Carpenter. 'I promise you.'

'It's hardly certain,' said Dr Carpenter. 'I'd like nothing better, of course.'

'After all,' said Mr Hewitt, 'you've contracted to lecture only for three months.'

'Anything may happen,' said Dr Carpenter.

'Whatever happens,' said Mrs Carpenter, beaming at them, 'he shall be back in England for Christmas. You may all believe me.'

They all believed her. The Doctor himself almost believed her. For ten years she had been promising him for dinner parties, garden parties, committees, heaven knows what, and the promises had always been kept.

The farewells began. There was a fluting of compliments on dear Hermione's marvellous arrangements. She and her husband would drive to Southampton that evening. They would embark the following day. No trains, no bustle, no last-minute worries. Certainly the Doctor was marvellously looked after. He would be a great success in America. Especially with Hermione to see to everything. She would have a wonderful time, too. She would see the skyscrapers. Nothing like that in Little Godwearing. But she must be very sure to bring him back. 'Yes, I will bring him back. You may rely upon it.' He mustn't be persuaded. No extensions. No wonderful post at some super-American hospital. Our infirmary needs him. And he must be back for Christmas. 'Yes,' Mrs Carpenter called to the last departing guest, 'I shall see to it. He shall be back by Christmas.'

The final arrangements for closing the house were very well managed. The maids soon had the tea things washed up; they came in, said good-bye, and were in time to catch the afternoon bus to Devizes.

Nothing remained but odds and ends, locking doors, seeing that everything was tidy. 'Go upstairs,' said Hermione, 'and change into your brown tweeds. Empty the pockets of that suit before you put it in your bag. I'll see to everything else. All you have to do is not to get in the way.'

The Doctor went upstairs and took off the suit he was wearing, but instead of the brown tweeds, he put on an old, dirty bath-gown, which he took from the back of his wardrobe. Then, after making one or two little arrangements, he leaned over the head of the stairs and called to his wife. 'Hermione! Have you a moment to spare?'

'Of course, dear. I'm just finished.'

'Just come up here for a moment. There's something rather extraordinary up here.'

Hermione immediately came up. 'Good heavens, my dear man!' she said, when she saw her husband. 'What are you lounging about in that filthy old thing for? I told you to have it burned long ago.'

'Who in the world,' said the Doctor, 'has dropped a gold chain down the bath-tub drain?'

'Nobody has, of course,' said Hermione. 'Nobody wears such a thing.'

'Then what is it doing there?' said the Doctor. 'Take this flashlight. If you lean right over, you can see it shining, deep down.'

'Some Woolworth's bangle off one of the maids,' said Hermione. 'It can be nothing else.' However, she took the flashlight and leaned over, squinting into the drain. The Doctor, raising a short length of lead pipe, struck two or three times with great force and precision, and tilting the body by the knees, tumbled it into the tub.

He then slipped off the bath-robe and, standing completely naked, unwrapped a towel full of implements and put them into the wash-basin. He spread several sheets of newspaper on the floor and turned once more to his victim.

She was dead, of course – horribly doubled up, like a somersaulter, at one end of the tub. He stood looking at her for a very long time, thinking of absolutely nothing at all. Then he saw how much blood there was and his mind began to move again.

First he pushed and pulled until she lay straight in the bath, then he removed her clothing. In a narrow bath-tub this was an extremely clumsy business, but he managed it at last and then turned on the taps. The water rushed into the tub, then dwindled, then died away, and the last of it gurgled down the drain.

'Good God!' he said. 'She turned it off at the main.'

There was only one thing to do: the Doctor hastily wiped his hands on a towel, opened the bathroom door with a clean corner of the towel, threw it back on to the bath stool, and ran downstairs, barefoot, light as a cat. The cellar door was in a corner of the entrance hall, under the stairs. He knew just where the cut-off was. He had reason to: he had been pottering about down there for some time past – trying to scrape out a bin for wine, he had told Hermione. He pushed open the cellar door, went down the steep steps, and just before the closing door plunged the cellar into pitch darkness, he put his hand on the tap and turned it on. Then he felt his way back along the grimy wall till he came to the steps. He was about to ascend them when the bell rang.

The Doctor was scarcely aware of the ringing as a sound. It was like a spike of iron pushed slowly up through his stomach. It went on until it reached his brain. Then something broke. He threw himself down in the coal dust on the floor and said, 'I'm through. I'm through.'

'They've got no right to come. Fools!' he said. Then he heard himself panting. 'None of this,' he said to himself. 'None of this.'

He began to revive. He got to his feet, and when the bell rang again the sound passed through him almost painlessly. 'Let them go away,' he said. Then he heard the front door open. He said, 'I don't care.' His shoulder came up, like that of a boxer, to shield his face. 'I give up,' he said.

He heard people calling. 'Herbert!' 'Hermione!' It was the Wallingfords. 'Damn them! They come butting in. People anxious to get off. All naked! And blood and coal dust! I'm done! I'm through! I can't do it.'

'Herbert!'

'Hermione!'

'Where the dickens can they be?'

'The car's there.'

'Maybe they've popped round to Mrs Liddell's.'

'We must see them.'

'Or to the shops, maybe. Something at the last minute.'

'Not Hermione. I say, listen! Isn't that someone having a bath? Shall I shout? What about whanging on the door?'

'Sh-h-h! Don't. It might not be tactful.'

'No harm in a shout.'

'Look, dear. Let's come in on our way back. Hermione said they wouldn't be leaving before seven. They're dining on the way, in Salisbury.'

'Think so? All right. Only I want a last drink with old Herbert. He'd be hurt.'

'Let's hurry. We can be back by half-past six.'

The Doctor heard them walk out and the front door close quietly behind them. He thought, 'Half-past six. I can do it.'

He crossed the hall, sprang the latch of the front door, went upstairs, and taking his instruments from the wash-basin, finished

61

what he had to do. He came down again, clad in his bath-gown, carrying parcel after parcel of towelling or newspaper neatly secured with safety-pins. These he packed carefully into the narrow, deep hole he had made in the corner of the cellar, shovelled in the soil, spread the coal dust over all, satisfied himself that everything was in order, and went upstairs again. He then thoroughly cleansed the bath, and himself, and the bath again, dressed, and took his wife's clothing and his bath-gown to the incinerator.

One or two more little touches and everything was in order. It was only quarter-past six. The Wallingfords were always late; he had only to get into the car and drive off. It was a pity he couldn't wait till after dusk, but he could make a detour to avoid passing through the main street, and even if he was seen driving alone, people would only think Hermione had gone on ahead for some reason and they would forget about it.

Still, he was glad when he finally got away, entirely unobserved, on the open road, driving into the gathering dusk. He had to drive very carefully; he found himself unable to judge distances, his reactions were abnormally delayed, but that was a detail. When it was quite dark he allowed himself to stop the car on the top of the downs, in order to think.

The stars were superb. He could see the lights of one or two little towns far away on the plain below him. He was exultant. Everything that was to follow was perfectly simple. Marion was waiting in Chicago. She already believed him to be a widower. The lecture people could be put off with a word. He had nothing to do but establish himself in some thriving out-of-the-way town in America and he was safe for ever. There were Hermione's clothes, of course, in the suitcases: they could be disposed of through the porthole. Thank heaven she wrote her letters on the typewriter – a little thing like handwriting might have prevented everything. 'But there you are,' he said. 'She was up-to-date, efficient all along the line. Managed everything. Managed herself to death, damn her!'

'There's no reason to get excited,' he thought. 'I'll write a few letters for her, then fewer and fewer. Write myself – always expecting to get back, never quite able to. Keep the house one year, then another, then another; they'll get used to it. Might even come back alone in a year or two and clear it up properly. Nothing easier. But not for Christmas!' He started up the engine and was off.

In New York he felt free at last, really free. He was safe. He could look back with pleasure – at least, after a meal, lighting his cigarette, he could look back with a sort of pleasure – to the minute he had passed in the cellar listening to the bell, the door, and the voices. He could look forward to Marion.

As he strolled through the lobby of his hotel, the clerk, smiling, held up letters for him. It was the first batch from England. Well, what did that matter? It would be fun dashing off the typewritten sheets in Hermione's downright style, signing them with her squiggle, telling everyone what a success his first lecture had been, how thrilled he was with America but how certainly she'd bring him back for Christmas. Doubts could creep in later.

He glanced over the letters. Most were for Hermione. From the Sinclairs, the Wallingfords, the vicar, and a business letter from Holt & Sons, Builders and Decorators.

He stood in the lounge, people brushing by him. He opened the letters with his thumb, reading here and there, smiling. They all seemed very confident he would be back for Christmas. They relied on Hermione. 'That's where they all make their big mistake,' said the Doctor, who had taken to American phrases. The builders' letter he kept to the last. Some bill, probably. It was:

Dear Madam,

We are in receipt of your kind acceptance of estimate as below, and also of key.

We beg to repeat you may have every confidence in same being ready in ample time for Christmas present as stated. We are setting men to work this week.

We are, Madam,

Yours faithfully,
Paul Holt & Sons

To excavating, building up, suitably lining one sunken wine bin in cellar as indicated, using best materials, making good, etc. £18 0 0

Before the Party

W. SOMERSET MAUGHAM

MRS SKINNER LIKED TO BE IN GOOD TIME. She was already dressed, in black silk as befitted her age and the mourning she wore for her son-in-law, and now she put on her toque. She was a little uncertain about it, since the egrets' feathers which adorned it might very well arouse in some of the friends she would certainly meet at the party acid expostulations; and of course it was shocking to kill those beautiful white birds, in the mating season too, for the sake of their feathers; but there they were, so pretty and stylish, and it would have been silly to refuse them, and it would have hurt her son-in-law's feelings. He had brought them all the way from Borneo and he expected her to be so pleased with them. Kathleen had made herself rather unpleasant about them, she must wish she hadn't now, after what had happened, but Kathleen had never really liked Harold. Mrs Skinner, standing at her dressing-table, placed the toque on her head, it was after all the only nice hat she had, and put in a pin with a large jet knob. If anybody spoke to her about the ospreys she had her answer.

'I know it's dreadful,' she would say, 'and I wouldn't dream of buying them, but my poor son-in-law brought them back the last time he was home on leave.'

That would explain her possession of them and excuse their use. Everyone had been very kind. Mrs Skinner took a clean handkerchief from a drawer and sprinkled a little *Eau de Cologne* on it. She never used scent, and she had always thought it rather fast, but *Eau de Cologne* was so refreshing. She was very nearly ready now, and her eyes wandered out of the window behind her looking-glass. Canon Heywood had a beautiful day for his garden-party. It was warm and the sky was blue; the trees had not yet lost the fresh green of the spring. She smiled as she saw her little grand-daughter in the strip of garden behind the house busily raking her very own flower-bed. Mrs Skinner wished Joan were not quite so pale, it was a mistake to have kept her so long in the tropics; and she was so grave for her age, you never saw her run about; she played quiet games of her own invention and watered her garden. Mrs Skinner gave the front of her dress a little pat, took up her gloves, and went downstairs.

Kathleen was at the writing-table in the window busy with lists she was making, for she was honorary secretary of the Ladies' Golf Club, and when there were competitions had a good deal to do. But she too was ready for the party.

'I see you've put on your jumper after all,' said Mrs Skinner.

They had discussed at luncheon whether Kathleen should wear her jumper or her black chiffon. The jumper was black and white, and Kathleen thought it rather smart, but it was hardly mourning. Millicent, however, was in favour of it.

'There's no reason why we should all look as if we'd just come from a funeral,' she said. 'Harold's been dead eight months.'

To Mrs Skinner it seemed rather unfeeling to talk like that. Millicent was strange since her return from Borneo.

'You're not going to leave off your weeds yet, darling?' she asked.

Millicent did not give a direct answer.

'People don't wear mourning in the way they used,' she said. She paused a little and when she went on there was a tone in her voice which Mrs Skinner thought quite peculiar. It was plain that Kathleen noticed it too, for she gave her sister a curious look. 'I'm sure Harold wouldn't wish me to wear mourning for him indefinitely.'

'I dressed early because I wanted to say something to Millicent,' said Kathleen in reply to her mother's observation.

'Oh?'

Kathleen did not explain. But she put her lists aside and with knitted brows read for the second time a letter from a lady who complained that the committee had most unfairly marked down her handicap from twenty-four to eighteen. It requires a good deal of tact to be honorary secretary to a ladies' golf club. Mrs Skinner began to put on her new gloves. The sun-blinds kept the room cool and dark. She looked at the great wooden hornbill, gaily painted, which Harold had left in her safekeeping; and it seemed a little odd and barbaric to her, but he had set much store on it. It had some religious significance and Canon Heywood had been greatly struck by it. On the wall, over the sofa, were Malay weapons, she forgot what they were called, and here and there on occasional tables pieces of silver and brass which Harold at various times had sent to them. She had liked Harold and involuntarily her eyes sought his photograph which stood on the piano with photographs of her two daughters, her grandchild, her sister and her sister's son.

'Why, Kathleen, where's Harold's photograph?' she asked.

Kathleen looked round. It no longer stood in its place.

'Someone's taken it away,' said Kathleen.

Surprised and puzzled, she got up and went over to the piano. The photographs had been rearranged so that no gap should show.

'Perhaps Millicent wanted to have it in her bedroom,' said Mrs Skinner.

'I should have noticed it. Besides, Millicent has several photographs of Harold. She keeps them locked up.'

Mrs Skinner had thought it very peculiar that her daughter should have no photographs of Harold in her room. Indeed she had spoken of it once, but Millicent had made no reply. Millicent had been strangely silent since she came back from Borneo, and had not encouraged the sympathy Mrs Skinner would have been so willing to show her. She seemed unwilling to speak of her great loss. Sorrow took people in different ways. Her husband had said the best thing was to leave her alone. The thought of him turned her ideas to the party they were going to.

'Father asked if I thought he ought to wear a top-hat,' she said. 'I said I thought it was just as well to be on the safe side.'

It was going to be quite a grand affair. They were having ices, strawberry and vanilla, from Boddy, the confectioner, but the Heywoods were making the iced coffee at home. Everyone would be there. They had been asked to meet the Bishop of Hong Kong, who was staying with the Canon, an old college friend of his, and he was going to speak on the Chinese missions. Mrs Skinner, whose daughter had lived in the East for eight years and whose son-in-law had been Resident of a district in Borneo, was in a flutter of interest. Naturally it meant more to her than to people who had never had anything to do with the Colonies and that sort of thing.

'What can they know of England who only England know?' as Mr Skinner said.

He came into the room at that moment. He was a lawyer, as his father had been before him, and he had offices in Lincoln's Inn Fields. He went up to London every morning and came down every evening. He was only able to accompany his wife and daughters to the Canon's garden-party because the Canon had very wisely chosen a Saturday to have it on. Mr Skinner looked very well in his tail-coat and pepper-and-salt trousers. He was not exactly dressy, but he was neat. He looked like a respectable family solicitor, which indeed he was; his firm never touched work that was not perfectly above board, and if a client went to him with some trouble that was not quite nice, Mr Skinner would look grave.

'I don't think this is the sort of case that we very much care to undertake,' he said. 'I think you'd do better to go elsewhere.'

He drew towards him his writing-block and scribbled a name and address on it. He tore off a sheet of paper and handed it to his client.

'If I were you I think I would go and see these people. If you mention my name I believe they'll do anything they can for you.'

Mr Skinner was clean-shaven and very bald. His pale lips were tight and thin, but his blue eyes were shy. He had no colour in his cheeks and his face was much lined.

'I see you've put on your new trousers,' said Mrs Skinner.

'I thought it would be a good opportunity,' he answered. 'I was wondering if I should wear a buttonhole.'

'I wouldn't, father,' said Kathleen. 'I don't think it's awfully good form.'

'A lot of people will be wearing them,' said Mrs Skinner.

'Only clerks and people like that,' said Kathleen. 'The Heywoods have had to ask everybody, you know. And besides, we are in mourning.'

'I wonder if there'll be a collection after the Bishop's address,' said Mr Skinner.

'I should hardly think so,' said Mrs Skinner.

'I think it would be rather bad form,' agreed Kathleen.

'It's as well to be on the safe side,' said Mr Skinner. 'I'll give for all of us. I was wondering if ten shillings would be enough or if I must give a pound.'

'If you give anything I think you ought to give a pound, father,' said Kathleen.

'I'll see when the time comes. I don't want to give less than anyone else, but on the other hand I see no reason to give more than I need.'

Kathleen put away her papers in the drawer of the writing-table and stood up. She looked at her wrist-watch.

'Is Millicent ready?' asked Mrs Skinner.

'There's plenty of time. We're only asked at four, and I don't think we ought to arrive much before half-past. I told Davis to bring the car round at four-fifteen.'

Generally Kathleen drove the car, but on grand occasions like this Davis, who was the gardener, put on his uniform and acted as chauffeur. It looked better when you drove up, and naturally Kathleen didn't want to drive herself when she was wearing her new jumper. The sight of her mother forcing her fingers one by one into her new gloves reminded her that she must put on her own. She smelt them to see if any odour of the cleaning still clung to them. It was very slight. She didn't believe anyone would notice.

At last the door opened and Millicent came in. She wore her widow's weeds. Mrs Skinner never could get used to them, but of course she knew that Millicent must wear them for a year. It was a pity they didn't suit her; they suited some people. She had tried on Millicent's bonnet once, with its white band and long veil, and thought she looked very well in it. Of course she hoped dear Alfred would survive her, but if he didn't she would never go out of weeds.

67

Queen Victoria never had. It was different for Millicent; Millicent was a much younger woman; she was only thirty-six: it was very sad to be a widow at thirty-six. And there wasn't much chance of her marrying again. Kathleen wasn't very likely to marry now, she was thirty-five; last time Millicent and Harold had come home she had suggested that they should have Kathleen to stay with them; Harold had seemed willing enough, but Millicent said it wouldn't do. Mrs Skinner didn't know why not. It would give her a chance. Of course they didn't want to get rid of her, but a girl ought to marry, and somehow all the men they knew at home were married already. Millicent said the climate was trying. It was true she was a bad colour. No one would think now that Millicent had been the prettier of the two. Kathleen had fined down as she grew older, of course some people said she was too thin, but now that she had cut her hair, with her cheeks red from playing golf in all weathers, Mrs Skinner thought her quite pretty. No one could say that of poor Millicent; she had lost her figure completely; she had never been tall, and now that she had filled out she looked stocky. She was a good deal too fat; Mrs Skinner supposed it was due to the tropical heat that prevented her from taking exercise. Her skin was sallow and muddy; and her blue eyes, which had been her best feature, had gone quite pale.

'She ought to do something about her neck,' Mrs Skinner reflected. 'She's becoming dreadfully jowly.'

She had spoken of it once or twice to her husband. He remarked that Millicent wasn't as young as she was; that might be, but she needn't let herself go altogether. Mrs Skinner made up her mind to talk to her daughter seriously, but of course she must respect her grief, and she would wait till the year was up. She was just as glad to have this reason to put off a conversation the thought of which made her slightly nervous. For Millicent was certainly changed. There was something sullen in her face which made her mother not quite at home with her. Mrs Skinner liked to say aloud all the thoughts that passed through her head, but Millicent when you made a remark (just to say something, you know) had an awkward habit of not answering, so that you wondered whether she had heard. Sometimes Mrs Skinner found it so irritating, that not to be quite sharp with Millicent she had to remind herself that poor Harold had only been dead eight months.

The light from the window fell on the widow's heavy face as she advanced silently, but Kathleen stood with her back to it. She watched her sister for a moment.

'Millicent, there's something I want to say to you,' she said. 'I was playing golf with Gladys Heywood this morning.'

'Did you beat her?' asked Millicent.

Gladys Heywood was the Canon's only unmarried daughter.

'She told me something about you which I think you ought to know.'

Millicent's eyes passed beyond her sister to the little girl watering flowers in the garden.

'Have you told Annie to give Joan her tea in the kitchen, mother?' she said.

'Yes, she'll have it when the servants have theirs.'

Kathleen looked at her sister coolly.

'The Bishop spent two or three days at Singapore on his way home,' she went on. 'He's very fond of travelling. He's been to Borneo, and he knows a good many of the people that you know.'

'He'll be interested to see you, dear,' said Mrs Skinner. 'Did he know poor Harold?'

'Yes, he met him at Kuala Solor. He remembers him very well. He says he was shocked to hear of his death.'

Millicent sat down and began to put on her black gloves. It seemed strange to Mrs Skinner that she received these remarks with complete silence.

'Oh, Millicent,' she said, 'Harold's photo has disappeared. Have you taken it?'

'Yes, I put it away.'

'I should have thought you'd like to have it out.'

Once more Millicent said nothing. It really was an exasperating habit.

Kathleen turned slightly in order to face her sister.

'Millicent, why did you tell us that Harold died of fever?'

The widow made no gesture, she looked at Kathleen with steady eyes, but her sallow skin darkened with a flush. She did not reply.

'What *do* you mean, Kathleen?' asked Mr Skinner, with surprise.

'The Bishop says that Harold committed suicide.'

Mrs Skinner gave a startled cry, but her husband put out a deprecating hand.

'Is it true, Millicent?'

'It is.'

'But why didn't you tell us?'

Millicent paused for an instant. She fingered idly a piece of Brunei brass which stood on the table by her side. That too had been a present from Harold.

'I thought it better for Joan that her father should be thought to have died of fever. I didn't want her to know anything about it.'

'You've put us in an awfully awkward position,' said Kathleen, frowning a little. 'Gladys Heywood said she thought it rather nasty of me not to have told her the truth. I had the greatest difficulty in

69

getting her to believe that I knew absolutely nothing about it. She said her father was rather put out. He says, after all the years we've known one another, and considering that he married you, and the terms we've been on, and all that, he does think we might have had confidence in him. And at all events, if we didn't want to tell him the truth we needn't have told him a lie.'

'I must say I sympathise with him there,' said Mr Skinner, acidly.

'Of course I told Gladys that we weren't to blame. We only told them what you told us.'

'I hope it didn't put you off your game,' said Millicent.

'Really, my dear, I think that is a most improper observation,' exclaimed her father.

He rose from his chair, walked over to the empty fireplace, and from force of habit stood in front of it with parted coat-tails.

'It was my business,' said Millicent, 'and if I chose to keep it to myself I didn't see why I shouldn't.'

'It doesn't look as if you had any affection for your mother if you didn't even tell her,' said Mrs Skinner.

Millicent shrugged her shoulders.

'You might have known it was bound to come out,' said Kathleen.

'Why? I didn't expect that two gossiping old parsons would have nothing else to talk about than me.'

'When the Bishop said he'd been to Borneo it's only natural that the Heywoods should ask him if he knew you and Harold.'

'All that's neither here nor there,' said Mr Skinner. 'I think you should certainly have told us the truth, and we could have decided what was the best thing to do. As a solicitor I can tell you that in the long run it only makes things worse if you attempt to hide them.'

'Poor Harold,' said Mrs Skinner, and the tears began to trickle down her raddled cheeks. 'It seems dreadful. He was always a good son-in-law to me. Whatever induced him to do such a dreadful thing?'

'The climate.'

'I think you'd better give us all the facts, Millicent,' said her father.

'Kathleen will tell you.'

Kathleen hesitated. What she had to say really was rather dreadful. It seemed terrible that such things should happen to a family like theirs.

'The Bishop says he cut his throat.'

Mrs Skinner gasped and she went impulsively up to her bereaved daughter. She wanted to fold her in her arms.

'My poor child,' she sobbed.

But Millicent withdrew herself.

'Please don't fuss me, mother. I really can't stand being mauled about.'

'Really, Millicent,' said Mr Skinner, with a frown.

He did not think she was behaving very nicely.

Mrs Skinner dabbed her eyes carefully with her handkerchief and with a sigh and a little shake of the head returned to her chair. Kathleen fidgeted with the long chain she wore round her neck.

'It does seem rather absurd that I should have to be told the details of my brother-in-law's death by a friend. It makes us all look such fools. The Bishop wants very much to see you, Millicent; he wants to tell you how much he feels for you.' She paused, but Millicent did not speak. 'He says that Millicent had been away with Joan and when she came back she found poor Harold lying dead on his bed.'

'It must have been a great shock,' said Mr Skinner.

Mrs Skinner began to cry again, but Kathleen put her hand gently on her shoulder.

'Don't cry, mother,' she said. 'It'll make your eyes red and people will think it so funny.'

They were all silent while Mrs Skinner, drying her eyes, made a successful effort to control herself. It seemed very strange to her that at this very moment she should be wearing in her toque the ospreys that poor Harold had given her.

'There's something else I ought to tell you,' said Kathleen.

Millicent looked at her sister again, without haste, and her eyes were steady, but watchful. She had the look of a person who is waiting for a sound which he is afraid of missing.

'I don't want to say anything to wound you, dear,' Kathleen went on, 'but there's something else and I think you ought to know it. The Bishop says that Harold drank.'

'Oh, my dear, how dreadful!' cried Mrs Skinner. 'What a shocking thing to say. Did Gladys Heywood tell you? What did you say?'

'I said it was entirely untrue.'

'This is what comes of making secrets of things,' said Mr Skinner, irritably. 'It's always the same. If you try and hush a thing up all sorts of rumours get about which are ten times worse than the truth.'

'They told the Bishop in Singapore that Harold had killed himself while he was suffering from delirium tremens. I think for all our sakes you ought to deny that, Millicent.'

'It's such a dreadful thing to have said about anyone who's dead,' said Mrs Skinner. 'And it'll be so bad for Joan when she grows up.'

'But what is the foundation of this story, Millicent?' asked her father. 'Harold was always very abstemious.'

'Here,' said the widow.

'Did he drink?'

'Like a fish.'

The answer was so unexpected, and the tone so sardonic, that all

71

three of them were startled.

'Millicent, how can you talk like that of your husband when he's dead?' cried her mother, clasping her neatly gloved hands. 'I can't understand you. You've been so strange since you came back. I could never have believed that a girl of mine could take her husband's death like that.'

'Never mind about that, mother,' said Mr Skinner. 'We can go into all that later.'

He walked to the window and looked out at the sunny little garden, and then walked back into the room. He took his pince-nez out of his pocket and, though he had no intention of putting them on, wiped them with his handkerchief. Millicent looked at him and in her eyes, unmistakably, was a look of irony which was quite cynical. Mr Skinner was vexed. He had finished his week's work and he was a free man till Monday morning. Though he had told his wife that this garden-party was a great nuisance and he would much sooner have tea quietly in his own garden, he had been looking forward to it. He did not care very much about Chinese missions, but it would be interesting to meet the Bishop. And now this! It was not the kind of thing he cared to be mixed up in; it was most unpleasant to be told on a sudden that his son-in-law was a drunkard and a suicide. Millicent was thoughtfully smoothing her white cuffs. Her coolness irritated him; but instead of addressing her he spoke to his younger daughter.

'Why don't you sit down, Kathleen? Surely there are plenty of chairs in the room.'

Kathleen drew forward a chair and without a word seated herself. Mr Skinner stopped in front of Millicent and faced her.

'Of course I see why you told us Harold had died of fever. I think it was a mistake, because that sort of thing is bound to come out sooner or later. I don't know how far what the Bishop has told the Heywoods coincides with the facts, but if you will take my advice you will tell us everything as circumstantially as you can, then we can see. We can't hope that it will go no further now that Canon Heywood and Gladys know. In a place like this people are bound to talk. It will make it easier for all of us if we at all events know the exact truth.'

Mrs Skinner and Kathleen thought he put the matter very well. They waited for Millicent's reply. She had listened with an impassive face; that sudden flush had disappeared and it was once more, as usual, pasty and sallow.

'I don't think you'll much like the truth if I tell it you,' she said.

'You must know that you can count on our sympathy and understanding,' said Kathleen gravely.

Millicent gave her a glance and the shadow of a smile flickered across her set mouth. She looked slowly at the three of them. Mrs

72

Skinner had an uneasy impression that she looked at them as though they were mannequins at a dressmaker's. She seemed to live in a different world from theirs and to have no connection with them.

'You know, I wasn't in love with Harold when I married him,' she said reflectively.

Mrs Skinner was on the point of making an exclamation when a rapid gesture of her husband, barely indicated, but after so many years of married life perfectly significant, stopped her. Millicent went on. She spoke with a level voice, slowly, and there was little change of expression in her tone.

'I was twenty-seven, and no one else seemed to want to marry me. It's true he was forty-four, and it seemed rather old, but he had a very good position, hadn't he? I wasn't likely to get a better chance.'

Mrs Skinner felt inclined to cry again, but she remembered the party.

'Of course I see now why you took his photograph away,' she said dolefully.

'Don't, mother,' exclaimed Kathleen.

It had been taken when he was engaged to Millicent and was a very good photograph of Harold. Mrs Skinner had always thought him quite a fine man. He was heavily built, tall and perhaps a little too fat, but he held himself well, and his presence was imposing. He was inclined to be bald, even then, but men did go bald very early nowadays, and he said that topees, sun-helmets, you know, were very bad for the hair. He had a small dark moustache, and his face was deeply burned by the sun. Of course his best feature was his eyes; they were brown and large, like Joan's. His conversation was interesting. Kathleen said he was pompous, but Mrs Skinner didn't think him so, she didn't mind it if a man laid down the law; and when she saw, as she very soon did, that he was attracted by Millicent she began to like him very much. He was always very attentive to Mrs Skinner, and she listened as though she were really interested when he spoke of his district, and told her of the big game he had killed. Kathleen said he had a pretty good opinion of himself, but Mrs Skinner came of a generation which accepted without question the good opinion that men had of themselves. Millicent saw very soon which way the wind blew, and though she said nothing to her mother, her mother knew that if Harold asked her she was going to accept him.

Harold was staying with some people who had been thirty years in Borneo and they spoke well of the country. There was no reason why a woman shouldn't live comfortably; of course the children had to come home when they were seven; but Mrs Skinner thought it unnecessary to trouble about that yet. She asked Harold to dine, and she told him they were always in to tea. He seemed to be at a loose end, and when his visit to his old friends was drawing to a close, she told him they would be very much pleased if he would come and spend a fortnight with them. It was towards the end of this that Harold and Millicent became engaged. They had a very pretty wedding, they went to Venice for their honeymoon, and then they started for the East. Millicent wrote from various ports at which the ship touched. She seemed happy.

'People were very nice to me at Kuala Solor,' she said. Kuala Solor was the chief town of the state of Sembulu. 'We stayed with the Resident and everyone asked us to dinner. Once or twice I heard men ask Harold to have a drink, but he refused; he said he had turned over a new leaf now he was a married man. I didn't know why they laughed. Mrs Gray, the Resident's wife, told me they were all so glad Harold was married. She said it was dreadfully lonely for a bachelor on one of the outstations. When we left Kuala Solor Mrs Gray said good-bye to me so funnily that I was quite surprised. It was as if she was solemnly putting Harold in my charge.'

They listened to her in silence. Kathleen never took her eyes off her sister's impassive face; but Mr Skinner stared straight in front of him at the Malay arms, krises and parangs, which hung on the wall above the sofa on which his wife sat.

'It wasn't till I went back to Kuala Solor a year and a half later, that I found out why their manner had seemed so odd.' Millicent gave a queer little sound like the echo of a scornful laugh. 'I knew then a good deal that I hadn't known before. Harold came to England that time in order to marry. He didn't much mind who it was. Do you remember how we spread ourselves out to catch him, mother? We needn't have taken so much trouble.'

'I don't know what you mean, Millicent,' said Mrs Skinner, not without acerbity, for the insinuation of scheming did not please her. 'I saw he was attracted by you.'

Millicent shrugged her heavy shoulders.

'He was a confirmed drunkard. He used to go to bed every night with a bottle of whisky and empty it before morning. The Chief Secretary told him he'd have to resign unless he stopped drinking. He said he'd give him one more chance. He could take his leave then and go to England. He advised him to marry so that when he got back he'd have someone to look after him. Harold married me because he wanted a keeper. They took bets in Kuala Solor on how long I'd make him stay sober.'

'But he was in love with you,' Mrs Skinner interrupted. 'You don't know how he used to speak to me about you, and at that time you're speaking of, when you went to Kuala Solor to have Joan, he wrote me such a charming letter about you.'

Millicent looked at her mother again and a deep colour dyed her sallow skin. Her hands, lying on her lap, began to tremble a little. She thought of those first months of her married life. The Government launch took them to the mouth of the river, and they spent the night at the bungalow which Harold said jokingly was their seaside residence. Next day they went up-stream in a prahu. From the novels she had read she expected the rivers of Borneo to be dark and strangely sinister, but the sky was blue, dappled with little white clouds, and the green of the mangroves and the nipahs, washed by the flowing water, glistened in the sun. On each side stretched the pathless jungle, and in the distance, silhouetted against the sky, was the rugged outline of a mountain. The air in the early morning was fresh and buoyant. She seemed to enter upon a friendly, fertile land, and she had a sense of spacious freedom. They watched the banks for monkeys sitting on the branches of the tangled trees, and once Harold pointed out something that looked like a log and said it was a crocodile. The Assistant Resident, in ducks and a topee, was at the landing-stage to meet them, and a dozen trim little soldiers were lined up to do them honour. The Assistant Resident was introduced to her. His name was Simpson.

'By Jove, sir,' he said to Harold, 'I'm glad to see you back. It's been deuced lonely without you.'

The Resident's bungalow, surrounded by a garden in which grew wildly all manner of gay flowers, stood on top of a low hill. It was a trifle shabby and the furniture was sparse, but the rooms were cool and of generous size.

'The kampong is down there,' said Harold, pointing.

Her eyes followed his gesture, and from among the coconut trees rose the beating of a gong. It gave her a queer little sensation in the heart.

Though she had nothing much to do the days passed easily enough. At dawn a boy brought them their tea and they lounged about the verandah, enjoying the fragrance of the morning (Harold in a singlet and a sarong, she in a dressing-gown) till it was time to dress for breakfast. Then Harold went to his office and she spent an hour or two learning Malay. After tiffin he went back to his office while she slept. A cup of tea revived them both, and they went for a walk or played golf on the nine-hole links which Harold had made on a level piece of cleared jungle below the bungalow. Night fell at six and Mr Simpson came along to have a drink. They chatted till their late dinner hour, and sometimes Harold and Mr Simpson played chess. The balmy evenings were enchanting. The fireflies turned the bushes just below the verandah into coldly-sparkling, tremulous beacons, and flowering trees scented the air with sweet odours. After dinner they read the papers which had left London six weeks before and

75

presently went to bed. Millicent enjoyed being a married woman, with a house of her own, and she was pleased with the native servants, in their gay sarongs, who went about the bungalow, with bare feet, silent but friendly. It gave her a pleasant sense of importance to be the wife of the Resident. Harold impressed her by the fluency with which he spoke the language, by his air of command, and by his dignity. She went into the court-house now and then to hear him try cases. The multifariousness of his duties and the competent way in which he performed them aroused her respect. Mr Simpson told her that Harold understood the natives as well as any man in the country. He had the combination of firmness, tact and good-humour which was essential in dealing with that timid, revengeful and suspicious race. Millicent began to feel a certain admiration for her husband.

They had been married nearly a year when two English naturalists came to stay with them for a few days on their way to the interior. They brought a pressing recommendation from the Governor, and Harold said he wanted to do them proud. Their arrival was an agreeable change. Millicent asked Mr Simpson to dinner (he lived at the Fort and only dined with them on Sunday nights) and after dinner the men sat down to play bridge. Millicent left them presently and went to bed, but they were so noisy that for some time she could not get to sleep. She did not know at what hour she was awakened by Harold staggering into the room. She kept silent. He made up his mind to have a bath before getting into bed; the bath-house was just below their room, and he went down the steps that led to it. Apparently he slipped, for there was a great clatter, and he began to swear. Then he was violently sick. She heard him sluice the buckets of water over himself and in a little while, walking very cautiously this time, he crawled up the stairs and slipped into bed. Millicent pretended to be asleep. She was disgusted. Harold was drunk. She made up her mind to speak about it in the morning. What would the naturalists think of him? But in the morning Harold was so dignified that she hadn't quite the determination to refer to the matter. At eight Harold and she, with their two guests, sat down to breakfast. Harold looked round the table.

'Porridge,' he said. 'Millicent, your guests might manage a little Worcester Sauce for breakfast, but I don't think they'll much fancy anything else. Personally I shall content myself with a whisky and soda.'

The naturalists laughed, but shamefacedly.

'Your husband's a terror,' said one of them.

'I should not think I had properly performed the duties of hospitality if I sent you sober to bed on the first night of your visit,' said Harold, with his round, stately way of putting things.

Millicent, smiling acidly, was relieved to think that her guests had been as drunk as her husband. The next evening she sat up with them and the party broke up at a reasonable hour. But she was glad when the strangers went on with their journey. Their life resumed its placid course. Some months later Harold went on a tour of inspection of his district and came back with a bad attack of malaria. This was the first time she had seen the disease of which she had heard so much, and when he recovered it did not seem strange to her that Harold was very shaky. She found his manner peculiar. He would come back from the office and stare at her with glazed eyes; he would stand on the verandah, swaying slightly, but still dignified, and make long harangues about the political situation in England; losing the thread of his discourse, he would look at her with an archness which his natural stateliness made somewhat disconcerting and say:

'Pulls you down dreadfully, this confounded malaria. Ah, little woman, you little know the strain it puts upon a man to be an empire builder.'

She thought that Mr Simpson began to look worried, and once or twice, when they were alone, he seemed on the point of saying something to her which his shyness at the last moment prevented. The feeling grew so strong that it made her nervous, and one evening when Harold, she knew not why, had remained later than usual at the office she tackled him.

'What have you got to say to me, Mr Simpson?' she broke out suddenly.

He blushed and hesitated.

'Nothing. What makes you think I have anything in particular to say to you?'

Mr Simpson was a thin, weedy youth of four and twenty, with a fine head of waving hair which he took great pains to plaster down very flat. His wrists were swollen and scarred with mosquito bites. Millicent looked at him steadily.

'If it's something to do with Harold don't you think it would be kinder to tell me frankly?'

He grew scarlet now. He shuffled uneasily on his rattan chair. She insisted.

'I'm afraid you'll think it awful cheek,' he said at last. 'It's rotten of me to say anything about my chief behind his back. Malaria's a rotten thing, and after one's had a bout of it one feels awfully down and out.'

He hesitated again. The corners of his mouth sagged as if he were going to cry. To Millicent he seemed like a little boy.

'I'll be as silent as the grave,' she said with a smile, trying to conceal her apprehension. 'Do tell me.'

'I think it's a pity your husband keeps a bottle of whisky at the office. He's apt to take a nip more often than he otherwise would.'

Mr Simpson's voice was hoarse with agitation. Millicent felt a sudden coldness shiver through her. She controlled herself, for she knew that she must not frighten the boy if she were to get out of him all there was to tell. He was unwilling to speak. She pressed him, wheedling, appealing to his sense of duty, and at last she began to cry. Then he told her that Harold had been drunk more or less for the last fortnight, the natives were talking about it, and they said that soon he would be as bad as he had been before his marriage. He had been in the habit of drinking a good deal too much then, but details of that time, notwithstanding all her attempts, Mr Simpson resolutely declined to give her.

'Do you think he's drinking now?' she asked.

'I don't know.'

Millicent felt herself on a sudden hot with shame and anger. The Fort, as it was called because the rifles and the ammunition were kept there, was also the court-house. It stood opposite the Resident's bungalow in a garden of its own. The sun was just about to set and she did not need a hat. She got up and walked across. She found Harold sitting in the office behind the large hall in which he administered justice. There was a bottle of whisky in front of him. He was smoking cigarettes and talking to three or four Malays who stood in front of him listening with obsequious and at the same time scornful smiles. His face was red.

The natives vanished.

'I came to see what you were doing,' she said.

He rose, for he always treated her with elaborate politeness, and lurched. Feeling himself unsteady he assumed an elaborate stateliness of demeanour.

'Take a seat, my dear, take a seat. I was detained by press of work.'

She looked at him with angry eyes.

'You're drunk,' she said.

He stared at her, his eyes bulging a little, and a haughty look gradually traversed his large and fleshy face.

'I haven't the remotest idea what you mean,' he said.

She had been ready with a flow of wrathful expostulation, but suddenly she burst into tears. She sank into a chair and hid her face. Harold looked at her for an instant, then the tears began to trickle down his own cheeks; he came towards her with outstretched arms and fell heavily on his knees. Sobbing, he clasped her to him.

'Forgive me, forgive me,' he said. 'I promise you it shall not happen again. It was that damned malaria.'

'It's so humiliating,' she moaned.

He wept like a child. There was something very touching in the self-abasement of that big dignified man. Presently Millicent looked up. His eyes, appealing and contrite, sought hers.

'Will you give me your word of honour that you'll never touch liquor again?'

'Yes, yes. I hate it.'

It was then she told him that she was with child. He was overjoyed.

'That is the one thing I wanted. That'll keep me straight.'

They went back to the bungalow. Harold bathed himself and had a nap. After dinner they talked long and quietly. He admitted that before he married her he had occasionally drunk more than was good for him; in outstations it was easy to fall into bad habits. He agreed to everything that Millicent asked. And during the months before it was necessary for her to go to Kuala Solor for her confinement, Harold was an excellent husband, tender, thoughtful, proud and affectionate; he was irreproachable. A launch came to fetch her, she was to leave him for six weeks, and he promised faithfully to drink nothing during her absence. He put his hands on her shoulders.

'I never break a promise,' he said in his dignified way. 'But even without it, can you imagine that while you are going through so much, I should do anything to increase your troubles?'

Joan was born. Millicent stayed at the Resident's and Mrs Gray, his wife, a kindly creature of middle age, was very good to her. The two women had little to do during the long days they were alone but to talk, and in course of time Millicent learnt everything there was to know of her husband's alcoholic past. The fact which she found most difficult to reconcile herself to was that Harold had been told that the only condition upon which he would be allowed to keep his post was that he should bring back a wife. It caused in her a dull feeling of resentment. And when she discovered what a persistent drunkard he had been, she felt vaguely uneasy. She had a horrified fear that during her absence he would not have been able to resist the craving. She went home with her baby and a nurse. She spent a night at the mouth of the river and sent a messenger in a canoe to announce her arrival. She scanned the landing-stage anxiously as the launch approached it. Harold and Mr Simpson were standing there. The trim little soldiers were lined up. Her heart sank, for Harold was swaying slightly, like a man who seeks to keep his balance on a rolling ship, and she knew he was drunk.

It wasn't a very pleasant home-coming. She had almost forgotten her mother and father and her sister who sat there silently listening to her. Now she roused herself and became once more aware of their presence. All that she spoke of seemed very far away.

'I knew that I hated him then,' she said. 'I could have killed him.'

'Oh, Millicent, don't say that,' cried her mother. 'Don't forget that he's dead, poor man.'

Millicent looked at her mother, and for a moment a scowl darkened her impassive face. Mr Skinner moved uneasily.

'Go on,' said Kathleen.

'When he found out that I knew all about him he didn't bother very much more. In three months he had another attack of D.Ts.'

'Why didn't you leave him?' asked Kathleen.

'What would have been the good of that? He would have been dismissed from the service in a fortnight. Who was to keep me and Joan? I had to stay. And when he was sober I had nothing to complain of. He wasn't in the least in love with me, but he was fond of me; I hadn't married him because I was in love with him, but because I wanted to be married. I did everything I could to keep liquor from him; I managed to get Mr Gray to prevent whisky being sent from Kuala Solor, but he got it from the Chinese. I watched him as a cat watches a mouse. He was too cunning for me. In a little while he had another outbreak. He neglected his duties. I was afraid complaints would be made. We were two days from Kuala Solor and that was our safeguard, but I suppose something was said, for Mr Gray wrote a private letter of warning to me. I showed it to Harold. He stormed and blustered, but I saw he was frightened, and for two or three months he was quite sober. Then he began again. And so it went on till our leave became due.

'Before we came to stay here I begged and prayed him to be careful. I didn't want any of you to know what sort of a man I had married. All the time he was in England he was all right and before we sailed I warned him. He'd grown to be very fond of Joan, and very proud of her, and she was devoted to him. She always liked him better than she liked me. I asked him if he wanted to have his child grow up, knowing that he was a drunkard, and I found out that at last I'd got a hold on him. The thought terrified him. I told him that *I* wouldn't allow it, and if he ever let Joan see him drunk I'd take her away from him at once. Do you know, he grew quite pale when I said it. I fell on my knees that night and thanked God, because I'd found a way of saving my husband.

'He told me that if I would stand by him he would have another try. We made up our minds to fight the thing together. And he tried so hard. When he felt as though he *must* drink he came to me. You know he was inclined to be rather pompous; with me he was so humble, he was like a child; he depended on me. Perhaps he didn't love me when he married me, but he loved me then, me and Joan. I'd hated him, because of the humiliation, because when he was drunk and tried to be dignified and impressive he was loathsome; but now I got a strange feeling in my heart. It wasn't love, but it was a queer, shy tenderness.

He was something more than my husband, he was like a child that I'd carried under my heart for long and weary months. He was so proud of me and, you know, I was proud too. His long speeches didn't irritate me any more, and I only thought his stately ways rather funny and charming. At last we won. For two years he never touched a drop. He lost his craving entirely. He was even able to joke about it.

'Mr Simpson had left us then and we had another young man called Francis.

' "I'm a reformed drunkard, you know, Francis," Harold said to him once. "If it hadn't been for my wife I'd have been sacked long ago. I've got the best wife in the world, Francis."

'You don't know what it meant to me to hear him say that. I felt that all I'd gone through was worth while. I was so happy.'

She was silent. She thought of the broad, yellow and turbid river on whose banks she had lived so long. The egrets, white and gleaming in the tremulous sunset, flew down the stream in a flock, flew low and swift, and scattered. They were like a ripple of snowy notes, sweet and pure and spring-like, which an unseen hand drew forth, a divine arpeggio, from an unseen harp. They fluttered along between the green banks, wrapped in the shadows of evening, like the happy thoughts of a contented mind.

'Then Joan fell ill. For three weeks we were very anxious. There was no doctor nearer than Kuala Solor and we had to put up with the treatment of a native dispenser. When she grew well again I took her down to the mouth of the river in order to give her a breath of sea air. We stayed there a week. It was the first time I had been separated from Harold since I went away to have Joan. There was a fishing village, on piles, not far from us, but really we were quite alone. I thought a great deal about Harold, so tenderly, and all at once I knew I loved him. I was so glad when the prahu came to fetch us back, because I wanted to tell him. I thought it would mean a good deal to him. I can't tell you how happy I was. As we rowed up-stream the headman told me that Mr Francis had had to go up-country to arrest a woman who had murdered her husband. He had been gone a couple of days.

'I was surprised that Harold was not on the landing-stage to meet me; he was always very punctilious about that sort of thing; he used to say that husband and wife should treat one another as politely as they treated acquaintances; and I could not imagine what business had prevented him. I walked up the little hill on which the bungalow stood. The ayah brought Joan behind me. The bungalow was strangely silent. There seemed to be no servants about, and I could not make it out; I wondered if Harold hadn't expected me so soon and was out. I went up the steps. Joan was thirsty and the ayah took her to

81

the servants' quarters to give her something to drink. Harold was not in the sitting-room. I called him, but there was no answer. I was disappointed because I should have liked him to be there. I went into our bedroom. Harold wasn't out after all; he was lying on the bed asleep. I was really very much amused, because he always pretended he never slept in the afternoon. He said it was an unnecessary habit that we white people got into. I went up to the bed softly. I thought I would have a joke with him. I opened the mosquito curtains. He was lying on his back, with nothing on but a sarong, and there was an empty whisky bottle by his side. He was drunk.

'It had begun again. All my struggles for so many years were wasted. My dream was shattered. It was all hopeless. I was seized with rage.'

Millicent's face grew once again darkly red and she clenched the arms of the chair she sat in.

'I took him by the shoulders and shook him with all my might. "You beast," I cried, "you beast." I was so angry I don't know what I did, I don't know what I said. I kept on shaking him. You don't know how loathsome he looked, that large fat man, half naked; he hadn't shaved for days, and his face was bloated and purple. He was breathing heavily. I shouted at him, but he took no notice. I tried to drag him out of bed, but he was too heavy. He lay there like a log. "Open your eyes," I screamed. I shook him again. I hated him. I hated him all the more because for a week I'd loved him with all my heart. He'd let me down. He'd let me down. I wanted to tell him what a filthy beast he was. I could make no impression on him. "You shall open your eyes," I cried. I was determined to make him look at me.'

The widow licked her dry lips. Her breath seemed hurried. She was silent.

'If he was in that state I should have thought it best to have let him go on sleeping,' said Kathleen.

'There was a parang on the wall by the side of the bed. You know how fond Harold was of curios.'

'What's a parang?' said Mrs Skinner.

'Don't be silly, mother,' her husband replied irritably. 'There's one on the wall immediately behind you.'

He pointed to the Malay sword on which for some reason his eyes had been unconsciously resting. Mrs Skinner drew quickly into the corner of the sofa, with a little frightened gesture, as though she had been told that a snake lay curled up beside her.

'Suddenly the blood spurted out from Harold's throat. There was a great red gash right across it.'

'Millicent,' cried Kathleen, springing up and almost leaping towards her, 'what in God's name do you mean?'

Mrs Skinner stood staring at her with wide startled eyes, her mouth open.

'The parang wasn't on the wall any more. It was on the bed. Then Harold opened his eyes. They were just like Joan's.'

'I don't understand,' said Mrs Skinner. 'How could he have committed suicide if he was in the state you describe?'

Kathleen took her sister's arm and shook her angrily.

'Millicent, for God's sake explain.'

Millicent released herself.

'The parang was on the wall, I told you. I don't know what happened. There was all the blood, and Harold opened his eyes. He died almost at once. He never spoke, but he gave a sort of gasp.'

At last Mr Skinner found his voice.

'But, you wretched woman, it was murder.'

Millicent, her face mottled with red, gave him such a look of scornful hatred that he shrank back. Mrs Skinner cried out.

'Millicent, you didn't do it, did you?'

Then Millicent did something that made them all feel as though their blood were turned to ice in their veins. She chuckled.

'I don't know who else did,' she said.

'My God,' muttered Mr Skinner.

Kathleen had been standing bolt upright with her hands to her heart, as though its beating were intolerable.

'And what happend then?' she said.

'I screamed. I went to the window and flung it open. I called for the ayah. She came across the compound with Joan. "Not Joan," I cried. "Don't let her come." She called the cook and told him to take the child. I cried to her to hurry. And when she came I showed her Harold. "The Tuan's killed himself!" I cried. She gave a scream and ran out of the house.

'No one would come near. They were all frightened out of their wits. I wrote a letter to Mr Francis, telling him what had happened and asking him to come at once.'

'How do you mean you told him what had happened?'

'I said, on my return from the mouth of the river, I'd found Harold with his throat cut. You know, in the tropics you have to bury people quickly. I got a Chinese coffin, and the soldiers dug a grave behind the Fort. When Mr Francis came, Harold had been buried for nearly two days. He was only a boy. I could do anything I wanted with him. I told him I'd found the parang in Harold's hand and there was no doubt he'd killed himself in an attack of delirium tremens. I showed him the empty bottle. The servants said he'd been drinking hard ever since I left to go to the sea. I told the same story at Kuala Solor. Everyone was very kind to me, and the Government granted me a pension.'

For a little while nobody spoke. At last Mr Skinner gathered himself together.

'I am a member of the legal profession. I'm a solicitor. I have certain duties. We've always had a most respectable practice. You've put me in a monstrous position.'

He fumbled, searching for the phrases that played at hide and seek in his scattered wits. Millicent looked at him with scorn.

'What are you going to do about it?'

'It was murder, that's what it was; do you think I can possibly connive at it?'

'Don't talk nonsense, father,' said Kathleen sharply. 'You can't give up your own daughter.'

'You've put me in a monstrous position,' he repeated.

Millicent shrugged her shoulders again.

'You made me tell you. And I've borne it long enough by myself. It was time that all of you bore it too.'

At that moment the door was opened by the maid.

'Davis has brought the car round, sir,' she said.

Kathleen had the presence of mind to say something, and the maid withdrew.

'We'd better be starting,' said Millicent.

'I can't go to the party now,' cried Mrs Skinner, with horror. 'I'm far too upset. How can we face the Heywoods? And the Bishop will want to be introduced to you.'

Millicent made a gesture of indifference. Her eyes held their ironical expression.

'We must go, mother,' said Kathleen. 'It would look so funny if we stayed away.' She turned on Millicent furiously. 'Oh, I think the whole thing is such frightfully bad form.'

Mrs Skinner looked helplessly at her husband. He went to her and gave her his hand to help her up from the sofa.

'I'm afraid we must go, mother,' he said.

'And me with the ospreys in my toque that Harold gave me with his own hands,' she moaned.

He led her out of the room, Kathleen followed close on their heels, and a step or two behind came Millicent.

'You'll get used to it, you know,' she said quietly. 'At first I thought of it all the time, but now I forget it for two or three days together. It's not as if there was any danger.'

They did not answer. They walked through the hall and out of the front door. The three ladies got into the back of the car and Mr Skinner seated himself beside the driver. They had no self-starter; it was an old car, and Davis went to the bonnet to crank it up. Mr

84

Skinner turned round and looked petulantly at Millicent.

'I ought never to have been told,' he said. 'I think it was most selfish of you.'

Davis took his seat and they drove off to the Canon's garden-party.

The Tell-Tale Heart

EDGAR ALLAN POE

TRUE! – NERVOUS – VERY, very dreadfully nervous I had been and am; but why *will* you say that I am mad? The disease had sharpened my senses – not destroyed – not dulled them. Above all was the sense of hearing acute. I heard all things in the heaven and in the earth. I heard many things in hell. How, then, am I mad? Harken! and observe how healthily – how calmly I can tell you the whole story.

It is impossible to say how first the idea entered my brain; but once conceived, it haunted me day and night. Object there was none. Passion there was none. I loved the old man. He had never wronged me. He had never given me insult. For his gold I had no desire. I think it was his eye! yes, it was this! One of his eyes resembled that of a vulture – a pale blue eye, with a film over it. Whenever it fell upon me, my blood ran cold; and so by degrees – very gradually – I made up my mind to take the life of the old man, and thus rid myself of the eye for ever.

Now this is the point. You fancy me mad. Madmen know nothing. But you should have seen *me*. You should have seen how wisely I proceeded – with what caution – with what foresight – with what dissimulation I went to work! I was never kinder to the old man than during the whole week before I killed him. And every night, about midnight, I turned the latch of his door and opened it – oh, so gently! And then, when I had made an opening sufficient for my head, I put in a dark lantern, all closed, closed, so that no light shone out, and then I thrust in my head. Oh, you would have laughed to see how cunningly I thrust it in! I moved it slowly – very, very slowly, so that I might not disturb the old man's sleep. It took me an hour to place my whole head within the opening so far that I could see him as he lay upon his bed. Ha! – would a madman have been so wise as this? And then, when my head was well in the room, I undid the lantern, cautiously – oh, so cautiously – cautiously (for the hinges creaked) I undid it just so much that a single thin ray fell upon the vulture eye. And this I did for seven long nights – every night just at midnight – but I found the eye always closed; and so it was impossible to do the work; for it was not the old man who vexed me, but his Evil Eye. And

86

every morning, when the day broke, I went boldly into the chamber, and spoke courageously to him, calling him by name in a hearty tone, and inquiring how he had passed the night. So you see he would have been a very profound old man, indeed, to suspect that every night, just at twelve, I looked upon him while he slept.

Upon the eighth night I was more than usually cautious in opening the door. A watch's minute hand moves more quickly than did mine. Never before that night had I *felt* the extent of my own powers – of my sagacity. I could scarcely contain my feelings of triumph. To think that there I was, opening the door, little by little, and he not even to dream of my secret deeds or thoughts. I fairly chuckled at the idea; and perhaps he heard me – for he moved on the bed suddenly, as if startled. Now you may think that I drew back – but no. His room was as black as pitch with the thick darkness (for the shutters were close-fastened, through fear of robbers), and so I knew that he could not see the opening of the door, and I kept pushing it on steadily, steadily.

I had my head in, and was about to open the lantern, when my thumb slipped upon the tin fastening, and the old man sprang up in the bed, crying out, 'Who's there?'

I kept quite still and said nothing. For a whole hour I did not move a muscle, and in the meantime I did not hear him lie down. He was still sitting up in the bed, listening – just as I have done, night after night, hearkening to the death-watches in the wall.

Presently I heard a groan, and I knew it was the groan of mortal terror. It was not a groan of pain or of grief – oh, no! – it was the low stifled sound that arises from the bottom of the soul when overcharged with awe. I knew the sound well. Many a night, just at midnight, when all the world slept, it has welled up from my own bosom, deepening, with its dreadful echo, the terrors that distracted me. I say I knew it well. I knew what the old man felt, and pitied him, although I chuckled at heart. I knew that he had been lying awake ever since the first slight noise, when he had turned in the bed. His fears had been ever since growing upon him. He had been trying to fancy them causeless, but could not. He had been saying to himself, 'It is nothing but the wind in the chimney – it is only a mouse crossing the floor,' or 'It is merely a cricket which has made a single chirp.' Yes, he had been trying to comfort himself with these suppositions; but he had found all in vain. *All in vain*; because Death, in approaching him, had stalked with his black shadow before him, and enveloped the victim. And it was the mournful influence of the unperceived shadow that caused him to feel – although he neither saw nor heard – to *feel* the presence of my head within the room.

When I had waited a long time, very patiently, without hearing him lie down, I resolved to open a little – a very, very little crevice in the lantern. So I opened it – you cannot imagine how stealthily, stealthily – until, at length, a single dim ray, like the thread of the spider, shot from out of the crevice and fell upon the vulture eye.

It was open – wide, wide open – and I grew furious as I gazed upon it. I saw it with perfect distinctness – all a dull blue, with a hideous veil over it that chilled the very marrow in my bones; but I could see nothing else of the old man's face or person, for I had directed the ray, as if by instinct, precisely upon the damned spot.

And now have I not told you that what you mistake for madness is but over-acuteness of the senses? – now, I say, there came to my ears a low, dull, quick sound, such as a watch makes when enveloped in cotton. I knew *that* sound well, too. It was the beating of the old man's heart. It increased my fury, as the beating of a drum stimulates the soldier into courage.

But even yet I refrained and kept still. I scarcely breathed. I held the lantern motionless. I tried how steadily I could maintain the ray upon the eye. Meantime the hellish tattoo of the heart increased. It grew quicker, and louder and louder every instant. The old man's terror *must* have been extreme! It grew louder, I say, louder every moment! – do you mark me well? I have told you that I am nervous: so I am. And now, at the dead hour of the night, amid the dreadful silence of that old house, so strange a noise as this excited me to uncontrollable terror. Yet, for some minutes longer, I refrained and stood still. But the beating grew louder, louder! I thought the heart must burst. And now a new anxiety seized me – the sound would be heard by a neighbour! The old man's hour had come! With a loud yell I threw open the lantern and leaped into the room. He shrieked once – once only. In an instant I dragged him to the floor, and pulled the heavy bed over him. I then smiled gaily, to find the deed so far done. But, for many minutes, the heart beat on with a muffled sound. This, however, did not vex me; it would not be heard through the wall. At length it ceased. The old man was dead. I removed the bed and examined the corpse. Yes, he was stone, stone dead. I placed my hand upon the heart and held it there many minutes. There was no pulsation. He was stone dead. His eye would trouble me no more.

If still you think me mad, you will think so no longer when I describe the wise precautions I took for the concealment of the body. The night waned, and I worked hastily, but in silence. First of all I dismembered the corpse. I cut off the head and the arms and the legs.

I then took up three planks from the flooring of the chamber and deposited all between the scantlings. I then replaced the boards so cleverly, so cunningly, that no human eye – not even *his* – could have detected anything wrong. There was nothing to wash out – no stain of any kind – no blood-spot whatever. I had been too wary for that.

A tub had caught all – ha! ha!

When I had made an end of these labours, it was four o'clock – still dark as midnight. As the bell sounded the hour, there came a knocking at the street door. I went down to open it with a light heart – for what had I *now* to fear? There entered three men, who introduced themselves, with perfect suavity, as officers of the police. A shriek had been heard by a neighbour during the night; suspicion of foul play had been aroused; information had been lodged at the police office, and they (the officers) had been deputed to search the premises.

I smiled – for *what* had I to fear? I bade the gentlemen welcome. The shriek, I said, was my own in a dream. The old man, I mentioned, was absent in the country. I took my visitors all over the house. I bade them search – search *well*. I led them, at length, to *his* chamber. I showed them his treasures, secure, undisturbed. In the enthusiasm of my confidence, I brought chairs into the room, and desired them *here* to rest from their fatigues, while I myself, in the wild audacity of my perfect triumph, placed my own seat upon the very spot beneath which reposed the corpse of the victim.

The officers were satisfied. My manner had convinced them. I was singularly at ease. They sat, and while I answered cheerily, they chatted of familiar things. But, ere long, I felt myself getting pale and wished them gone. My head ached, and I fancied a ringing in my ears; but still they sat and still chatted. The ringing became more distinct – it continued and became more distinct. I talked more freely to get rid of the feeling; but it continued and gained definitiveness – until, at length, I found that the noise was *not* within my ears.

No doubt I now grew very pale; but I talked more fluently, and with a heightened voice. Yet the sound increased – and what could I do? It was *a low, dull, quick sound – much such a sound as a watch makes when enveloped in cotton.* I gasped for breath – and yet the officers heard it not. I talked more quickly – more vehemently; but the noise steadily increased. I arose and argued about trifles, in a high key and with violent gesticulations; but the noise steadily increased. Why *would* they not be gone? I paced the floor to and fro with heavy strides, as if excited to fury by the observations of the men – but the noise steadily increased. Oh God! what *could* I do? I foamed – I raved – I swore! I swung the chair upon which I had been sitting, and grated it upon the boards, but the noise arose over all continually increased. It grew louder – louder – *louder!* And still the men chatted pleasantly, and smiled. Was it possible they heard not? Almighty God! – no, no! They heard! – they suspected! – they *knew!* – they were making a mockery of my horror! – this I thought, and this I think. But anything was better than this agony! Anything was more tolerable than this derision! I could bear those hypocritical smiles no longer! I felt that I must scream or die! – and now – again! hark! louder! louder! louder! *louder!*——

'Villains!' I shrieked, 'dissemble no more! I admit the deed! – tear up the planks! – here, here! – it is the beating of his hideous heart!'

The Evidence of the Altar-Boy

GEORGES SIMENON

I

A FINE COLD RAIN WAS falling. The night was very dark; only at the far end of the street, near the barracks from which, at half past five, there had come the sound of bugle calls and the noise of horses being taken to be watered, was there a faint light shining in someone's window – an early riser, or an invalid who had lain awake all night.

The rest of the street was asleep. It was a broad, quiet, newish street, with almost identical one- or two-storied houses such as are to be seen in the suburbs of most big provincial towns.

The whole district was new, devoid of mystery, inhabited by quite unassuming people, clerks and commercial travellers, retired men and peaceful widows.

Maigret, with his overcoat collar turned up, was huddling in the angle of a carriage gateway, that of the boys' school; he was waiting, watch in hand, and smoking his pipe.

At a quarter to six exactly, bells rang out from the parish church behind him, and he knew that, as the boy had said, it was the 'first stroke' for six o'clock Mass.

The sound of the bells was still vibrating in the damp air when he heard, or rather guessed at, the shrill clamour of an alarm clock. This lasted only a few seconds. The boy must already have stretched a hand out of his warm bed and groped in the darkness for the safety-catch that would silence the clock. A few minutes later, the attic window on the second floor lit up.

It all happened exactly as the boy had said. He must have risen noiselessly, before anyone else, in the sleeping house. Now he must be picking up his clothes, his socks, washing his face and hands and combing his hair. As for his shoes, he had declared:

'I carry them downstairs and put them on when I get to the last step, so as not to wake up my parents.'

This had happened every day, winter and summer, for nearly two years, ever since Justin had first begun to serve at Mass at the hospital.

He had asserted, furthermore: 'The hospital clock always strikes

91

three or four minutes later than the parish church clock.'

And this had proved to be the case. The inspectors of the Flying Squad to which Maigret had been seconded for the past few months had shrugged their shoulders over these tiresome details about first bells and second bells.

Was it because Maigret had been an altar-boy himself for a long time that he had not dismissed the story with a smile?

The bells of the parish church rang first, at a quarter to six. Then Justin's alarm clock went off, in the attic where the boy slept. Then a few moments later came the shriller, more silvery sound of the hospital chapel bells, like those of a convent.

He still had his watch in his hand. The boy took barely more than four minutes to dress. Then the light went out. He must be groping his way down the stairs, anxious not to waken his parents, then sitting down on the bottom step to put on his shoes, and taking down his coat and cap from the bamboo coat-rack on the right in the passage.

The door opened. The boy closed it again without making a sound, looked up and down the street anxiously and then saw the Superintendent's burly figure coming up to him.

'I was afraid you might not be there.'

And he started walking fast. He was a thin, fair-haired little twelve-year-old with an obstinate look about him.

'You want me to do just what I usually do, don't you? I always walk fast, for one thing because I've worked out to the minute how long it takes, and for another, because in winter, when it's dark, I'm frightened. In a month it'll be getting light by this time in the morning.'

He took the first turning on the right into another quiet, somewhat shorter street, which led on to an open square planted with elms and crossed diagonally by tramlines.

And Maigret noted tiny details that reminded him of his own childhood. He noticed, for one thing, that the boy did not walk closely to the houses, probably because he was afraid of seeing someone suddenly emerge from a dark doorway. Then, that when he crossed the square he avoided the trees in the same way, because a man might have been hiding behind them.

He was a brave boy, really, since for two whole winters, in all weathers, sometimes in thick fog or in the almost total darkness of a moonless night, he had made the same journey every morning all alone.

'When we get to the middle of the Rue Sainte-Catherine you'll hear the second bell for Mass from the parish church . . .'

'At what time does the first tram pass?'

'At six o'clock. I've only seen it two or three times, when I was late . . . once because my alarm clock hadn't rung, another time because I'd fallen asleep again. That's why I jump out of bed as soon as it rings.'

A pale little face in the rainy night, with eyes that still retained something of the fixed stare of a sleepwalker, and a thoughtful expression with just a slight tinge of anxiety.

'I shan't go on serving at Mass. It's because you insisted that I've come today. . . .'

They turned left down the Rue Saint-Catherine, where, as in all the streets in this district, there was a lamp every fifty metres, each of them shedding a pool of light; and the child unconsciously quickened his pace each time he left the reassuring zone of brightness.

The noises from the barracks could still be heard in the distance. A few windows lit up. Footsteps sounded in a side street; probably a workman going to his job.

'When you got to the corner of the street, did you see nothing?'

This was the trickiest point, for the Rue Sainte-Catherine was very straight and empty, with its rectilinear pavements and its street lamps at regular intervals, leaving so little shadow between them that one could not have failed to see a couple of men quarrelling even at a hundred metres' distance.

'Perhaps I wasn't looking in front of me . . . I was talking to myself, I remember . . . I often do talk to myself in a whisper, when I'm going along there in the morning . . . I wanted to ask mother something when I got home and I was repeating to myself what I was going to say to her . . .'

'What did you want to say to her?'

'I've wanted a bike for ever such a long time . . . I've already saved up three hundred francs out of my church money.'

Was it just an impression? It seemed to Maigret that the boy was keeping further away from the houses. He even stepped off the pavement, and returned to it a little further on.

'It was here. . . . Look. . . . There's the second bell ringing for Mass at the parish church.'

And Maigret endeavoured, in all seriousness, to enter into the world which was the child's world every morning.

'I must have looked up suddenly. . . . You know, like when you're running without looking where you're going and find yourself in front of a wall. . . . It was just here.'

He pointed to the line on the pavement dividing the darkness from the lamplight, where the drizzle formed a luminous haze.

'First I saw that there was a man lying down and he looked so big that I could have sworn he took up the whole width of the pavement.'

That was impossible, for the pavement was at least two and a half

93

metres across.

'I don't know what I did exactly . . . I must have jumped aside . . . I didn't run away immediately, for I saw the knife stuck in his chest, with a big handle made of brown horn. I noticed it because my uncle Henri has a knife just like it and he told me it was made out of a stag's horn. I'm certain the man was dead . . .'

'Why?'

'I don't know. . . . He looked like a corpse.'

'Were his eyes shut?'

'I didn't notice his eyes . . . I don't know. . . . But I had the feeling he was dead. . . . It all happened very quickly, as I told you yesterday in your office. . . . They made me repeat the same thing so many times yesterday that I'm all muddled. . . . Specially when I feel people don't believe me . . .'

'And the other man?'

'When I looked up I saw that there was somebody a little further on, five metres away maybe, a man with very pale eyes who looked at me for a moment and then started running. It was the murderer . . .'

'How do you know that?'

'Because he ran off as fast as he could.'

'In which direction?'

'Right over there . . .'

'Towards the barracks?'

'Yes. . . .'

It was a fact that Justin had been interrogated at least ten times the previous day. Before Maigret appeared in the office the detectives had even made a sort of game of it. His story had never varied in a single detail.

'And what did you do?'

'I started running too. . . . It's hard to explain. . . . I think it was when I saw the man running away that I got frightened. . . . And then I ran as hard as I could . . .'

'In the opposite direction?'

'Yes.'

'Did you not think of calling for help?'

'No . . . I was too frightened . . . I was specially afraid my legs might give way, for I could scarcely feel them . . . I turned right-about as far as the Place du Congrès . . . I took the other street, that leads to the hospital too after making a bend.'

'Let's go on.'

More bells, the shrill-toned bells of the chapel. After walking some fifty metres they reached a crossroads, on the left of which were the walls of the barracks, pierced with loopholes, and on the right a huge gateway dimly lit and surmounted by a clockface of greenish glass.

It was three minutes to six.

'I'm a minute late. . . . Yesterday I was on time in spite of it all, because I ran . . .'

There was a heavy knocker on the solid oak door; the child lifted it, and the noise reverberated through the porch. A porter in slippers opened the door, let Justin go in but barred the way to Maigret, looking at him suspiciously.

'What is it?'

'Police.'

'Let's see your card?'

Hospital smells were perceptible as soon as they entered the porch. They went on through a second door into a huge courtyard surrounded by various hospital buildings. In the distance could be glimpsed the white head-dresses of nuns on their way to the chapel.

'Why didn't you say anything to the porter yesterday?'

'I don't know . . . I was in a hurry to get there . . .'

Maigret could understand that. The haven was not the official entrance with its crabbed, mistrustful porter, nor the unwelcoming courtyard through which stretchers were being carried in silence; it was the warm vestry near the chapel, where a nun was lighting candles on the altar.

'Are you coming in with me?'

'Yes.'

Justin looked vexed, or rather shocked, probably at the thought that this policeman, who might be an unbeliever, was going to enter into his hallowed world. And this, too, explained to Maigret why every morning the child had the courage to get up so early and overcome his fears.

The chapel had a warm and intimate atmosphere. Patients in the blue-grey hospital uniform, some with bandaged heads, some with crutches or with their arms in slings, were already sitting in the pews of the nave. Up in the gallery the nuns formed a flock of identical figures, and all their white cornets bowed simultaneously in pious worship.

'Follow me.'

They went up a few steps, passing close to the altar where candles were already burning. To the right was a vestry panelled in dark wood, where a tall gaunt priest was putting on his vestments, while a surplice edged with fine lace lay ready for the altar-boy. A nun was busy filling the holy vessels.

It was here that, on the previous day, Justin had come to a halt at last, panting and weak-kneed. It was here that he had shouted: 'A man's been killed in the Rue Sainte-Catherine!'

A small clock set in the wainscot pointed to six o'clock exactly. Bells

95

were ringing again, sounding fainter here than outside. Justin told the nun who was helping him on with his surplice: 'This is the Police Superintendent . . .'

And Maigret stood waiting while the child went in, ahead of the chaplain, the skirts of his red cassock flapping as he hurried towards the altar steps.

The vestry nun had said: 'Justin is a good little boy, who's very devout and who's never lied to us. . . . Occasionally he's failed to come and serve at Mass. . . . He might have pretended he'd been ill. . . . Well, he never did; he always admitted frankly that he'd not had the courage to get up because it was too cold, or because he'd had a nightmare during the night and was feeling too tired . . .'

And the chaplain, after saying Mass, had gazed at the Superintendent with the clear eyes of a saint in a stained glass window: 'Why should the child have invented such a tale?'

Maigret knew, now, what had gone on in the hospital chapel on the previous morning. Justin, his teeth chattering, at the end of his tether, had been in a state of hysterics. The service could not be delayed; the vestry nun had informed the Sister Superior and had herself served at Mass in place of the child, who was meanwhile being attended to in the vestry.

Ten minutes later, the Sister Superior had thought of informing the police. She had gone out through the chapel, and everyone had realized that something was happening.

At the local police station the sergeant on duty had failed to understand.

'What's that? . . . The Sister Superior? . . . Superior to what?'

And she had told him, in the hushed tone they use in convents, that there had been a crime in the Rue Sainte-Catherine; and the police had found nothing, no victim, and, needless to say, no murderer . . .

Justin had gone to school at half past eight, just as usual, as though nothing had happened; and it was in his classroom that Inspector Besson, a strapping little fellow who looked like a boxer and who liked to act tough, had picked him up at 9.30 as soon as the Flying Squad had got the report.

Poor kid! For two whole hours, in a dreary office that reeked of tobacco fumes and the smoke from a stove that wouldn't draw, he had been interrogated not as a witness but as a suspect.

Three inspectors in turn, Besson, Thiberge and Vallin, had tried to catch him out, to make him contradict himself.

To make matters worse his mother had come too. She sat in the waiting-room, weeping and snivelling and telling everybody: 'We're decent people and we've never had anything to do with the police.'

Maigret, who had worked late the previous evening on a case of drug-smuggling, had not reached his office until eleven o'clock.

'What's happening?' he had asked when he saw the child standing there, dry-eyed but as stiffly defiant as a little fighting-cock.

'A kid who's been having us on. . . . He claims to have seen a dead body in the street and a murderer who ran away when he got near. But a tram passed along the same street four minutes later and the driver saw nothing. . . . It's a quiet street, and nobody heard anything. . . . And finally when the police were called, a quarter of an hour later, by some nun or other, there was absolutely nothing to be seen on the pavement, not the slightest trace of a bloodstain. . . .'

'Come along into my office, boy.'

And Maigret was the first of them, that day, not to address Justin by the familiar *tu*, the first to treat him not as a fanciful or malicious urchin but as a small man.

He had listened to the boy's story simply and quietly, without interrupting or taking any notes.

'Shall you go on serving at Mass in the hospital?'

'No. I don't want to go back. I'm too frightened.'

And yet it meant a great sacrifice for him. Not only was he a devout child, deeply responsive to the poetry of that early Mass in the warm and somewhat mysterious atmosphere of the chapel; but in addition, he was paid for his services – not much, but enough to enable him to get together a little nest-egg. And he so badly wanted a bicycle which his parents could not afford to buy for him!

'I should like you to go just once more, tomorrow morning.'

'I shan't dare.'

'I'll go along with you. . . . I'll wait for you in front of your home. You must behave exactly as you always do.'

This was what had been happening, and Maigret, at seven in the morning, was now standing alone outside the door of the hospital, in a district which, on the previous day, he had known only from having been through it by car or in a tram.

An icy drizzle was still falling from the sky which was now paler, and it clung to the Superintendent's shoulders; he sneezed twice. A few pedestrians hurried past, their coat collars turned up and their hands in their pockets; butchers and grocers had begun taking down the shutters of their shops.

It was the quietest, most ordinary district imaginable. At a pinch one might picture a quarrel between two men, two drunks for instance, at five minutes to six on the pavement of the Rue Sainte-Catherine. One might even conceive of an assault by some ruffian on an early passer-by.

97

But the sequel was puzzling. According to the boy, the murderer had run off when he came near, and it was then five minutes to six. At six o'clock, however, the first tram had passed, and the driver had declared that he had seen nothing.

He might, of course, have been inattentive, or looking in the other direction. But at five minutes past six two policemen on their beat had walked along that very pavement. And they had seen nothing!

At seven or eight minutes past six a cavalry officer who lived three houses away from the spot indicated by Justin had left home, as he did every morning, to go to the barracks.

And he had seen nothing either!

Finally, at twenty-past six, the police cyclists dispatched from the local station had found no trace of the victim.

Had someone come in the meantime to remove the body in a car or van? Maigret had deliberately and calmly sought to consider every hypothesis, and this one had proved as unreliable as all the rest. At no. 42 in the same street, there was a sick woman whose husband had sat up with her all night. He had asserted categorically:

'We hear all the noises outside. I notice them all the more because my wife is in great pain, and the least noise makes her wince. The tram woke her when she'd only just dropped off. . . . I can give you my word no car came past before seven o'clock. The dustcart was the earliest.'

'And you heard nothing else?'

'Somebody running, at one point . . .'

'Before the tram?'

'Yes, because my wife was asleep . . . I was making myself some coffee on the gas-ring.'

'One person running?'

'More like two.'

'You don't know in which direction?'

'The blind was down. . . . As it creaks when you lift it I didn't try to look out.'

This was the only piece of evidence in Justin's favour. There was a bridge two hundred metres further on. And the policeman on duty there had seen no car pass.

Could one assume that barely a few minutes after he'd run away the murderer had come back, picked up his victim's body and carried it off somewhere or other, without attracting attention?

Worse still, there was one piece of evidence which made people shrug their shoulders when they talked about the boy's story. The place he had indicated was just opposite no. 61. Inspector Thiberge had called at this house the day before, and Maigret, who left nothing to chance, now visited it himself.

It was a new house of pinkish brick; three steps led up to a shiny pitchpine door with a letter-box of gleaming brass.

Although it was only 7.30 in the morning, the Superintendent had been given to understand that he might call at that early hour.

A gaunt old woman with a moustache peered through a spy-hole and argued before letting him into the hall, where there was a pleasant smell of fresh coffee.

'I'll go and see if the Judge will see you.'

For the house belonged to a retired magistrate, who was reputed to have private means and who lived there alone with a housekeeper.

Some whispering went on in the front room, which should by rights have been a drawing-room. Then the old woman returned and said sourly:

'Come in. . . . Wipe your feet, please. . . . You're not in a stable.'

The room was no drawing-room; it bore no resemblance to what one usually thinks of as such. It was very large, and it was part bedroom, part study, part library and part junk-room, being cluttered with the most unexpected objects.

'Have you come to look for the corpse?' said a sneering voice that made the Superintendent jump.

Since there was a bed, he had naturally looked towards it, but it was empty. The voice came from the chimney corner, where a lean old man was huddled in the depths of an armchair, with a plaid over his legs.

'Take off your overcoat, for I adore heat and you'll not be able to stand it here.'

It was quite true. The old man, holding a pair of tongs, was doing his best to encourage the biggest possible blaze from a log fire.

'I have thought that the police had made some progress since my time and had learnt to mistrust evidence given by children. Children and girls are the most unreliable of witnesses, and when I was on the Bench . . .'

He was wearing a thick dressing-gown, and in spite of the heat of the room, he had a scarf as broad as a shawl round his neck.

'So the crime is supposed to have been committed in front of my house? And if I'm not mistaken, you are the famous Superintendent Maigret, whom they have graciously sent to our town to reorganize our Flying Squad?'

His voice grated. It was that of a spiteful, aggressive, savagely sarcastic old man.

'Well, my dear Superintendent, unless you're going to accuse me of being in league with the murderer, I am sorry to tell you, as I told

99

your young inspector yesterday, that you're on the wrong track.

'You've probably heard that old people need very little sleep. Moreover there are people who, all their life long, sleep very little. Erasmus was one such, for instance, as was also a gentleman known as Voltaire . . .'

He glanced smugly at the bookshelves where volumes were piled ceiling-high.

'This has been the case with many other people whom you're not likely to know either. . . . It's the case with me, and I pride myself on not having slept more than three hours a night during the last thirteen years. . . . Since for the past ten my legs have refused to carry me, and since furthermore I've no desire to visit any of the places to which they might take me, I spend my days and nights in this room which, as you can see for yourself, gives directly on to the street.

'By four in the morning I am sitting in this armchair, with all my wits about me, believe me . . . I could show you the book in which I was deep yesterday morning, only it was by a Greek philosopher and I can't imagine you'd be interested.

'The fact remains that if an incident of the sort described by your over-imaginative young friend had taken place under my window, I can promise you I should have noticed it. . . . My legs are weak, as I've said, but my hearing is still good.

'Moreover, I have retained enough natural curiosity to take an interest in all that happens in the street, and if it amuses you I could tell you at what time every housewife in the neighbourhood goes past my window to do her shopping.'

He was looking at Maigret with a smile of triumph.

'So you usually hear young Justin passing in front of the house?' the Superintendent asked in the meekest and gentlest of tones.

'Naturally.'

'You both hear him and see him?'

'I don't follow.'

'For most of the year, for almost two-thirds of the year, it's broad daylight at six in the morning. . . . Now the child served at six o'clock Mass both summer and winter.'

'I used to see him go past.'

'Considering that this happened every day with as much regularity as the passing of the first tram, you must have been attentively aware of it . . .'

'What do you mean?'

'I mean that, for instance, when a factory siren sounds every day at the same time in a certain district, when somebody passes your window with clockwork regularity, you naturally say to yourself: Hullo, it must be such and such a time.

'And if one day the siren doesn't sound, you think: Why, it's Sunday. And if the person doesn't come past you wonder: What can have happened to him? Perhaps he's ill?'

The judge was looking at Maigret with sharp, sly little eyes. He seemed to resent being taught a lesson.

'I know all that . . .' he grumbled, cracking his bony finger-joints. 'I was a magistrate before you were a policeman.'

'When the altar-boy went past . . .'

'I used to hear him, if that's what you're trying to make me admit.'

'And if he didn't go past?'

'I might have happened to notice it. But I might have happened not to notice it. As in the case of the factory siren you mentioned. One isn't struck every Sunday by the silence of the siren . . .'

'What about yesterday?'

Could Maigret be mistaken? He had the impression that the old magistrate was scowling, that there was something sullen and savagely secretive about his expression. Old people sometimes sulk, like children; they often display the same puerile stubbornness.

'Yesterday?'

'Yes . . .'

Why did he repeat the question, unless to give himself time to make a decision?

'I noticed nothing.'

'Not that he had passed?'

'No . . .'

'Nor that he hadn't passed?'

'No . . .'

One or the other answer was untrue, Maigret was convinced. He was anxious to continue the test, and he went on with his questions:

'Nobody ran past your windows?'

'No.'

This time the *no* was spoken frankly and the old man must have been telling the truth.

'You heard no unusual sound?'

'No' again, uttered with the same downrightness and almost with a note of triumph.

'No sound of trampling, of groaning, no sound of a body falling?'

'Nothing at all.'

'I'm much obliged to you.'

'Don't mention it.'

'Seeing that you've been a magistrate I need not of course ask you if you are willing to repeat your statement under oath?'

'Whenever you like.'

And the old man said that with a kind of delighted impatience.

101

'I apologise for disturbing you, Judge.'

'I wish you all success in your enquiry, Superintendent.'

The old housekeeper must have been hiding behind the door, for she was waiting on the threshold to show out the Superintendent and shut the front door behind him.

Maigret experienced a curious sensation as he re-emerged into everyday life in that quiet suburban street where housewives were beginning their shopping and children were on their way to school.

It seemed to him that he had been hoaxed, and yet he could have sworn that the judge had not withheld the truth except on one point. He had the impression, furthermore, that at a certain moment he had been about to discover something very odd, very elusive, very unexpected; that he would only have had to make a tiny effort but that he had been unable to do so.

Once again he pictured the boy, he pictured the old man; he tried to find a link between them.

Slowly he filled his pipe, standing on the kerb. Then, since he had had no breakfast, not even a cup of coffee on rising, and since his wet overcoat was clinging to his shoulders, he went to wait at the corner of the Place du Congrès for the tram that would take him home.

II

Out of the heaving mass of sheets and blankets an arm emerged, and a red face glistening with sweat appeared on the pillow; finally a sulky voice growled: 'Pass me the thermometer.'

And Madame Maigret, who was sewing by the window – she had drawn aside the net curtain so as to see in the gathering dusk – rose with a sigh and switched on the electric light.

'I thought you were asleep. It's not half an hour since you last took your temperature.'

Resignedly, for she knew from long marital experience that it was useless to cross the big fellow, she shook the thermometer to bring down the mercury and slipped the tip of it between his lips.

He asked, meanwhile: 'Has anybody come?'

'You'd know if they had, since you've not been asleep.'

He must have dozed off though, if only for a few minutes. But he was continually being roused from his torpor by that blasted jingle from down below.

They were not in their own home. Since his mission in this provincial town was to last for six months at least, and since Madame Maigret could not bear the thought of letting her husband eat in restaurants for so long a period, she had followed him, and they had rented a furnished flat in the upper part of the town.

102

It was too bright, with flowery wallpaper, gimcrack furniture and a bed that groaned under the Superintendent's weight. They had, at any rate, chosen a quiet street, where, as the landlady Madame Danse had told them, not a soul passed.

What she had failed to add was that, the ground floor of the house being occupied by a dairy, the whole place was pervaded by a sickly smell of cheese. Another fact which she had not revealed but which Maigret had just discovered for himself, since this was the first time he had stayed in bed in the daytime, was that the door of the dairy was equipped not with a bell but with a strange contraption of metal tubes which, whenever a customer came in, clashed together with a prolonged jingling sound.

'How high?'

'38.5 . . .'

'A little while ago it was 38.8.'

'And by tonight it'll be over 39.'

He was furious. He was always bad tempered when he was ill, and he glowered resentfully at Madame Maigret, who obstinately refused to go out when he was longing to fill himself a pipe.

It was still pouring with rain, the same fine rain that clung to the windows and fell in mournful silence, giving one the impression of living in an aquarium. A crude glare shone down from the electric light bulb which swung, unshaded, at the end of its cord. And one could imagine an endless succession of streets equally deserted, windows lighting up one after the other, people caged in their rooms, moving about like fishes in a bowl.

'You must have another cup of tisane.'

It was probably the tenth since twelve o'clock, and then all that lukewarm water had to be sweated away into his sheets, which ended up as damp as compresses.

He must have caught flu or tonsillitis while waiting for the boy in the cold early morning rain outside the school, or else afterwards while he was roaming the streets. By ten o'clock, when he was back in his room in the Flying Squad's offices, and while he was poking the stove with what had become almost a ritual gesture, he had been seized with the shivers. Then he had felt too hot. His eyelids were smarting and when he looked at himself in the bit of mirror in the cloakroom, he had seen round staring eyes that were glistening with fever.

Moreover his pipe no longer tasted the same, and that was a sure sign.

'Look here, Besson: if by any chance I shouldn't come back this afternoon, will you carry on investigating the altar-boy problem?'

And Besson, who always thought himself cleverer than anybody

103

else: 'Do you really think, Chief, that there *is* such a problem, and that a good spanking wouldn't put an end to it?'

'All the same, you must get one of your colleagues, Vallin for instance, to keep an eye on the Rue Sainte-Catherine.'

'In case the corpse comes back to lie down in front of the judge's house?'

Maigret was too dazed by his incipient fever to follow Besson on to that ground. He had just gone on deliberately giving instructions.

'Draw up a list of all the residents in the street. It won't be a big job, because it's a short street.'

'Shall I question the kid again?'

'No . . .'

And since then he had felt too hot; he was conscious of drops of sweat beading on his skin, he had a sour taste in his mouth, he kept hoping to sink into oblivion but was constantly disturbed by the ridiculous jingle of the brass tubes from the dairy.

He loathed being ill because it was humiliating and also because Madame Maigret kept a fierce watch to prevent him from smoking his pipe. If only she'd had to go out and buy something at the pharmacist's! But she was always careful to take a well-stocked medicine chest about with her.

He loathed being ill, and yet there were moments when he almost enjoyed it, moments when, closing his eyes, he felt ageless because he experienced once again the sensations of his childhood.

Then he remembered the boy Justin, whose pale face already showed such strength of character. All that morning's scenes recurred to his mind, not with the precision of everyday reality nor with the sharp outline of things seen, but with the peculiar intensity of things felt.

For instance he could have described almost in detail the attic room that he had never seen, the iron bedstead, the alarm clock on the bedside table, the boy stretching out his arm, dressing silently, the same gestures invariably repeated . . .

Invariably the same gestures! It seemed to him an important and obvious truth. When you've been serving at Mass for two years at a regular time, your gestures become almost completely automatic. . . . The first bell at a quarter to six. . . . The alarm clock. . . . The shriller sound of the chapel bells. . . . Then the child would put on his shoes at the foot of the stairs, open the front door and meet the cold breath of early morning.

'You know, Madame Maigret, he's never read any detective stories.' For as long back as they could remember, possibly because it had begun as a joke, they had called one another Maigret and Madame Maigret, and they had almost forgotten that they had

Christian names like other people . . .

'He doesn't read the papers either . . .'

'You'd better try to sleep.'

He closed his eyes, after a longing glance at his pipe, which lay on the black marble mantelpiece.

'I questioned his mother at great length; she's a decent woman, but she's mightily in awe of the police . . .'

'Go to sleep!'

He kept silence for a while. His breathing became deeper; it sounded as if he was really dozing off.

'She declares he's never seen a dead body. . . . It's the sort of thing you try to keep from children.'

'Why is it important?'

'He told me the body was so big that it seemed to take up the whole pavement. . . . Now that's the impression that a dead body lying on the ground makes on one. . . . A dead person always looks bigger than a living one. . . . D'you understand?'

'I can't think why you're worrying, since Besson's looking after the case.'

'Besson doesn't believe in it.'

'In what?'

'In the dead body.'

'Shall I put out the light?'

In spite of his protests, she climbed on to a chair and fastened a band of waxed paper round the bulb so as to dim its light.

'Now try to get an hour's sleep, then I'll make you another cup of tisane. You haven't been sweating enough . . .'

'Don't you think if I were to have just a tiny puff at my pipe . . .'

'Are you mad?'

She went into the kitchen to keep an eye on the vegetable broth, and he heard her tiptoeing back and forth. He kept picturing the same section of the Rue Saint-Catherine, with street lamps every fifty metres.

'The judge declares he heard nothing . . .'

'What are you saying?'

'I bet they hate one another . . .'

And her voice reached him from the far end of the kitchen:

'Who are you talking about? You see I'm busy . . .'

'The judge and the altar-boy. They've never spoken to one another, but I'll take my oath they hate each other. You know, very old people, particularly old people who live by themselves, end up by becoming like children. . . . Justin went past every morning, and every morning the old Judge was behind his window. . . . He looks like an owl!'

'I don't know what you're trying to say . . .'

105

She stood framed in the doorway, a steaming ladle in her hand.

'Try to follow me. The judge declares that he heard nothing, and it's too serious a matter for me to suspect him of lying.'

'You see! Try to stop thinking about it.'

'Only he dared not assert that he had or had not heard Justin go past yesterday morning.'

'Perhaps he went back to sleep.'

'No. . . . He daren't tell a lie, and so he's deliberately vague. And the husband at no. 42 who was sitting up with his sick wife heard somebody running in the street.'

He kept reverting to that. His thoughts, sharpened by fever, went round in a circle.

'What would have become of the corpse?' objected Madame Maigret with her womanly common sense. 'Don't think any more about it! Besson knows his job, you've often said so youself . . .'

He slumped back under the blankets, discouraged, and tried hard to go to sleep, but was inevitably haunted before long by the image of the altar-boy's face, and his pallid legs above black socks.

'There's something wrong . . .'

'What did you say? Something wrong? Are you feeling worse? Shall I ring the doctor?'

Not that. He started again from scratch, obstinately; he went back to the threshold of the boys' school and crossed the Place du Congrès.

'And this is where there's something amiss.'

For one thing, because the judge had heard nothing. Unless one was going to accuse him of perjury it was hard to believe that a fight could have gone on under his window, just a few metres away, that a man had started running off towards the barracks while the boy had rushed off in the opposite direction.

'Listen, Madame Maigret . . .'

'What is it now?'

'Suppose they had both started running in the same direction?'

With a sigh, Madame Maigret picked up her needlework and listened, dutifully, to her husband's monologue interspersed with wheezy gasps.

'For one thing, it's more logical . . .'

'What's more logical?'

'That they should both have run in the same direction. . . . Only in that case it wouldn't have been towards the barracks.'

'Could the boy have been running after the murderer?'

'No. The murderer would have run after the boy . . .'

'What for, since he didn't kill him?'

'To make him hold his tongue, for instance.'

'He didn't succeed, since the child spoke . . .'

'Or to prevent him from telling something, from giving some particular detail. . . . Look here, Madame Maigret.'

'What is it you want?'

'I know you'll start by saying no, but it's absolutely necessary. . . . Pass me my pipe and my tobacco. . . . Just a few puffs. . . . I've got the feeling that I'm going to understand the whole thing, that in a few minutes – if I don't lose the thread.'

She went to fetch his pipe from the mantelpiece and handed it to him resignedly, sighing: 'I knew you'd think of some good excuse. . . . In any case tonight I'm going to make you a poultice whether you like it or not.'

Luckily there was no telephone in the flat and one had to go down into the shop to ring up from behind the counter.

'Will you go downstairs, Madame Maigret, and call Besson for me? It's seven o'clock. He may still be at the office. Otherwise call the *Café du Centre*, where he'll be playing billiards with Thiberge.'

'Shall I ask him to come here?'

'To bring me as soon as possible a list, not of all the residents in the street but of the tenants of the houses on the left side of it, between the Place du Congrès and the Judge's house.'

'Do try to keep covered up . . .'

Barely had she set foot on the staircase when he thrust both legs out of bed and rushed, barefooted, to fetch his tobacco pouch and fill himself a fresh pipe; then he lay back innocently between the sheets.

Through the flimsy floorboards he could hear a hum of voices and Madame Maigret's, speaking on the telephone. He smoked his pipe in greedy little puffs, although his throat was very sore. He could see raindrops slowly sliding down the dark panes, and this again reminded him of his childhood, of childish illnesses when his mother used to bring him caramel custard in bed.

Madame Maigret returned, panting a little, glanced round the room as if to take note of anything unusual, but did not think of the pipe.

'He'll be here in about an hour.'

'I'm going to ask you one more favour, Madame Maigret. . . . Will you put on your coat . . .'

She cast a suspicious glance at him.

'Will you go to young Justin's home and ask his parents to let you bring him to me. . . . Be very kind to him. . . . If I were to send a policeman he'd undoubtedly take fright, and he's liable enough to be prickly as it is. . . . Just tell him I'd like a few minutes' chat with him.'

'And suppose his mother wants to come with him?'

'Work out your own plan, but I don't want the mother.'

Left to himself, he sank back into the hot, humid depths of the bed, the tip of his pipe emerging from the sheets and emitting a slight cloud of smoke. He closed his eyes, and he could keep picturing the corner of the Rue Sainte-Catherine; he was no longer Superintendent Maigret, he had become the altar-boy who hurried along, covering the same ground every morning at the same time and talking to himself to keep up his courage.

As he turned into the Rue Sainte-Catherine: 'Maman, I wish you'd buy me a bike . . .'

For the kid had been rehearsing the scene he would play for his mother when he got back from the hospital. It would have to be more complicated; he must have thought up subtler approaches.

'You know, maman, if I had a bike, I could. . . .' Or else, 'I've saved three hundred francs already. . . . If you'd lend me the rest, which I promise to pay back with what I earn from the chapel, I could . . .'

The corner of the Rue Sainte-Catherine . . . a few seconds before the bells of the parish church rang out for the second time. And there were only a hundred and fifty metres of dark empty street to go through before reaching the safe haven of the hospital. . . . A few jumps between the pools of brightness shed by the street lamps . . .

Later the child was to declare: 'I looked up and I saw . . .'

That was the whole problem. The judge lived practically in the middle of the street, half way between the Place du Congrès and the corner of the barracks, and he had seen nothing and heard nothing.

The husband of the sick woman, the man from no. 42, lived closer to the Place du Congrès, on the right side of the street, and he had heard the sound of running footsteps.

Yet, five minutes later, there had been no dead or injured body on the pavement. And no car or van had passed. The policeman on duty on the bridge, the others on the beat at various spots in the neighbourhood, had seen nothing unusual such as, for instance, a man carrying another man on his back.

Maigret's temperature was certainly going up but he no longer thought of consulting the thermometer. Things were fine as they were; words evoked images, and images assumed unexpected sharpness.

It was just like when he was a sick child and his mother, bending over him, seemed to have grown so big that she took up the whole house.

There was that body lying across the pavement, looking so long because it was a dead body, with a brown-handled knife sticking out of its chest.

And a few metres away a man, a pale-eyed man who had begun running. . . . Running towards the barracks, whereas Justin ran for all

108

he was worth in the opposite direction.

'That's it!'

That's what? Maigret had made the remark out loud, as though it contained the solution of the problem, as though it had actually been the solution of the problem, and he smiled contentedly as he drew on his pipe with ecstatic little puffs.

Drunks are like that. Things suddenly appear to them self-evidently true, which they are nevertheless incapable of explaining, and which dissolve into vagueness as soon as they are examined coolly.

Something was untrue, that was it! And Maigret, in his feverish imagining, felt sure that he had put his finger on the weak point in the story.

Justin had not made it up. . . . His terror, his panic on arriving at the hospital had been genuine. Neither had he made up the picture of the long body sprawling across the pavement. Moreover there was at least one person in the street who had heard running footsteps.

What had the judge with the sneering smile remarked? 'You haven't yet learned to mistrust the evidence of children?' . . . or something of the sort.

However the judge was wrong. Children are incapable of inventing because one cannot construct truths out of nothing. One needs materials. Children transpose maybe, they don't invent.

And that was that! At each stage, Maigret repeated that self-congratulatory *voilà*!

There had been a body on the pavement. . . . And no doubt there had been a man close by. Had he had pale eyes? Quite possibly. And somebody had run.

And the old judge, Maigret could have sworn, was not the sort of man to tell a deliberate lie.

He felt hot. He was bathed in sweat, but nonetheless he left his bed to go and fill one last pipe before Madame Maigret's return. While he was up, he took the opportunity to open the cupboard and drink a big mouthful of rum from the bottle. What did it matter if his temperature was up that night? Everything would be finished by then!

And it would be quite an achievement; a difficult case solved from a sick-bed! Madame Maigret was not likely to appreciate that, however.

The judge had not lied, and yet he must have tried to play a trick on the boy whom he hated as two children of the same age can hate one another.

Customers seemed to be getting fewer down below, for the ridiculous chimes over the door sounded less frequently. Probably the dairyman and his wife, with their daughter whose cheeks were as pink as ham, were dining together in the room at the back of the shop.

There were steps on the pavement; there were steps on the stair. Small feet were stumbling. Madame Maigret opened the door and ushered in young Justin, whose navy-blue duffel coat was glistening with rain. He smelt like a wet dog.

'Here, my boy, let me take off your coat.'

'I can take it off myself.'

Another mistrustful glance from Madame Maigret. Obviously she could not believe he was still smoking the same pipe. Who knows, perhaps she even suspected the shot of rum?

'Sit down, Justin,' said the Superintendent, pointing to a chair.

'Thanks, I'm not tired.'

'I asked you to come so that we could have a friendly chat together for a few minutes. What were you busy with?'

'My arithmetic homework.'

'Because in spite of all you've been through you've gone back to school?'

'Why shouldn't I have gone?'

The boy was proud. He was on his high horse again. Did Maigret seem to him bigger and longer than usual, now that he was lying down?

'Madame Maigret, be an angel and go and look after the vegetable broth in the kitchen, and close the door.'

When that was done he gave the boy a knowing wink.

'Pass me my tobacco pouch, which is on the mantelpiece. . . . And the pipe, which must be in my overcoat pocket. . . . Yes, the one that's hanging behind the door. . . . Thanks, my boy. . . . Were you frightened when my wife came to fetch you?'

'No.' He said that with some pride.

'Were you annoyed?'

'Because everyone keeps saying that I've made it up.'

'And you haven't, have you?'

'There was a dead man on the pavement and another who . . .'

'Hush!'

'What?'

'Not so quick. . . . Sit down. . . .'

'I'm not tired.'

'So you've said, but I get tired of seeing you standing up. . . .'

He sat down on the very edge of the chair, and his feet didn't touch the ground; his legs were dangling, his bare knobbly knees protruding between the short pants and the socks.

'What sort of trick did you play on the judge?'

A swift, instinctive reaction: 'I never did anything to him.'

'You know what judge I mean?'

'The one who's always peering out of his window and who looks like an owl?'

'Just how I'd described him. . . . What happened between you?'

'In winter I didn't see him because his curtains were drawn when I went past.'

'But in summer?'

'I put out my tongue at him.'

'Why?'

'Because he kept looking at me as if he was making fun of me; he sniggered to himself as he looked at me.'

'Did you often put out your tongue at him?'

'Every time I saw him . . .'

'And what did he do?'

'He laughed in a spiteful sort of way . . . I thought it was because I served at Mass and he's an unbeliever . . .'

'Has he told a lie, then?'

'What did he say?'

'That nothing happened yesterday morning in front of his house, because he would have noticed.'

The boy stared intently at Maigret, then lowered his head.

'He was lying, wasn't he?'

'There was a body on the pavement with a knife stuck in its chest.'

'I know . . .'

'How do you know?'

'I know because it's the truth . . .' repeated Maigret gently. 'Pass me the matches . . . I've let my pipe go out.'

'Are you too hot?'

'It's nothing . . . just the flu . . .'

'Did you catch it this morning?'

'Maybe. . . . Sit down.'

He listened attentively and then called: 'Madame Maigret! Will you run downstairs? I think I heard Besson arriving and I don't want him to come up before I'm ready. . . . Will you keep him company downstairs? My friend Justin will call you . . .'

Once more, he said to his young companion: 'Sit down. . . . It's true, too, that you both ran . . .'

'I told you it was true . . .'

'And I believe you. . . . Go and make sure there's nobody behind the door and that it's properly shut.'

The child obeyed without understanding, impressed by the importance that his actions had suddenly acquired.

'Listen, Justin, you're a brave little chap.'

'Why do you say that?'

'It was true about the corpse. It was true about the man running.'

The child raised his head once again, and Maigret saw his lip

111

quivering.

'And the judge, who didn't lie, because a judge would not dare to lie, didn't tell the whole truth . . .'

The room smelt of flu and rum and tobacco. A whiff of vegetable broth came in under the kitchen door, and raindrops were still falling like silver tears on the black window pane beyond which lay the empty street. Were the two now facing one another still a man and a small boy? Or two men, or two small boys?

Maigret's head felt heavy; his eyes were glistening. His pipe had a curious medical flavour that was not unpleasant, and he remembered the smells of the hospital, its chapel and its vestry.

'The judge didn't tell the whole truth because he wanted to rile you. And you didn't tell the whole truth either. . . . Now I forbid you to cry. We don't want everyone to know what we've been saying to each other. . . . You understand, Justin?'

The boy nodded.

'If what you described hadn't happened at all, the man at no. 42 wouldn't have heard running footsteps.'

'I didn't make it up.'

'Of course not! But if it had happened just as you said, the judge would not have been able to say that he had heard nothing. . . . And if the murderer had run away towards the barracks, the old man would not have sworn that nobody had run past his house.'

The child sat motionless, staring down at the tips of his dangling feet.

'The judge was being honest, on the whole, in not daring to assert that you had gone past his house yesterday morning. But he might perhaps have asserted that you had not gone past. That's the truth, since you ran off in the opposite direction. . . . He was telling the truth, too, when he declared that no man had run past on the pavement under his window. . . . For the man did not go in that direction.'

'How do you know?'

He had stiffened, and was staring wide-eyed at Maigret as he must have stared on the previous night at the murderer or his victim.

'Because the man inevitably rushed off in the same direction as yourself, which explains why the husband in no. 42 heard him go past. . . . Because, knowing that you had seen him, that you had seen the body, that you could get him caught, he ran *after* you . . .'

'If you tell my mother, I . . .'

'Hush! . . . I don't wish to tell your mother or anyone else anything at all. . . . You see, Justin my boy, I'm going to talk to you like a man. . . . A murderer clever and cool enough to make a corpse disappear without trace in a few minutes would not have been foolish enough to

112

let you escape after seeing what you had seen.'

'I don't know . . .'

'But I do. . . . It's my job to know. . . . The most difficult thing is not to kill a man, it's to make the body disappear afterwards, and this one disappeared magnificently. . . . It disappeared, even though you had seen it and seen the murderer. . . . In other words, the murderer's a really smart guy. . . . And a really smart guy, with his life at stake, would never have let you get away like that.'

'I didn't know . . .'

'What didn't you know?'

'I didn't know it mattered so much . . .'

'It doesn't matter at all now, since everything has been put right.'

'Have you arrested him?'

There was immense hope in the tone in which these words were uttered.

'He'll be arrested before long. . . . Sit still; stop swinging your legs . . .'

'I won't move.'

'For one thing, if it had all happened in front of the judge's house, that's to say in the middle of the street, you'd have been aware of it from further off, and you'd have had time to run away. . . . That was the only mistake the murderer made, for all his cleverness . . .'

'How did you guess?'

'I didn't guess. But I was once an altar-boy myself, and I served at six o'clock Mass like you. . . . You wouldn't have gone a hundred metres along the street without looking in front of you. . . . So the corpse must have been closer, much closer, just round the corner of the street.'

'Five houses past the corner.'

'You were thinking of something else, of your bike, and you may have gone twenty metres without seeing anything.'

'How can you possibly know?'

'And when you saw, you ran towards the Place du Congrès to get to the hospital by the other street. The man ran after you . . .'

'I thought I should die of fright.'

'Did he grab you by the shoulder?'

'He grabbed my shoulders with both hands. I thought he was going to strangle me . . .'

'He asked you to say . . '

The child was crying, quietly. He was pale and the tears were rolling slowly down his cheeks.

'If you tell my mother she'll blame me all my life long. She's always nagging at me.'

'He ordered you to say that it had happened further on . . .'

113

'Yes.'

'In front of the judge's house?'

'It was me that thought of the judge's house, because of putting out my tongue at him. . . . The man only said the other end of the street, and that he'd run off towards the barracks.'

'And so we very nearly had a perfect crime, because nobody believed you, since there was no murderer and no body, no traces of any sort, and it all seemed impossible . . .'

'But what about you?'

'I don't count. It just so happens that I was once an altar-boy, and that today I'm in bed with flu. . . . What did he promise you?'

'He told me that if I didn't say what he wanted me to, he would always be after me, wherever I went, in spite of the police, and that he would wring my neck like a chicken's.'

'And then?'

'He asked me what I wanted to have . . .'

'And you said a bike . . .?'

'How do you know?'

'I've told you, I was once an altar-boy too.'

'And you wanted a bike?'

'That, and a great many other things that I've never had. . . . Why did you say he had pale eyes?'

'I don't know. I didn't see his eyes. He was wearing thick glasses. But I didn't want him to be caught . . .'

'Because of the bike?'

'Maybe. . . . You're going to tell my mother, aren't you?'

'Not your mother nor anyone else. . . . Aren't we pals now? . . . Look, you hand me my tobacco pouch and don't tell Madame Maigret that I've smoked three pipes since we've been here together. . . . You see, grown-ups don't always tell the whole truth either. . . . Which door was it in front of, Justin?'

'The yellow house next door to the delicatessen.'

'Go and fetch my wife.'

'Where is she?'

'Downstairs. . . . She's with Inspector Besson, the one who was so beastly to you.'

'And who's going to arrest me?'

'Open the wardrobe . . .'

'Right . . .'

'There's a pair of trousers hanging there . . .'

'What am I to do with it?'

'In the left hand pocket you'll find a wallet.'

'Here it is.'

'In the wallet there are some visiting-cards.'

'Do you want them?'

'Hand me one. . . . And also the pen that's on the table . . '

With which, Maigret wrote on one of the cards that bore his name:
Supply bearer with one bicycle.

III

'Come in, Besson.'

Madame Maigret glanced up at the dense cloud of smoke that hung round the lamp in its waxed-paper shade; then she hurried into the kitchen, because she could smell something burning there.

As for Besson, taking the chair just vacated by the boy, for whom he had only a disdainful glance, he announced:

'I've got the list you asked me to draw up. I must tell you right away . . .'

'That it's useless. . . . Who lives in no. 14?'

'One moment. . . .' He consulted his notes. 'Let's see . . . no. 14. . . . There's only a single tenant there.'

'I suspected as much.'

'Oh?' An uneasy glance at the boy. 'It's a foreigner, name of Frankelstein, a dealer in jewellery.'

Maigret had slipped back among his pillows; he muttered, with an air of indifference: 'A fence.'

'What did you say, Chief?'

'A fence. . . . Possibly the boss of a gang.'

'I don't understand.'

'That doesn't matter. . . . Be a good fellow, Besson, pass me the bottle of rum that's in the cupboard. Quickly, before Madame Maigret comes back. . . . I bet my temperature's soaring and I'll need to have my sheets changed a couple of times tonight . . . Frankelstein . . . Get a search warrant from the examining magistrate. . . . No. . . . At this time of night, it'll take too long, for he's sure to be out playing bridge somewhere. . . . Have you had dinner? . . . Me, I'm waiting for my vegetable broth. . . . There are some blank warrants in my desk – left-hand drawer. Fill one in. Search the house. You're sure to find the body, even if it means knocking down a cellar wall.'

Poor Besson stared at his Chief in some anxiety, then glanced at the boy, who was sitting waiting quietly in a corner.

'Act quickly, old man. . . . If he knows that the kid's been here tonight, you won't find him in his lair. . . . He's a tough guy, as you'll find out.'

He was indeed. When the police rang at his door, he tried to escape through backyards and over walls; it took them all night to catch him, which they finally did among the roof-tops. Meanwhile other policemen searched the house for hours before discovering the corpse,

115

decomposing in a bath of quicklime.

It had obviously been a settling of accounts. A disgruntled and frustrated member of the gang had called on the boss in the small hours; Frankelstein had done him in on the doorstep, unaware that an altar-boy was at that very instant coming round the street corner.

'What does it say?' Maigret no longer had the heart to look at the thermometer himself.

'39.3 . . .'

'Aren't you cheating?'

He knew that she was cheating, that his temperature was higher than that, but he didn't care; it was good, it was delicious to sink into unconsciousness, to let himself glide at a dizzy speed into a misty, yet terribly real world where an altar-boy bearing a strong resemblance to Maigret as he had once been was tearing wildly down the street, sure that he was either going to be strangled or to win a shiny new bicycle.

'What are you talking about?' asked Madame Maigret, whose plump fingers held a scalding hot poultice which she was proposing to apply to her husband's throat.

He was muttering nonsense like a feverish child, talking about the first bell and the second bell.

'I'm going to be late . . .'

'Late for what?'

'For Mass. . . . Sister. . . . Sister . . .'

He meant the vestry-nun, the sacristine, but he could not find the word.

He fell asleep at last, with a huge compress round his neck, dreaming of Mass in his own village and of Marie Titin's inn, past which he used to run because he was afraid.

Afraid of what? . . .

'I got him, all the same . . .'

'Who?'

'The judge.'

'What judge?'

It was too complicated to explain. The judge reminded him of somebody in his village at whom he used to put out his tongue. The blacksmith? No. . . . It was the baker's wife's stepfather. . . . It didn't matter. Somebody he disliked. And it was the judge who had misled him the whole way through, in order to be revenged on the altar-boy and to annoy people. . . . He said he had heard no footsteps *in front of his house* . . .

But he had not said that he had heard two people running off in the opposite direction . . .

Old people become childish. And they quarrel with children. Like children.

Maigret was satisfied, in spite of everything. He had cheated by three whole pipes, even four. . . . He had a good taste of tobacco in his mouth and he could let himself drift away . . .

And tomorrow, since he had flu, Madame Maigret would make him some caramel custard.

The Hand

GUY DE MAUPASSANT

A CIRCLE HAD FORMED round Monsieur Bermutier, the Examining Magistrate, who was giving his opinion about the mysterious Saint-Cloud affair. For the past month this unsolved crime had been the talk of Paris. No one could explain it.

Monsieur Bermutier was standing with his back to the fireplace, talking. He marshalled the evidence, discussed a variety of theories, but could reach no conclusion.

Several ladies had left their chairs to get closer to him, and they remained standing, with their eyes on the magistrate's clean-shaven lips, from which fell words of the utmost gravity. They shuddered and were thrilled. That strange fear had hold of them, that avid and insatiable love of being frightened which haunts all women and torments them like a physical hunger.

A brief silence had fallen, and one of these ladies, who looked paler than the others, broke it.

'It is positively horrifying,' she said. 'There is something almost supernatural about it. I don't suppose we shall ever know what really happened.'

The magistrate turned to her:

'That is extremely probable, Madame. But this I can tell you, that the word *supernatural*, which you have just used, is entirely out of place in this connection. We are dealing with a crime which was skilfully planned, most adroitly carried out, and so wrapped in mystery that we have completely failed to free it from the impenetrable circumstances which surround it. But I once had to inquire into an affair about which there really was an element of the fantastic. There, too, the investigation had to be abandoned, for lack of evidence.'

Several of the ladies exclaimed, with such unanimity that their voices sounded as one:

'Oh, do tell us about it!'

Monsieur Bermutier's smile was sober and serious, as the smile of an Examining Magistrate should be. He continued:

'Please do not think for a single moment that I suppose there to have been anything supernatural about the case in question. I believe

118

only in natural causes. It would be a great deal better if we used the word "inexplicable" rather than "supernatural" to describe matters we know nothing of. Be that as it may, what really interested me in the occurrence I am about to describe, were the attendant, the preparatory circumstances. Here are the facts.

'At the time of which I am speaking I was Examining Magistrate at Ajaccio, a small white town standing on the shore of a lovely bay surrounded on all sides by high mountains.

'I was chiefly concerned with matters having to do with *vendetta*. This tradition of private warfare is rich in superb, infinitely dramatic, fierce and heroic incidents. It provides us with the most wonderful stories of vengeance imaginable – hatred kept alive from generation to generation, momentarily appeased but never allowed to die, stratagems of the most horrible description, murders on such a scale as to deserve the name of massacres, and almost epic deeds. For two years I heard of nothing but blood-feuds, of that terrible Corsican obsession which insists that a man must take vengeance not only on an enemy, but on his descendants and his relatives. I have known of old men, children, cousins having their throats cut in the name of that bloodstained doctrine. I have heard more stories of *vendetta* than I care to remember.

'I learned one day that an Englishman had taken the lease of a house, at the far end of the bay, for several years. He had brought with him a French servant whom he had engaged when passing through Marseilles.

'It was not long before the whole neighbourhood was buzzing with gossip about this strange character, who lived all alone in his house and never left it except to shoot and fish. He talked to nobody, never went into town, and spent an hour or two every morning practising with a revolver and a carbine.

'He became the subject of many legends. Some said that he was a man of high rank who had fled from his country for political reasons; others, that he was hiding in order to escape the consequences of a detestable crime. People went so far as to give details of a more than usually blood-curdling nature.

'It was natural that, as an Examining Magistrate, I should wish to find out all I could about the fellow. But to learn much turned out to be impossible. He went by the name of Sir John Rowell.

'I had to be content with keeping such watch as I could upon him, but, even so, I could discover nothing in any way suspicious in his activities.

'Since, however, rumours continued to circulate, to grow and to become widespread, I thought it my duty to make personal contact with this foreigner, and, with this end in view, I took to shooting

119

regularly near his property. I had to wait some time for the chance I needed. But it came at last, in the form of a partridge at which I took a pot shot and happened to bring down under the very nose of the Englishman. My dog recovered it, and I went at once, with the bird in my hand, to apologize for my bad manners and to ask Sir John to accept the victim of my gun.

'He was a big man, with red hair and a beard, very tall, very broad, in fact, a sort of urbane and quiet-mannered Hercules. There was nothing of the traditional British stiffness about him, and he thanked me warmly for my civility. He spoke French with an accent which undoubtedly hailed from across the Channel. By the end of a month, we had chattered together on five or six occasions.

'Then one evening, when I happened to be passing his door, I saw him sitting astride a chair in his garden, smoking his pipe. I raised my hat, and he asked me in for a glass of beer. Needless to say, I did not wait to be asked twice. He received me with scrupulous English courtesy, was loud in his praise of France and of Corsica, and declared that he had developed a great fondness for "this country" and "this stretch of coast".

'With the utmost care, and pretending a lively interest, I questioned him about his life and his plans. He showed no embarrassment, and told me that he had travelled a great deal in Africa, India, and America, adding with a laugh:

' "I have had my full share of adventures."

'Then I started to talk shooting with him, and he told me many curious details about his experiences when hunting hippopotamuses, tigers, elephants, and even gorillas.

' "Those are all very dangerous animals," I said.

'He smiled: "But there is none more dangerous than man."

'All of a sudden, he laughed outright, and his laugh was that of a solid, satisfied Englishman.

' "I have hunted a good many men, too, in my time."

'Then he switched the talk to firearms, and asked me into the house to look at his collection of guns and rifles.

'The hangings in his drawing-room were black – black silk embroidered in gold. Great yellow flowers sprawled all over the dark material, glittering like flame.

' "It is a Japanese fabric," he said.

'But, in the middle of the largest panel, a strange object caught my eye. On a square of red velvet something black stood out in strong relief. I went closer. It was a hand, a human hand, not the hand of a skeleton, white and clean, but a shrivelled black hand with yellow nails. The sinews had been laid bare, and there were traces of dried blood, like a scab, on the bones, which had been cleanly severed about half way up the forearm.

'Round the wrist was an enormous iron chain, riveted and soldered to the unsavoury limb, and attached to the wall. It looked strong enough to tether an elephant.

' "What is that?" I asked.

'With complete composure the Englishman replied: "That belonged to my best enemy. Comes from America – cut off with a sabre, and the skin scraped away with a sharp stone. Left to dry in the sun for eight days. It was a bit of luck for me, I can tell you."

'I touched the grisly relic, which must have belonged to a man of tremendous size. The abnormally long fingers were attached to enormous sinews to which, in places, strips of skin were still adhering. Flayed like that, the hand was a disgusting sight, and seemingly bore witness to some act of savage vengeance.

'I said: "He must have been very strong."

'Very quietly, my host replied: "He was: but I was stronger. I put that chain on to hold him down."

'I thought he was joking, and said: "But there is no reason for the chain now. That hand isn't going to run away!"

'In a perfectly serious voice, Sir John Rowell said: "It was always trying to get free: I had to chain it."

'I shot a quick inquiring look at him. Was he, I wondered, a madman or just a practical joker?

'But his face remained inscrutable, calm, and benignant. I changed the subject, and much admired his collection of guns.

'I noticed however, that there were three loaded revolvers lying about on various pieces of furniture, as though the man were living in constant fear of attack.

'I revisited him on several occasions. Then I stopped going. The locals had grown used to him, and nobody now gave him a thought.'

'A year went by, and then, one morning towards the end of November, my servant woke me with the news that Sir John Rowell had been murdered during the night.

'I went to the Englishman's house with the Chief Constable and the Captain of Gendarmes. The dazed and distracted valet was blubbering in front of the door. I immediately suspected him, but he was, as it turned out, innocent.

'The identity of the murderer was never established.

'On going into the drawing-room, the first thing I saw was the body of Sir John lying in the middle of the floor.

'His waistcoat was torn open, and one sleeve of the coat was hanging by a thread. There had obviously been a fierce struggle.

'The Englishman had been strangled. His black and swollen face

121

was horrible to see and, in his eyes, there was a look of the most appalling terror. There was something between his clenched teeth, and his neck, pierced in five places by some sharp instrument, was covered in blood.

'A doctor joined us. He made a prolonged examination of the finger-marks on the dead man's neck, and then uttered these strange words.

' "Looks to me as though he'd been strangled by a skeleton!"

'A shiver went down my back, and I looked at the wall where I had once seen that dreadful flayed hand. It was no longer there. The chain had been broken and was hanging loose.

'Then I bent over the corpse. The object between its teeth was one of the fingers of the vanished hand, but cut, or rather bitten through at the second joint.

'A search was made but without producing any new evidence. Not a door, nor a window, had been forced. None of the furniture showed signs of violence. The two watch-dogs seemed to have slept through whatever had happened.

'Here in brief, is the gist of the servant's deposition.

'For the last month, he said, his master had seemed to be uneasy and on edge. He had received a number of letters which he had thrown on the fire as soon as they arrived.

'He frequently took a hunting-crop, and, in a fit more of madness than of rage, had lashed blindly at the withered hand, which, at the moment of the crime, had been spirited away from its place on the wall, no one could say how.

'He went to bed very late, and was careful to lock all the doors and windows. He always had some weapon within easy reach. He would frequently speak in a loud voice during the night. He seemed to be quarrelling with somebody.

'On the night in question, however, he made no noise, and it was only when his servant went into his room to open the shutters, that he found Sir John murdered. He could think of no possible suspect.

'I communicated all I knew about the dead man to the civil authorities and the police. The whole island was combed, but without result.

'About three months after the crime, I had a most terrifying nightmare. I dreamed that I saw that horrible hand scuttling like a scorpion or a spider along my walls and curtains. Three times I woke up: three times I fell asleep again, and three times I saw that hideous relic galloping round the room, moving its fingers like legs.

'Next morning it was brought to me. It had been found in the churchyard on Sir John Rowell's grave – for in the absence of any discoverable relative, he had been buried on the spot. The index finger was missing.

'And that, ladies, is my story. I know nothing more.'

The ladies were horror-stricken, pale, and trembling. One of them exclaimed:

'But you have suggested no solution, no explanation of the mystery! I am sure none of us will sleep unless you tell us at least what you *think* happened!'

The Magistrate smiled, but his eyes remained severe.

'I fear that, so far as dreams are concerned, I shall be a wet blanket. My theory, such as it is, is very simple, namely that the owner of the hand was not dead at all, but came to look for it. What he did, I have no idea, but I am inclined to think that the whole affair had something to do with a *vendetta*.'

'No,' murmured one of the ladies: 'that *can't* be the explanation!'

The Magistrate, still smiling, concluded:

'I told you that you would not like my theory.'

Tickled to Death

SIMON BRETT

IF A DEAD BODY COULD ever be funny, this one was. Only intimations of his own mortality prevented Inspector Walsh from smiling at the sight.

The corpse in the greenhouse was dressed in a clown's costume. Bald plastic cranium with side-tufts of ropey orange hair. Red jacket, too long. Black and white check trousers suspended on elastic braces to a hooped waistband. Shoes three foot long pointing upwards in strange semaphore.

'Boy, he's really turned his toes up,' said Sergeant Trooper, who was prone to such witticisms even when the corpse was less obviously humorous.

The clown's face could not be seen. The back of a plate supplied a moonlike substitute which fitted well with the overall image.

'Going to look good on the report,' Sergeant Trooper continued. 'Cause of death – suffocation. Murder weapon – a custard pie.'

'I suppose that *was* the cause . . . Let the photographers and fingerprint boys do their bit and we'll have a look.'

These formalities concluded, Inspector Walsh donned rubber gloves and cautiously prised the plate away. Over its make-up, the face was covered with pink goo. It was clogged in the nostrils and in the slack, painted mouth.

'Yes, Sergeant Trooper, it looks like suffocation.'

'Course it does. What's your alternative? Poisoned custard in the pie?'

'Well, it's certainly not custard.' The Inspector poked at the congealed mess. It was hard and crumbly. 'Even school custard wasn't this bad. No, it's plaster of Paris or something. They don't usually use that for slapstick, do they?'

Sergeant Trooper shook his head. 'Nope. Foam, flour and water, dough . . . not plaster of Paris.'

'Hmm. Which probably means the crime was premeditated.'

The Sergeant thought this too obvious to merit a response. Inspector Walsh bent down and felt in the capacious pockets of the red jacket.

124

'What are you looking for? I don't think clowns carry credit cards or passports.'

'No,' Inspector Walsh agreed, producing a string of cloth sausages and a jointless rubber fish.

'Wonder if there's anything else.' He felt again in the pockets. His rubber-gloved hand closed round a soft oval object. He squeezed it gently.

'Bloody hell,' said Sergeant Trooper.

Thin jets of water found their way through the caked white beneath the clown's eyes. Inspector Walsh drew out a rubber bulb attached to a plastic tube.

'Old clown's prop – squirting eyes.'

He reached into the other pocket and found what felt like a switch. He pressed it.

The two tufts of orange hair shot out at right angles from the clown's bald head. As they did so, the noise of a klaxon escaped from somewhere inside the jacket.

Inspector Walsh stood up. 'I don't know,' he said. 'It's a funny business.'

'The fact is,' objected the Teapot, 'it's damnably inconvenient. These people are our guests. We can't just keep them here against their will.'

'No, we can't,' the Pillar-box agreed shrilly. 'What will they think of our hospitality?'

The Yorkshire terrier, scampering around the study, barked its endorsement of their anger.

'I'm sorry,' Inspector Walsh leant coolly back against the leather-topped desk. 'But a murder has been committed and we cannot allow anyone to leave the building until we have taken their statements.'

'Well, I may be forced to speak to your superior,' snapped the Teapot. 'I am not without influence in this area.'

'I'm sure you're not,' the Inspector soothed. 'Now why don't you take your lid off and sit down?'

The Teapot flounced angrily, but did remove its hatlike lid and, hitching up its wired body, perched on a low stool.

'You may as well sit down too, madam.' The Inspector pointed to a second stool and the Pillar-box, with equally bad grace, folded on to it. Pale blue eyes flashed resentment through the posting slit.

'And can we get rid of that bloody dog?' A uniformed policeman ushered the reluctant Yorkshire terrior out of the study. 'Oh, and get us some tea while you're at it, could you, constable?' The Inspector smiled perfunctorily. 'Now let's just get a few facts straight. You are Mr and Mrs Alcott?'

The two heads nodded curt agreement.

125

'And this is your house?'

Two more nods.

'And, Mr Alcott, you have no doubt that the dead man is your business partner, Mr Cruikshank?'

Alcott's head, rising tortoise-like from the top of the Teapot, twitched from side to side. 'No doubt at all.'

'He had been wearing a clown costume all evening?'

'Yes. It's one of our most popular lines. As partners, we always try to demonstrate both the traditional and the new. Mr Cruikshank was wearing one of Festifunn's oldest designs, while I –' Unconsciously, he smoothed down the Teapot frame with his spout. '– chose one of the most recent.' He gestured proudly to the Pillar-box. 'My wife's is also a new design.'

Some response seemed to be required. The Inspector murmured, 'Very nice too,' which he hoped was appropriate.

'And your guests?'

'They're all dressed in our lines too.'

'Yes. That wasn't really what I was going to ask. I wished to inquire about your guest-list. Are all the people here personal friends?'

'Not so much friends as professional associates,' replied the Teapot tartly.

'So they would all have known Mr Cruikshank?'

'Oh, certainly. Mr Cruikshank always made a point of getting to know our staff and clients personally.' The Teapot's tone implied disapproval of this familiarity.

'So I would be correct in assuming that this Fancy Dress Party is a business function?'

The Teapot was vehement in its agreement with this statement. The party was very definitely part of Festifunn's promotional campaign, and as such (though this was implied rather than stated) tax-deductible.

'You don't think we do this for fun, do you?' asked the crumpled Pillar-box.

'No, of course we don't.' The Teapot assumed an accent of self-denying righteousness. 'It's just an opportunity to demonstrate the full range of our stock to potential customers. And also it's a kind of thank-you to the staff. Something that I wouldn't do voluntarily, I hasten to add, but something they demand these days as a right. And one daren't cross them. Even the novelty industry,' he concluded darkly, 'is not immune to the destructive influence of the trade unions.'

'But presumably everyone has a good time?'

Mr Alcott winced at the Inspector's suggestion. 'The Fancy Dress

Party was not originally my idea,' he said in further self-justification.

'Mr Cruikshank's,' Walsh deduced smoothly.

'Yes.'

'Then why is it held in your house?'

'Have you recently examined the cost of hiring outside premises?'

'I meant why not in Mr Cruikshank's house?'

The Pillar-box tutted at the idea. 'Mr Cruikshank's house would be totally unsuitable for a function of this nature. It's a terrible mess, full of odd machinery and designs he's working on . . . most unsalubrious. I'm afraid his style of living, too, is – was – most irregular. He drank, you know.'

The Inspector let that go for the moment. 'Mr. Alcott, would you say Mr Cruikshank had any enemies?'

'Well . . .'

'I mean, did he tend to annoy people?'

'Certainly.'

'In what way?'

'Well, I have no wish to speak ill of the dead . . .'

'But?'

'But Mr Cruikshank was . . .' The Teapot formed the words with distaste. '. . . a practical joker.'

'Ah.' The Inspector smiled. 'Good thing to be in your line of business.'

'By no means,' the Teapot contradicted. 'Most unsuitable.'

Again Walsh didn't pursue it. Time enough for that. 'Right now, I would like from you a list of your guests before I start interviewing them.' He took a notebook from his pocket, then turned round to the desk and picked up a pencil that lay beside an old-fashioned biscuit-barrel.

'Well, there's Mr Brickett, our Sales Manager . . .'

Inspector Walsh bent to write the name down. The pencil squashed softly against the paper. It was made of rubber.

'I'm sorry. That's one of our BJ153s. Joke Pencil – Many Minutes of Mirth.'

'Ah.'

At that moment the uniformed constable arrived with the tea-tray. The three helped themselves and then, when the Inspector again looked round for something to write with, the Teapot said, 'There's a ball-point pen just the other side of the biscuit-barrel.'

'Thank you.' The Inspector picked it up to continue his list.

'Sugar?' the Pillar-box offered, adding righteously, 'We don't.'

'Well, I do.' He took two lumps, put them in the tea, and reached for a spoon. When he looked back, the lumps of sugar were floating in the top of his cup.

'I'm sorry, Inspector,' said the Teapot. 'You've got some of our GW34s. Silly Sugar – Your Friends Will Be Tickled To Death.'

The young man looked sheepish. Since he was dressed as a Sheep, this wasn't difficult.

'Might I ask, Mr O'Brien . . .' Despite the request for permission, Inspector Walsh was clearly going to ask anyway. '. . . why you went out to the greenhouse at the time that you discovered the body?'

'Well, I . . . er . . . well, um . . .' the young man bleated.

'I think you'd do better to tell me.' Walsh advised portentously.

'Yes. Well, the fact was, I was . . . um, there was a young lady involved.'

'You mean a young lady was with you when you found Mr Cruikshank?'

'No. No, no, she was still in the house, but I was . . . er . . . sort of scouting out the . . . er . . . lie of the land. Do I make myself clear?'

'No.'

'Oh. Am I going to have to spell it out?'

'Yes.'

'Well, you see, this young lady and I are . . . er . . . rather good friends. I'm at Festifunn in Indoor Firework Testing and she's in Fancy Dress Design, so we see quite a lot of each other and . . . er . . . you know how it is . . .'

The Inspector nodded indulgently, awaiting further information.

'Unfortunately, her father doesn't approve of our . . . er, er . . . friendship. He thinks, as a profession, Indoor Fireworks is too . . . er . . . volatile. And my landlady's a bit old-fashioned, so we can only really meet at work, or in secret . . .'

'Yes?'

'Which, I mean, is OK. It works all right, but it sometimes leads to complications. Like tonight.'

'What happened tonight?'

'Well, um . . .' Insofar as it is possible for a sheep to blush, the Sheep blushed. 'You see, it comes down to . . . sex.'

'It often does,' Walsh observed sagely.

'Yes. Well, um . . . do I really have to tell you this?'

'Yes.'

'Right. Well, normally we . . . um . . . go into my car for . . . um . . .'

'I understand.'

'Thank you. But you see, this is where feminine vanity raises problems. At least it did tonight. You see, my friend, as any woman would, was anxious to look her best for the party and, since she works in Fancy Dress Design, nothing would stop her from coming in her latest creation. No woman could resist such an opportunity to show off her skills.'

'No,' Walsh agreed with a worldly shake of his head. 'And may I ask you what your friend is dressed as?'

'An Orange,' the Sheep replied miserably.

'Ah.'

'And I've only got a Mini.'

'I begin to understand why you were checking out the greenhouse, Mr O'Brien.'

The Sheep looked, if it were possible, even more sheepish.

'And what happened to the trifle?'

'The top flipped off, there was a loud squeak, and I saw the mouse in the bottom of the dish.'

'Would that be a real mouse?' Inspector Walsh asked cautiously.

Joan of Arc was so surprised at the question that she removed the cigarette which drooped from her generously lipsticked mouth. 'No, a rubber one. It's just the basic BT3, Squeaking Mouse, incorporated into the HM200, Tricky Trifle.'

'Oh, I see. And Mr Cruikshank offered it to you?'

'Yes. I shouldn't have fallen for it. Good Lord, I handle half a dozen HM200s a day in the shop. But it was a party, you know, I wasn't concentrating – perhaps even a bit tiddly.' She simpered. 'Honestly, me – a couple of Babychams and I'm anybody's.'

She moved her body in a manner calculated to display her bosom (a wasted effort for someone dressed in complete armour).

'I see,' said Inspector Walsh again, more to change the subject than for any other reason. 'Why I'm asking about the incident, Mrs Dancer, is because we believe you may have been the last person – except, of course, for his murderer – to see Mr Cruikshank alive.'

'Oh, fancy that.'

'And handing you the Tricky Trifle may have been his last action before his death.'

'Good Lord.' Joan of Arc paused, then set her painted face in an expression of piety, as if prepared to hear voices. 'Oh well, I'm glad I fell for it then. It's how he'd have wanted to go.'

'I'm sorry?'

She elaborated. 'He loved his jokes, Mr Cruikshank did. He designed almost all the novelties at Festifunn. Always working on something new. His latest idea was a customised Jack-in-a-Box. Really novel. Clown pops out when the box opens and a personal recorded message starts up. You know, you get different ones – jolly for kids' parties, fruity for stag nights, and so on.

'Full of ideas, Mr Cruikshank always was. Really loved jokes. So, you see, I'm glad about the Tricky Trifle. Because if he had to die,

129

he'd have been really chuffed to die after catching someone out with one of his own novelties.'

The Inspector was tempted to ask how anyone could be 'chuffed' while being suffocated by a custard pie, but contented himself with another 'I see.' (In his early days as a detective, Walsh had worried about how often he said 'I see' during interrogations, but long since he had come to accept it as just an occupational hazard.) 'And before this evening, Mrs Dancer, when did you last see Mr Cruikshank?'

'Well, funnily enough, I saw him this afternoon.'

'Ah.'

'Yes, he came into the shop.'

'Was that unusual?'

'Not unusual for him to come in, no – he liked to keep in touch with what was happening in the business – but unusual for him to come in two days running.'

'I see. What did he come in for?'

'Oh, a chat. See how the stock was going. He was particularly worried about the Noses. Always get a run on Noses this time of year. We're very low on Red Drunken and Warty Witch's – and completely out of Long Rubbery.'

'Oh dear,' the Inspector commiserated. 'And this afternoon, when Mr Cruikshank came into the shop, did you notice anything unusual about him?'

'No.' Joan of Arc stubbed her cigarette out on her cuirass as she reconsidered this answer. But she didn't change her mind. 'No. Well, he had a knife through his head, but –'

'I beg your pardon?'

'Knife-Through-Head – JL417. As opposed to Tomahawk-Through-Head – JL418 – and Nail-Through-Head – JL419.'

'Uhuh.' Curiosity overcame Inspector Walsh's customary reserve. 'Which one of these is the most popular?'

'Oh, 417,' Joan of Arc replied without hesitation. 'Sell a few Nails, but very little call for Tomahawks these days. It's because they're not making so many Westerns – all these space films instead. Mr Cruikshank was trying to come up with a Laser-Beam-Through-Head, but it's not as easy as it sounds.'

'No, I suppose not.' Walsh digested this gobbet of marketing information before continuing. 'And did Mr Cruikshank often come into the shop with a knife through his head?'

'Yes. Well, that or some other novelty. Boil-On-Face, Vampire Teeth, Safety-Pin-Through-Nose, that sort of thing. Lived for his work, Mr Cruikshank.'

'And he didn't say anything strange that afternoon?'

'No.' She pondered. 'Well, yes, I suppose he did, in a way.'

130

'Ah.'

'He said he'd come to say goodbye.'

'Goodbye?'

'Yes, he said someone was out to kill him, and he didn't think he'd live more than twenty-four hours.'

Walsh sat bolt-upright. 'What! Did he say who was out to kill him?'

'Oh yes.' Joan of Arc reached casually into her habergeon and brought out a packet of Players Number Six. She put one in her mouth, reached past the biscuit-barrel and picked up a box of matches. She opened it and a green snake jumped out. 'BK351,' she said dismissively.

'Mrs Dancer, who? *Who* did he say was out to kill him?'

'Oh, Mr Alcott.'

'But that's terribly important. Why on earth didn't you mention it before?'

'Oh, I thought it was just another of Mr Cruikshank's jokes.'

'So what did you do when he told you?'

'Oh, I just offered him some Squirting Chocolate and went back to stock-taking the Severed Fingers.'

'You have to understand that I'm a professional accountant . . .' The Baby self-importantly hitched up his nappy and adjusted the dummy-string around his neck. '. . . and I am bound by a code of discretion in relation to the affairs of my clients.'

'This *is* a police investigation, Mr McCabe . . .'

'I am aware of that, Inspector Walsh.'

'. . . into the most serious crime one human being can commit against another.'

'Yes.'

'So I suggest you save time and answer all my questions as fully as possible.'

'Oh, very well.' With bad grace, the Baby threw his rattle on the desk and sat down.

'I'm going to ask you a direct question, Mr McCabe, and I require you to give me a direct answer.'

The Baby's bald head wrinkled with disapproval at this proposal. But he said nothing, just stared pointedly upwards at the ornate ceiling-rose over the desk.

'Right, Mr McCabe, was there any cause for dissension between the two partners in Festifunn?'

'Well . . . As you have probably gathered, Inspector, Mr Alcott and Mr Cruikshank were men of very different personalities . . .'

'I had gathered that, yes.'

'And so, inevitably, they did not always see eye to eye on the daily

131

minutiae of the business.'

'There were arguments?'

'Yes, there were.'

'Threats?'

'Occasionally.'

'What form did the threats take?'

'Well, they –' The Baby stopped short and coloured. The flush spread from his head to just above the navel. 'Inspector, are you suggesting that Mr Alcott . . .'

'We have to consider every possibility, Mr McCabe. In our experience, people are most commonly murdered by their loved ones. Since, in this case, Mr Cruikshank had no immediate family, we are forced to consider those who worked closely with him.'

'If you're making accusations against Mr Alcott, I don't think I can answer any further questions without a solicitor present.'

The Baby sat back complacently after this repetition of something he'd heard on television. Then Inspector Walsh spoiled it by asking, 'Whose solicitor?'

'I beg your pardon?'

'Whose? Yours? Mr Alcott's?'

'Oh. Um . . .'

'Anyway, I'm not making accusations at the moment, so just answer the questions!'

The Baby was suitably cowed.

'Right, was there any recent cause for more serious disagreement between the two partners of Festifunn?'

'Well . . .'

'Answer!'

'Yes, right, fine.' The words came out quickly. 'There has recently been an offer to take over the firm. An offer from the Jollijests Corporaton.'

'And the partners disagreed about the advisability of accepting the offer?'

'Precisely. Mr Alcott recognized it for the good business proposition it was. Mr Cruikshank opposed it on the somewhat whimsical grounds that he didn't want Festifunn's output limited to the manufacture of party hats and squeakers.'

'Sounds a reasonable objection.'

The Baby gave a patronising smile. 'When you've been in the novelty business as long as I have, Inspector, you will understand that it is not an area where sentiment should be allowed to overrule common sense.'

'I see. So the argument about the proposed take-over was quite violent?'

132

'Certainly. At the last board meeting, Mr Cruikshank's behaviour was most unseemly. He used language that was distinctly unparliamentary.' Then, after a pause, 'He drank, you know.'

'Yes, I did know. But he wouldn't accept the deal?'

'Under no circumstances. In fact he said, if it were to take place, it would be *over his dead body.*'

The words were out before the Baby realized their significance and coloured again.

At first, Walsh restricted himself to another 'I see.' Then, piecing his question together slowly, he asked, 'So, from the point of view of Mr Alcott's plans for the future of Festifunn, Mr Cruikshank's death couldn't have come at a more convenient time?'

Mr McCabe rose with all the dignity that a fifty-year-old accountant in a nappy can muster. 'I don't see that I have to answer any further questions, Inspector. You can't make me. I suggest that you carry on the rest of your investigation without my assistance.'

'Fair enough.' Walsh didn't bother to argue. 'Thank you, anyway, for all the invaluable help you've already given me.'

The Baby, moving away, turned his head to flash a venomous look at his interrogator.

'Hey, watch out! That Yorkshire terrier's misbehaved.' The Inspector pointed to where the Baby's knobbly-veined foot was about to land. Neatly on the carpet, like a pointed cottage loaf, lay the brown, glistening lump of a dog's mess.

The Baby sneered openly. 'When you've been in the novelty business as long as I have, Inspector, you will learn to recognize the product. That, if I'm not very much mistaken, is an AR88 – Naughty Puppy – All Plastic, Made in Taiwan.' He bent down to pick it up. 'Oh.'

He was very much mistaken.

Sergeant Trooper broke into Mr Brickett, the Sales Manager's, disquisition on the boom in Revolving Bow-ties in the Tyneside area. 'I put it down to unemployment,' he was saying. 'People got time on their hands, that's when they need a laugh and we –'

'Sorry to butt in, sir, but it's important. Got the preliminary medical report, Inspector.' The Sergeant handed over a buff envelope.

'Oh, thank you. Mr Brickett, if you'd mind just stepping outside, and we'll continue when . . .'

'Fine, fine.' Mr Brickett, who was dressed as the Tin Man from *The Wizard of Oz*, obligingly squeaked his way out of the door.

'This is very interesting,' commented Inspector Walsh, as he scanned the report.

'Yes. Looks like he would have died of the overdose of sleeping pills without the custard pie. Mogadon, they reckon.'

The Inspector looked sternly at his underling. 'You aren't meant to read this.'

'No, well, I –' Trooper tried to get off the hook by changing the subject. 'I've checked. Mrs Alcott uses Mogadon. What's more, there are twenty-five tablets missing from her supply. She knows, because she started a new bottle last night.'

'Hmm. That's very good, Trooper, but it doesn't change the fact that you shouldn't have looked at –'

'And, on top of that, the boys were looking round Mr Alcott's workshop and, shoved under a couple of old sacks, they found – this.'

On the word, the Sergeant dramatically produced an old paint-pot lid, to which clung the powdery traces of a thick pinkish substance.

'Polyfilla, sir,' he announced with a dramatic efficiency which he then weakened by lapsing into another of his jokes. 'What they stuff dead parrots with.'

Receiving not the slightest encouragement to further humour, he hurried on. 'And exactly, according to the forensic boys, what the custard pie was made of.'

'Hmm. Prospect doesn't look too promising for Mr Alcott, does it, Trooper?'

'No, sir. Interesting thing is, though, this bit of the report suggests he needn't have gone to all that trouble.'

Inspector Walsh didn't even bother to remonstrate as he followed his Sergeant's stubby finger to the relevant paragraph.

'My investigation,' the Inspector began, 'is now nearly complete, and I have gathered you all here because I wish to piece together the murder, and some of you may be able to confirm as facts details which at the moment are mere supposition.'

He paused impressively, and looked around the crowded study. Towering over the assembly were the built-up shoulders of Charles I, whose head dangled nonchalantly from its owner's fingers. The Teapot, which had resumed its lid, sat primly behind its desk, with the Pillar-box, equally prim, at its side. A Salt Cellar and a Pepper Mill leant sleepily against each other. A Nun had her hand inside Julius Caesar's toga. A large cigar protruded from the Gorilla's bared teeth. A Rolling Pin, whose year at secretarial college hadn't prepared her for the effects of gin on an empty stomach, swayed gently. The Front Half of the Pantomime Horse had collapsed in a heap on the floor, while the Back Half had its arm lasciviously round The-Princess-Of-Wales-On-Her-Wedding-Day. Hereward the Wake snored contentedly in the corner, and Atilla the Hun ate a jelly with a plastic spoon.

There was little movement, except from the Orange, which kept slipping off the Sheep's knee, and from the Baby, who kept sniffing his hands apprehensively.

'Right, now,' the Inspector continued, 'what has happened here this evening has been a crime of vicious premeditation. There is one person in this room who has always borne a grudge against the deceased, Mr Cruikshank, and seen him as an obstacle to the advance of his own career.

'That person planned this crime with great – but, alas, insufficient – care. That person appropriated some of Mrs Alcott's sleeping pills and, probably by crushing them into his drinks, forced Mr Cruikshank to take a fatal overdose.

'Then, not content to let the old man slip quietly away to oblivion, that person made assurance doubly sure by mixing a cruel custard pie of Pollyfilla – and with that he asphyxiated his already incapable victim.'

The Inspector allowed another impressive pause. This time there was no movement. The Orange defied gravity on the Sheep's knee. The Baby ceased momentarily to worry about the smell of his hands. Even the Rolling Pin stopped swaying.

'There is only one person in this room who had the motivation and the opportunity to commit this despicable crime. And that person is . . .'

Long experience of denouements had taught him now to extend this pause almost interminably.

It had also taught him how suddenly to swing round, point his finger at the Teapot and boom in the voice of the Avenging Angel, 'Mr Alcott!'

All colour drained from the face framed by pot and lid. The pale mouth twitched, unable to form sounds. You could have heard a pin drop. The Rolling Pin, deserted by all faculties but a sense of timing, dropped.

'What? It's not true!' the Teapot finally managed to gasp.

'But it is, Mr Alcott,' Inspector Walsh continued implacably. 'All the evidence points to you. There is no question about it.'

'No!'

'Yes. And the sad irony of the whole crime, Mr Alcott, is that it was unnecessary. Our medical report reveals that Mr Cruikshank was suffering from terminal cancer. Had you only waited a couple of months, nature would have removed the obstacle to your plans.'

'What?' the Teapot hissed.

'I am afraid I am obliged to put you under arrest, Mr Alcott. And I would advise you not to make any trouble.'

'No!' the Teapot screamed. 'You will not arrest me!' And its handle

135

shot out to a desk drawer, only to reappear holding a small, black automatic.

Inspector Walsh checked his advance for a second, but then continued forward. 'You're being very foolish, Mr Alcott. Threatening a police officer is a very serious –'

'Stop or I'll shoot!'

'*Shooting* a police officer is an even more serious –'

'I'll fire!'

The room was silent. Except that she hadn't recovered from the last time, you could have heard a Pin drop again. And still the Inspector advanced on the Teapot behind the desk.

'I will fire! One – two – three. Right, you've asked for it!'

The entire room winced as the Teapot pulled the trigger.

There was a click and a flash of movement at the end of the gun.

When they opened their eyes, they all saw the little banner hanging from the barrel. BANG! it said in red letters.

The Orange began to giggle. Others would have followed her example but for the sudden movement behind the desk. The Teapot's spout had reached into the other drawer and emerged with a gleaming knife appended.

'Out of my way, Inspector!'

Walsh stood his ground. The Teapot came lunging at him, knife upraised.

Suddenly, Joan of Arc interposed her body between the Inspector and certain death. The knife plunged up to its hilt into her chest.

The room winced again, waiting for the spurt of blood and her collapse.

But neither came. Joan of Arc pulled the knife from the Teapot's nerveless spout. 'NH257,' she said contemptuously. 'Retractable-Blade-Dagger. Recognize it anywhere.'

This second failure (and the accompanying laugh) was too much for the Teapot. Clasping its handle to its lid, it collapsed backwards into the chair behind the desk. Then it slumped forward and, with cries of 'Damn! Damn! Damn!' began to beat clenched handle and spout against the desk-top.

It must have been this which animated the biscuit-barrel. With a shrieking whistle, the lid flew off and a model clown on a long spring leapt into the air.

Then, over the screams and giggles, a disembodied voice sounded. It was an old voice, a tired voice, but a voice warmed by a sense of mischief.

'Hello, everyone,' it said, and the reaction showed that everyone recognized it. 'If all's gone according to plan, Rodney Alcott should by now have been arrested for my murder. And I will have pulled off

136

the greatest practical joke of my career.

'The fact is, I'm afraid, that Rodney didn't kill me. I, Hamish Cruikshank, killed myself. I heard from my doctor last week that my body is riddled with cancer. I had at best three months to live and, rather than waste away, I decided it was better to choose my own manner of departure. About which you all, I'm sure, will now know. I have prepared the custard pie, will shortly take the overdose of Mogadon and, as I feel drowsiness creep over me, will bury my face in the soft blanket of Polyfilla. Oh, Mr Cruikshank, I hear you all saying – plastered again.

'But, by my death, I will take my revenge on Rodney Alcott for what I have always regarded as his unpardonable crime. No, not his meanness. Nor his selfishness. What I refer to is his total lack of sense of humour, his inability ever to laugh at any joke – whether mine or someone else's – and the fact that he had never in his life provided anyone with that most precious of wordly commodities – laughter.

'Well, it may have taken my death to do it, but let me tell you – Rodney Alcott's going to give you a good laugh now!'

The recorded voice stopped with a click. Whether it was that or some other invention of the old man's fertile mind that triggered the device, Hamish Cruikshank's timing, to the end, remained perfect.

The ceiling-rose above the swivel chair opened, and a deluge of bilious yellow custard descended on to the Teapot below.

And the staff and clients of Festifunn laughed and laughed and laughed. And Inspector Walsh and Sergeant Trooper couldn't help joining in.

'And you're not even going to charge him with threatening behaviour?' asked the Sergeant.

'No. He's paid his dues. Gone to bed now with one of the Pillar-box's remaining Mogadon. No, case is finished now. Just have another cup of tea, and we'll be on our way. Mrs Dancer, do you think tea's possible?'

Joan of Arc, who had lingered after the others had left, smiled a motherly acquiescence. 'Don't see why not.'

'All I want to do is put my feet up for ten minutes.'

The Inspector sank heavily into an armchair. As he did so, a loud flubbering fart broke the silence of the room.

At the door, Joan of Arc, without even turning round, said, 'KT47. Whoopee Cushion. Hours of Fun. Your Friends Will Roar.'

Miss Marple Tells a Story

AGATHA CHRISTIE

I DON'T THINK I'VE EVER told you, my dears – you, Raymond, and you, Joan, about the rather curious little business that happened some years ago now. I don't want to seem *vain* in any way – of course I know that in comparison with you young people I'm not clever at all – Raymond writes those very modern books all about rather unpleasant young men and women – and Joan paints those very remarkable pictures of square people with curious bulges on them – very clever of you, my dear, but as Raymond always says (only quite kindly, because he is the kindest of nephews) I am hopelessly Victorian. I admire Mr Alma-Tadema and Mr Frederic Leighton and I suppose to you they seem hopelessly *vieux jeu*. Now let me see, what was I saying? Oh, yes – that I didn't want to appear vain – but I couldn't help being just a teeny weeny bit pleased with myself, because, just by applying a little common sense, I believe I really did solve a problem that had baffled cleverer heads than mine. Though really I should have thought the whole thing was *obvious* from the beginning . . .

Well, I'll tell you my little story, and if you think I'm inclined to be conceited about it, you must remember that I did at least help a fellow creature who was in very grave distress.

The first I knew of this business was one evening about nine o'clock when Gwen – (you remember Gwen? My little maid with red hair) well – Gwen came in and told me that Mr Petherick and a gentleman had called to see me. Gwen had shown them into the drawing-room – quite rightly. I was sitting in the dining-room because in early spring I think it is so wasteful to have two fires going.

I directed Gwen to bring in the cherry brandy and some glasses and I hurried into the drawing-room. I don't know whether you remember Mr Petherick? He died two years ago, but he had been a friend of mine for many years as well as attending to all my legal business. A very shrewd man and a really clever solicitor. His son does my business for me now – a very nice lad and very up to date – but somehow I don't feel quite the *confidence* I had in Mr Petherick.

I explained to Mr Petherick about the fires and he said at once that he and his friend would come into the dining-room – and then he introduced his friend – a Mr Rhodes. He was a youngish man – not much over forty – and I saw at once that there was something very wrong. His manner was most *peculiar*. One might have called it *rude* if one hadn't realized that the poor fellow was suffering from *strain*.

When we were settled in the dining-room and Gwen had brought the cherry brandy, Mr Petherick explained the reason for his visit.

'Miss Marple,' he said, 'you must forgive an old friend for taking a liberty. What I have come here for is a consultation.'

I couldn't understand at all what he meant, and he went on:

'In a case of illness one likes two points of view – that of the specialist and that of the family physician. It is the fashion to regard the former as of more value, but I am not sure that I agree. The specialist has experience only in his own subject – the family doctor has, perhaps, less knowledge – but a wider experience.'

I knew just what he meant, because a young niece of mine not long before had hurried her child off to a very well-known specialist in skin disease without consulting her own doctor whom she considered an old dodderer, and the specialist had ordered some very expensive treatment, and later they found that all the child was suffering from was rather an unusual form of measles.

I just mention this – though I have a horror of *digressing* – to show that I appreciate Mr Petherick's point – but I still hadn't any idea what he was driving at.

'If Mr Rhodes is ill –' I said, and stopped – because the poor man gave a most dreadful laugh.

He said: 'I expect to die of a broken neck in a few months' time.'

And then it all came out. There had been a case of murder lately in Barnchester – a town about twenty miles away. I'm afraid I hadn't paid much attention to it at the time, because we had been having a lot of excitement in the village about our district nurse, and outside occurrences like an earthquake in India and a murder in Barnchester, although of course far more important really – had given way to our own little local excitements. I'm afraid villages are like that. Still, I *did* remember having read about a woman having been stabbed in a hotel, though I hadn't remembered her name. But now it seemed that this woman had been Mr Rhodes's wife – and as if that wasn't bad enough – he was actually under suspicion of having murdered her himself.

All this Mr Petherick explained to me very clearly, saying that, although the Coroner's jury had brought in a verdict of murder by a person or persons unknown, Mr Rhodes had reason to believe that he would probably be arrested within a day or two, and that he had come to Mr Petherick and placed himself in his hands. Mr Petherick went on to say that they had that afternoon consulted Sir Malcolm Olde,

KC, and that in the event of the case coming to trial Sir Malcolm had been briefed to defend Mr Rhodes.

Sir Malcolm was a young man, Mr Petherick said, very up to date in his methods, and he had indicated a certain line of defence. But with that line of defence Mr Petherick was not entirely satisfied.

'You see, my dear lady,' he said, 'it is tainted with what I call the specialist's point of view. Give Sir Malcolm a case and he sees only one point – the most likely line of defence. But even the best line of defence may ignore completely what is, to my mind, the vital point. It takes no account of what actually happened.'

Then he went on to say some very kind and flattering things about my acumen and judgement and my knowledge of human nature, and asked permission to tell me the story of the case in the hopes that I might be able to suggest some explanation.

I could see that Mr Rhodes was highly sceptical of my being of any use and he was annoyed at being brought here. But Mr Petherick took no notice and proceeded to give me the facts of what occurred on the night of March 8th.

Mr and Mrs Rhodes had been staying at the Crown Hotel in Barnchester. Mrs Rhodes who (so I gathered from Mr Petherick's careful language) was perhaps just a shade of a hypochondriac, had retired to bed immediately after dinner. She and her husband occupied adjoining rooms with a connecting door. Mr Rhodes, who is writing a book on prehistoric flints, settled down to work in the adjoining room. At eleven o'clock he tidied up his papers and prepared to go to bed. Before doing so, he just glanced into his wife's room to make sure that there was nothing she wanted. He discovered the electric light on and his wife lying in bed stabbed through the heart. She had been dead at least an hour – probably longer. The following were the points made. There was another door in Mrs Rhodes's room leading into the corridor. This door was locked and bolted on the inside. The only window in the room was closed and latched. According to Mr Rhodes nobody had passed through the room in which he was sitting except a chambermaid bringing hot water bottles. The weapon found in the wound was a stiletto dagger which had been lying on Mrs Rhodes's dressing-table. She was in the habit of using it as a paper knife. There were no fingerprints on it.

The situation boiled down to this – no one but Mr Rhodes and the chambermaid had entered the victim's room.

I inquired about the chambermaid.

'That was our first line of inquiry,' said Mr Petherick. 'Mary Hill is a local woman. She had been chambermaid at the Crown for ten years. There seems absolutely no reason why she should commit a sudden assault on a guest. She is, in any case, extraordinarily stupid, almost half-witted. Her story has never varied. She brought Mrs Rhodes her hot water bottle and says the lady was drowsy – just dropping off to sleep. Frankly, I cannot believe, and I am sure no jury would believe, that she committed the crime.'

Mr Petherick went on to mention a few additional details. At the head of the staircase in the Crown Hotel is a kind of miniature lounge where people sometimes sit and have coffee. A passage goes off to the right and the last door in it is the door to the room occupied by Mr Rhodes. The passage then turns sharply to the right again and the first door round the corner is the door to Mrs Rhodes's room. As it happened, both these doors could be seen by witnesses. The first door – that into Mr Rhodes's room, which I will call A, could be seen by four people, two commercial travellers and an elderly married couple who were having coffee. According to them nobody went in or out of door A except Mr Rhodes and the chambermaid. As to the other door in passage B, there was an electrician at work there and he also swears that nobody entered or left door B except the chambermaid.

It was certainly a very curious and interesting case. On the face of it, it looked as though Mr Rhodes *must* have murdered his wife. But I could see that Mr Petherick was quite convinced of his client's innocence and Mr Petherick was a very shrewd man.

At the inquest Mr Rhodes had told a hesitating and rambling story about some woman who had written threatening letters to his wife. His story, I gathered, had been unconvincing in the extreme. Appealed to by Mr Petherick, he explained himself.

'Frankly,' he said, 'I never believed it. I thought Amy had made most of it up.'

Mrs Rhodes, I gathered, was one of those romantic liars who go through life embroidering everything that happens to them. The amount of adventures that, according to her own account, happened to her in a year was simply incredible. If she slipped on a bit of banana peel it was a case of near escape from death. If a lampshade caught fire she was rescued from a burning building at the hazard of her life. Her husband got into the habit of discounting her statements. Her tale as to some woman whose child she had injured in a motor accident and who had vowed vengeance on her – well – Mr Rhodes had simply not taken any notice of it. The incident had happened before he married his wife and although she had read him letters couched in crazy language, he had suspected her of composing them herself. She had actually done such a thing once or twice before. She was a woman of hysterical tendencies who craved ceaselessly for excitement.

Now, all that seemed to me very natural – indeed, we have a young woman in the village who does much the same thing. The danger with

141

such people is that when anything at all extraordinary really does happen to them, nobody believes they are speaking the truth. It seemed to me that that was what had happened in this case. The police, I gathered, merely believed that Mr Rhodes was making up this unconvincing tale in order to avert suspicion from himself.

I asked if there had been any women staying by themselves in the hotel. It seems there were two – a Mrs Granby, an Anglo-Indian widow, and a Miss Carruthers, rather a horsy spinster who dropped her g's. Mr Petherick added that the most minute inquiries had failed to elicit anyone who had seen either of them near the scene of the crime and there was nothing to connect either of them with it in any way. I asked him to describe their personal appearance. He said that Mrs Granby had reddish hair rather untidily done, was sallow-faced and about fifty years of age. Her clothes were rather picturesque, being made mostly of native silk, etc. Miss Carruthers was about forty, wore pince-nez, had close-cropped hair like a man and wore mannish coats and skirts.

'Dear me,' I said, 'that makes it very difficult.'

Mr Petherick looked inquiringly at me, but I didn't want to say any more just then, so I asked what Sir Malcolm Olde had said.

Sir Malcolm Olde, it seemed, was going all out for suicide. Mr Petherick said the medical evidence was dead against this, and there was the absence of fingerprints, but Sir Malcolm was confident of being able to call conflicting medical testimony and to suggest some way of getting over the fingerprint difficulty. I asked Mr Rhodes what he thought and he said all doctors were fools but he himself couldn't really believe that his wife had killed herself. 'She wasn't that kind of woman,' he said simply – and I believed him. Hysterical people don't usually commit suicide.

I thought a minute and then I asked if the door from Mrs Rhodes's room led straight into the corridor. Mr Rhodes said no – there was a little hallway with bathroom and lavatory. It was the door from the bedroom to the hallway that was locked and bolted on the inside.

'In that case,' I said, 'the whole thing seems to me remarkably simple.'

And really, you know, it *did* . . . The simplest thing in the world. And yet no one seemed to have seen it that way.

Both Mr Petherick and Mr Rhodes were staring at me so that I felt quite embarrassed.

'Perhaps,' said Mr Rhodes, 'Miss Marple hasn't quite appreciated the difficulties.'

'Yes,' I said, 'I think I have. There are four possibilities. Either Mrs Rhodes was killed by her husband, or by the chambermaid, or she committed suicide, or she was killed by an outsider whom nobody saw enter or leave.'

'And that's impossible,' Mr Rhodes broke in. 'Nobody could come in or go out through my room without my seeing them, and even if anyone did manage to come in through my wife's room without the electrician seeing them, how the devil could they go out again leaving the door locked and bolted on the inside?'

Mr Petherick looked at me and said: 'Well, Miss Marple?' in an encouraging manner.

'I should like,' I said, 'to ask a question. Mr Rhodes, what did the chambermaid look like?'

He said he wasn't sure – she was tallish, he thought – he didn't remember if she was fair or dark. I turned to Mr Petherick and asked the same question.

He said she was of medium height, had fairish hair and blue eyes and rather a high colour.

Mr Rhodes said: 'You are a better observer than I am, Petherick.'

I ventured to disagree. I then asked Mr Rhodes if he could describe the maid in my house. Neither he nor Mr Petherick could do so.

'Don't you see what that means?' I said. 'You both came here full of your own affairs and the person who let you in was only a *parlourmaid*. The same applies to Mr Rhodes at the hotel. He saw only a *chambermaid*. He saw her uniform and her apron. He was engrossed by his work. But Mr Petherick has interviewed the same woman in a different capacity. He has looked at her as a *person*.

'That's what the woman who did the murder counted upon.'

As they still didn't see, I had to explain.

'I think,' I said, 'that this is how it went. The chambermaid came in by door A, passed through Mr Rhodes's room into Mrs Rhodes's room with the hot water bottle and went out through the hallway into the passage B. X – as I will call our murderess – came in by door B into the little hallway, concealed herself in – well, in a certain apartment, ahem – and waited until the chambermaid had passed out. Then she entered Mrs Rhodes's room, took the stiletto from the dressing-table – (she had doubtless explored the room earlier in the day) went up to the bed, stabbed the dozing woman, wiped the handle of the stiletto, locked and bolted the door by which she had entered, and then passed out through the room where Mr Rhodes was working.'

Mr Rhodes cried out: 'But I should have *seen* her. The electrician would have seen her go in.'

'No,' I said. 'That's where you're wrong. You wouldn't see her – *not if she were dressed as a chambermaid*.' I let it sink in, then I went on, 'You were engrossed in your work – out of the tail of your eye you saw a chambermaid come in, go into your wife's room, come back and go out. It was the same *dress* – but not the same woman. That's what the people having coffee saw – a chambermaid go in and a chambermaid come out. The electrician did the same. I dare say if a chambermaid were very pretty a gentleman might notice her face – human nature being what it is – but if she were just an ordinary middle-aged woman – well – it would be the chambermaid's *dress* you would see – not the woman herself.'

Mr Rhodes cried: 'Who was she?'

'Well,' I said, 'that is going to be a little difficult. It must be either Mrs Granby or Miss Carruthers. Mrs Granby sounds as though she might wear a wig normally – so she could wear her own hair as a chambermaid. On the other hand, Miss Carruthers with her close-cropped mannish head might easily put on a wig to play her part. I dare say you will find out easily enough which of them it is. Personally, I incline myself to think it will be Miss Carruthers.'

And really, my dears, that is the end of the story. Carruthers was a false name, but she was the woman all right. There was insanity in her family. Mrs Rhodes, who was a most reckless and dangerous driver, had run over her little girl, and it had driven the poor woman off her head. She concealed her madness very cunningly except for writing distinctly insane letters to her intended victim. She had been following her about for some time, and she laid her plans very cleverly. The false hair and maid's dress she posted in a parcel first thing the next morning. When taxed with the truth she broke down and confessed at once. The poor thing is in Broadmoor now. Completely unbalanced of course, but a very cleverly planned crime.

Mr Petherick came to me afterwards and brought me a very nice letter from Mr Rhodes – really, it made me blush. Then my old friend said to me: 'Just one thing – why did you think it was more likely to be Carruthers than Granby? You'd never seen either of them.'

'Well,' I said. 'It was the g's. You said she dropped her g's. Now, that's done by a lot of hunting people in books, but I don't know many people who do it in reality – and certainly no one under sixty. You said this woman was forty. Those dropped g's sounded to me like a woman who was playing a part and over-doing it.'

I shan't tell you what Mr Petherick said to that – but he was very complimentary – and I really couldn't help feeling just a teeny weeny bit pleased with myself.

And it's extraordinary how things turn out for the best in this world. Mr Rhodes has married again – such a nice, sensible girl – and they've got a dear little baby and – what do you think? – they asked me to be godmother. Wasn't it nice of them?

Now I do hope you don't think I've been running on too long . . .

Browdean Farm

A. M. BURRAGE

MOST PEOPLE WITH LIMITED vocabularies such as mine would describe the house loosely and comprehensively as picturesque. But it was more than beautiful in its venerable age. It had certain subtle qualities which are called Atmosphere. It invited you, as you approached it along the rough and narrow road which is ignored by those maps which are sold for the use of motorists. In the language of very old houses it said plainly: 'Come in. Come in.'

It said 'Come in' to Rudge Jefferson and me. In one of the front windows there was a notice, inscribed in an illiterate hand, to the effect that the house was to be let, and that the keys were to be obtained at the first cottage down the road. We went and got them. The woman who handed them over to us remarked that plenty of people looked over the house, but nobody ever took it. It had been empty for years.

'Damp and falling to pieces, I suppose,' said Rudge as we returned. 'There's always a snag about these old places.'

The house – 'Browdean Farm' it was called – stood some thirty yards back from the road, at the end of a strip of garden not much wider than its façade. Most of the building was plainly Tudor, but part of it was even earlier. Time was when it had been the property of prosperous yeomen, but now its acres had been added to those of another farm, and it stood shorn of all its land save the small, untended gardens in front and behind, and half an acre of apple orchard.

As in most houses of that description the kitchen was the largest room. It was long and lofty and its arched roof was supported by mighty beams which stretched across its breadth. There was a huge range with a noble oven. One could fancy, in the old days of plenty, a score of harvesters supping there after their work, and beer and cider flowing as freely as spring brooks.

To our surprise the place showed few signs of damp, considering the length of time it had been untenanted, and it needed little in the way of repairs. There was not a stick of furniture in the house, but we could tell that its last occupants had been people of refinement and

145

taste. The wallpapers upstairs, the colours of the faded paints and distempers, the presence of a bathroom – that great rarity in old farmhouses – all pointed to the probability of its having been last in the hands of an amateur of country cottages.

Jefferson told me that he knew in his bones – and for once I agreed with his bones – that Nina would love the farm. He was engaged to my sister, and they were waiting until he had saved sufficient money to give them a reasonable material start in matrimony. Like most painstaking writers of no particular reputation Jefferson had to take care of the pence and the shillings, but, like Nina's, his tastes were inexpensive, and it was an understood thing that they were to live quietly together in the country.

We inquired about the rent. It was astonishingly low. Jefferson had to live somewhere while he finished a book, and he was already paying storage for the furniture which he had bought. I could look forward to some months of idleness before returning to India. There was a trout stream in the neighbourhood which would keep me occupied and out of mischief. We laid our heads together.

Jefferson did not want a house immediately, but bargains of that sort are not everyday affairs in these hard times. Besides, with me to share expenses for the next six months, the cost of living at Browdean Farm would be very low, and it seemed a profitable speculation to take the house then and there on a seven years' lease. This is just what Jefferson did – or rather, the agreement was signed by both parties within a week.

Rudge Jefferson and I were old enough friends to understand each other thoroughly, and make allowances for each other's temperaments. We were neither of us morose but often one or both of us would not be anxious to talk. There were indefinite hours when Rudge felt either impelled or compelled to write. We found no difficulty in coming to a working agreement. We did not feel obliged to converse at meals. We could bring books to the table if we so wished. Rudge could go to his work when he chose, and I could go off fishing or otherwise amuse myself. Only when we were both inclined for companionship need we pay any attention to each other's existence.

And, from the April evening when we arrived half an hour after the men with the furniture, it worked admirably.

We lived practically in one room, the larger of the two front sitting-rooms. There we took our meals, talked and smoked and read. The smaller sitting-room Rudge commandeered for a study. He retired thither when the spirit moved him to invoke the Muses and tap at his typewriter. Our only servant was the woman who had lately had charge of the keys. She came in every day to cook our meals and do the housework, and, as for convenience we dined in the middle of the

146

day, we had the place to ourselves immediately after tea. The garden we decided to tend ourselves, but although we began digging and planting with the early enthusiasm of most amateurs we soon tired of the job and let wild nature take its course.

Our first month was ideal and idyllic. The weather was kind, and everything seemed to go in our favour. The trout gave me all the fun I could have hoped for, and Rudge was satisfied with the quality and quantity of his output. I had no difficulty in adapting myself to his little ways, and soon discovered that his best hours for working were in the mornings and the late evenings, so I left him to himself at those times. We took our last meal, a light cold supper, at about half-past nine, and very often I stayed out until that hour.

You must not think that we lived like two recluses under the same roof. Sometimes Rudge was not in the mood for work and hinted at a desire for companionship. Then we went out for long walks, or he came to watch me fish. He was himself a ham-handed angler and seldom attempted to throw a fly. Often we went to drink light ale at the village inn, a mile distant. And always after supper we smoked and talked for an hour or so before turning in.

It was then, while we were sitting quietly, that we discovered that the house, which was mute by day, owned strange voices which gave tongue after dark. They were the noises which, I suppose, one ought to expect to hear in an old house half full of timber when the world around it is hushed and sleeping. They might have been nerve-racking if one of us had been there alone, but as it was we took little notice at first. Mostly they proceeded from the kitchen, whence we heard the creaking of beams, sobbing noises, gasping noises, and queer indescribable scufflings.

While neither of us believed in ghosts we laughingly agreed that the house ought to be haunted, and by something a little more sensational than the sounds of timber contracting and the wind in the kitchen chimney. We knew ourselves to be the unwilling hosts of rats, which was in itself sufficient to account for most nocturnal noises. Rudge said that he wanted to meet the ghost of an eighteenth-century miser, who couldn't rest until he had shown where the money was hidden. There was some practical use in that sort of bogey. And although, as time went on, these night noises became louder and more persistent, we put them down to 'natural causes' and made no effort to investigate them. It occurred to us both that some more rats had discovered a good home, and although we talked of trapping them our talk came to nothing.

We had been at the farm about a month before Rudge Jefferson began to show symptoms of 'nerves'. All writers are the same. Neurotic brutes! But I said nothing to him and waited for him to

147

diagnose his own trouble and ease up a little with his work.

It was at about that time that I, walking homewards one morning just about lunch-time, with my rod over my shoulder, encountered the local policeman just outside the village inn. He wished me a good day which was at once hearty and respectful, and at the same time passed the back of his hand over a thirsty-looking moustache. The hint was obvious, and only a heart of stone could have refrained from inviting him inside. Besides, I believe in keeping in with the police.

He was one of those country constables who become fixtures in quiet, out-of-the-way districts, where they live and let live, and often go into pensioned retirement without bringing more than half a dozen cases before the petty sessions. This worthy was named Hicks, and I had already discovered that everybody liked him. He did not look for trouble. He had rabbits from the local poachers, beer from local cyclists who rode after dark without lights, and more beer from the landlord who chose to exercise his own discretion with regard to closing-time.

PC Hicks drank a pint of bitter with me and gave me his best respects. He asked me how we were getting on up at the farm. Admirably, I told him; and then he looked at me closely, as if to see if I were sincere, or, rather, to search my eyes for the passing of some afterthought.

Having found me guileless, as it seemed, he went on to tell me of his length of service – he had been eighteen years on the one beat – and of how little trouble he had been to anybody. There was something pathetic in the protestations of the middle-aged Bobby that, to all the world, he had been a man and a brother. He seemed tacitly to be asking for reciprocity, and his own vagueness drew me out of my depth.

You know those beautifully vague men, who pride themselves for being diplomatists on the principle that a nod is as good as a wink to a blind horse? The people who will hint and hint and hint, the asses who will wander round and round and round the haystack with hardly a nibble at it? He was one of them. He wanted to tell me something without actually telling me, to exact from me a promise about something he chose not to mention.

I found myself in dialectical tangles with him, and at last I laughingly gave up the task of trying to follow his labyrinthine thoughts. I ordered two more bitters and then He said:

'Well, sir, if anything 'appens up at the farm, you needn' get talkin' about it. We done our best. What's past is past, and can't be altered. There isn't no sense in settin' people against *us*.'

I knew from his inflection on the word that 'us' was the police. He did not look at me while he spoke. He was staring at something straight across the counter, and I happened by sheer chance to follow the direction of his gaze.

Opposite us, and hanging from a shelf so as to face the customers, was a little tear-off calendar. The date recorded there was the nineteenth of May.

Two evenings later – which is to say the evening of May 21st – I returned home at half-past nine full of suppressed excitement. I had a story to tell Rudge, and I was yet not sure if I should be wise in telling it. His nerves had grown worse during the past two days, but after all there are nerves and nerves, and my tale might interest without harming him.

It was only just dusk and not a tithe of the stars were burning as I walked up the garden path, inhaling the rank scents of those hardy flowers which had sprung up untended in that miniature wilderness. The sitting-room window was dark, but the subdued light of an oil lamp burned behind the curtains of Rudge's study. I found the door unbarred, walked in, and entered the study. You see, it was supper-time, and Rudge might safely be intruded upon.

Rather to my surprise the room was empty, but I surmised that Rudge had gone up to wash. That he had lately been at work was evident from the fact that a sheet of paper, half used, lay in the roller of the typewriter. I sat down in the revolving chair to see what he had written – I was allowed that privilege – and was astonished to see that he had ended in the middle of a sentence. In some respects he was a methodical person, and this was unlike him. The last word he had written was 'the', and the last letter of that word was black and prominent as if he had slammed down the key with unnecessary force.

Two minutes later, while I was still reading, a probable explanation was revealed to me. I heard the gate click and footfalls on the path. Naturally I guessed that Rudge, temperamental as he was, had suddenly tired of his work and gone out for a walk. I heard the footsteps come to within a few yards of the house, when they left the path, fell softer on the grass and weeds, and approached the window. The curtain obscured my view, but on the glass I heard the tap of fingertips and the clink of nails.

I did not pause to reflect that Rudge, if he had gone out, must know that he had left the door on the latch, or that he could have no reason to suppose that I was already in the house. One does not consider these things in so brief a time. I just called out, 'Right ho,' and went round to the front door to let him in.

Having opened the front door I leaned out and saw him – Rudge, I imagined – peering in at the study window. He was no more than a dark, bent shadow in the dusk, crowned by a soft felt hat, such as he generally wore. 'Right ho,' I said again, and, leaving the door wide open for him, I hurried into the kitchen. There was some salad left in to soak which had to be shaken and wiped before bringing it to the table. I remember that, as I walked through to the sink, one of the beams over my head creaked noisily.

I washed the salad and returned towards the dining-room. As I turned into the hall a gust of air from the still open door passed like a cool caress across my face. Then, before I had time to enter the dining-room, I heard the gate click at the end of the garden path, and footfalls on the gravel. I waited to see who it was. It was Rudge – and he was bareheaded.

He produced a book at supper, and sat scowling at it over his left arm while he ate. This was permitted by our rules, but I had something to tell him, and after a while I forced my voice upon his attention.

'Rudge,' I said, 'I've made a discovery this evening. I know how you got this place so cheap.'

He sat up with a start, stared at me, and winced.

'How?' he demanded.

'This is Stanley Stryde's old house. Don't you remember Stanley Stryde?'

He was pale already, but I saw him turn paler still.

'I remember the name vaguely,' he said. 'Wasn't he a murderer?'

'He was,' I answered, 'I didn't remember the case very well. But my memory's been refreshed today. Everybody here thought we knew, and the curious delicacy of the bucolic mind forbade mentioning it to us. It was rather a grisly business, and the odd thing is that local opinion is all in favour of Stryde's innocence, although he was hanged.'

Rudge's eyes had grown larger.

'I remember the name,' he said, 'but I forget the case. Tell me.'

'Well, Stanley Stryde was an artist who took this place. He'd got himself entangled with the daughter of a neighbouring farmer – the family has left here since – and then he found himself morally and socially compelled to marry her. At the same time he fell in love with another girl, so he lured the old one here and did her in. Don't you remember now?'

Rudge wrinkled his nose.

'Yes, vaguely,' he said. 'Didn't he bury the body and afterwards try to make out she'd committed suicide? So this is the house, is it? Funny nobody told us before.'

'They thought we knew,' I repeated, 'and nobody liked to mention it. As if it were some disgrace to *us*, you know! Oh, and, of course, the house is haunted.'

Rudge stared at me and frowned.

'I don't know about "haunted",' he said, 'but it's been a damned uncomfortable house to sit in for the past few evenings. I mean at twilight, when I've been waiting for you. My nerves have been pretty raw lately. Tonight I couldn't stand it, so I went out for a stroll.'

'Left in the middle of a sentence,' I remarked.

'Oh, so you noticed that, did you?'

'By the way,' I asked, 'what made you go out a second time?'

'I didn't.'

'But my dear chap, you did! Because the first time you came in you wore a hat, and two minutes later I saw you walking up the garden without one.'

'That's when I did come back. I haven't worn a hat at all this evening.'

'Then who –' I began.

'And that reminds me,' he continued quickly, 'when *you* come in of an evening you needn't sneak up to the window and tap on it with your fingers. It doesn't frighten me, but it's disconcerting. You can always walk into the room to let me know you've come back.'

I sat and looked at him and laughed.

'But, my dear chap, I haven't done such a thing yet.'

'You old liar!' he exclaimed with an uneasy laugh, 'you've been doing it every evening for the past week – until tonight, when I didn't give you the chance.'

'I swear I haven't, Rudge. But if you thought that, it explains why you did the same thing to me tonight.'

I saw from his face that I had made some queer mistake, and interrupted his denial to ask:

'Then who was the man I saw peering in at the window? I saw him from the door. I thought you'd tapped at the window to be let in, not knowing that the door was open. So I went round and saw – I thought it was you – and called out, "Right ho".'

We looked at each other again and laughed uneasily.

'It seems we've got our ghost after all,' Rudge said half jestingly.

'Or somebody's trying to pull our leg,' I amended.

'I don't know that I should fancy meeting the ghost of a murderer. But, joking apart, the house *has* been getting on my nerves of late. And those noises we've always heard have been getting louder and more mysterious lately.'

As if to corroborate a statement which needed no evidence so far as I was concerned we heard a scuffling sound from the kitchen followed by the loud creaking of timber. We laughed again, puzzled uneasy laughter, for the thing was still half a joke.

'There you are!' said Rudge, and got upon his legs. 'I'm going to

151

investigate this.'

He crossed the room and suddenly halted. I knew why. Then he turned about with an odd, shamed chuckle.

'No,' he said, 'there's no sense in it. I shall find nothing there. Why should I pander to my nerves?'

I had nothing to say. But I knew that in turning back he was pandering to cowardice, because just then I would have done almost anything rather than enter that kitchen. Had anybody asked me then where the murder was done I could have told them with as much certainty as if I had just been reading about it in the papers.

Rudge sat down again.

'Don't laugh at me,' he said. 'I know this is all rot, but I've got a hideous feeling that things hidden and unseen around us are moving steadily to a crisis.'

'Cheerful brute,' I said, smiling.

'I know, it's only my nerves, of course, I don't want to infect you with them. But the noises we hear, and the fellow who comes and taps at the window – they want some explaining away, don't they?'

'Especially now that we know that somebody was murdered here,' I agreed. 'I'm beginning to wish we didn't know about that.'

Rudge went early to bed that night, but I sat up reading. As often happens to me I fell asleep over my book, and when I woke I was almost in darkness, for the lamp needed filling. The last jagged, blue flame swelled and dwindled, fluttering like a moth and tapping against the glass. And as I watched it I became suddenly aware of the cause of my waking. I had heard the latch snap on the garden gate. And in that moment I began to hear them – the footfalls.

I heard the rhythmic crunch of gravel and then the swish of long grass and plantains, and then a shadow nodded on the blind. It loomed up large and suddenly became stationary. A loose pane rattled under the impact of fingers.

Perhaps there was a moon, perhaps not, but there was at least bright starlight in the world outside. The drawn blind looked like dim bluish glass, and the shadow of something outside was cut as cleanly as a silhouette clipped away with scissors. I saw only the head and shoulders of a man, who wore a dented felt hat. His head lolled over on to his left shoulder, just as I had always imagined a man's head would loll, if, well, if he had been hanged. And I knew in my blood that he was a Horror and that he wanted me for something.

I felt my hair bristle and suddenly I was streaming with sweat. I don't remember turning and running, but I have a vague recollection of cannoning off the door post and stumbling in the hall. And when I reached my bed I don't know if I fainted or fell asleep.

No, I didn't tell Rudge next day. His nerves were in a bad enough state already. Besides, in the fresh glory of a May morning it was easy to persuade myself that the episode had been an evil dream. But I did question Mrs Jaines, our charwoman, when she arrived, and I saw a look half stubborn and half guilty cross her face.

Yes, of course, she remembered the murder happening, but she didn't remember much about it. Mr Stryde was quite a nice gentleman, although rather a one for the ladies, and she had worked for him sometimes. Stryde's defence was that the poor girl had committed suicide and that he'd lost his head and buried the body when he found it. Lots of people thought that was true, but they'd hanged Mr Stryde for it all the same. And that was all I could get out of Mrs Jaines.

I smiled grimly to myself. As if the woman didn't remember every detail. As if the neighbourhood had talked of anything else for the two following years! And then I remembered the policeman's strange words and how he had been staring at the calendar while he spoke.

So the morning when I called at the inn for my usual glass of beer, I too looked at the calendar, and asked the landlord if he could tell me the date of the murder.

'Yes, sir,' he said, 'it was May the –' And then he stopped himself. 'Why, it was eight years ago, tonight!' he said.

I went out again that evening and came in at the usual hour. But that evening Rudge came down the path to meet me. He was white and sick-looking.

'He's been here again,' he said, 'half an hour ago.'

'You saw him this time?' I asked jerkily.

'Yes, I did as you did and went round to the door.' He paused and added quite soberly: 'He *is* a ghost, you know.'

'What happened?' I asked, looking uneasily around me.

'Oh! I went round to the door when I heard him tapping at the window, and there he was, as you saw him yesterday evening, trying to look through into the room. He must have heard me, for he turned and stared. His head was drooping all on one side, like a poppy on a broken stem. He came towards me, and I couldn't stand that, so I turned and ran into the house and locked the door.'

He spoke in a tone half weary, half matter of fact, and suddenly I knew that it was all true. I don't mean that I knew that just his story was true. I knew that the house was haunted and that the thing which we had both seen was part of the man who had once been Stanley Stryde.

When once one has accepted the hitherto incredible it is strange how soon one can adapt oneself to the altered point of view.

'This is the anniversary of the – the murder,' I said quietly. 'I

153

should think something – something worse will happen tonight. Shall we see it through or shall we beat it?'

And almost in a whisper Rudge said:

'Poor devil! Oughtn't one to pity? He wants to tell us something, you know.'

'Yes,' I agreed, 'or show us something.'

Together we walked into the house. We were braver in each other's company, and we did not again discuss the problem of going or staying. We stayed.

I can pass over the details of how we spent that evening. They are of no importance to the story. We were left in peace until just after eleven o'clock, when once more we heard the garden gate being opened, and footfalls which by this time we were able to recognize came up the path and through the long grass to the window. We could see nothing, for our lamp was alight, but I knew what it looked like – the thing that stood outside and now tapped softly upon the glass. And in spite of having Rudge for company, I lost my head and screamed at it.

'Get back to hell! Get back to hell, I tell you!' I heard myself shout.

And it was Rudge, Rudge the sensitive neurotic, who kept his head, for human psychology is past human understanding.

'No,' he called out in a thin quaver, 'come in. Come in if we can help you.'

And then, as if regretting his courage on the instant, he caught my hand and held it, drawing me towards him.

The front door was locked, but it was no barrier to that which responded to the invitation. We heard slow footfalls shuffling through the hall, the footfalls, it seemed to me, of a man whose head was a burden to him. I died a thousand deaths as they approached the door of our room, but they passed and died away up the passage. And then I heard a whisper from Rudge.

'He's gone through into the kitchen. I think he wants us to follow.'

I shouldn't have gone if Rudge hadn't half dragged me by the hand. And as I went the sweat from the roots of my stiffened hair ran down my cheeks.

The kitchen door was closed, and we halted outside it, both of us breathing as if we had been running hard. Then Rudge held his breath for a moment, lifted the latch, and took a quick step across the threshold. And in that same instant he froze my chilled blood with a scream such as I had heard in wartime from a wounded horse.

He had almost fainted when he fell into my arms, but he had the presence of mind to pull the door after him, so that I saw nothing. I half dragged, half carried him into the dining-room and gave him brandy. And suddenly I became aware that a great peace had settled upon the house. I can only liken it to the freshness and the sweetness of the earth after a storm has passed. Rudge felt it too, for presently he began to talk.

'What was he – doing?' I asked in a whisper.

'He? He wasn't there – not in the kitchen.'

'Not in the kitchen? Then what – who –'

'It was She. Only She. She was kicking and struggling. From the middle of the beam, you know. And there was an overturned chair at her feet.'

He shuddered convulsively.

'She was worse than he,' he said presently – 'far worse.'

And then later.

'Poor devil! So he didn't do it, you see!'

Next morning we had it out with Mrs Jaines, and we did not permit her theory to be hazy or defective. She must have known that we had seen something, and presently she burst into tears.

'He said he'd found her hanging in the kitchen, poor gentleman, and that he'd buried her because he was afraid people would say he'd done it. But the jury wouldn't believe him, and the doctors all said that it wasn't true, and that the marks on her neck were where he'd strangled her with a rope. I don't believe to this day that he did it. I don't! But nothing can't ever bring him back.' She paused at that and added, 'Not back to life, I mean – real life, like you and me, I mean.'

And that was all we heard and all we wished to hear.

Afterwards Rudge said to me:

'For his sake, the truth as we know it ought to be told to everybody. I suppose the police know?'

'Yes,' I said, 'the police know – now. But as Mrs Jaines said, it can't bring him back.'

'Who wants to bring him back?' exclaimed Rudge with a shudder. 'But perhaps if people knew – as we know – it might let him rest. I am sure that was what he wanted – just that people should know.'

He paused and drew a long breath through his lips.

'You write it,' he said jerkily, 'I can't!'

And so I have.

A Nice Touch

MANN RUBIN

THE PHONE RANG THREE times before it woke him. It took another two rings for him to move from the dark bedroom, down the hallway, into the still darker living-room, find the instrument and lift it to his ear.

'New York calling,' said the operator's voice. 'I have a person-to-person call for Mr Larry Preston of Los Angeles.'

'Speaking,' he mumbled, his voice hung over with sleep. 'Go ahead, I'll take the call.'

There was a pause and then he heard her. Her voice was hurried, breathless.

'Honey, this is Janice. I woke you, didn't I? I'm awfully sorry. Only I had to talk to you. I'm half out of my mind.'

Last remnants of sleep lifted, drifted from his head, silhouettes in the room began taking shape. He leaned backwards feeling for the couch next to the telephone table and settled into it.

'Take it easy,' he said. 'Tell me what happened.' It had been almost three days since he had last spoken to her.

'Oh, Larry, it was terrible. He came to the apartment tonight. A half-hour ago. He was drunk, dead drunk. He started hitting me.' Her voice fell away into sobs.

'How did he find out where you were living?'

'He said he called my office. They gave him the new address. Listen, he said he wasn't ever going to give me a divorce. You should have seen him; he was crying and swearing he'd never give me up without a fight. Oh, honey, what are we going to do? I'm so mixed up, so lost . . .' The crying started again, this time deeper.

'Easy,' said the man.

'I wish you were here with me. I need you so much. When are you coming home?' Her voice was tortured, pleading. In the darkness, he could visualize what her face looked like at the moment, drawn, frantic, the blonde hair in wild disorder.

'Soon,' he said. 'As soon as the picture's finished. Another month or so.'

'That's too long. Let me come out to you. I'll hitch-hike, I'll walk, I'll fly, anything. Only let's be together. I need you so bad.'

156

'You know that's impossible,' he chided. 'Right now I can't afford any sort of scandal. I've been waiting for this break all my life.'

'I know, honey. Forgive me for even asking. You're a good actor, a wonderful actor. I'd be the last one in the world to hurt your chances.'

He waited until he was sure of his control. 'Where is he now?'

'You mean Al? He passed out on the floor. I don't know what's going to happen when he comes to.'

The man reached for a pack of cigarettes he remembered leaving near the phone. His mouth tasted dry, lifeless. In the darkness, his hand brushed against an empty beer can, almost knocking it over. Finally, he made contact with the cigarettes, then matches. The woman was crying again. He lit a cigarette and waited.

'I'm sorry,' she said after a minute. 'I just can't help it. I was already asleep. Since you're gone I go to bed early every night. I watch television; that's all I do.'

He interrupted her, brought her back on the track. 'How'd he get to you? I mean is his car outside?'

'Yeah, that grey Ford of his. I can see it from where I'm standing. It's right in front of the house.'

'Anybody see him come in?' he asked, trying to keep the tone steady.

'It's almost four o'clock here. Nobody's up. And anyway, you know this street, mostly factories. You haven't forgotten all that since you're gone, have you?'

The man mumbled that he hadn't. He was quiet a long time. He could hear her waiting for him, her breath making static three thousand miles away.

'Larry?'

'I'm here.'

'What am I going to do? He hurt me. What if he means it and won't give me a divorce?'

'That is a problem.'

'Why are you so quiet?'

'I'm thinking,' he said. He was too. Quickly, efficiently, his mind criss-crossed with thoughts. He marvelled at how astute his brain became the first few minutes after sleep. Everything was so simple, so stripped to the bare essentials.

'You love me, Janice?' he asked.

'Oh, honey, darling, why do you even ask? You know there's nothing I wouldn't do for you.'

'Then listen to me.' He bent forward as if to make himself closer to her. 'I'm afraid your husband is getting to be a pest. You gave me your word there would be no trouble, that everything was agreed to. I have a reputation to think of. My whole future's at stake.'

'What are you trying to say to me?' asked the girl.

'Just that I'm tired of meeting in dark restaurants and sneaking around back alleys. I thought it would be settled by now. Instead it's as futile as ever.'

'It isn't,' she said, her voice begging, pleading.

'It is as long as he's hanging over our heads.'

She became tearful again. 'Larry, I don't know what to do. I don't like you talking like that. You scare me. Tell me what to do. I'll do anything you say.'

He waited through the inhale-exhale of the cigarette, then spoke slowly, softly. He hoped the operator was off the line; it was a chance he'd have to take.

'He has to be taken care of, Janice. While he's around, you and I'll never make it.'

'I don't understand.'

'Yes, you do,' he coaxed. 'You understand perfectly. It's either one way or the other, me or him.'

He heard her suck in her breath. She was caught. The protests would be there, the qualms, but he knew she was hooked.

'Larry, you sound so crazy.'

'Me or him,' he repeated. 'I mean it. This is showdown night.'

'But how? What are you asking? What do you want from me?' Her voice sounded choked, broken like something starting to drown.

'He's lying there unconscious, isn't he? You told me after drinking he sometimes passes out for hours. It would be simple. You said no one saw him coming in. The streets are deserted. Who would ever know?'

'But how?' He could almost touch the tension in her voice, it was that fierce, that tight.

'You know the big pillow you keep on the bed? The one I bought you the time I played Atlantic City.'

'Oh, Larry, no, I couldn't. I couldn't.' She had caught on quick.

He continued as if she hadn't spoken. 'Go get the pillow, Janice. You said he's small. You always said you could eat peanuts off his head. Cover his face, press down and hold him that way five minutes.'

'Larry, I beg you.'

'He's dead to the world. Make him deader.'

The weeping came on heavy this time, all the pain, all the uncertainty striving to reach across three thousand miles of telephone wire. He had patience. On the ceiling above him, he watched the reflected headlights of a car make shadows as it drove by outside. There was the silence of night and its small sounds. He studied the glowing tip of his cigarette.

'Larry . . .' her voice pleaded.

'I mean it, Janice. You've wished him dead a hundred times. Now's your chance. He's been a shadow on every happy moment we've had.'

'But he's a human being . . . my husband.'

'He's a curse. That's all he is; that's all he'll ever be unless you do something now.' He stopped then, letting the silence convey his impatience and anger. When he spoke again, his words were tight. 'There's nothing else I can say, Janice.'

'Larry!' she screamed. 'Larry, don't hang up on me. Please, Larry, I'd kill myself if I lost you.'

'Then do as I say.'

'Yes, yes, anything . . . Only I'm frightened. I need you here. I need your arms around me.'

'Soon . . . very soon,' he soothed.

'I'm shaking like I was a little girl. My face is all swollen where he hit me. I wish you could see.'

'Pick up the pillow, Janice. Reach out now and take it. Let's be free of him once and for all.'

'I have it. Honey, I love you. Say you love me.'

'I love you,' said the man. 'Just imagine I'm there beside you.'

'Yes, yes, together.'

'Go ahead, baby. I'll wait for you.'

'Larry . . .'

'No more words. Remember what he stands for. Get it over with. I'll be here thinking of what to do next.'

'And you'll never leave me again?'

'Never.'

'Oh, God, I'm afraid . . .' She was weakening again.

'For me, baby. For us. I love you.'

'I'll do it now,' said the woman. 'Wait for me.'

He heard her put the phone down; then silence. He lit another cigarette and blew smoke into the blackness. He held up his hand before him to see if he were shaking, but the room was too dark. He kept the receiver pressed tightly against his ear. Faintly, the sound of music drifted over the wire. She must have fallen asleep with the radio still on. She had often done that. He thought of the small white radio on the table near her bed. How innocent the music sounded, how unrelated to the action going on. Sweat trickled down the inside of his arm. He wondered what the weather was like in New York. He smoked and waited, waited and smoked. Once he thought he heard a rustling noise, another time he thought he caught the sound of sobbing.

How long he waited he couldn't be sure. After a time the phone seemed an extension of himself, as important to his survival as an arm or a leg. The music had faded into silence. It was as if all sound, all

159

stirring from that point three thousand miles away had been shut off. Only static, unrelieved, rhythmic, made contact with his ear. More sweat ran down his chest. His heart was beating wildly. Surely five minutes, perhaps even ten minutes had passed. Nothing, nothing . . . then her voice, faint, caved-in, dead.

'Larry?'

'Janice.'

'It's done, Larry. He's dead. I killed him. Just like you asked. It was like putting him to sleep. He looks so small and quiet.'

'Are you positive?'

'Very. I held my pocket mirror against his mouth like they do in the movies. There was nothing. He's dead.' The words sounded harsh and final. 'Talk to me, Larry. It's so quiet here. Please, please, say anything.'

'There's nothing to worry about.'

'He's lying there so still.'

'Janice, listen to me, you have to get started.'

'How soon you coming home?'

'Before you know it.'

'And you'll never leave me again?'

'I told you I wouldn't.'

'I'm sorry, I just need to hear you say it – that's all. What do you want me to do now?'

'Take the blanket off your bed. Cover him with it.'

'Then what?'

'Make sure the street is clear. Then bring the car around as close as you can. Drag him into it as quickly as possible.'

'I don't think I can.'

'You have to. He's small, a lightweight, you told me yourself.'

'Honey, I'm so scared.'

'I'm counting on you, Janice.'

'I love you, Larry.'

'Will you get started?'

'Yes, only tell me how it's going to be.'

'It's going to be fine.'

'And you'll be home in a month?'

'Yes.'

'And we'll get married?'

'Sure.'

'And you'll love me, won't you? You'll never leave me again?'

'No.'

'And you'll be a great actor. And every night when you come home from work I'll have dinner ready. And the house will be clean. And we'll drink wine. And kiss each other all the time. Tell me it's going to be like that.'

'Janice.'

'Tell me. Please. I need it so bad. I killed him. I killed my poor drunken husband. He was only forty-three years old.'

'Sure. It'll be just that way. Just the way you said. I'll get home as soon as I can.'

'That's what I wanted to hear. I'll be okay.'

'You'll manage with the body?'

'I'll manage.'

'After you put him in the car, drive down the East River Drive. Make sure you keep the blanket covering him. Remember that dock we used to park on, the one near 16th Street.'

'I remember. The first time you kissed me was there. Oh, darling . . .'

'That's the one. Drive to it. Make sure it's deserted, then dump the body over the side. After that take the car and leave it a few blocks from the house. Wear gloves. Walk back to the apartment.'

There was silence.

'Janice, you hear me? It's got to be done quickly.'

'I hear you,' said the woman weakly.

'That's my girl.'

'I did it for you, Larry. I'd never do this for anyone else.'

'I know that, baby. I know,' said the man petting her with his voice. 'You're part of me, I'm part of you.'

'It's the same with me. Only you better get started before it gets too light.'

'Will you call me?'

'In an hour. You should have finished it by then.'

'I wish you were here.'

'I do too,' said the man. 'But we've got to be realistic.'

'I'll be thinking of you every second.'

'Me too.'

'Do you hate me for what I did?'

'No, I love you.'

'Say it again.'

'I love you.'

'I can do anything now.' She paused. 'Call me in an hour.'

'I said I would.'

'It's getting lighter out.'

'Better hurry then.'

'Yes . . . Larry?'

'Yes?'

'Nothing . . . Oh, God, I'm scared.'

'Steady. Steady.'

161

'Good night, darling. Be with me.'

'All the way.'

He heard the click and the line went dead. Gently he put the receiver back in its cradle. The room was still dark, cool. Of all the features he liked about California, the nights were way out in front. He lit the last cigarette in the pack and crushed the empty wrapper in his clenched hand. After a minute, he picked up the phone again, dialled the operator and asked for the Los Angeles Police Department. He cleared his throat while the connection was being made. It would all have to be very convincing.

'My name is Larry Preston,' he told the police sergeant who answered. 'I'm an actor. I live on North Yucca Street just off Sunset. About ten minutes ago I received a long-distance call from New York City. It was the wife of a friend of mine. She was hysterical, incoherent, so I don't know if she was telling the truth, but she swore she had just killed her husband. She said she couldn't take his beatings any more. She was going to carry his body to their car and dump it in the East River off a dock on 16th Street. She sounded half-crazy. I think the New York Police should be alerted.'

He described the car as a grey Ford and told the sergeant the route she said she'd be taking. He was sorry he couldn't supply the licence number. The sergeant thanked him for his co-operation and promised to call back as soon as they heard any word from the New York Police and hung up.

He sat motionless another minute going over in his mind all the questionable points of his story, so that if he were called to testify the pieces would link in perfect symmetry. When he was satisfied it jelled enough to ward off the slightest hint of complicity or collusion, he took a final drag at his cigarette and crushed it out in an ash tray. Then he stood up and walked through the darkness to the bedroom. He slid into the bed and pulled the covers around him. The sheets were still warm. He lay very still, his eyes on the ceiling, hardly breathing. Sleep was gone.

Next to him the brunette stirred, changed her position. 'Who was that?' she asked.

'A friend,' he answered.

'You were gone a long time,' said the girl, her voice still creamy with sleep and promises.

'Had some business to finish.'

'Did you get it done?'

His eyes grew accustomed to the room and he saw her long dark hair on the pillow, caught the scent of her expensive French perfume. He touched her hair, winding a strand around his finger.

'I think so,' he said.

'I missed you,' said the brunette.

'Tell me more.' He dropped his hand and began to stroke her back gently. Her name was Darlene and she was under contract to M-G-M as an actress, and already the Hollywood columnists were linking them as an item.

'Hmmmm, you have a nice touch,' she said.

'Don't I, though.' He smiled and continued to trace his hand gently, caressingly along the curve of her back until she purred and reached for him again.

Light Verse
ISAAC ASIMOV

THE VERY LAST PERSON anyone would expect to be a murderer was Mrs Avis Lardner. Widow of the great astronaut-martyr, she was a philanthropist, an art collector, a hostess extraordinary, and, everyone agreed, an artistic genius. But above all, she was the gentlest and kindest human being one could imagine.

Her husband, William J. Lardner, died, as we all know, of the effects of radiation from a solar flare, after he had deliberately remained in space so that a passenger vessel might make it safely to Space Station 5.

Mrs Lardner had received a generous pension for that, and she had then invested wisely and well. By late middle age, she was very wealthy.

Her house was a showplace, a veritable museum containing a small but extremely select collection of extraordinarily beautiful jeweled objects. From a dozen different cultures, she had obtained relics of almost every conceivable artifact that could be embedded with jewels and made to serve the aristocracy of that culture. She had one of the first jeweled wristwatches manufactured in America, a jeweled dagger from Cambodia, a jeweled pair of spectacles from Italy, and so on almost endlessly.

All was open for inspection. The artifacts were not insured, and there were no ordinary security provisions. There was no need for anything conventional, for Mrs Lardner maintained a large staff of robot-servants, all of whom could be relied on to guard every item with imperturbable concentration, irreproachable honesty and irrevocable efficiency.

Everyone knew the existence of those robots and there is no record of any attempt at theft – ever.

And then, of course, there was her light-sculpture. How Mrs Lardner discovered her own genius at the art, no guest at her many lavish entertainments could guess. On each occasion, however, when her house was thrown open to guests, a new symphony of light shone throughout the rooms; three-dimensional curves and solids in melting color, some pure and some fusing in startling, crystalline effects that bathed every guest in wonder and somehow always adjusted itself so as to make Mrs Lardner's blue-white hair and soft, unlined face gently beautiful.

It was for the light-sculpture more than anything else that the guests came. It was never the same twice, and never failed to explore new experimental avenues of art. Many people who could afford light-consoles prepared light-sculptures for amusement, but no one could approach Mrs Lardner's expertise. Not even those who considered themselves professional artists.

She herself was charmingly modest about it. 'No, no,' she would protest when someone waxed lyrical. 'I wouldn't call it "poetry in light." That's far too kind. At most, I would say it was mere "light verse." ' And everyone smiled at her gentle wit.

Though she was often asked, she would never create light-sculptures for any occasion but her own parties. 'That would be commercialization,' she said.

She had no objection, however, to the preparation of elaborate holograms of her sculptures so that they might be made permanent and reproduced in museums of art all over the world. Nor was there ever a charge for any use that might be made of her light-sculptures.

'I couldn't ask a penny,' she said, spreading her arms wide. 'It's free to all. After all, I have no further use for it myself.' It was true! She never used the same light-sculpture twice.

When the holograms were taken, she was cooperation itself. Watching benignly at every step, she was always ready to order her robot-servants to help. 'Please, Courtney,' she would say, 'would you be so kind as to adjust the stepladder?'

It was her fashion. She always addressed her robots with the most formal courtesy.

Once, years before, she had been almost scolded by a government functionary from the Bureau of Robots and Mechanical Men. 'You can't do that,' he said, severely. 'It interferes with their efficiency. They are constructed to follow orders, and the more clearly you give those orders, the more efficiently they follow them. When you ask with elaborate politeness, it is difficult for them to understand an order is being given. They react more slowly.'

Mrs Lardner lifted her aristocratic head. 'I do not ask for speed and efficiency,' she said. 'I ask goodwill. My robots love me.'

The government functionary might have explained that robots cannot love, but he withered under her hurt but gentle glance.

It was notorious that Mrs Lardner never even returned a robot to the factory for adjustment. Their positronic brains are enormously complex and once in ten times or so, the adjustment is not perfect as it leaves the factory. Sometimes the error does not show up for a period

165

of time, but whenever it does, US Robots and Mechanical Men, Inc., always makes the adjustment free of charge.

Mrs Lardner shook her head. 'Once a robot is in my house,' she said, 'and has performed his duties, any minor eccentricities must be borne with. I will not have him manhandled.'

It was the worst thing possible to try to explain that a robot was but a machine. She would say, very stiffly, 'Nothing that is as intelligent as a robot can ever be nothing *but* a machine. I treat them as people.'

And that was that!

She kept even Max, although he was almost helpless. He could scarcely understand what was expected of him. Mrs Lardner denied that strenuously, however. 'Not at all,' she would say, firmly. 'He can take hats and coats and store them very well, indeed. He can hold objects for me. He can do many things.'

'But why not have him adjusted?' asked a friend, once.

'Oh, I couldn't. He's himself. He's very lovable, you know. After all, a positronic brain is so complex that no one can ever tell in just what way it's off. If he were made perfectly normal there would be no way to adjust him back to the lovability he now has. I won't give that up.'

'But if he's maladjusted,' said the friend, looking at Max nervously, 'might he not be dangerous?'

'Never,' laughed Mrs Lardner. 'I've had him for years. He's completely harmless and quite a dear.'

Actually he looked like all the other robots: smooth, metallic, vaguely human but expressionless.

To the gentle Mrs Lardner, however, they were all individual, all sweet, all lovable. It was the kind of woman she was.

How could she commit murder?

The very last person anyone would expect to be murdered would be John Semper Travis. Introverted and gentle, he was in the world but not of it. He had that peculiar mathematical turn of mind that made it possible for him to work out in his mind the complicated tapestry of the myriad positronic brain-paths in a robot's mind.

He was chief engineer of US Robots and Mechanical Men, Inc.

But he was also an enthusiastic amateur in light-sculpture. He had written a book on the subject, trying to show that the type of mathematics he used in working out positronic brain-paths might be modified into a guide to the production of aesthetic light-sculpture.

His attempt at putting theory into practice was a dismal failure, however. The sculptures he himself produced, following his mathematical principles, were stodgy, mechanical and uninteresting.

It was the only reason for unhappiness in his quiet, introverted and secure life, and yet it was reason enough for him to be very unhappy indeed. He *knew* his theories were right, yet he could not make them work. If he could but produce *one* great piece of light-sculpture . . .

Naturally, he was aware of Mrs Lardner's light-sculpture. She was universally hailed as a genius, yet Travis knew she could not understand even the simplest aspect of robotic mathematics. He had corresponded with her but she consistently refused to explain her methods, and he wondered if she had any at all. Might it not be mere intuition? But even intuition might be reduced to mathematics. Finally, he managed to receive an invitation to one of her parties. He simply had to see her.

Mr Travis arrived rather late. He had made one last attempt at a piece of sculpture and had failed dismally.

He greeted Mrs Lardner with a kind of puzzled respect and said, 'That was a peculiar robot who took my hat and coat.'

'That is Max,' said Mrs Lardner.

'He is quite maladjusted, and he's a fairly old model. How is it you did not return it to the factory?'

'Oh, no,' said Mrs Lardner. 'It would be too much trouble.'

'None at all, Mrs Lardner,' said Travis. 'You would be surprised how simple a task it was. Since I am with US Robots, I took the liberty of adjusting him myself. It took no time and you'll find he is now in perfect working order.'

A queer change came over Mrs Lardner's face. Fury found a place on it for the first time in her gentle life and it was as though the lines did not know how to form.

'You adjusted him?' she shrieked. 'But it was *he* who created my light-sculptures. It was the maladjustment, the *maladjustment*, which you will never be able to restore, that . . . that . . .'

It was really unfortunate that she had been showing her collection at the time and that the jeweled dagger from Cambodia was on the marble tabletop before her.

Travis's face was also distorted. 'You mean if I had studied his uniquely maladjusted positronic brain-paths, I might have learned . . .'

She lunged with the knife too quickly for anyone to stop her and he did not try to dodge. Some said he came to meet it . . . as though he *wanted* to die.

Composed of Cobwebs
EDDY C. BERTIN

AS HE SAT THERE, RESTING his head on his hands, two scrawled white spots on the icy steering-wheel, his thoughts seemed to be composed of cobwebs; they drifted in his face as if brought by a playful wind, but before he could touch them to discover what they really were, they dissolved into silken threads, which broke and tore as he reached out to clasp them.

He had just got back inside the car, after having rung the door bell in vain at Radstone's flat. The windows were cold and unlighted, and there was no answer to his ringing. He had seen the darkened windows as soon as he arrived, but he had tried anyway, not wanting to face the thought that Radstone wasn't home. Radstone was always home, ready for a drink and a chat, and maybe some TV if there was an interesting programme or a late-night film. Where could he have gone to? Well, it hardly mattered, he wasn't home, and that was it. The saving heaven he had driven to so gladly was empty and cold.

Spots danced before his eyes, and he closed them for a few seconds, willing the spots to disappear. As soon as he had closed his eyelids, however, the shadows were there too, shrouding the world with their abominable darkness, and he jerked his eyes open again. The shadows were so close already, he couldn't risk them getting any nearer. Even now he spotted them in the driving mirror, a dark grey lingering mist, weaving ghostly fingers at him. The street lights beyond shivered faintly through the shadows.

They had never been as close as now, which was why he had finally driven to Radstone (with whom he wasn't that friendly after all) just to be with someone, anyone. A few strong drinks on his empty stomach and an evening of small talk would have kept them away, at least for tonight. Still his fingers hesitated on the ignition key, not wanting to turn the engine on yet. Why shouldn't he wait a few minutes? Maybe Radstone had just gone out to get cigarettes, or for a short drink, and would be coming home any minute now. But that was ridiculous, Radstone never went out for a drink. Still he decided to wait a few minutes, just in case.

His head was aching again, and he tried to recall how it all had

168

started; he couldn't focus his thoughts, nothing appeared in its proper perspective in the foggy grey blur of his mind. The headaches, that had been the starting point, the headaches which had begun troubling him. He had been working too much and too late, never getting enough sleep or time for a rest. Every day i.1 a stuffy office, then in the evening hours trying to break into the writing business, sitting up hammering on an old typewriter whose keys always jammed, keeping himself awake with strong coffee, till two, three o'clock in the morning, and then again to the office. He thought of his evenings, coming home to find the rejection slips and returned stories and articles in the mail. It began to get frustrating, spending all that time and money for nothing but he had shut the anger in himself, fed on it, and had continued. Then the spots had begun to appear, coloured spots and circles and dots, dancing before him in the air. He had his eyes tested, but they were all right, there was no reason for him to see spots, except that he needed rest. The office had become more demanding, mountains of paper work which could be done by any imbecile, and he often wondered if this was why he had spent all those years at school.

He shook his head to make the thoughts go away but they stayed with him. He started the engine again, and drove away. Maybe Lucy and Brett would be home? It wasn't so very far to their place. Looking back, he saw the shadows starting to follow him, keeping the same velocity as his car, fat darkish slugs crawling over the pavement stones, along the walls of the houses on both sides of the street.

While driving, the thoughts kept on striking him with black wings. He was always tired, shivering with cold even in the warmth of a summer day. Waking up in the morning was immediately followed by the feeling of not having slept at all, or else by immense gratitude for being awake, cutting off his nightmarish walks through the haunted dimensions of his mind. He never could remember exactly the face of the terrors that assaulted him during his sleep, they were vague, undefined. Some of the dreams were clear however, so much so that somehow they seemed more real than the car he was driving right now. He remembered sitting in his working room very late, writing or correcting some first-draft manuscripts. Just beside the room was a small stairway, leading upwards to an untenanted room used to store away old junk. He remembered the footsteps coming down those stairs, immensely slow and hollow and threatening, footfalls coming from somewhere where no one lived. He remembered sitting, shivering with unknown dread, unable to move, only his eyes alive, watching the door which separated him from whatever came downwards. Then the endless moment as the footsteps halted, and something turned the handle of the door, then pushed, and the door

169

opened . . . and he awoke screaming. Then the nightmare where he was walking along an empty but fully lighted street, just thinking, and suddenly an icy hand touched the back of his head, freezing him into immobility, during minutes which seemed to stretch into eternity, before he dared turn around, and there was nothing at all behind him. He tried fighting off the nightmares with sleeping pills, but then he began to oversleep too often and got into fights with the superiors at the office, so he had to stop taking them.

That was when the dizzy spells had appeared. Suddenly his body would seem to feel as rigid as a corpse's, seem to freeze, while his mind began spinning around an uncertain centre somewhere in space. Sometimes he saw his own face and body, while his mind drifted away into an unknown and unknowable darkness. Then the fit passed, and he discovered that his body hadn't stopped moving for even a split second, his movements hadn't faltered one instant. If he had been lighting a cigarette, he was still doing so, and if he had been walking, he still was. No time-lag had passed.

His view cleared and the brakes shrieked loudly as his foot crashed down on the pedal. The screaming car came to stop only a few feet before a bright red traffic light. The idiots, imagine putting lights here where almost no traffic came by. It was like that when the accident with Marciella had happened. No, he didn't want to remember that right now, it was all past and gone, gone, goddamn you idiot, why did you have to think of it? But it was too late, his wandering mind had grasped the scene, and again it flashed through his brain with horrible clarity. He had fallen in love with Marciella two years ago, never thinking himself capable of loving anyone and having proved himself wrong. He had met her at one of those silly parties where everybody knows everybody without really knowing anybody, and made sure to meet her again. When he worked it out for himself, he was surprised to find that though he loved her he hadn't even thought yet of going to bed with her, that had seemed something so far away. Anyway, winning her love didn't turn out as easily as he had expected: she was friendly and kind enough, but she had a steady boy friend. He had tried to win Marciella without exactly knowing where and how to start, so the results were negligible. They went dancing a few times together when her boy friend had other things to do, and twice they even slept together, but she made it clear that she had no intention of leaving her boy friend. It wasn't exactly turning out as he had wanted; he didn't only want her body, he wanted her love, fully and completely.

Then one evening he had seen them leaving her flat, and suddenly he had found his hand on the ignition key of his car, ready to start the engine and crush lover boy against the nearest wall. He checked himself in time, but the hatred had been too real and too deadly, his body had been soaked with sweat, and he had been shaking uncontrollably. He stopped seeing her for some time, but then met them again by accident in a nightclub. They still lived together. They got to chatting about old times, had a drink, and another one, and then a long series of drinks. He had offered to drive them home, and his head had started spinning as soon as he sat down. The steering-wheel felt unreal in his hands. Marciella got in the back of the car, and her boy friend sat beside him in the front. He got the engine running at the second try, and with some difficulty got out of the car park. All radio programmes were off the air, and they started singing while he drove. He still heard the tune in his ears, one of those monotonous melodies which keep on returning in the back of one's mind, and he recalled some of the words too, a strange and sad song:

> *'Alone I stand in my ruins,*
> *at home to the wind,*
> *what is left of the walls,*
> *a jagged edge outlined in daylight;*
> *I wonder why my poems*
> *are all composed of cobwebs,*
> *that shine in the light*
> *of a setting sun . . .'*

A haunting song, whose words he then had noticed for the first time, and had never been able to forget. Long afterwards, he had learned that the song was titled 'In Ruins' and had been recorded. He had hunted a long time for the record, and when he had finally found a copy, he hadn't been able to play it. After the first words, he had crashed his fist down on the record, silencing the song forever, hoping that maybe it would also be silenced in his mind.

It had been raining heavily during that afternoon, and the evening was quite cold. There was a slight fog, which was getting thicker, but he never slowed the speed of his car. Feeling her so close to him, and yet further away than ever, had seemed to burn his mind, and he drove like a madman while they sang. When the car slipped, it had almost seemed funny, like sitting in a ferris wheel, going round and round, with flashes of light and darkness, before the crash came, and then silence.

He had stumbled out of the car in a daze, blood running from between his lips, where he felt broken teeth as his mouth had smashed into the steering-wheel. One side of the car had ended up against a concrete pillar, and her lover was sitting straight up, his eyes and face cut to shreds by pieces of glass. Then he slowly toppled sideways,

171

showing what was left of one side of his head. She had been unconscious when the ambulance arrived; he visited her at the hospital, but she hadn't said a word. She had only looked at him with those eyes, and he had left and never returned. Three weeks later she was released from hospital, and the next week she took two dozen sleeping pills. Someone told him when the funeral was, but he didn't go. He had tried to forget it, but it always came back, those staring grey eyes, and the fear of what they might have known about him that he didn't dare to face himself.

He brought the car to a halt at Lucy and Brett's place, and got out. His hands were wet and clammy, and he rubbed them against his jacket as he went up the stairs to their apartment. Silence met him. He knocked a few times on the door. No one answered. He swore, hesitated, then boldly knocked again. Nothing. He turned and went down. Through the door he could see the shadows, watching him; but they drifted away from him as he left the apartment and went to the car. He had been careless, the lights were still blazing. He put them out, started the car and just in time remembered to put them on again. He *had* to be with someone this evening, being alone in his rooms would drive him mad. Joey and his wife lived in the other part of the city, but he could as well drive over to them. It was late already, but they never went to bed early. Besides, they were used to him dropping in at the weirdest hours. They wouldn't mind. He drove carefully now, trying to straighten things out in his mind which seemed a white mass of moving fog and shadow fragments. His thoughts sped through his brain as a cloud of little black wings, quick and impossible to catch. Then there had been the troubles at the office. Sure, he knew he had been neglecting things a bit, but he had kept up with the new schedules, hadn't he? And he hadn't exactly been working badly, there had been no big mistakes to report, only a few small things which he had been careless about. Surely that couldn't be the real reason for the warning they had given him? The bastards! Of course he knew they had just been waiting for those small slips to get at him. The fools had always secretly envied him, and probably hated him. They had been after him from the first time he had entered the office, with their blunt jokes he thought vulgar and obscene, and their stupid practical jokes. They enjoyed making him feel small, and how he hated them for it! How often hadn't he felt the insane desire, the *need* to pick up something heavy, just anything as long as it was hard enough to smash their skulls into a bloody pulp. But he kept it all inside, all the choked-up anger, the never-released fury. That's when the fits got stronger, bringing a red patterned web before his eyes, a blood dripping maze from which there was no escape. It changed his vision into a pool of dark red fog, through which he wanted to reach out and burn them with his hatred. But he locked it up inside, there was no one else he could talk to about it, he had forgotten the habit of talking, *really talking* to people who could understand him; or maybe there were just no such people left.

He drove up the big highway, pushing his foot down on the accelerator as on an enemy's face, wanting to lose the shadows, but he knew they were following him at the same speed as his car, drifting over the highway behind him as a palpitating moving cloud.

He remembered when he had found the diary. A pretty little book, one of those expensive strongly-coloured Japanese imports, bound in silk. It had been hidden in the lowest drawer of his desk, the one where he kept the only picture he had ever had of Marciella, the only drawer which was always locked. He remembered himself straightening up the small book in his hands, wondering where it had come from. He had hesitantly opened it, fearfully seeing the first words, scrawled in an unsteady handwriting right across the page. 'Marciella, I love you,' it said, and then another handwriting over it, stating 'Rot in hell, you bitch'. The second handwriting continued through the book, beginning on the next page with 'Dear Allan. You won't mind me addressing you, I know. How you must hate me, dear beloved Allan. In fact it must be easy for you to hate me. I, who am self-confident and assured, while you are in fact just a self-pitying fool. You always talk so nicely, Allan, a friendly word for everyone, isn't it? Never angry, never a mad gesture, and yet you are burning up, devoured by . . .'

He had shut the book, standing there shivering, the words addressed to him, Allan, dancing in the air before his eyes. The diary was written to him, and the handwriting was his own, but he couldn't remember writing it. He had burned the book, and taken a week off work. It hadn't helped much, his days had been spent wandering aimlessly in town, or making long pointless drives to places he wasn't interested in seeing at all, and his nights had been horror-filled walks through the empty dark places inside his head. Sometimes the mad desire to pick up something and smash everything around him became almost too much to bear, but he kept clinging on to his precious self-control, always turning on a smiling face.

Then the shadows had come. The first time, he had been looking out of the window and had seen them. He remembered thinking that there was a slight fog coming on, then he had watched more closely and he had seen that the mist had fingers. The mist didn't go away, and two days later it had looked through the window inside. He had looked for the faces to go with the hands and claw-like fingers, but there weren't any.

Startled by the lights of another car passing him, he looked up, and,

173

cursing, he noticed that he had passed the turning to Joey's place. He had to continue for another ten minutes, before he was able to leave the highway on a crossroad. He finally stopped in front of Joey's house, and a deep feeling of warmth and happiness spread over him as he noticed the light spilling through the curtains of their windows. He put out the lights, closed the door behind him and walked up to their front door. As he stretched his finger out to push the bell, he heard the TV set blaring loudly inside, some wild pop programme. Fine, this was exactly what he needed to keep the morbid thoughts out of his mind. The lurking shadows behind him were already crawling over his car like fat slugs. A few hours with a loud TV set and overpowering music, a few drinks and afterwards some jokes and small talk, and then he would drive home again; the drinks would hide the shadows. Maybe he could even stay with Joey and his wife, they did have a spare bedroom, and he had slept there before when sometimes it was too late to drive home, or he had had a bit too much to drink. The bell rang, a sharp and angry sound which tore through his naked brain. There was a moment of stunned silence when the sound of the TV set was shut off, as if the house itself was surprised and wondering who the visitor was. Footsteps came to the door. It was opened, and the face of a young boy with blond hair looked at him with startled eyes. 'Yes, sir?' the face asked.

'I . . . I . . . aren't the Joey's at home?' Allan asked. Already something small and terribly cold began scrambling around in his stomach. 'No, sir, sorry,' replied the boy. 'They're out – at a party. Who can I say called?'

'I . . . No, they weren't expecting me . . . I just passed by and saw the lights still burning so I . . . thought . . . I decided to drop in . . . Just say a friend called . . .'

He turned around and almost ran back to his car. As he reached it, he heard the door close, shutting him off from the real world. He fumbled with his keys, dropped them, and had to get down on his knees, soiling his suit, to get them back from under the car, while misty fingers also were groping for them. Finally he was back inside, frantically trying to remember who he was.

As he sat there now, resting his head on his hands, two scrawled white spots on the icy driving-wheel, his thoughts all seemed to be composed of cobwebs; they drifted in his face as brought in by a playful wind, but before he could touch them to discover what they really were, they dissolved into silken threads, which broke and tore as he reached out to clasp them. There was a horrible feeling of *déjà vu* lurking at the edge of his mind. As the shadows approached again, he started the car and aimlessly drove into the outskirts of the city. He could have gone to a dance or a pub, but he knew it would be worse

174

then: he would carry his isolation as a glass cage around him, through which even the music wouldn't be able to reach him.

He finally parked the car and got out, not bothering to lock it behind him. He left the car standing there, both doors wide open, and all lights on, a blazing beacon in a sea of dark silence. He began walking; his shoes making strange empty noises on the pavement. There were many doors, and they were all closed and silent, abnormally silent. Surely no city where thousands of people lived could be as silent as this one? There were many bells, and he didn't ring a single one, because if no one came and answered his late call, then he would know with certainty that they were all empty, all those houses, empty and silent. Cobwebbed, with dust covering the carpets and the chairs and the cupboards, with dried-out food in the refrigerator and mould creeping along the walls. Only the street lights were real, and he began counting them as he passed underneath them, but the most he could see at once were two or three, because the shadows were moving with him, covering all the others from his sight.

Sometimes they came nearer now, stretching out their fading hands towards him, but they didn't dare touch him yet, not yet; he was still safe from them, if he could only find someone to protect him in this dead city. Memories began to spin through his mind, faces of people he knew or had known, and eyes coldly staring at him, not saying anything, just staring, grey knowing eyes. Hell, how long would he have to walk this city of the dead before the shadows reached him? They were closer, always closer, they took their strength from him, like vampires, they fed on his fears, on his loneliness. 'Find someone,' his mind shrieked, 'you can't be the last one' . . . But what if he was? What if the world was really dead, and he was the last one alive? No, that couldn't be, he . . . who was he? He still couldn't recall his name, but he had to, he needed an identity. I am Edgar Allan Poe, he thought, I am walking alone and proud, and then I'm deliriously dying in the gutter of Baltimore, and there's no Virginia Clemm waiting for me. I am Howard Phillips Lovecraft, noting down the symptoms of my sickness, and none of my friends know that I'm dying, but I know. Damn you all, what is my name, who am I? Who am I?

The shadows followed, silently, waiting, always nearer.

He began running, his feet drumming nightmarishly on the pavement. The shadows always kept the same distance, before and after him, shrouding the houses and the street.

They were all dead, he was sure now, the houses were only skulls, empty sentinels, catacombs, pyramids, enormous tombs holding nothing but crumbling and rotting corpses. The shadows had killed them all, and now they would kill him too if they got him. He didn't look where he was running, and stumbled over some digging tools, where for some reason or another workmen had been opening up the street. Weren't they afraid someone would steal their tools? But no, they were dead too, as all the rest, so who would come and steal them?

Then, as he approached the corner of the street, he stopped. Could it be? Footsteps were nearing, idly walking, closer now, closer. A blackness came from behind the corner, as he stood face to face with a surprised policeman. The policeman looked at him with a slight frown of distaste. 'Well, sir, what's the matter? Why are you in such a hurry?'

Allan started to cry, and it all came out, in an unsteady spilling fountain of words, the dead city, the shadows, Marciella, the baby-sitter, his night drive, the emptiness of the streets. He was holding the policeman's shoulder, shaking uncontrollably, and it flew out of him as from a well which had been opened. 'You're alive,' he shrieked, 'I'll go with you, you're alive, *you're alive!*'

'Now, easy, sir,' the policeman said, 'let's not make such a noise, we wouldn't want to wake people up, would we? After all, it's nearly one o'clock now. Listen, why don't you go home? You'd better leave your car right where you parked it, you can come and get it first thing in the morning. Walking will do you a lot of good, sir, if I may say so. I have to finish my round, you know.'

'But I . . . I want to go with you!' Allan screamed. 'You can't send me away. You'll have to lock me up, that's what you'll have to do. You can't leave me alone with the shadows. Please, please take me with you, please!'

The policeman looked with disgust at the wailing man. He had covered a long beat already, and his feet were aching in his new shoes. He was tired, he only wanted to check in at the station, report that there was nothing to report, and then check out. His feet needed their warm slippers, and his stomach cried out for a steaming cup of coffee. He wasn't going to do poorly paid overtime work for this idiot. If they wanted to get drunk, that was all right with him, but why did they have to make such a nuisance of themselves? He tried again. 'Listen, sir,' he said as calmly but severely as possible, 'why don't you just be a good boy, and go home? Just sleep it off. I can see you're no tramp, and I don't like to run a gentleman in just because he had a bit more than his stomach could take. Listen, there's a phone box on the next corner, I'll phone a cab for you, and you just wait here till it arrives and takes you home safely. I'll go and lock your car for you, and then I'll forget I met you and go home also. A good night's sleep, and you'll see, you'll be a new man in the morning. Good night, sir.'

The policeman turned his back, and walked away.

Allan stood there, watching him, the tears running down his cheeks, his hands aimlessly stretched out for help, and help from anybody. The shadows were hovering over him, grinning down on his helplessness. They were long and dark now, borne on cloudy dark membraneous wings which obscured the night sky, and they had eyes now, glowing eyes which were watching him all the time, sardonically, mercilessly. They would get him, he knew now, they would finally get him as they had been certain to do from the very start. All his running away, all his pleas and trials, they had all been in vain. He had been a fly in a spider's web, trying to escape, and they had let him try, mocking him, making fun of him his whole life through.

And that man walking away, he too was no more than the empty houses and the silent streets. He was just another puppet they had put in his way, for fun, for amusement. The man was an empty walking doll, manipulated on strings by the shadows, he would soon now turn the corner of the street, and then the shadows would loosen the strings, he would drop down and never move again. A puppet, an empty puppet, making fun of him! He took a few shaky steps backwards, again stumbling over the workmen's tools, and fell to his knees. His hands dropped to the earth, and his fingers touched something cold, which he picked up. It was a pick-axe, smooth ice in his hands, the only reality in this nightmare world of the dead and the shadows. He had to fight them, it was the only escape left. He stood up, taking the heavy axe with him. First a few sneaking steps, and then he broke into a run, bringing the axe up, screaming. It came down on the head of the empty walking doll in the policeman's uniform, and up and down, up and down, the hands of the clock of time, the executioner's sword, up and down, up and down. And see, the man wasn't empty at all, as he had thought, on the contrary, he was full of weak soft flesh and hot red blood. Up and down, slower and slower, as a mechanism running down.

He let the axe fall, and looked down on the empty man at his feet, then at the silent street; lights came on in some houses, there were sounds of voices, and doors opening, and the dead came out, mummified and crumbling rotting corpses as he had known they would be, and some of the older houses fell into ashes, as he began to see through the general illusion.

'You're dead,' he screamed into the darkness which began shrouding him as a heavy muffling cloak of utter silence, 'you're all dead, you're all dead, damn you!'

Then the shadows closed in on him completely, finally.

The lines from the poem, giving this story its title, are from 'In Ruins' and are reprinted here with the kind permission of the author, Glen E. Symonds, from his poetry collection, Dark Voices © *1971.*

The Boscombe Valley Mystery

SIR ARTHUR CONAN DOYLE

WE WERE SEATED AT BREAKFAST one morning, my wife and I, when the maid brought in a telegram. It was from Sherlock Holmes, and ran in this way:

'Have you a couple of days to spare? Have just been wired for from the West of England in connection with Boscombe Valley tragedy. Shall be glad if you will come with me. Air and scenery perfect. Leave Paddington by the 11.15.'

'What do you say, dear?' said my wife, looking across at me. 'Will you go?'

'I really don't know what to say. I have a fairly long list at present.'

'Oh, Anstruther would do your work for you. You have been looking a little pale lately. I think that the change would do you good, and you are always so interested in Mr Sherlock Holmes' cases.'

'I should be ungrateful if I were not, seeing what I gained through one of them,' I answered. 'But if I am to go I must pack at once, for I have only half an hour.'

My experience of camp life in Afghanistan had at least had the effect of making me a prompt and ready traveller. My wants were few and simple, so that in less than the time stated I was in a cab with my valise, rattling away to Paddington Station. Sherlock Holmes was pacing up and down the platform, his tall, gaunt figure made even gaunter and taller by his long grey travelling-cloak and close-fitting cloth cap.

'It is really very good of you to come, Watson,' said he. 'It makes a considerable difference to me, having someone with me on whom I can thoroughly rely. Local aid is always either worthless or else biased. If you will keep the two corner seats I shall get the tickets.'

We had the carriage to ourselves save for an immense litter of papers which Holmes had brought with him. Among these he rummaged and read, with intervals of note-taking and of meditation, until we were past Reading. Then he suddenly rolled them all into a gigantic ball, and tossed them up on to the rack.

'Have you heard anything of the case?' he asked.

'Not a word. I have not seen a paper for some days.'

178

'The London press has not had very full accounts. I have just been looking through all the recent papers in order to master the particulars. It seems, from what I gather, to be one of those simple cases which are so extremely difficult.'

'That sounds a little paradoxical.'

'But it is profoundly true. Singularity is almost invariably a clue. The more featureless and commonplace a crime is, the more difficult is it to bring it home. In this case, however, they have established a very serious case against the son of the murdered man.'

'It is murder, then?'

'Well, it is conjectured to be so. I shall take nothing for granted until I have the opportunity of looking personally into it. I will explain the state of things to you, as far as I have been able to understand it, in a very few words.

'Boscombe Valley is a country district not very far from Ross, in Herefordshire. The largest landed proprietor in that part is a Mr John Turner, who made his money in Australia, and returned some years ago to the old country. One of the farms which he held, that of Hatherley, was let to Mr Charles McCarthy, who was also an ex-Australian. The men had known each other in the Colonies, so that it was not unnatural that when they came to settle down they should do so as near each other as possible. Turner was apparently the richer man, so McCarthy became his tenant, but still remained, it seems, upon terms of perfect equality, as they were frequently together. McCarthy had one son, a lad of eighteen, and Turner had an only daughter of the same age, but neither of them had wives living. They appear to have avoided the society of the neighbouring English families, and to have led retired lives, though both the McCarthys were fond of sport, and were frequently seen at the race meetings of the neighbourhood. McCarthy kept two servants – a man and a girl. Turner had a considerable household, some half-dozen at the least. That is as much as I have been able to gather about the families. Now for the facts.

'On June 3 – that is, on Monday last – McCarthy left his house at Hatherley about three in the afternoon, and walked down to the Boscombe Pool, which is a small lake formed by the spreading out of the stream which runs down the Boscombe Valley. He had been out with his serving-man in the morning at Ross, and he had told the man that he must hurry, as he had an appointment of importance to keep at three. From that appointment he never came back alive.

'From Hatherley Farm-house to the Boscombe Pool is a quarter of a mile, and two people saw him as he passed over this ground. One was an old woman, whose name is not mentioned, and the other was William Crowder, a gamekeeper in the employ of Mr Turner. Both these witnesses depose that Mr McCarthy was walking alone. The gamekeeper adds that within a few minutes of his seeing Mr McCarthy pass he had seen his son, Mr James McCarthy, going the same way with a gun under his arm. To the best of his belief, the father was actually in sight at the time, and the son was following him. He thought no more of the matter until he heard in the evening of the tragedy that had occurred.

'The two McCarthys were seen after the time when William Crowder, the gamekeeper, lost sight of them. The Boscombe Pool is thickly wooded round, with just a fringe of grass and of reeds round the edge. A girl of fourteen, Patience Moran, who is the daughter of the lodge-keeper of the Boscombe Valley Estate, was in one of the woods picking flowers. She states that while she was there she saw, at the border of the wood and close by the lake, Mr McCarthy and his son, and that they appeared to be having a violent quarrel. She heard Mr McCarthy the elder using very strong language to his son, and she saw the latter raise up his hand as if to strike his father. She was so frightened by their violence that she ran away, and told her mother when she reached home that she had left the two McCarthys quarrelling near Boscombe Pool, and that she was afraid that they were going to fight. She had hardly said the words when young Mr McCarthy came running up to the lodge to say that he had found his father dead in the wood, and to ask for the help of the lodge-keeper. He was much excited, without either his gun or his hat, and his right hand and sleeve were observed to be stained with fresh blood. On following him they found the dead body of his father stretched out upon the grass beside the Pool. The head had been beaten in by repeated blows of some heavy and blunt weapon. The injuries were such as might very well have been inflicted by the butt-end of his son's gun, which was found lying on the grass within a few paces of the body. Under these circumstances the young man was instantly arrested, and a verdict of "Wilful Murder" having been returned at the inquest on Tuesday, he was on Wednesday brought before the magistrates at Ross, who have referred the case to the next assizes. Those are the main facts of the case as they came out before the coroner and at the police-court.'

'I could hardly imagine a more damning case,' I remarked. 'If ever circumstantial evidence pointed to a criminal it does so here.'

'Circumstantial evidence is a very tricky thing,' answered Holmes thoughtfully; 'it may seem to point very straight to one thing, but if you shift your own point of view a little, you may find it pointing in an equally uncompromising manner to something entirely different. It must be confessed, however, that the case looks exceedingly grave against the young man, and it is very possible that he is indeed the culprit. There are several people in the neighbourhood, however, and

180

among them Miss Turner, the daughter of the neighbouring landowner, who believe in his innocence, and who have retained Lestrade, whom you may remember in connection with the Study in Scarlet, to work out the case in his interest. Lestrade, being rather puzzled, has referred the case to me, and hence it is that two middle-aged gentlemen are flying westward at fifty miles an hour, instead of quietly digesting their breakfasts at home.'

'I am afraid,' said I, 'that the facts are so obvious that you will find little credit to be gained out of this case.'

'There is nothing more deceptive than an obvious fact,' he answered, laughing. 'Besides, we may chance to hit upon some other obvious facts which may have been by no means obvious to Mr Lestrade. You know me too well to think that I am boasting when I say that I shall either confirm or destroy his theory by means which he is quite incapable of employing, or even of understanding. To take the first example to hand, I very clearly perceive that in your bedroom the window is upon the right-hand side, and yet I question whether Mr Lestrade would have noted even so self-evident a thing as that.'

'How on earth———!'

'My dear fellow, I know you well. I know the military neatness which characterizes you. You shave every morning, and in this season you shave by the sunlight, but since your shaving is less and less complete as we get farther back on the left side, until it becomes positively slovenly as we get round the angle of the jaw, it is surely very clear that that side is less well illuminated than the other. I could not imagine a man of your habits looking at himself in an equal light, and being satisfied with such a result. I only quote this as a trivial example of observation and inference. Therein lies my *métier*, and it is just possible that it may be of some service in the investigation which lies before us. There are one or two minor points which were brought out in the inquest, and which are worth considering.'

'What are they?'

'It appears that his arrest did not take place at once, but after the return to Hatherley Farm. On the inspector of constabulary informing him that he was a prisoner, he remarked that he was not surprised to hear it, and that it was no more than his deserts. This observation of his had the natural effect of removing any traces of doubt which might have remained in the minds of the coroner's jury.'

'It was a confession,' I ejaculated.

'No, for it was followed by a protestation of innocence.'

'Coming on the top of such a damning series of events, it was at least a most suspicious remark.'

'On the contrary,' said Holmes, 'it is the brightest rift which I can at present see in the clouds. However innocent he might be, he could

181

not be such an absolute imbecile as not to see that the circumstances were very black against him. Had he appeared surprised at his own arrest, or feigned indignation at it, I should have looked upon it as highly suspicious, because such surprise or anger would not be natural under the circumstances, and yet might appear to be the best policy to a scheming man. His frank acceptance of the situation marks him as either an innocent man, or else a man of considerable self-restraint and firmness. As to his remark about his deserts, it was also not unnatural if you consider that he stood by the dead body of his father, and that there is no doubt that he had that very day so far forgotten his filial duty as to bandy words with him, and even, according to the little girl whose evidence is so important, to raise his hand as if to strike him. The self-reproach and contrition which are displayed in his remark appear to me to be the signs of a healthy mind, rather than of a guilty one.'

I shook my head. 'Many men have been hanged on far slighter evidence,' I remarked.

'So they have. And many men have been wrongfully hanged.'

'What is the young man's own account of the matter?'

'It is, I am afraid, not very encouraging to his supporters, though there are one or two points in it which are suggestive. You will find it here, and may read it for yourself.'

He picked out from his bundle a copy of the local Herefordshire paper, and having turned down the sheet, he pointed out the paragraph in which the unfortunate young man had given his own statement of what had occurred. I settled myself down in the corner of the carriage, and read it very carefully. It ran in this way:

'Mr James McCarthy, the only son of the deceased, was then called, and gave evidence as follows: "I had been away from home for three days at Bristol, and had only just returned upon the morning of last Monday, the 3rd. My father was absent from home at the time of my arrival, and I was informed by the maid that he had driven over to Ross with John Cobb, the groom. Shortly after my return I heard the wheels of his trap in the yard, and, looking out of my window, I saw him get out and walk rapidly out of the yard, though I was not aware in which direction he was going. I then took my gun, and strolled out in the direction of the Boscombe Pool, with the intention of visiting the rabbit warren which is upon the other side. On my way I saw William Crowder, the gamekeeper, as he has stated in his evidence; but he is mistaken in thinking that I was following my father. I had no idea that he was in front of me. When about a hundred yards from the Pool I heard a cry of 'Cooee!' which was a usual signal between my father and myself. I then hurried forward, and found him standing by the Pool. He appeared to be much surprised at seeing me, and asked me rather roughly what I was doing there. A conversation ensued, which led to high words, and almost to blows, for my father was a man of a very violent temper. Seeing that his passion was becoming ungovernable, I left him, and returned towards Hatherley Farm. I had not gone more than one hundred and fifty yards, however, when I heard a hideous outcry behind me, which caused me to run back again. I found my father expiring on the ground, with his head terribly injured. I dropped my gun, and held him in my arms, but he almost instantly expired. I knelt beside him for some minutes, and then made my way to Mr Turner's lodge-keeper, his house being the nearest, to ask for assistance. I saw no one near my father when I returned, and I have no idea how he came by his injuries. He was not a popular man, being somewhat cold and forbidding in his manners; but he had, as far as I know, no active enemies. I know nothing further of the matter."

'The Coroner: Did your father make any statement to you before he died?

'Witness: He mumbled a few words, but I could only catch some allusion to a rat.

'The Coroner: What did you understand by that?

'Witness: It conveyed no meaning to me. I thought that he was delirious.

'The Coroner: What was the point upon which you and your father had this final quarrel?

'Witness: I should prefer not to answer.

'The Coroner: I am afraid that I must press it.

'Witness: It is really impossible for me to tell you. I can assure you that it has nothing to do with the sad tragedy which followed.

'The Coroner: That is for the Court to decide. I need not point out to you that your refusal to answer will prejudice your case considerably in any future proceedings which may arise.

'Witness: I must still refuse.

'The Coroner: I understand that the cry of "Cooee" was a common signal between you and your father?

'Witness: It was.

'The Coroner: How was it, then, that he uttered it before he saw you, and before he even knew that you had returned from Bristol?

'Witness (with considerable confusion): I do not know.

'A Juryman: Did you see nothing which aroused your suspicions when you returned on hearing the cry, and found your father fatally injured?

'Witness: Nothing definite.

'The Coroner: What do you mean?

'Witness: I was so disturbed and excited as I rushed out into the open, that I could think of nothing except my father. Yet I have a vague impression that as I ran forward something lay upon the ground to the left of me. It seemed to me to be something grey in colour, a coat of some sort, or a plaid perhaps. When I rose from my father I looked round for it, but it was gone.

' "Do you mean that it disappeared before you went for help?"

' "Yes, it was gone."

' "You cannot say what it was?"

' "No, I had a feeling something was there."

' "How far from the body?"

' "A dozen yards or so."

' "And how far from the edge of the wood?"

' "About the same."

' "Then if it was removed it was while you were within a dozen yards of it?"

' "Yes, but with my back towards it."

'This concluded the examination of the witness.'

'I see,' said I, as I glanced down the column, 'that the coroner in his concluding remarks was rather severe upon young McCarthy. He calls attention, and with reason, to the discrepancy about his father having signalled to him before seeing him, also to his refusal to give details of his conversation with his father, and his singular account of his father's dying words. They are all, as he remarks, very much against the son.'

Holmes laughed softly to himself, and stretched himself out upon the cushioned seat. 'Both you and the coroner have been at some pains,' said he, 'to single out the very strongest points in the young man's favour. Don't you see that you alternately give him credit for having too much imagination and too little? Too little, if he could not invent a cause of quarrel which would give him the sympathy of the jury; too much, if he evolved from his own inner consciousness anything so *outré* as a dying reference to a rat, and the incident of the vanishing cloth. No, sir, I shall approach this case from the point of view that what this young man says is true, and we shall see whither that hypothesis will lead us. And now here is my pocket Petrarch, and not another word shall I say of this case until we are on the scene of action. We lunch at Swindon, and I see that we shall be there in twenty minutes.'

It was nearly four o'clock when we at last, after passing through the beautiful Stroud Valley and over the broad gleaming Severn, found ourselves at the pretty little country town of Ross. A lean, ferret-like man, furtive and sly-looking, was waiting for us upon the platform. In spite of the light brown dust-coat and leather leggings which he wore in deference to his rustic surroundings, I had no difficulty in recognizing Lestrade, of Scotland Yard. With him we drove to the 'Hereford Arms,' where a room had already been engaged for us.

'I have ordered a carriage,' said Lestrade, as we sat over a cup of tea. 'I knew your energetic nature, and that you would not be happy until you had been on the scene of the crime.'

'It was very nice and complimentary of you,' Holmes answered. 'It is entirely a question of barometric pressure.'

Lestrade looked startled. 'I do not quite follow,' he said.

'How is the glass? Twenty-nine, I see. No wind, and not a cloud in the sky. I have a caseful of cigarettes here which need smoking, and the sofa is very much superior to the usual country hotel abomination. I do not think that it is probable that I shall use the carriage tonight.'

Lestrade laughed indulgently. 'You have, no doubt, already formed your conclusions from the newspapers,' he said. 'The case is as plain as a pikestaff, and the more one goes into it the plainer it becomes. Still, of course, one can't refuse a lady, and such a very positive one, too. She had heard of you, and would have your opinion, though I repeatedly told her that there was nothing which you could do which I had not already done. Why, bless my soul! here is her carriage at the door.'

He had hardly spoken before there rushed into the room one of the most lovely young women that I have ever seen in my life. Her violet eyes shining, her lips parted, a pink flush upon her cheeks, all thought of her natural reserve lost in her overpowering excitement and concern.

'Oh, Mr Sherlock Holmes!' she cried, glancing from one to the other of us, and finally, with a woman's quick intuition, fastening upon my companion, 'I am so glad that you have come. I have driven down to tell you so. I know that James didn't do it. I know it, and I want you to start upon your work knowing it, too. Never let yourself doubt upon that point. We have known each other since we were little children, and I know his faults as no one else does; but he is too tender-hearted to hurt a fly. Such a charge is absurd to anyone who really knows him.'

'I hope we may clear him, Miss Turner,' said Sherlock Holmes. 'You may rely upon my doing all that I can.'

'But you have read the evidence. You have formed some conclusion? Do you not see some loophole, some flaw? Do you not yourself think that he is innocent?'

'I think that it is very probable.'

'There now!' she cried, throwing back her head and looking defiantly at Lestrade. 'You hear! He gives me hope.'

185

Lestrade shrugged her shoulders. 'I am afraid that my colleague has been a little quick in forming his conclusions,' he said.

'But he is right. Oh! I know that he is right. James never did it. And about his quarrel with his father, I am sure that the reason why he would not speak about it to the coroner was because I was concerned in it.'

'In what way?' asked Holmes.

'It is no time for me to hide anything. James and his father had many disagreements about me. Mr McCarthy was very anxious that there should be a marriage between us. James and I have always loved each other as brother and sister, but of course he is young and has seen very little of life yet, and – and – well, he naturally did not wish to do anything like that yet. So there were quarrels, and this, I am sure, was one of them.'

'And your father?' asked Holmes. 'Was he in favour of such a union?'

'No, he was averse to it also. No one but Mr McCarthy was in favour of it.' A quick blush passed over her fresh young face as Holmes shot one of his keen, questioning glances at her.

'Thank you for this information,' said he. 'May I see your father if I call tomorrow?'

'I am afraid the doctor won't allow it.'

'The doctor?'

'Yes, have you not heard? Poor father has never been strong for years back, but this has broken him down completely. He has taken to his bed, and Dr Willows says that he is a wreck, and that his nervous system is shattered. Mr McCarthy was the only man alive who had known dad in the old days in Victoria.'

'Ha! In Victoria! That is important.'

'Yes, at the mines.'

'Quite so; at the gold mines, where, as I understand, Mr Turner made his money.'

'Yes, certainly.'

'Thank you, Miss Turner. You have been of material assistance to me.'

'You will tell me if you have any news tomorrow. No doubt you will go to the prison to see James. Oh, if you do, Mr Holmes, do tell him that I know him to be innocent.'

'I will, Miss Turner.'

'I must go home now, for dad is very ill, and he misses me so if I leave him. Good-bye, and God help you in your undertaking.' She hurried from the room as impulsively as she had entered, and we heard the wheels of her carriage rattle off down the street.

'I am ashamed of you, Holmes,' said Lestrade with dignity, after a few minutes' silence. 'Why should you raise up hopes which you are bound to disappoint? I am not over-tender of heart, but I call it cruel.'

'I think that I see my way to clearing James McCarthy,' said Holmes. 'Have you an order to see him in prison?'

'Yes, but only for you and me.'

'Then I shall reconsider my resolution about going out. We have still time to take a train to Hereford and see him tonight?'

'Ample.'

'Then let us do so. Watson, I fear that you will find it very slow, but I shall only be away a couple of hours.'

I walked down to the station with them, and then wandered through the streets of the little town, finally returning to the hotel, where I lay upon the sofa and tried to interest myself in a yellow-backed novel. The puny plot of the story was so thin, however, when compared to the deep mystery through which we were groping, and I found my attention wander so constantly from the fiction to the fact, that I at last flung it across the room, and gave myself up entirely to a consideration of the events of the day. Supposing that this unhappy young man's story was absolutely true, then what hellish thing, what absolutely unforeseen and extraordinary calamity, could have occurred between the time when he parted from his father and the moment when, drawn back by his screams, he rushed into the glade? It was something terrible and deadly. What could it be? Might not the nature of the injuries reveal something to my medical instincts? I rang the bell, and called for the weekly county paper, which contained a verbatim account of the inquest. In the surgeon's deposition it was stated that the posterior third of the left parietal bone and the left half of the occipital bone had been shattered by a heavy blow from a blunt weapon. I marked the spot upon my own head. Clearly such a blow must have been struck from behind. That was to some extent in favour of the accused, as when seen quarrelling he was face to face with his father. Still, it did not go for very much, for the older man might have turned his back before the blow fell. Still, it might be worth while to call Holmes' attention to it. Then there was the peculiar dying reference to a rat. What could that mean? It could not be delirium. A man dying from a sudden blow does not commonly become delirious. No, it was more likely to be an attempt to explain how he met his fate. But what could it indicate? I cudgelled my brains to find some possible explanation. And then the incident of the grey cloth, seen by young McCarthy. If that were true, the murderer must have dropped some part of his dress, presumably his overcoat, in his flight, and must have had the hardihood to return and carry it away at the instant when the son was kneeling with his back turned not a dozen paces off. What a tissue of mysteries and improbabilities the whole thing was! I did not wonder at Lestrade's opinion, and yet I had so much faith in Sherlock Holmes' insight that I could not lose hope as long as every fresh fact seemed to strengthen his conviction of young McCarthy's innocence.

It was late before Sherlock Holmes returned. He came back alone, for Lestrade was staying in lodgings in the town.

'The glass still keeps very high,' he remarked, as he sat down. 'It is of importance that it should not rain before we are able to go over the ground. On the other hand, a man should be at his very best and keenest for such nice work as that, and I did not wish to do it when fagged by a long journey. I have seen young McCarthy.'

'And what did you learn from him?'

'Nothing.'

'Could he throw no light?'

'None at all. I was inclined to think at one time that he knew who had done it, and was screening him or her, but I am convinced now that he is as puzzled as everyone else. He is not a very quick-witted youth, though comely to look at, and, I should think, sound at heart.'

'I cannot admire his taste,' I remarked, 'if it is indeed a fact that he was averse to a marriage with so charming a young lady as this Miss Turner.'

'Ah, thereby hangs a rather painful tale. This fellow is madly, insanely in love with her, but some two years ago, when he was only a lad, and before he really knew her, for she had been away five years at a boarding-school, what does the idiot do but get into the clutches of a barmaid in Bristol, and marry her at a registry office! No one knows a word of the matter, but you can imagine how maddening it must be to him to be upbraided for not doing what he would give his very eyes to do, but what he knows to be absolutely impossible. It was sheer frenzy of this sort which made him throw his hands up into the air when his father, at their last interview, was goading him on to propose to Miss Turner. On the other hand, he had no means of supporting himself, and his father, who was by all accounts a very hard man, would have thrown him over utterly had he known the truth. It was with his barmaid wife that he had spent the last three days in Bristol, and his father did not know where he was. Mark that point. It is of importance. Good has come out of evil, however, for the barmaid, finding from the papers that he is in serious trouble, and likely to be hanged, has thrown him over utterly, and has written to him to say that she has a husband already in the Bermuda Dockyard, so that there is really no tie between them. I think that that bit of news has consoled young McCarthy for all that he has suffered.'

'But if he is innocent, who has done it?'

'Ah! who? I would call your attention very particularly to two points. One is that the murdered man had an appointment with someone at the Pool, and that the someone could not have been his son, for his son was away, and he did not know when he would return. The second is that the murdered man was heard to cry "Cooee!" before he knew that his son had returned. Those are the crucial points upon which the case depends. And now let us talk about George Meredith, if you please, and we shall leave minor points until tomorrow.'

There was no rain, as Holmes had foretold, and the morning broke bright and cloudless. At nine o'clock Lestrade called for us with the carriage, and we set off for Hatherley Farm and the Boscombe Pool.

'There is serious news this morning,' Lestrade observed. 'It is said that Mr Turner, of the Hall, is so ill that his life is despaired of.'

'An elderly man, I presume?' said Holmes.

'About sixty; but his constitution has been shattered by his life abroad, and he has been in failing health for some time. This business has had a very bad effect upon him. He was an old friend of McCarthy's, and, I may add, a great benefactor to him, for I have learned that he gave him Hatherley Farm rent free.'

'Indeed! That is interesting,' said Holmes.

'Oh, yes! In a hundred other ways he has helped him. Everybody about here speaks of his kindness to him.'

'Really! Does it not strike you as a little singular that this McCarthy, who appears to have had little of his own, and to have been under such obligations to Turner, should still talk of marrying his son to Turner's daughter, who is, presumably, heiress to the estate, and that in such a very cocksure manner, as if it was merely a case of a proposal and all else would follow? It is the more strange since we know that Turner himself was averse to the idea. The daughter told us as much. Do you not deduce something from that?'

'We have got to the deductions and the inferences,' said Lestrade, winking at me. 'I find it hard enough to tackle facts, Holmes, without flying away after theories and fancies.'

'You are right,' said Holmes demurely; 'you do find it very hard to tackle the facts.'

'Anyhow, I have grasped one fact which you seem to find it difficult to get hold of,' replied Lestrade with some warmth.

'And that is?'

'That McCarthy, senior, met his death from McCarthy, junior, and that all theories to the contrary are the merest moonshine.'

'Well, moonshine is a brighter thing than fog,' said Holmes, laughing. 'But I am very much mistaken if this is not Hatherley Farm upon the left.'

'Yes, that is it.' It was a widespread, comfortable-looking building,

189

two-storied, slate-roofed, with great yellow blotches of lichen upon the grey walls. The drawn blinds and the smokeless chimneys, however, gave it a stricken look, as though the weight of this horror still lay heavy upon it. We called at the door, when the maid, at Holmes' request, showed us the boots which her master wore at the time of his death, and also a pair of the son's, though not the pair which he had then had. Having measured these very carefully from seven or eight different points, Holmes desired to be led to the courtyard, from which we all followed the winding track which led to Boscombe Pool.

Sherlock Holmes was transformed when he was hot upon such a scent as this. Men who had only known the quiet thinker and logician of Baker Street would have failed to recognize him. His face flushed and darkened. His brows were drawn into two hard, black lines, while his eyes shone out from beneath them with a steely glitter. His face was bent downwards, his shoulders bowed, his lips compressed, and the veins stood out like whip-cord in his long, sinewy neck. His nostrils seemed to dilate with a purely animal lust for the chase, and his mind was so absolutely concentrated upon the matter before him, that a question or remark fell unheeded upon his ears, or at the most only provoked a quick, impatient snarl in reply. Swiftly and silently he made his way along the track which ran through the meadows, and so by way of the woods to the Boscombe Pool. It was damp, marshy ground, as is all that district, and there were marks of many feet, both upon the path and amid the short grass which bounded it on either side. Sometimes Holmes would hurry on, sometimes stop dead, and once he made quite a little *détour* into the meadow. Lestrade and I walked behind him, the detective indifferent and contemptuous, while I watched my friend with the interest which sprang from the conviction that every one of his actions was directed towards a definite end.

The Boscombe Pool, which is a little reed-girt sheet of water some fifty yards across, is situated at the boundary between the Hatherley Farm and the private park of the wealthy Mr Turner. Above the woods which lined it upon the farther side we could see the red jutting pinnacles which marked the site of the rich landowner's dwelling. On the Hatherley side of the Pool the woods grew very thick, and there was a narrow belt of sodden grass twenty paces across between the edge of the trees and the reeds which lined the lake. Lestrade showed us the exact spot at which the body had been found, and indeed, so moist was the ground, that I could plainly see the traces which had been left by the fall of the stricken man. To Holmes, as I could see by his eager face and peering eyes, very many other things were to be read upon the trampled grass. He ran round, like a dog who is picking up a scent, and then turned upon my companion.

190

'What did you go into the Pool for?' he asked.

'I fished about with a rake. I thought there might be some weapon or other trace. But how on earth——?'

'Oh, tut, tut! I have no time. That left foot of yours with its inward twist is all over the place. A mole could trace it, and there it vanishes among the reeds. Oh, how simple it would all have been had I been here before they came like a herd of buffalo, and wallowed all over it. Here is where the party with the lodge-keeper came, and they have covered all tracks for six or eight feet round the body. But here are three separate tracks of the same feet.' He drew out a lens, and lay down upon his waterproof to have a better view, talking all the time rather to himself than to us. 'These are young McCarthy's feet. Twice he was walking, and once he ran swiftly so that the soles are deeply marked, and the heels hardly visible. That bears out his story. He ran when he saw his father on the ground. Then here are the father's feet as he paced up and down. What is this, then? It is the butt end of the gun as the son stood listening. And this? Ha, ha! What have we here? Tip-toes, tip-toes! Square, too, quite unusual boots! They come, they go, they come again – of course that was for the cloak. Now where did they come from?' He ran up and down, sometimes losing, sometimes finding the track, until we were well within the edge of the wood and under the shadow of a great beech, the largest tree in the neighbourhood. Holmes traced his way to the farther side of this, and lay down once more upon his face with a little cry of satisfaction. For a long time he remained there, turning over the leaves and dried sticks, gathering up what seemed to me to be dust into an envelope, and examining with his lens not only the ground, but even the bark of the tree as far as he could reach. A jagged stone was lying among the moss, and this also he carefully examined and retained. Then he followed a pathway through the wood until he came to the high-road, where all traces were lost.

'It has been a case of considerable interest,' he remarked, returning to his natural manner. 'I fancy that this grey house on the right must be the lodge. I think that I will go in and have a word with Moran, and perhaps write a little note. Having done that, we may drive back to our luncheon. You may walk to the cab, and I shall be with you presently.'

It was about ten minutes before we regained our cab, and drove back into Ross, Holmes still carrying with him the stone which he had picked up in the wood.

'This may interest you, Lestrade,' he remarked, holding it out. 'The murder was done with it.'

'I see no marks.'

'There are none.'

191

'How do you know, then?'

'The grass was growing under it. It had only lain there a few days. There was no sign of a place whence it had been taken. It corresponds with the injuries. There is no sign of any other weapon.'

'And the murderer?'

'Is a tall man, left-handed, limps with the right leg, wears thick-soled shooting-boots and a grey cloak, smokes Indian cigars, uses a cigar-holder, and carries a blunt penknife in his pocket. There are several other indications, but these may be enough to aid us in our search.'

Lestrade laughed. 'I am afraid that I am still a sceptic,' he said. 'Theories are all very well, but we have to deal with a hard-headed British jury.'

'*Nous verrons*,' answered Holmes calmly. 'You work your own method, and I shall work mine. I shall be busy this afternoon, and shall probably return to London by the evening train.'

'And leave your case unfinished?'

'No, finished.'

'But the mystery?'

'It is solved.'

'Who was the criminal, then?'

'The gentleman I describe.'

'But who is he?'

'Surely it would not be difficult to find out. This is not such a populous neighbourhood.'

Lestrade shrugged his shoulders. 'I am a practical man,' he said, 'And I really cannot undertake to go about the country looking for a left-handed gentleman with a game leg. I should become the laughing-stock of Scotland Yard.'

'All right,' said Holmes quietly. 'I have given you the chance. Here are your lodgings. Good-bye. I shall drop you a line before I leave.'

Having left Lestrade at his rooms we drove to our hotel, where we found lunch upon the table. Holmes was silent and buried in thought, with a pained expression upon his face, as one who finds himself in a perplexing position.

'Look here, Watson,' he said, when the cloth was cleared; 'just sit down in this chair and let me preach to you for a little. I don't quite know what to do, and I should value your advice. Light a cigar, and let me expound.'

'Pray do so.'

'Well, now, in considering this case there are two points about young McCarthy's narrative which struck us both instantly, although they impressed me in his favour and you against him. One was the fact that his father should, according to his account, cry

192

"Cooee!" before seeing him. The other was his singular dying reference to a rat. He mumbled several words, you understand, but that was all that caught the son's ear. Now from this double point our research must commence, and we will begin it by presuming that what the lad says is absolutely true.'

'What of this "Cooee!" then?'

'Well, obviously it could not have been meant for the son. The son, as far as he knew, was in Bristol. It was mere chance that he was within earshot. The "Cooee!" was meant to attract the attention of whoever it was that he had the appointment with. But "Cooee" is a distinctly Australian cry, and one which is used between Australians. There is a strong presumption that the person whom McCarthy expected him to meet at Boscombe Pool was someone who had been in Australia.'

'What of the rat, then?'

Sherlock Holmes took a folded paper from his pocket and flattened it out on the table. 'This is the map of the Colony of Victoria,' he said. 'I wired to Bristol for it last night.' He put his hand over part of the map. 'What do you read?' he asked.

'ARAT,' I read.

'And now?' He raised his hand.

'BALLARAT.'

'Quite so. That was the word the man uttered, and of which his son only caught the last two syllables. He was trying to utter the name of his murderer. So-and-so of Ballarat.'

'It is wonderful!' I exclaimed.

'It is obvious. And now, you see, I had narrowed the field down considerably. The possession of a grey garment was a third point which, granting the son's statement to be correct, was a certainty. We have come now out of mere vagueness to the definite conception of an Australian from Ballarat with a grey cloak.'

'Certainly.'

'And one who was at home in the district, for the Pool can only be approached by the farm or by the estate, where strangers could hardly wander.'

'Quite so.'

'Then comes our expedition of today. By an examination of the ground I gained the trifling details which I gave to that imbecile Lestrade, as to the personality of the criminal.'

'But how did you gain them?'

'You know my method. It is founded upon the observance of trifles.'

'His height I know that you might roughly judge from the length of his stride. His boots, too, might be told from their traces.'

'Yes, they were peculiar boots.'

'But his lameness?'

'The impression of his right foot was always less distinct than his left. He put less weight upon it. Why? Because he limped – he was lame.'

'But his left-handedness?'

'You were yourself struck by the nature of the injury as recorded by the surgeon at the inquest. The blow was struck from immediately behind, and yet was upon the left side. Now, how can that be unless it were by a left-handed man? He had stood behind that tree during the interview between the father and son. He had even smoked there. I found the ash of a cigar, which my special knowledge of tobacco ashes enabled me to pronounce as an Indian cigar. I have, as you know, devoted some attention to this, and written a little monograph on the ashes of 140 different varieties of pipe, cigar, and cigarette tobacco. Having found the ash, I then looked round and discovered the stump among the moss where he had tossed it. It was an Indian cigar, of the variety which are rolled in Rotterdam.'

'And the cigar-holder?'

'I could see that the end had not been in his mouth. Therefore he used a holder. The tip had been cut off, not bitten off, but the cut was not a clean one, so I deduced a blunt penknife.'

'Holmes,' I said, 'you have drawn a net round this man from which he cannot escape, and you have saved an innocent human life as truly as if you had cut the cord which was hanging him. I see the direction in which all this points. The culprit is –'

'Mr John Turner,' cried the hotel waiter, opening the door of our sitting-room, and ushering in a visitor.

The man who entered was a strange and impressive figure. His slow, limping step and bowed shoulders gave the appearance of decrepitude, and yet his hard, deeplined, craggy features, and his enormous limbs showed that he was possessed of unusual strength of body and of character. His tangled beard, grizzled hair, and outstanding, drooping eyebrows combined to give an air of dignity and power to his appearance, but his face was of an ashen white, while his lips and the corners of his nostrils were tinged with a shade of blue. It was clear to me at a glance that he was in the grip of some deadly chronic disease.

'Pray sit down on the sofa,' said Holmes gently. 'You had my note?'

'Yes, the lodge-keeper brought it up. You said that you wished to see me here to avoid scandal.'

'I thought people would talk if I went to the Hall.'

'And why did you wish to see me?' He looked across at my companion with despair in his weary eyes, as though his question were already answered.

'Yes,' said Holmes, answering the look rather than the words. 'It is so. I know all about McCarthy.'

The old man sank his face in his hands. 'God help me!' he cried. 'But I would not have let the young man come to harm. I give you my word that I would have spoken out if it went against him at the Assizes.'

'I am glad to hear you say so,' said Holmes gravely.

'I would have spoken now had it not been for my dear girl. It would break her heart – it will break her heart when she hears that I am arrested.'

'It may not come to that,' said Holmes.

'What!'

'I am no official agent. I understand that it was your daughter who required my presence here, and I am acting in her interests. Young McCarthy must be got off, however.'

'I am a dying man,' said old Turner. 'I have had diabetes for years. My doctor says it is a question whether I shall live a month. Yet I would rather die under my own roof than in a gaol.'

Holmes rose and sat down at the table with his pen in his hand and a bundle of paper before him. 'Just tell us the truth,' he said. 'I shall jot down the facts. You will sign it, and Watson here can witness it. Then I could produce your confession at the last extremity to save young McCarthy. I promise you that I shall not use it unless it is absolutely needed.'

'It's as well,' said the old man; 'it's a question whether I shall live to the Assizes, so it matters little to me, but I should wish to spare Alice the shock. And now I will make the thing clear to you; it has been a long time in the acting, but will not take me long to tell.

'You didn't know this dead man, McCarthy. He was a devil incarnate. I tell you that. God keep you out of the clutches of such a man as he. His grip has been upon me these twenty years, and he has blasted my life. I'll tell you first how I came to be in his power.

'It was in the early 'sixties at the diggings. I was a young chap then, hot-blooded and reckless, ready to turn my hand to anything; I got among bad companions, took to drink, had no luck with my claim, took to the bush, and, in a word, became what you would call over here a highway robber. There were six of us, and we had a wild, free life of it, sticking up a station from time to time, or stopping the wagons on the road to the diggings. Black Jack of Ballarat was the name I went under, and our party is still remembered in the colony as the Ballarat Gang.

'One day a gold convoy came down from Ballarat to Melbourne, and we lay in wait for it and attacked it. There were six troopers and six of us, so it was a close thing, but we emptied four of their saddles at the first volley. Three of our boys were killed, however, before we got the swag. I put my pistol to the head of the wagon-driver, who was this very man McCarthy. I wish to the Lord that I had shot him then, but I spared him, though I saw his wicked little eyes fixed on my face, as though to remember every feature. We got away with the gold, became wealthy men, and made our way over to England without being suspected. There I parted from my old pals, and determined to settle down to a quiet and respectable life. I bought this estate, which chanced to be in the market, and I set myself to do a little good with my money, to make up for the way in which I had earned it. I married, too, and though my wife died young, she left me my dear little Alice. Even when she was just a baby her wee hand seemed to lead me down the right path as nothing else had ever done. In a word, I turned over a new leaf, and did my best to make up for the past. All was going well when McCarthy laid his grip upon me.

'I had gone up to town about an investment, and I met him in Regent Street with hardly a coat to his back or a boot to his foot.

' "Here we are, Jack," says he, touching me on the arm; "we'll be as good as a family to you. There's two of us, me and my son, and you can have the keeping of us. If you don't – it's a fine, law-abiding country is England, and there's always a policeman within hail."

'Well, down they came to the West Country, there was no shaking them off, and there they have lived rent free on my best land ever since. There was no rest for me, no peace, no forgetfulness; turn where I would, there was his cunning, grinning face at my elbow. It grew worse as Alice grew up, for he soon saw I was more afraid of her knowing my past than of the police. Whatever he wanted he must have; and whatever it was I gave him without question, land, money, houses, until at last he asked for a thing which I could not give. He asked for Alice.

'His son, you see, had grown up, and so had my girl, and as I was known to be in weak health, it seemed a fine stroke to him that his lad should step into the whole property. But there I was firm. I would not have his cursed stock mixed with mine; not that I had any dislike to the lad, but his blood was in him, and that was enough. I stood firm. McCarthy threatened. I braved him to do his worst. We were to meet at the Pool midway between our houses to talk it over.

'When I went down there I found him talking with his son, so I smoked a cigar, and waited behind a tree until he should be alone. But as I listened to his talk all that was black and bitter in me seemed to come uppermost. He was urging his son to marry my daughter with as little regard for what she might think as if she were a slut from off the streets. It drove me mad to think that I and all that I held most dear should be in the power of such a man as this. Could I not snap the bond? I was already a dying and a desperate man. Though clear of mind and fairly strong of limb, I knew that my own fate was sealed. But my memory and my girl! Both could be saved, if I could but silence that foul tongue. I did it, Mr Holmes. I would do it again. Deeply as I have sinned, I have led a life of martyrdom to atone for it. But that my girl should be entangled in the same meshes which held me was more than I could suffer. I struck him down with no more compunction than if he had been some foul and venomous beast. His cry brought back his son; but I had gained the cover of the wood, though I was forced to go back to fetch the cloak which I had dropped in my flight. That is the true story, gentlemen, of all that occurred.'

'Well, it is not for me to judge you,' said Holmes, as the old man signed the statement which had been drawn out. 'I pray that we may never be exposed to such a temptation.'

'I pray not, sir. And what do you intend to do?'

'In view of your health, nothing. You are yourself aware that you will soon have to answer for your deed at a higher court than the Assizes. I will keep your confession, and, if McCarthy is condemned, I shall be forced to use it. If not, it shall never be seen by mortal eye; and your secret, whether you be alive or dead, shall be safe with us.'

'Farewell! then,' said the old man solemnly. 'Your own death-beds, when they come, will be the easier for the thought of the peace which you have given to mine.' Tottering and shaking in all his giant frame, he stumbled slowly from the room.

'God help us!' said Holmes, after a long silence. 'Why does Fate play such tricks with poor helpless worms? I never hear of such a case as this that I do not think of Baxter's words, and say: "There, but for the grace of God, goes Sherlock Holmes." '

James McCarthy was acquitted at the Assizes, on the strength of a number of objections which had been drawn out by Holmes, and submitted to the defending counsel. Old Turner lived for seven months after our interview, but he is now dead; and there is every prospect that the son and daughter may come to live happily together, in ignorance of the black cloud which rests upon their past.

The Man Who Knew How

DOROTHY SAYERS

FOR PERHAPS THE TWENTIETH time since the train had left Carlisle, Pender glanced up from *Murder at the Manse* and caught the eye of the man opposite.

He frowned a little. It was irritating to be watched so closely, and always with that faint, sardonic smile. It was still more irritating to allow oneself to be so much disturbed by the smile and the scrutiny. Pender wrenched himself back to his book with a determination to concentrate upon the problem of the minister murdered in the library. But the story was of the academic kind that crowds all its exciting incidents into the first chapter, and proceeds thereafter by a long series of deductions to a scientific solution in the last. The thin thread of interest, spun precariously upon the wheel of Pender's reasoning brain, had been snapped. Twice he had to turn back to verify points that he had missed in reading. Then he became aware that his eyes had followed three closely argued pages without conveying anything whatever to his intelligence. He was not thinking about the murdered minister at all – he was becoming more and more actively conscious of the other man's face. A queer face, Pender thought.

There was nothing especially remarkable about the features in themselves; it was their expression that daunted Pender. It was a secret face, the face of one who knew a great deal to other people's disadvantage. The mouth was a little crooked and tightly tucked in at the corners, as though savouring a hidden amusement. The eyes, behind a pair of rimless pince-nez, glittered curiously; but that was possibly due to the light reflected in the glasses. Pender wondered what the man's profession might be. He was dressed in a dark lounge suit, a raincoat and a shabby soft hat; his age was perhaps about forty.

Pender coughed unnecessarily and settled back into his corner, raising the detective story high before his face, barrier-fashion. This was worse than useless. He gained the impression that the man saw through the manœuvre and was secretly entertained by it. He wanted to fidget, but felt obscurely that his doing so would in some way constitute a victory for the other man. In his self-consciousness he held himself so rigid that attention to his book became a sheer physical impossibility.

There was no stop now before Rugby, and it was unlikely that any passenger would enter from the corridor to break up this disagreeable *solitude à deux*. But something must be done. The silence had lasted so long that any remark, however trivial, would – so Pender felt – burst upon the tense atmosphere with the unnatural clatter of an alarm clock. One could, of course, go out into the corridor and not return, but that would be an acknowledgment of defeat. Pender lowered *Murder at the Manse* and caught the man's eye again.

'Getting tired of it?' asked the man.

'Night journeys are always a bit tedious,' replied Pender, half relieved and half reluctant. 'Would you like a book?'

He took *The Paper-Clip Clue* from his attaché-case and held it out hopefully. The other man glanced at the title and shook his head.

'Thanks very much,' he said, 'but I never read detective stories. They're so – inadequate, don't you think so?'

'They are rather lacking in characterization and human interest, certainly,' said Pender, 'but on a railway journey——'

'I don't mean that,' said the other man. 'I am not concerned with humanity. But all these murderers are so incompetent – they bore me.'

'Oh, I don't know,' replied Pender. 'At any rate they are usually a good deal more imaginative and ingenious than murderers in real life.'

'Than the murderers who are found out in real life, yes,' admitted the other man.

'Even some of those did pretty well before they got pinched,' objected Pender. 'Crippen, for instance; he need never have been caught if he hadn't lost his head and run off to America. George Joseph Smith did away with at least two brides quite successfully before fate and the *News of the World* intervened.'

'Yes,' said the other man, 'but look at the clumsiness of it all; the elaboration, the lies, the paraphernalia. Absolutely unnecessary.'

'Oh, come!' said Pender. 'You can't expect committing a murder and getting away with it to be as simple as shelling peas.'

'Ah!' said the other man. 'You think that, do you?'

Pender waited for him to elaborate this remark, but nothing came of it. The man leaned back and smiled in his secret way at the roof of the carriage; he appeared to think the conversation not worth going on with. Pender, taking up his book again, found himself attracted by his companion's hands. They were white and surprisingly long in the fingers. He watched them gently tapping upon their owner's knee – then resolutely turned a page – then put the book down once more and said:

199

'Well, if it's so easy, how would *you* set about committing a murder?'

'I?' repeated the man. The light on his glasses made his eyes quite blank to Pender, but his voice sounded gently amused. 'That's different; *I* should not have to think twice about it.'

'Why not?'

'Because I happen to know how to do it.'

'Do you indeed?' muttered Pender, rebelliously.

'Oh yes; there's nothing in it.'

'How can you be sure? You haven't tried, I suppose?'

'It isn't a case of trying,' said the man. 'There's nothing tentative about my method. That's just the beauty of it.'

'It's easy to say that,' retorted Pender, 'but what *is* this wonderful method?'

'You can't expect me to tell you that, can you?' said the other man, bringing his eyes back to rest on Pender's. 'It might not be safe. You look harmless enough, but who could look more harmless than Crippen? Nobody is fit to be trusted with *absolute* control over other people's lives.'

'Bosh!' exclaimed Pender. 'I shouldn't think of murdering anybody.'

'Oh, yes, you would,' said the other man, 'if you really believed it was safe. So would anybody. Why are all these tremendous artificial barriers built up around murder by the Church and the law? Just because it's everybody's crime, and just as natural as breathing.'

'But that's ridiculous!' cried Pender, warmly.

'You think so, do you? That's what most people would say. But I wouldn't trust 'em. Not with sulphate of thanatol to be bought for twopence at any chemist's.'

'Sulphate of what?' asked Pender sharply.

'Ah! you think I'm giving something away. Well, it's a mixture of that and one or two other things – all equally ordinary and cheap. For ninepence you could make up enough to poison the entire Cabinet – and even you would hardly call that a crime, would you? But of course one wouldn't polish the whole lot off at once; it might look funny if they all died simultaneously in their baths.'

'Why in their baths?'

'That's the way it would take them. It's the action of the hot water that brings on the effect of the stuff, you see. Any time from a few hours to a few days after administration. It's quite a simple chemical reaction and it couldn't possibly be detected by analysis. It would just look like heart failure.'

Pender eyed him uneasily. He did not like the smile; it was not only derisive, it was smug, it was almost – gloating – triumphant! He could not quite put a name to it.

'You know,' pursued the man, thoughtfully pulling a pipe from his pocket and beginning to fill it, 'it is very odd how often one seems to read of people being found dead in their baths. It must be a very common accident. Quite temptingly so. After all, there is a fascination about murder. The thing grows upon one – that is, I imagine it would, you know.'

'Very likely,' said Pender.

'Look at Palmer. Look at Gesina Gottfried. Look at Armstrong. No, I wouldn't trust anybody with that formula – not even a virtuous young man like yourself.'

The long white fingers tamped the tobacco firmly into the bowl and struck a match.

'But how about you?' said Pender, irritated. (Nobody cares to be called a virtuous young man.) 'If nobody is fit to be trusted——'

'I'm not, eh?' replied the man. 'Well, that's true, but it's past praying for now, isn't it? I know the thing and I can't unknow it again. It's unfortunate, but there it is. At any rate you have the comfort of knowing that nothing disagreeable is likely to happen to *me*. Dear me! Rugby already. I get out here. I have a little bit of business to do at Rugby.'

He rose and shook himself, buttoned his raincoat about him and pulled the shabby hat more firmly down above his enigmatic glasses. The train slowed down and stopped. With a brief goodnight and a crooked smile the man stepped on to the platform. Pender watched him stride quickly away into the drizzle beyond the radius of the gaslight.

'Dotty or something,' said Pender, oddly relieved. 'Thank goodness, I seem to be going to have the carriage to myself.'

He returned to *Murder at the Manse*, but his attention still kept wandering.

'What was the name of that stuff the fellow talked about?'

For the life of him he could not remember.

It was on the following afternoon that Pender saw the news item. He had bought the *Standard* to read at lunch, and the word 'Bath' caught his eye; otherwise he would probably have missed the paragraph altogether, for it was only a short one.

'WEALTHY MANUFACTURER DIES IN BATH
WIFE'S TRAGIC DISCOVERY

A distressing discovery was made early this morning by Mrs John Brittlesea, wife of the well-known head of Brittlesea's Engineering Works at Rugby. Finding that her husband, whom

201

she had seen alive and well less than an hour previously, did not come down in time for his breakfast, she searched for him in the bathroom, where, on the door being broken down, the engineer was found lying dead in his bath, life having been extinct, according to the medical men, for half an hour. The cause of the death is pronounced to be heart failure. The deceased manufacturer . . .'

'That's an odd coincidence,' said Pender. 'At Rugby. I should think my unknown friend would be interested – if he is still there, doing his bit of business. I wonder what his business is, by the way.'

It is a very curious thing how, when once your attention is attracted to any particular set of circumstances, that set of circumstances seems to haunt you. You get appendicitis: immediately the newspapers are filled with paragraphs about statesmen suffering from appendicitis and victims dying of it; you learn that all your acquaintances have had it, or know friends who have had it, and either died of it, or recovered from it with more surprising and spectacular rapidity than yourself; you cannot open a popular magazine without seeing its cure mentioned as one of the triumphs of modern surgery, or dip into a scientific treatise without coming across a comparison of the vermiform appendix in men and monkeys. Probably these references to appendicitis are equally frequent at all times, but you only notice them when your mind is attuned to the subject. At any rate, it was in this way that Pender accounted to himself for the extraordinary frequency with which people seemed to die in their baths at this period.

The thing pursued him at every turn. Always the same sequence of events: the hot bath, the discovery of the corpse, the inquest; always the same medical opinion: heart failure following immersion in too-hot water. It began to seem to Pender that it was scarcely safe to enter a hot bath at all. He took to making his own bath cooler and cooler every day, until it almost ceased to be enjoyable.

He skimmed his paper each morning for headlines about baths before settling down to read the news; and was at once relieved and vaguely disappointed if a week passed without a hot-bath tragedy.

One of the sudden deaths that occurred in this way was that of a young and beautiful woman whose husband, an analytical chemist, had tried without success to divorce her a few months previously. The coroner displayed a tendency to suspect foul play, and put the husband through a severe cross-examination. There seemed, however, to be no getting behind the doctor's evidence. Pender, brooding fancifully over the improbable possible, wished, as he did every day of the week, that he could remember the name of that drug the man in the train had mentioned.

Then came the excitement in Pender's own neighbourhood. An old Mr Skimmings, who lived alone with a housekeeper in a street just round the corner, was found dead in his bathroom. His heart had never been strong. The housekeeper told the milkman that she had always expected something of the sort to happen, for the old gentleman would always take his bath so hot. Pender went to the inquest.

The housekeeper gave her evidence. Mr Skimmings had been the kindest of employers, and she was heartbroken at losing him. No, she had not been aware that Mr Skimmings had left her a large sum of money, but it was just like his goodness of heart. The verdict was Death by Misadventure.

Pender, that evening, went out for his usual stroll with his dog. Some feeling of curiosity moved him to go round past the late Mr Skimming's house. As he loitered by, glancing up at the blank windows, the garden-gate opened and a man came out. In the light of a street lamp, Pender recognized him at once.

'Hullo!' he said.

'Oh, it's you, is it?' said the man. 'Viewing the site of the tragedy, eh? What do *you* think about it all?'

'Oh, nothing very much,' said Pender. 'I didn't know him. Odd, our meeting again like this.'

'Yes, isn't it? You live near here, I suppose.'

'Yes,' said Pender; and then wished he hadn't. 'Do you live in these parts too?'

'Me?' said the man. 'Oh, no. I was only here on a little matter of business.'

'Last time we met,' said Pender, 'you had business at Rugby.' They had fallen into step together, and were walking slowly down to the turning Pender had to take in order to reach his house.

'So I had,' agreed the other man. 'My business takes me all over the country. I never know where I may be wanted next.'

'It was while you were at Rugby that old Brittlesea was found dead in his bath, wasn't it?' remarked Pender carelessly.

'Yes. Funny thing, coincidence.' The man glanced up at him sideways through his glittering glasses. 'Left all his money to his wife, didn't he? She's a rich woman now. Good-looking girl – a lot younger than he was.'

They were passing Pender's gate. 'Come in and have a drink,' said Pender, and again immediately regretted the impulse.

The man accepted, and they went into Pender's bachelor study.

'Remarkable lot of these bath-deaths there have been lately, haven't there?' observed Pender carelessly, as he splashed soda into the tumblers.

'You think it's remarkable?' said the man, with his usual irritating trick of querying everything that was said to him. 'Well, I don't know. Perhaps it is. But it's always a fairly common accident.'

'I suppose I've been taking more notice on account of that conversation we had in the train.' Pender laughed, a little self-consciously. 'It just makes me wonder – you know how one does – whether anybody else had happened to hit on that drug you mentioned – what was its name?'

The man ignored the question.

'Oh, I shouldn't think so,' he said. 'I fancy I'm the only person who knows about that. I only stumbled on the thing by accident myself when I was looking for something else. I don't imagine it could have been discovered simultaneously in so many parts of the country. But all these verdicts just show, don't they, what a safe way it would be of getting rid of a person.'

'You're a chemist, then?' asked Pender, catching at the one phrase which seemed to promise information.

'Oh, I'm a bit of everything. Sort of general utility-man. I do a good bit of studying on my own, too. You've got one or two interesting books here, I see.'

Pender was flattered. For a man in his position – he had been in a bank until he came into a little bit of money – he felt that he had improved his mind to some purpose, and he knew that his collection of modern first editions would be worth money some day. He went over to the glass-fronted bookcase and pulled out a volume or two to show his visitor.

The man displayed intelligence, and presently joined him in front of the shelves.

'These, I take it, represent your personal tastes?' He took down a volume of Henry James and glanced at the fly-leaf. 'That your name? E. Pender?'

Pender admitted that it was. 'You have the advantage of me,' he added.

'Oh! I am one of the great Smith clan,' said the other with a laugh, 'and work for my bread. You seem to be very nicely fixed here.'

Pender explained about the clerkship and the legacy.

'Very nice, isn't it?' said Smith. 'Not married? No. You're one of the lucky ones. Not likely to be needing any sulphate of . . . any useful drugs in the near future. And you never will, if you stick to what you've got and keep off women and speculation.'

He smiled up sideways at Pender. Now that his hat was off, Pender saw that he had a quantity of closely curled grey hair, which made him look older than he had appeared in the railway carriage.

'No, I shan't be coming to you for assistance yet awhile,' said Pender, laughing. 'Besides, how should I find you if I wanted you?'

'You wouldn't have to,' said Smith. '*I* should find *you*. There's never any difficulty about that.' He grinned, oddly. 'Well, I'd better be getting on. Thank you for your hospitality. I don't expect we shall meet again – but we may, of course. Things work out so queerly, don't they?'

When he had gone, Pender returned to his own arm-chair. He took up his glass of whisky, which stood there nearly full.

'Funny!' he said to himself. 'I don't remember pouring that out. I suppose I got interested and did it mechanically.' He emptied his glass slowly, thinking about Smith.

What in the world was Smith doing at Skimmings's house?

An odd business altogether. If Skimmings's housekeeper had known about the money . . . But she had not known, and if she had, how could she have found out about Smith and his sulphate of . . . the word had been on the tip of his tongue then.

'You would not need to find me. *I* should find *you*.' What had the man meant by that? But this was ridiculous. Smith was not the devil, presumably. But if he really had this secret – if he liked to put a price upon it – nonsense.

'Business at Rugby – a little bit of business at Skimmings's house.' Oh, absurd!

'Nobody is fit to be trusted. *Absolute* power over another man's life . . . it grows on you.'

Lunacy! And, if there was anything in it, the man was mad to tell Pender about it. If Pender chose to speak he could get the fellow hanged. The very existence of Pender would be dangerous.

That whisky!

More and more, thinking it over, Pender became persuaded that he had never poured it out. Smith must have done it while his back was turned. Why that sudden display of interest in the bookshelves? It had had no connection with anything that had gone before. Now Pender came to think of it, it had been a very stiff whisky. Was it imagination, or had there been something about the flavour of it?

A cold sweat broke out on Pender's forehead.

A quarter of an hour later, after a powerful dose of mustard and water, Pender was downstairs again, very cold and shivering, huddling over the fire. He had had a narrow escape – if he had escaped. He did not know how the stuff worked, but he would not take a hot bath again for some days. One never knew.

Whether the mustard and water had done the trick in time, or whether the hot bath was an essential part of the treatment, Pender's life was saved for the time being. But he was still uneasy. He kept the front door on the chain and warned his servant to let no strangers into the house.

He ordered two more morning papers and the *News of the World* on Sundays, and kept a careful watch upon their columns. Deaths in baths became an obsession with him. He neglected his first editions and took to attending inquests.

Three weeks later he found himself in Lincoln. A man had died of heart failure in a Turkish bath – a fat man, of sedentary habits. The jury added a rider to their verdict of Misadventure, to the effect that the management should exercise a stricter supervision over the bathers and should never permit them to be left unattended in the hot room.

As Pender emerged from the hall he saw ahead of him a shabby hat that seemed familiar. He plunged after it, and caught Mr Smith about to step into a taxi.

'Smith,' he cried, gasping a little. He clutched him fiercely by the shoulder.

'What, you again?' said Smith. 'Taking notes of the case, eh? *Can I do anything for you?*'

'You devil!' said Pender. 'You're mixed up in this! You tried to kill me the other day.'

'Did I? Why should I do that?'

'You'll swing for this,' shouted Pender menacingly.

A policeman pushed his way through the gathering crowd.

'Here!' said he, 'what's all this about?'

Smith touched his forehead significantly.

'It's all right, officer,' said he. 'The gentleman seems to think I'm here for no good. Here's my card. The coroner knows me. But he attacked me. You'd better keep an eye on him.'

'That's right,' said a bystander.

'This man tried to kill me,' said Pender.

The policeman nodded.

'Don't worry about that, sir,' he said. 'You think better of it. The 'eat in there has upset you a bit. All right, *all* right.'

'But I want to charge him,' said Pender.

'I wouldn't do that if I was you,' said the policeman.

'I tell you,' said Pender, 'that this man Smith has been trying to poison me. He's a murderer. He's poisoned scores of people.'

The policeman winked at Smith.

'Best be off, sir,' he said. 'I'll settle this. Now, my lad' – he held Pender firmly by the arms – 'just you keep cool and take it quiet. That gentleman's name ain't Smith nor nothing like it. You've got a bit mixed up like.'

'Well, what is his name?' demanded Pender.

'Never you mind,' replied the constable. 'You leave him alone, or you'll be getting yourself into trouble.'

The taxi had driven away. Pender glanced round at the circle of amused faces and gave in.

'All right, officer,' he said. 'I won't give you any trouble. I'll come round with you to the police-station and tell you about it.'

'What do you think o' that one?' asked the inspector of the sergeant when Pender had stumbled out of the station.

'Up the pole an' 'alf-way round the flag, if you ask me,' replied his subordinate. 'Got one o' them ideez fix what they talk about.'

'H'm!' replied the inspector. 'Well, we've got his name and address. Better make a note of 'em. He might turn up again. Poisoning people so as they die in their baths, eh? That's a pretty good 'un. Wonderful how these barmy ones thinks it all out, isn't it?'

The spring that year was a bad one – cold and foggy. It was March when Pender went down to an inquest at Deptford, but a thick blanket of mist was hanging over the river as though it were November. The cold ate into your bones. As he sat in the dingy little court, peering through the yellow twilight of gas and fog, he could scarcely see the witnesses as they came to the table. Everybody in the place seemed to be coughing. Pender was coughing too. His bones ached, and he felt as though he were about due for a bout of influenza.

Straining his eyes, he thought he recognized a face on the other side of the room, but the smarting fog which penetrated every crack stung and blinded him. He felt in his overcoat pocket, and his hand closed comfortably on something thick and heavy. Ever since that day in Lincoln he had gone about armed for protection. Not a revolver – he was no hand with firearms. A sandbag was much better. He had bought one from an old man wheeling a barrow. It was meant for keeping out draughts from the door – a good, old-fashioned affair.

The inevitable verdict was returned. The spectators began to push their way out. Pender had to hurry now, not to lose sight of his man. He elbowed his way along, muttering apologies. At the door he almost touched the man, but a stout woman intervened. He plunged past her, and she gave a little squeak of indignation. The man in front turned his head, and the light over the door glinted on his glasses.

Pender pulled his hat over his eyes and followed. His shoes had crêpe rubber soles and made no sound on the sticking pavement. The man went on, jogging quietly up one street and down another, and never looking back. The fog was so thick that Pender was forced to

207

keep within a few yards of him. Where was he going? Into the lighted streets? Home by 'bus or tram? No. He turned off to the left, down a narrow street.

The fog was thicker here. Pender could no longer see his quarry, but he heard the footsteps going on before him at the same even pace. It seemed to him that they were two alone in the world – pursued and pursuer, slayer and avenger. The street began to slope more rapidly. They must be coming out somewhere near the river.

Suddenly the dim shapes of the houses fell away on either side. There was an open space, with a lamp vaguely visible in the middle. The footsteps paused. Pender, silently hurrying after, saw the man standing close beneath the lamp, apparently consulting something in a notebook.

Four steps, and Pender was upon him. He drew the sandbag from his pocket. The man looked up.

'I've got you this time,' said Pender, and struck with all his force.

Pender had been quite right. He did get influenza. It was a week before he was out and about again. The weather had changed, and the air was fresh and sweet. In spite of the weakness left by the malady he felt as though a heavy weight had been lifted from his shoulders. He tottered down to a favourite bookshop of his in the Strand, and picked up a D. H. Lawrence 'first' at a price which he knew to be a bargain. Encouraged by this, he turned into a small chop-house, chiefly frequented by Fleet Street men, and ordered a grilled cutlet and a half-tankard of bitter.

Two journalists were seated at the next table.

'Going to poor old Buckley's funeral?' asked one.

'Yes,' said the other. 'Poor devil! Fancy his getting sloshed on the head like that. He must have been on his way down to interview the widow of that fellow who died in a bath. It's a rough district. Probably one of Jimmy the Card's crowd had it in for him. He was a great crime-reporter – they won't get another like Bill Buckley in a hurry.'

'He was a decent sort, too. Great old sport. No end of a leg-puller. Remember his great stunt about sulphate of thanatol?'

Pender started. *That* was the word that had eluded him for so many months. A curious dizziness came over him and he took a pull at the tankard to steady himself.

'. . . looking at you as sober as a judge,' the journalist was saying. 'He used to work off that wheeze on poor boobs in railway carriages to see how they'd take it. Would you believe that one chap actually offered him——'

'Hullo!' interrupted his friend. 'That bloke over there has fainted. I thought he was looking a bit white.'

The Hands of Mr Ottermole

THOMAS BURKE

AT SIX O'CLOCK OF A JANUARY evening Mr Whybrow was walking home through the cobweb alleys of London's East End. He had left the golden clamour of the great High Street to which the tram had brought him from the river and his daily work, and was now in the chess-board of byways that is called Mallon End. None of the rush and gleam of the High Street trickled into these byways. A few paces south – a flood-tide of life, foaming and beating. Here – only slow shuffling figures and muffled pulses. He was in the sink of London, the last refuge of European vagrants.

As though in tune with the street's spirit, he too walked slowly, with head down. It seemed that he was pondering some pressing trouble, but he was not. He had no trouble. He was walking slowly because he had been on his feet all day, and he was bent in abstraction because he was wondering whether the Missis would have herrings for his tea, or haddock; and he was trying to decide which would be the more tasty on a night like this. A wretched night it was, of damp and mist, and the mist wandered into his throat and his eyes, and the damp had settled on pavement and roadway, and where the sparse lamplight fell it sent up a greasy sparkle that chilled one to look at. By contrast it made his speculation more agreeable, and made him ready for that tea – whether herring or haddock. His eye turned from the glum bricks that made his horizon, and went forward half a mile. He saw a gas-lit kitchen, a flamy fire and a spread tea-table. There was toast in the hearth and a singing kettle on the side and a piquant effusion of herrings, or maybe of haddock, or perhaps sausages. The vision gave his aching feet a throb of energy. He shook imperceptible damp from his shoulders, and hastened towards its reality.

But Mr Whybrow wasn't going to get any tea that evening – or any other evening. Mr Whybrow was going to die. Somewhere within a hundred yards of him another man was walking: a man much like Mr Whybrow and much like any other man, but without the only quality that enables mankind to live peaceably together and not as madmen in a jungle. A man with a dead heart eating into itself and bringing forth the foul organisms that arise from death and corruption. And

209

that thing in a man's shape, on a whim or a settled idea – one cannot know – had said within himself that Mr Whybrow should never taste another herring. Not that Mr Whybrow had injured him. Not that he had any dislike of Mr Whybrow. Indeed, he knew nothing of him save as a familiar figure about the streets. But, moved by a force that had taken possession of his empty cells, he had picked on Mr Whybrow with that blind choice that makes us pick one restaurant table that has nothing to mark it from four or five other tables, or one apple from a dish of half a dozen equal apples; or that drives Nature to send a cyclone upon one corner of this planet, and destroy five hundred lives in that corner, and leave another five hundred in the same corner unharmed. So this man had picked on Mr Whybrow, as he might have picked on you or me, had we been within his daily observation; and even now he was creeping through the blue-toned streets, nursing his large white hands, moving ever closer to Mr Whybrow's tea-table, and so closer to Mr Whybrow himself.

He wasn't, this man, a bad man. Indeed, he had many of the social and amiable qualities, and passed as a respectable man, as most successful criminals do. But the thought had come into his mouldering mind that he would like to murder somebody, and, as he held no fear of God or man, he was going to do it, and would then go home to *his* tea. I don't say that flippantly, but as a statement of fact. Strange as it may seem to the humane, murderers must and do sit down to meals after a murder. There is no reason why they shouldn't, and many reasons why they should. For one thing, they need to keep their physical and mental vitality at full beat for the business of covering their crime. For another, the strain of their effort makes them hungry, and satisfaction at the accomplishment of a desired thing brings a feeling of relaxation towards human pleasures. It is accepted among non-murderers that the murderer is always overcome by fear for his safety and horror at his act; but this type is rare. His own safety is, of course, his immediate concern, but vanity is a marked quality of most murderers, and that, together with the thrill of conquest, makes him confident that he can secure it, and when he has restored his strength with food he goes about securing it as a young hostess goes about the arranging of her first big dinner – a little anxious, but no more. Criminologists and detectives tell us that *every* murderer, however intelligent or cunning, always makes one slip in his tactics – one slip that brings the affair home to him. But that is only half true. It is true only of the murderers who are caught. Scores of murderers are not caught: therefore scores of murderers do not make any mistake at all. This man didn't.

As for horror or remorse, prison chaplains, doctors, and lawyers have told us that of murderers they have interviewed under condemnation and the shadow of death, only one here and there has expressed any contrition for his act, or shown any sign of mental misery. Most of them display only exasperation at having been caught when so many have gone undiscovered, or indignation at being condemned for a perfectly reasonable act. However normal and humane they may have been before the murder, they are utterly without conscience after it. For what is conscience? Simply a polite nickname for superstition, which is a polite nickname for fear. Those who associate remorse with murder are, no doubt, basing their ideas on the world-legend of the remorse of Cain, or are projecting their own frail minds into the mind of the murderer, and getting false reactions. Peaceable folk cannot hope to make contact with this mind, for they are not merely different in mental type from the murderer: they are different in their personal chemistry and construction. Some men can and do kill, not one man, but two or three, and go calmly about their daily affairs. Other men could not, under the most agonizing provocation, bring themselves even to wound. It is men of this sort who imagine the murderer in torments of remorse and fear of the law, whereas he is actually sitting down to his tea.

The man with the large white hands was as ready for his tea as Mr Whybrow was, but he had something to do before he went to it. When he had done that something, and made no mistake about it, he would be even more ready for it, and would go to it as comfortably as he went to it the day before, when his hands were stainless.

Walk on, then Mr Whybrow, walk on; and as you walk, look your last upon the familiar features of your nightly journey. Follow your jack-o'-lantern tea-table. Look well upon its warmth and colour and kindness; feed your eyes with it, and tease your nose with its gentle domestic odours; for you will never sit down to it. Within ten minutes' pacing of you a pursuing phantom has spoken in his heart, and you are doomed. There you go – you and phantom – two nebulous dabs of mortality, moving through green air along pavements of powder-blue, the one to kill, the other to be killed. Walk on. Don't annoy your burning feet by hurrying, for the more slowly you walk, the longer you will breathe the green air of this January dusk, and see the dreamy lamplight and the little shops, and hear the agreeable commerce of the London crowd and the haunting pathos of the street-organ. These things are dear to you, Mr Whybrow. You don't know it now, but in fifteen minutes you will have two seconds in which to realize how inexpressibly dear they are.

Walk on, then, across this crazy chess-board. You are in Lagos Street now, among the tents of the wanderers of Eastern Europe. A minute or so, and you are in Loyal Lane, among the lodging-houses

211

that shelter the useless and the beaten of London's camp-followers. The lane holds the smell of them, and its soft darkness seems heavy with the wail of the futile. But you are not sensitive to impalpable things, and you plod through it, unseeing, as you do every evening, and come to Blean Street, and plod through that. From basement to sky rise the tenements of an alien colony. Their windows slit the ebony of their walls with lemon. Behind those windows strange life is moving, dressed with forms that are not of London or of England, yet, in essence, the same agreeable life that you have been living, and tonight will live no more. From high above you comes a voice crooning *The Song of Katta*. Through a window you see a family keeping a religious rite. Through another you see a woman pouring out tea for her husband. You see a man mending a pair of boots; a mother bathing her baby. You have seen all these things before, and never noticed them. You do not notice them now, but if you knew that you were never going to see them again, not because your life has run its natural course, but because a man whom you have often passed in the street has at his own solitary pleasure decided to usurp the awful authority of nature, and destroy you. So perhaps it's as well that you don't notice them, for your part in them is ended. No more for you these pretty moments of our earthly travail: only one moment of terror, and then a plunging darkness.

Closer to you this shadow of massacre moves, and now he is twenty yards behind you. You can hear his footfalls, but you do not turn your head. You are familiar with footfalls. You are in London, in the easy security of your daily territory, and footfalls behind you, your instinct tells you, are no more than a message of human company.

But can't you hear something in those footfalls – something that goes with a widdershins beat? Something that says: *Look out, look out. Beware, beware.* Can't you hear the very syllables of *murd-er-er, murd-er-er?* No; there is nothing in footfalls. They are neutral. The foot of villainy falls with the same quiet note as the foot of honesty. But those footfalls, Mr Whybrow, are bearing on to you a pair of hands, and there *is* something in hands. Behind you that pair of hands is even now stretching its muscles in preparation for your end. Every minute of your days you have been seeing human hands. Have you ever realized the sheer horror of hands – those appendages that are a symbol of our moments of trust and affection and salutation? Have you thought of the sickening potentialities that lie within the scope of that five-tentacled member? No, you never have; for all the human hands that you have seen have been stretched to you in kindness or fellowship. Yet, though the eyes can hate, and the lips can sting, it is only that dangling member that can gather the accumulated essence of evil, and electrify it into currents of destruction. Satan may enter

212

into man by many doors, but in the hands alone can he find the servants of his will.

Another minute, Mr Whybrow, and you will know all about the horror of human hands.

You are nearly home now. You have turned into your street – Caspar Street – and you are in the centre of the chess-board. You can see the front window of your little four-roomed house. The street is dark, and its three lamps give only a smut of light that is more confusing than darkness. It is dark – empty, too. Nobody about; no lights in the front parlours of the houses, for the families are at tea in their kitchens; and only a random glow in a few upper rooms occupied by lodgers. Nobody about but you and your following companion, and you don't notice him. You see him so often that he is never seen. Even if you turned your head and saw him, you would only say 'Good evening' to him, and walk on. A suggestion that he was a possible murderer would not even make you laugh. It would be too silly.

And now you are at your gate. And now you have found your door key. And now you are in, and hanging up your hat and coat. The Missis has just called a greeting from the kitchen, whose smell is an echo of that greeting (herring!) and you have answered it, when the door shakes under a sharp knock.

Go away, Mr Whybrow. Go away from that door. Don't touch it. Get right away from it. Get out of the house. Run with the Missis to the back garden, and over the fence. Or call the neighbours. But don't touch that door. Don't, Mr Whybrow, don't open . . .

Mr Whybrow opened the door.

That was the beginning of what became known as London's Strangling Horrors. Horrors they were called because they were something more than murders: they were motiveless, and there was an air of black magic about them. Each murder was committed at a time when the street where the bodies were found was empty of any perceptible or possible murderer. There would be an empty alley. There would be a policeman at its end. He would turn his back on the empty alley for less than a minute. Then he would look round and run into the night with news of another strangling. And in any direction he looked nobody to be seen and no report to be had of anybody being seen. Or he would be on duty in a long quiet street, and suddenly be called to a house of dead people whom a few seconds earlier he had seen alive. And, again, whichever way he looked nobody to be seen; and although police whistles put an immediate cordon around the area, and all the houses were searched, no possible murderer to be found.

The first news of the murder of Mr and Mrs Whybrow was brought

213

by the station sergeant. He had been walking through Caspar Street on his way to the station for duty, when he noticed the open door of No. 98. Glancing in, he saw by the gaslight of the passage a motionless body on the floor. After a second look he blew his whistle, and when the constables answered him he took one to join him in a search of the house, and sent others to watch all neighbouring streets, and make inquiries at adjoining houses. But neither in the house nor in the streets was anything found to indicate the murderer. Neighbours on either side, and opposite, were questioned, but they had seen nobody about, and had heard nothing. One had heard Mr Whybrow come home – the scrape of his latchkey in the door was so regular an evening sound, he said, that you could set your watch by it for half-past six – but he had heard nothing more than the sound of the opening door until the sergeant's whistle. Nobody had been seen to enter the house or leave it, by front or back, and the necks of the dead people carried no finger-prints or other traces. A nephew was called in to go over the house, but he could find nothing missing; and anyway his uncle possessed nothing worth stealing. The little money in the house was untouched, and there were no signs of any disturbance of the property, or even of struggle. No signs of anything but brutal and wanton murder.

Mr Whybrow was known to neighbours and work-mates as a quiet, likeable, home-loving man; such a man as could not have any enemies. But, then, murdered men seldom have. A relentless enemy who hates a man to the point of wanting to hurt him seldom wants to murder him, since to do that puts him beyond suffering. So the police were left with an impossible situation: no clue to the murderer and no motive for the murders; only the fact that they had been done.

The first news of the affair sent a tremor through London generally, and an electric thrill through all Mallon End. Here was murder of two inoffensive people, not for gain and not for revenge; and the murderer, to whom, apparently, killing was a casual impulse, was at large. He had left no traces, and, provided he had no companions, there seemed no reason why he should not remain at large. Any clear-headed man who stands alone, and has no fear of God or man, can, if he chooses, hold a city, even a nation, in subjection; but your everyday criminal is seldom clear-headed, and dislikes being lonely. He needs, if not the support of confederates, at least somebody to talk to; his vanity needs the satisfaction of perceiving at first hand the effect of his work. For this he will frequent bars and coffee-shops and other public places. Then, sooner or later, in a glow of comradeship, he will utter the one word too much; and the nark, who is everywhere, has an easy job.

But though the doss-houses and saloons and other places were 'combed' and set with watches, and it was made known by whispers that good money and protection were assured to those with information, nothing attaching to the Whybrow case could be found. The murderer clearly had no friends and kept no company. Known men of this type were called up and questioned, but each was able to give a good account of himself; and in a few days the police were at a dead end. Against the constant public gibe that the thing had been done almost under their noses, they became restive, and for four days each man of the force was working his daily beat under a strain. On the fifth day they became still more restive.

It was the season of annual teas and entertainments for the children of the Sunday Schools, and on an evening of fog, when London was a world of groping phantoms, a small girl, in the bravery of best Sunday frock and shoes, shining face and new-washed hair, set out from Logan Passage of St Michael's Parish Hall. She never got there. She was not actually dead until half-past six, but she was as good as dead from the moment she left her mother's door. Somebody like a man, pacing the street from which the Passage led, saw her come out; and from that moment she was dead. Through the fog somebody's large white hands reached after her, and in fifteen minutes they were about her.

At half-past six a whistle screamed trouble, and those answering it found the body of little Nellie Vrinoff in a warehouse entry in Minnow Street. The sergeant was first among them, and he posted his men to useful points, ordering them here and there in the tart tones of repressed rage, and berating the officer whose beat the street was. 'I saw you, Magson, at the end of the lane. What were you up to there? You were there ten minutes before you turned.' Magson began an explanation about keeping an eye on a suspicious-looking character at that end, but the sergeant cut him short; 'Suspicious characters be damned. You don't want to look for suspicious characters. You want to look for *murderers*. Messing about . . . and then this happens right where you ought to be. Now think what they'll say.'

With the speed of ill news came the crowd, pale and perturbed; and on the story that the unknown monster had appeared again, and this time to a child, their faces streaked the fog with spots of hate and horror. But then came the ambulance and more police, and swiftly they broke up the crowd; and as it broke the sergeant's thought was thickened into words, and from all sides came low murmurs of 'Right under their noses.' Later inquiries showed that four people of the district, above suspicion, had passed that entry at intervals of seconds before the murder, and seen nothing and heard nothing. None of them had passed the child alive or seen her dead. None of them had seen anybody in the street except themselves. Again the police were left with no motive and with no clue.

215

And now the district, as you will remember, was given over, not to panic, for the London public never yields to that, but to apprehension and dismay. If these things were happening in their familiar streets, then anything might happen. Wherever people met – in the streets, the markets and the shops – they debated the one topic. Women took to bolting their windows and doors at the first fall of dusk. They kept their children closely under their eye. They did their shopping before dark, and watched anxiously, while pretending they weren't watching, for the return of their husbands from work. Under the Cockney's semi-humorous resignation to disaster, they hid an hourly foreboding. By the whim of one man with a pair of hands the structure and tenor of their daily life were shaken, as they always can be shaken by any man contemptuous of humanity and fearless of its laws. They began to realize that the pillars that supported the peaceable society in which they lived were mere straws that anybody could snap; that laws were powerful only so long as they were obeyed; that the police were potent only so long as they were feared. By the power of his hands this one man had made a whole community do something new: he had made it think, and left it gasping at the obvious.

And then, while it was yet gasping under his first two strokes, he made his third. Conscious of the horror that his hands had created, and hungry as an actor who has once tasted the thrill of the multitude, he made fresh advertisement of his presence; and on Wednesday morning, three days after the murder of the child, the papers carried to the breakfast tables of England the story of a still more shocking outrage.

At 9.32 on Tuesday night a constable was on duty in Jarnigan Road, and at that time spoke to a fellow-officer named Peterson at the top of Clemming Street. He had seen this officer walk down that street. He could swear that the street was empty at that time, except for a lame boot-black whom he knew by sight, and who passed him and entered a tenement on the side opposite that on which his fellow-officer was walking. He had the habit, as all constables had just then, of looking constantly behind him and around him, whichever way he was walking, and he was certain that the street was empty. He passed his sergeant at 9.33, saluted him, and answered his inquiry for anything seen. He reported that he had seen nothing, and passed on. His beat ended at a short distance from Clemming Street, and, having paced it, he turned and came again at 9.34 to the top of the street. He had scarcely reached it before he heard the hoarse voice of the sergeant: 'Gregory! You there? Quick. Here's another. My God, it's Peterson! Garrotted. Quick, call 'em up!'

That was the third of the Strangling Horrors, of which there were to be a fourth and a fifth; and the five horrors were to pass into the unknown and unknowable. That is, unknown as far as authority and the public were concerned. The identity of the murderer *was* known, but to two men only. One was the murderer himself; the other was a young journalist.

This young man, who was covering the affairs for his paper, the *Daily Torch*, was no smarter than the other zealous newspaper men who were hanging about these byways in the hope of a sudden story. But he was patient, and he hung a little closer to the case than the other fellows, and by continually staring at it he at last raised the figure of the murderer like a genie from the stones on which he had stood to do his murders.

After the first few days the men had given up any attempt at exclusive stories, for there was none to be had. They met regularly at the police station, and what little information there was they shared. The officials were agreeable to them, but no more. The sergeant discussed with them the details of each murder; suggested possible explanations of the man's methods; recalled from the past those cases that had some similarity; and on the matter of motive reminded them of the motiveless Neil Cream and the wanton John Williams, and hinted that work was being done which would soon bring the business to an end; but about that work he would say not a word. The inspector, too, was gracefully garrulous on the theme of murder, but whenever one of the party edged the talk towards what was being done in this immediate matter, he glided past it. Whatever the officials knew, they were not giving it to newspaper men. The business had fallen heavily upon them, and only by a capture made by their own efforts could they rehabilitate themselves in official and public esteem. Scotland Yard, of course, was at work, and had all the station's material; but the station's hope was that they themselves would have the honour of settling the affair; and however useful the co-operation of the Press might be in other cases they did not want to risk a defeat by a premature disclosure of their theories and plans.

So the sergeant talked at large, and propounded one interesting theory after another, all of which the newspaper men had thought of themselves.

The young man soon gave up these morning lectures on the Philosophy of Crime, and took to wandering about the streets and making bright stories out of the effect of the murders on the normal life of the people. A melancholy job was made more melancholy by the district. The littered roadways, the crestfallen houses, the bleared windows – all held the acid misery that evokes no sympathy: the misery of the frustrated poet. The misery was the creation of the aliens, who were living in this makeshift fashion because they had no settled homes, and would neither take the trouble to make a home

217

where they *could* settle, nor get on with their wandering.

There was little to be picked up. All he saw and heard were indignant faces and wild conjectures of the murderer's identity and of the secret of his trick of appearing and disappearing unseen. Since a policeman himself had fallen a victim, denunciations of the force had ceased, and the unknown was now invested with a cloak of legend. Men eyed other men, as though thinking: It might be *him*. It might be *him*. They were no longer looking for a man who had the air of a Madame Tussaud murderer; they were looking for a man, or perhaps some harridan woman, who had done these particular murders. Their thoughts ran mainly on the foreign set. Such ruffianism could scarcely belong to England, nor could the bewildering cleverness of the thing. So they turned to Rumanian gypsies and Turkish carpet-sellers. There, clearly, would be found the 'warm' spot. These Eastern fellows – they knew all sorts of tricks, and they had no real religion – nothing to hold them within bounds. Sailors returning from those parts had told tales of conjurors who made themselves invisible; and there were tales of Egyptian and Arab potions that were used for abysmally queer purposes. Perhaps it *was* possible to them; you never knew. They were so slick and cunning, and they had such gliding movements; no Englishman could melt away as they could. Almost certainly the murderer would be found to be one of that sort – with some dark trick of his own – and just because they were sure that he *was* a magician, they felt that it was useless to look for him. He was a power, able to hold them in subjection and to hold himself untouchable. Superstition, which so easily cracks the frail shell of reason, had got into them. He could do anything he chose; he would never be discovered. These two points they settled, and they went about the streets in a mood of resentful fatalism.

They talked of their ideas to the journalist in half-tones, looking right and left as though *HE* might overhear them and visit them. And though all the district was thinking of him and ready to pounce upon him, yet, so strongly had he worked upon them, that if any man in the street – say, a small man of commonplace features and form – had cried '*I* am the monster!' would their stifled fury have broken into flood and have borne him down and engulfed him? Or would they not suddenly have seen something unearthly in that everyday face and figure, something unearthly about his hat, something that marked him as one whom none of their weapons could alarm or pierce? And would they not momentarily have fallen back from this devil, as the devil fell back from the cross made by the sword of Faust, and so have given him time to escape? I do not know; but so fixed was their belief in his invincibility that it is at least likely that they would have made this hesitation, had such an occasion arisen. But it never did. Today

218

THE HANDS OF MR OTTERMOLE

this commonplace fellow, his murder-lust glutted, is still seen and observed among them as he was seen and observed all the time; but because nobody then dreamt, or now dreams, that he was what he was, they observed him then, and observe him now, as people observe a lamp-post.

Almost was their belief in his invincibility justified; for five days after the murder of the policeman Petersen, when the experience and inspiration of the whole detective force of London were turned towards his identification and capture, he made his fourth and fifth strokes.

At nine o'clock that evening, the young newspaper man, who hung about every night until his paper was away, was strolling along Richards Lane. Richards Lane is a narrow street, partly a stall-market, and partly residential. The young man was in the residential section, which carries on one side small working-class cottages, and on the other the wall of a railway goods yard. The great wall hung a blanket of shadow over the lane, and the shadow and the cadaverous outline of the now deserted market stalls gave it the appearance of a living lane that had been turned to frost in the moment between breath and death. The very lamps, that elsewhere were nimbuses of gold, had here the rigidity of gems. The journalist, feeling this message of frozen eternity, was telling himself that he was tired of the whole thing, when in one stroke the frost was broken. In the moment between one pace and another silence and darkness were racked by a high scream and through the scream a voice: 'Help! help! *He's here!*'

Before he could think what movement to make, the lane came to life. As though its invisible populace had been waiting on that cry, the door of every cottage was flung open, and from them and from the alleys poured shadowy figures bent in question-mark form. For a second or so they stood as rigid as the lamps; then a police whistle gave them direction, and the flock of shadows sloped up the street. The journalist followed them, and others followed him. From the main street and from surrounding streets they came, some risen from unfinished suppers, some disturbed in their ease of slippers and shirt sleeves, some stumbling on infirm limbs, and some upright, and armed with pokers or the tools of their trade. Here and there above the wavering cloud of heads moved the bold helmets of policemen. In one dim mass they surged upon a cottage whose doorway was marked by the sergeant and two constables; and voices of those behind urged them on with 'Get in! Find him! Run round the back! Over the wall!' and those in front cried: 'Keep back! Keep back!'

And now the fury of a mob held in thrall by unknown peril broke loose. He was here – on the spot. Surely this time he *could not* escape. All minds were bent upon the cottage; all energies thrust towards its doors and windows and roof; all thought was turned upon one unknown man and his extermination. So that no one man saw any other man. No man saw the narrow, packed lane and the mass of struggling shadows, and all forgot to look among themselves for the monster who never lingered upon his victims. All forgot, indeed, that they, by their mass crusade of vengeance, were affording him the perfect hiding-place. They saw only the house, and they heard only the rending of woodwork and the smash of glass at back and front, and the police giving orders or crying with the chase; and they pressed on.

But they found no murderer. All they found was news of murder and a glimpse of the ambulance, and for their fury there was no other object than the police themselves, who fought against this hampering of their work.

The journalist managed to struggle through to the cottage door, and to get the story from the constable stationed there. The cottage was the home of a pensioned sailor and his wife and daughter. They had been at supper, and at first it appeared that some noxious gas had smitten all three in mid-action. The daughter lay dead on the hearthrug, with a piece of bread and butter in her hand. The father had fallen sideways from his chair, leaving on his plate a filled spoon of rice-pudding. The mother lay half under the table, her lap filled with the pieces of a broken cup and splashes of cocoa. But in three seconds the idea of gas was dismissed. One glance at their necks showed that this was the Strangler again; and the police stood and looked at the room and momentarily shared the fatalism of the public. They were helpless.

This was his fourth visit, making seven murders in all. He was to do, as you know, one more – and to do it that night; and then he was to pass into history as the unknown London horror, and return to the decent life that he had always led, remembering little of what he had done, and worried not at all by the memory. Why did he stop? Impossible to say. Why did he begin? Impossible again. It just happened like that; and if he thinks at all of those days and nights, I surmise that he thinks of them as we think of foolish or dirty little sins that we committed in childhood. We say that they were not really sins, because we were not then consciously ourselves: we had not come to realization; and we look back at that foolish little creature that we once were, and forgive him because he didn't know. So, I think, with this man.

There are plenty like him. Eugene Aram, after the murder of Daniel Clark, lived a quiet, contented life for fourteen years, unhaunted by his crime and unshaken in his self-esteem. Dr Crippen murdered his wife, and then lived pleasantly with his mistress in the house under whose floor he had buried his wife. Constance Kent, found Not Guilty of the murder of her young brother, led a peaceful life for five years before she confessed. George Joseph Smith and William Palmer lived amiably among their fellows untroubled by fear or by remorse for their poisonings and drownings. Charles Peace, at the time he made his one unfortunate essay, had settled down into a respectable citizen with an interest in antiques. It happened that, after a lapse of time, these men were discovered, but more murderers than we guess are living decent lives today, and will die in decency, undiscovered and unsuspected. As this man will.

But he had a narrow escape, and it was perhaps this narrow escape that brought him to a stop. The escape was due to an error of judgment on the part of the journalist.

As soon as he had the full story of the affair, which took some time, he spent fifteen minutes on the telephone, sending the story through, and at the end of the fifteen minutes, when the stimulus of the business had left him, he felt physically tired and mentally dishevelled. He was not yet free to go home; the paper would not go away for another hour; so he turned into a bar for a drink and some sandwiches.

It was then, when he had dismissed the whole business from his mind, and he was looking about the bar and admiring the landlord's taste in watch-chains and his air of domination, and was thinking that the landlord of a well-conducted tavern had a more comfortable life than a newspaper man, that his mind received from nowhere a spark of light. He was not thinking about the Strangling Horrors; his mind was on his sandwich. As a public-house sandwich, it was a curiosity. The bread had been thinly cut, it was buttered, and the ham was not two months stale; it was ham as it should be. His mind turned to the inventor of this refreshment, the Earl of Sandwich, and then to George the Fourth, and then to the Georges, and then to the legend of that George who was worried to know how the apple got into the apple-dumpling. He wondered whether George would have been equally puzzled to know how the ham got into the ham sandwich, and how long it would have been before it occurred to him that the ham could not have got there unless somebody had put it there. He got up to order another sandwich, and in that moment a little active corner of his mind settled the affair. If there was ham in his sandwich, somebody must have put it there. If seven people had been murdered, somebody must have been there to murder them. There was no aeroplane or automobile that would go into a man's pocket; therefore that somebody must have escaped either by running away or standing still; and again therefore –

He was visualizing the front page story that his paper would carry if

221

his theory were correct, and if – a matter of conjecture – his editor had the necessary nerve to make a bold stroke, when a cry of 'Time, gentleman, please! All out!' reminded him of the hour. He got up and went out into a world of mist, broken by the ragged disks of roadside puddles and the streaming lightning of motor buses. He was certain that he had *the* story, but, even if it were proved, he was doubtful whether the policy of his paper would permit him to print it. It had one great fault. It was truth, but it was impossible truth. It rocked the foundations of everything that newspaper readers believed and that newspaper editors helped them to believe. They might believe that Turkish carpet-sellers had the gift of making themselves invisible. They would not believe this.

As it happened, they were not asked to, for the story was never written. As his paper had by now gone away, and as he was nourished by his refreshment and stimulated by his theory, he thought he might put in an extra half-hour by testing that theory. So he began to look about for the man he had in mind – a man with white hair, and large white hands; otherwise an everyday figure whom nobody would look twice at. He wanted to spring his idea on this man without warning, and he was going to place himself within reach of a man armoured in legends of dreadfulness and grue. This might appear to be an act of supreme courage – that one man, with no hope of immediate outside support, should place himself at the mercy of one who was holding a whole parish in terror. But it wasn't. He didn't think about the risk. He didn't think about his duty to his employers or loyalty to his paper. He was moved simply by an instinct to follow a story to its end.

He walked slowly from the tavern and crossed into Fingal Street, making for Deever Market, where he had hope of finding his man. But his journey was shortened. At the corner of Lotus Street he saw him – or a man who looked like him. This street was poorly lit, and he could see little of the man; but he *could* see white hands. For some twenty paces he stalked him; then drew level with him; and at a point where the arch of a railway crossed the street, he was sure that this was his man. He approached him with the current conversational phrase of the district: 'Well, seen anything of the murderer?' The man stopped to look sharply at him; then, satisfied that the journalist was not the murderer, said:

'Eh? No, nor's anybody else, curse it. Doubt if they ever will.'

'I don't know. I've been thinking about them, and I've got an idea.'

'So?'

'Yes. Came to me all of a sudden. Quarter of an hour ago. And I'd felt that we'd all been blind. It's been staring us in the face.'

The man turned again to look at him, and the look and the movement held suspicion of this man who seemed to know so much. 'Oh? Has it?

222

Well, if you're so sure, why not give us the benefit of it?'

'I'm going to.' They walked level, and were nearly at the end of the little street where it meets Deever Market, when the journalist turned casually to the man. He put a finger on his arm. 'Yes, it seems to me quite simple now. But there's still one point I don't understand. One little thing I'd like to clear up. I mean the motive. Now, as man to man, tell me, Sergeant Ottermole, just *why* did you kill those inoffensive people?'

The sergeant stopped, and the journalist stopped. There was just enough light from the sky, which held the reflected light of the continent of London, to give him a sight of the sergeant's face, and the sergeant's face was turned to him with a wide smile of such urbanity and charm that the journalist's eyes were frozen as they met it. The smile stayed for some seconds. Then said the sergeant: 'Well, to tell you the truth, Mister Newspaper Man, I don't know. I really don't know. In fact, I've been worried about it myself. But I've got an idea – just like you. Everybody knows that we can't control the workings of our minds. Don't they? Ideas come into our minds without asking. But everybody's supposed to be able to control his body. Why? Eh? We get our minds from lord-knows-where – from people who were dead hundreds of years before we were born. Mayn't we get our bodies in the same way? Our faces – our legs – our heads – they aren't completely ours. We don't make 'em. They come to us. And couldn't ideas come into our bodies like ideas come into our minds? Eh? Can't ideas live in nerve and muscle as well as brain? Couldn't it be that parts of our bodies aren't really us, and couldn't ideas come into those parts all of a sudden, like ideas come into – into' – he shot his arms out, showing the great white-gloved hands and hairy wrists; shot them out so swiftly to the journalist's throat that his eyes never saw them – 'into *my hands*.'

You Got to Have Brains

ROBERT BLOCH

MUST HAVE BEEN ABOUT a year ago, give or take a month when Mr Goofy first showed up here on the street.

We get all kinds here, you know – thousands of bums and winos floating in and out every day of the year. Nobody knows where they come from and nobody cares where they go. They sleep in flophouses, sleep in bars, and in doorways – sleep right out in the gutter if you let 'em. Just so's they get their kicks. Wine jags, shot-an'-beers, canned heat, reefers – there was one guy, he used to go around and bust up thermometers and drink the juice, so help me!

When you work behind the bar, like me, you get so you hardly notice people any more. But this Mr Goofy was different.

He came in one night in winter, and the joint was almost empty. Most of the regulars, right after New Year's, they get themselves jugged and do ninety. Keeps 'em out of the cold.

So it was quiet when Mr Goofy showed up, around supper time. He didn't come to the bar, even though he was all alone. He headed straight for a back booth, plunks down, and asked Ferd for a couple of hamburgers. That's when I noticed him.

What's so screwy about that? Well, it's because he was lugging about ten or fifteen pounds of scrap metal with him, that's why. He banged it down in the booth alongside him and sat there with his hands held over it like he was one of them guards at Fort Knox or wherever.

I mean, he had all this here dirty scrap metal – tin and steel and twisted old engine parts covered with mud. He must have dug it out of the dumps around Canal Street, some place like that. So when I got a chance I come down to this end of the bar and looked this character over. He sure was a sad one.

He was only about five feet high and weighed about a hunnerd pounds, just a little dried-up futz of a guy. He had a kind of bald head and he wore old twisted-up glasses with the ear-pieces all bent, and he had trouble with the hamburgers on account of his false choppers. He was dressed in them War Surplus things – leftovers from World War I, yet. And a cap.

224

Go out on the street right now and you'll see plenty more just like him, but Mr Goofy was different. Because he was clean. Sure, he looked beat-up, but even his old duds was neat.

Another thing. While he waited for the hamburgers he kept writing stuff. He had this here pencil and notebook out and he was scribbling away for dear life. I got the idea he was figuring out some kind of arithametics.

Well, I was all set to ask him the score when somebody come in and I got busy. It happens that way; next thing I know the whole place was crowded and I forgot all about Mr Goofy for maybe two hours. Then I happened to look over and by gawd if he ain't still sitting there, with that pencil going like crazy!

Only by this time the old juke is blasting, and he kind of frowns and takes his time like he didn't care for music but was, you know, concentrated on his figures, like.

He sees me watching him and wiggles his fingers like so, and I went over there and he says, 'Pardon me – but could you lower the volume of that instrument?'

Just like that he says it, with a kind of funny accent I can't place. But real polite and fancy for a foreigner.

So I says, 'Sure, I'll switch it down a little.' I went over and fiddled with the control to cut it down, like we do late at night.

But just then Stakowsky come up to me. This Stakowsky used to be a wheel on the street – owned two-three flop-houses and fleabag hotels, and he comes in regular to get loaded. He was kind of mean, but a good spender.

Well, Stakowsky come up and he stuck his big red face over the bar and yelled. 'Whassa big idea, Jack? I puts in my nickel, I wanna hear my piece. You wanna busted nose or something?'

Like I say, he was a mean type.

I didn't know right off what to tell him, but it turned out I didn't have to tell him nothing. Because the little guy in the booth stood up and he tapped Stakowsky on the shoulder and said, real quiet, 'Pardon me, but it was I who requested that the music be made softer.'

Stakowsky turned around and he said, 'Yeah? And who in hell you think you are – somebody?'

The little guy said, 'You know me. I rented the top of the loft from you yesterday.'

Stakowsky looks at him again and then says, 'Awright. So you rent. So you pay a month advance. Awright. But that ain't got to do with how I play music. I want it should be turned up, so me and my friends can hear it good.'

By this time the number is over and half the bar has come down to get in on the deal. They was all standing around waiting for the next pitch.

The little guy says, 'You don't understand, Mr Stakowsky. It happens I am doing some very important work and require freedom from distraction.'

I bet Stakowsky never heard no two-dollar words before. He got redder and redder and at last he says, 'You don't understand so good, neither. You wanna figure, go by your loft. Now I turn up the music. Are you gonna try and stop me?' And he takes a swipe at the little futz with his fist.

Little guy never batted an eye. He just sort of ducked, and when he come up again he had a shiv in his hand. But it wasn't no regular shiv, and it wasn't nothing he found in no junk-heap.

This one was about a foot long, and sharp. The blade was sharp and the tip was sharp, and the little guy didn't look like he was just gonna give Stakowsky a shave with it.

Stakowsky, he didn't think so either. He whitened up fast and backed away to the bar and says, 'All right, all right,' over and over again.

It happened all in a minute, and then the knife was gone and the little guy picked up his scrap metal and walked out without even looking back once.

Then everybody was hollering, and I poured Stakowsky a fast double, and then another. Of course he made off like he hadn't been scared and he talked plenty loud – but we all knew.

'Goofy,' he says. 'That's who he is. Mr Goofy. Sure, he rents from me. You know, by the Palace Rooms, where I live. He rents the top – a great big loft up there. Comes yesterday, a month rent in advance he pays too. I tell him, "Mister, you're goofy. What do you want with such a big empty loft? A loft ain't no good in winter, unless you want to freeze. Why you don't take a nice warm room downstairs by the steam heat?" But no, he wants the loft, and I should put up a cot for him. So I do, and he moves in last night.'

Stakowsky got red in the face. 'All day today that Mr Goofy, he's bringing up his crazy outfits. Iron and busted machinery. Stuff like that. I ask him what he's doing and he says he's building. I ask him what he's building and he says – well, he just don't say. You saw how he acted tonight? Now you know. He's goofy in the head. I ain't afraid of no guys, but those crazy ones you got to watch out for. Lofts and machinery and knives – you ever hear anything like that Mr Goofy?'

So that's how he got his name. And I remembered him. One of the reasons was, I was staying at the Palace Rooms myself. Not in the flops, but a nice place on the third floor, right next to Stakowsky's room. And right upstairs from us was this loft. An attic, like. I never went up there, but there were stairs in back.

The next couple of days I kept my eyes open, figuring on seeing Mr Goofy again. But I didn't. All I did was hear him. Nights, he kept banging and pounding away, him and his scrap metal or whatever it was, and he moved stuff across the floor. Me, I'm a pretty sound sleeper and Stakowsky was always loaded when he turned in, so it didn't bother him neither. But Mr Goofy never seemed to sleep. He was always working up there. And on what?

I couldn't figure it out. Day after day he'd come in and out with some more metal. I don't know where he got it all, but he must have lugged up a couple of thousand pounds, ten or fifteen each trip. It got to bothering me because he was the sort of a mystery you feel you've got to know more about.

Next time I saw him was when he started coming into the place regular, to eat. And always he had the pencil and notebook with him. He took the same booth every night – and nobody bothered him with loud music after the story got around about him and his shiv.

He'd just sit there and figure and mumble to himself and walk out again, and pretty soon they were making up all kinds of stories about the guy.

Some said he was a Red on account of that accent, you know, and he was building one of them there atomic bombs. One of the winos says no, he passed the place one night about 4 am and he heard a big clank like machinery working. He figured Mr Goofy was a counterfitter. Which was the kind of crazy idea you'd expect from a wino.

Anyways, the closest anybody come was Manny Schreiber from the hock shop, and he guessed Goofy was a inventor and maybe he was building a rowbot. You know, a rowbot, like in these scientist magazines. Mechanical men, they run by machinery.

One day, about an hour before I went on shift, I was sitting in my room when Stakowsky knocked on the door. 'Come on,' he says. 'Mr Goofy just went out. I'm gonna take a look around up there.'

Well, I didn't care one way or the other. Stakowsky, he was the landlord, and I figured he had a right. So we sneaked up and he used his key and we went inside the loft.

It was a big barn of a place with a cot in the corner. Next to the cot was a table with a lot of notes piled up, and maybe twenty-five or thirty books. Foreign books they were, and I couldn't make out the names. In the other corners there were piles of scrap metal and what looked like a bunch of old radio sets from a repair shop.

And in the center of the room was this machine. At least, it looked like a machine, even though it must have been thirty feet long. It was higher than my head, too. And there was a door in it, and you could get inside the machinery that was all tangled up on the sides and sit

227

down in a chair. In front of the chair was a big board with a lot of switches on it.

And everywhere was gears and pistons and coils and even glass tubes. Where he picked up all that stuff, I dunno. But he'd patched it all together somehow and when you looked at it – it made sense. I mean, you could tell the machine would do something, if you could only figure out what.

Stakowsky looked at me and I looked at him and we both looked at the machine.

'That Mr Goofy!' says Stakowsky. 'He does all this in a month. You know something, Jack?'

'What?' I says.

'You tell anybody else and I'll kill you. But I'm scared to even come near Mr Goofy. This machine of his, I don't like it. Tomorrow his month is up. I'm going to tell him he should move. Get out. I don't want crazy people around here.'

'But how'll he move this thing out?'

'I don't care how. Tomorrow he gets the word. And I'm going to have Lippy and Stan and the boys here. He don't pull no knife on me again. Out he goes.'

We went downstairs and I went to work. All night long I tried to figure that machine of his. There wasn't much else to do, because there was a real blizzard going and nobody came in.

I kept remembering the way the machine looked. It had a sort of framework running around the outside, and if it got covered over with some metal it would be like a submarine or one of them rockets. And there was a part inside, where a big glass globe connected up to some wires leading to the switchboard, or whatever it was. And a guy could sit in there. It all made some kind of crazy sense.

I sat there, thinking it over, until along about midnight. Then Mr Goofy came in.

This time he didn't head for his booth. He come right up to the bar and sat down on a stool. His face was red, and he brushed snow off his coat. But he looked happy.

'Do you have any decent brandy?' he asked.

'I think so,' I told him. I found a bottle and opened it up.

'Will you be good enough to have a drink with me?'

'Sure, thanks.' I looked at him. 'Celebrating?'

'That's right,' says Mr Goofy. 'This is a great occasion. My work is finished. Tonight I put on the sheaths. Now I am almost ready to demonstrate.'

'Demonstrate what?'

Well, he dummied up on me right away. I poured him another drink and another, and he just sat there grinning. Then he sort of loosened up. That brandy was plenty powerful.

'Look,' he says. 'I will tell you all about it. You have been kind to me, and I can trust you. Besides, it is good to share a moment of triumph.'

He says, 'So long I have worked, but soon they will not laugh at me any more. Soon the smart Americans, the men over here who call themselves Professors, will take note of my work. They did not believe me when I offered to show them my plans. They would not accept my basic theory. But I knew I was right. I knew I could do it. Part of it must be mechanical, yes. But the most important part is the mind itself. You know what I told them? To do this, and to do it right, you've got to have brains.'

He sort of chuckled, and poured another drink. 'Yes. That is the whole secret. More than anything else, you need brains. Not mechanical formula alone. But when I spoke of harnessing the mind, powering it with mental energy rather than physical, they laughed. Now we'll see.'

I brought myself a drink, and I guess he realized I wasn't in on the pitch, because he says, 'You don't understand, do you?'

I shook my head.

'What would you say, my friend, if I told you I have just successfully completed the construction of the first practical space-ship?'

Oh-oh, I thought to myself. Mr Goofy!

'But not a model, not a theory in metal – an actual, practical machine for travel to the moon?'

Mr Goofy and his knife, I thought. Making a crazy thing out of old scrap iron. Mr Goofy!

'If I wish, I can go tonight,' he said. 'Or tomorrow. Any time. No astronomy. No calculus. Mental energy is the secret. Harness the machinery to a human brain and it will be guided automatically to its destination in a moment, if properly controlled. That's all it takes – a single instant. Long enough to direct the potential energy of the cortex.'

Maybe you think it's funny the way I can remember all those big words, but I'll never forget anything Mr Goofy said.

And he told me, 'Who has ever estimated the power of the human brain – its unexploited capacity for performance? Using the machine for autohypnosis, the brain is capable of tremendous effort. The electrical impulses can be stepped up, magnified ten millionfold. Atomic energy is insignificant in comparison. Now do you see what I have achieved?'

I thought about it for a minute or so – him sitting there all steamed up over his dizzy junk heap. Then I remembered what was happening to him tomorrow.

I just didn't have the heart to let him go on and on about how his life-work was realized, and how he'd be famous in Europe and America and he'd reach the moon and all that crud. I didn't have the heart. He was so little and so whacky. Mr Goofy!

So I says, 'Look, I got to tell you something. Stakowsky, he's bouncing you out tomorrow. That's right. He's gonna kick you and your machine into the street. He says he can't stand it around.'

'Machine?' says Mr Goofy. 'What does he know of my machine?'

Well, I had to tell him then. I had to. About how we went upstairs and looked.

'Before the sheath was on, you saw?' he asked.

'That's the way it was,' I told him. 'I saw it, and so did Stakowsky. And he'll kick you out.'

'But he cannot! I mean, I chose this spot carefully, so I could work unobserved. I need privacy. And I cannot move the ship now. I must bring people to see it when I make the announcement. I must make the special arrangements for the tests. It is a very delicate matter. Doesn't he understand? He'll be famous, too, because of what happened in his miserable hole of a place –'

'He's probably famous tonight,' I said. 'I'll bet he's down the street somewheres right now, babbling about you and your machine, and how he's gonna toss you out.'

Mr Goofy looked so sad I tried to make a joke. 'What's the matter with you? You say yourself it works by brain power. So use your brain and move it some place else. Huh?'

He looked even sadder. 'Don't you realize it is designed only for space-travel? And properly, my brain must be free to act as the control agent. Still, you are right about that man. He is a wicked person, and he hates me. I must do something. I wonder if –'

Then you know what he does, this Mr Goofy? He whips out his pencil and notebook and starts figuring. Just sits there and scribbles away. And he says, 'Yes, it is possible. Change the wires leading to the controls. It is only a matter of a few moments. And what better proof could I ask than an actual demonstration? Yes. It is fated to be this way. Good.'

Then he stood up and stuck out his mitt. 'Good-by, Jack,' he says. 'And thank you for your suggestion.'

'What suggestion?'

But he doesn't answer me, and then he's out of the door and gone.

I closed up the joint about 1.30. The boss wasn't around and I figured what the hell, it was a blizzard.

There was nobody out on the street this time of night, not with the wind off the lake and the snow coming down about a foot a minute. I couldn't see in front of my face.

I crossed the street in front of the Palace Rooms – it must have been quarter to two or thereabouts – and all of a sudden it happened.

Whoom!

Like that it goes, a big loud blast you can hear even over the wind and the blizzard. On account of the snow being so thick I couldn't see nothing. But let me tell you. I sure heard it.

At first I thought maybe it was some kind of explosion, so I quick run across to the Palace and up the stairs. All the winos in the flops was asleep – those guys, they get a jag on and they'll sleep even if you set fire to the mattress. But I had to find out if anything was wrong.

I didn't smell no smoke and my room was okay, and it was all quiet in the hall. Except the back door leading to the attic was open, and the air was cold.

Right away I figured maybe Mr Goofy had pulled something off, so I ran up the stairs. And I saw it.

Mr Goofy was gone. The junk was still scattered all over the room, but he'd burned all his notes and he was gone. The great big machine, or spaceship, or whatever it was – that was gone, too.

How'd he get it out of the room and where did he take it? You can search me, brother.

All I know is there was a big charred spot burned away in the center of the floor where the machine had stood. And right above there was a big round hole punched smack through the roof of the loft.

So help me, I just stood there. What else could I do? Mr Goofy said he built a spaceship that could take him to the moon. He said he could go there in a flash, just like that. He said all it took was brains.

And what do I know about this here autohypnosis deal, or whatever he called it, and about electricity-energy, and force fields, and all that stuff?

He was gone. The machine or ship was gone. And there was this awful hole in the roof. That's all I knew.

Maybe Stakowsky would know the rest. It was worth a try, anyhow. So I run down to Stakowsky's room.

After that, things didn't go so good.

The cops started to push me around when they got there, and if it hadn't been for my boss putting the old pressure on, they'd have given me a real rough time. But they could see I was sorta like out of my head – and I was, too, for about a week.

I kept yelling about this Mr Goofy and his crazy invention and his big knife and his trip to the moon, and it didn't make no sense to the cops. Of course, nothing ever made any sense to them, and they had to drop the whole case – hush it up. The whole thing was too screwy to

231

ever let leak out.

Anyhow, I felt rugged until I moved out of the Palace Rooms and got back to work. Now I scarcely ever think about Mr Goofy any more, or Stakowsky – or the whole cockeyed mess.

I don't like to think about the mess.

The mess was when I ran down the stairs that night and looked for Stakowsky in his room. He was there all right, but he didn't care about Goofy or the trip to the moon or the hole in his loft roof either.

Because he was very, very dead.

And Mr Goofy's foot-long knife was laying right next to him on the bed. So that part was easy to figure out. Mr Goofy come right back there from the tavern, and he killed him.

But after that?

After that, your guess is as good as mine. The cops never found out a bit – not even Mr Goofy's real name, or where he came from, or where he got this here theory about spaceships and power to run them.

Did he really have a invention that would take him to the moon? Could he change some wires and controls and just scoot off through the roof with his mental energy hooked up?

Nobody knows. Nobody ever will know. But I can tell you this.

There was a mess, one awful mess, in Stakowsky's room. Mr Goofy must have taken his knife and gone to work on Stakowsky's head. There was nothing left on top but a big round hole, and it was empty.

Stakowsky's head was empty.

Mr Goofy took out what was inside and fixed his machine and went to the moon.

That's all.

Like Mr Goofy says, you got to have brains . . .

How the Third Floor Knew the Potteries

AMELIA B. EDWARDS

I AM A PLAIN MAN, MAJOR, and you may not dislike to hear a plain statement of facts from me. Some of those facts lie beyond my understanding. I do not pretend to explain them. I only know that they happened as I relate them, and that I pledge myself for the truth of every word of them.

I began life roughly, down among the Potteries. I was an orphan; and my earliest recollections are of a great porcelain manufactory in the country of the Potteries, where I helped about the yard, picked up what halfpence fell in my way, and slept in a harness-loft over the stable. Those were hard times; but things bettered themselves as I grew older and stronger, especially after George Barnard had come to be foreman of the yard.

George Barnard was a Wesleyan – we were mostly dissenters in the Potteries – sober, clear-headed, somewhat sulky and silent, but a good fellow every inch of him, and my best friend at the time when I most needed a good friend. He took me out of the yard, and set me to the furnace-work. He entered me on the books at a fixed rate of wages. He helped me to pay for a little cheap schooling four nights a week; and he led me to go with him on Sundays to the chapel down by the river-side, where I first saw Leah Payne. She was his sweetheart, and so pretty that I used to forget the preacher and everybody else, when I looked at her. When she joined in the singing, I heard no voice but hers. If she asked me for the hymn-book, I used to blush and tremble. I believe I worshipped her, in my stupid ignorant way; and I think I worshipped Barnard almost as blindly, though after a different fashion. I felt I owed him everything. I knew that he had saved me, body and mind; and I looked up to him as a savage might look up to a missionary.

Leah was the daughter of a plumber, who lived close by the chapel. She was twenty, and George about seven or eight-and-thirty. Some captious folks said there was too much difference in their ages; but she was so serious-minded, and they loved each other so earnestly and quietly, that, if nothing had come between them during their courtship, I don't believe the question of disparity would ever have

233

troubled the happiness of their married lives. Something did come, however; and that something was a Frenchman, called Louis Laroche. He was a painter on porcelain, from the famous works at Sèvres; and our master, it was said, had engaged him for three years certain, at such wages as none of our own people, however skilful, could hope to command. It was about the beginning or middle of September when he first came among us. He looked very young; was small, dark, and well made; had little white soft hands, and a silky moustache; and spoke English nearly as well as I do. None of us liked him; but that was only natural, seeing how he was put over the head of every Englishman in the place. Besides, though he was always smiling and civil, we couldn't help seeing that he thought himself ever so much better than the rest of us; and that was not pleasant. Neither was it pleasant to see him strolling about the town, dressed just like a gentleman, when working hours were over; smoking good cigars, when we were forced to be content with a pipe of common tobacco; hiring a horse on Sunday afternoons, when we were trudging a-foot; and taking his pleasure as if the world was made for him to enjoy, and us to work in.

'Ben, boy,' said George, 'there's something wrong about that Frenchman.'

It was on a Saturday afternoon, and we were sitting on a pile of empty seggars against the door of my furnace-room, waiting till the men should all have cleared out of the yard. Seggars are deep earthen boxes in which the pottery is put, while being fired in the kiln.

I looked up, inquiringly.

'About the Count?' said I, for that was the nickname by which he went in the pottery.

George nodded, and paused for a moment with his chin resting on his palms.

'He has an evil eye,' said he; 'and a false smile. Something wrong about him.'

I drew nearer, and listened to George as if he had been an oracle.

'Besides,' added he, in his slow quiet way, with his eyes fixed straight before him as if he was thinking aloud, 'there's a young look about him that isn't natural. Take him just at sight, and you'd think he was almost a boy; but look close at him – see the little fine wrinkles under his eyes, and the hard lines about his mouth, and then tell me his age, if you can! Why, Ben, boy, he's as old as I am, pretty near; ay, and as strong, too. You stare; but I tell you that, slight as he looks, he could fling you over his shoulder as if you were a feather. And as for his hands, little and white as they are, there are muscles of iron inside them, take my word for it.'

'But, George, how can you know?'

'Because I have a warning against him,' replied George, very gravely. 'Because, whenever he is by, I feel as if my eyes saw clearer, and my ears heard keener, than at other times. Maybe it's presumption, but I sometimes feel as if I had to call to guard myself and others against him. Look at the children, Ben, how they shrink away from him; and see there, now! Ask Captain what he thinks of him! Ben, that dog likes him no better than I do.'

I looked, and saw Captain crouching by his kennel with his ears laid back, growling audibly, as the Frenchman came slowly down the steps leading from his own workshop at the upper end of the yard. On the last step he paused; lighted a cigar; glanced round, as if to see whether anyone was by; and then walked straight over to within a couple of yards of the kennel. Captain gave a short angry snarl, and laid his muzzle close down upon his paws, ready for a spring. The Frenchman folded his arms deliberately, fixed his eyes on the dog, and stood calmly smoking. He knew exactly how far he dared go, and kept just that one foot out of harm's way. All at once he stopped, puffed a mouthful of smoke in the dog's eyes, burst into a mocking laugh, turned lightly on his heel, and walked away; leaving Captain straining at his chain, and barking after him like a mad creature.

Days went by, and I, at work in my own department, saw no more of the Count. Sunday came – the third, I think, after I had talked with George in the yard. Going with George to chapel, as usual, in the morning, I noticed that there was something strange and anxious in his face, and that he scarcely opened his lips to me on the way. Still I said nothing. It was not my place to question him; and I remember thinking to myself that the cloud would all clear off as soon as he found himself by Leah's side, holding the same book, and joining in the same hymn. It did not, however, for no Leah was there. I looked every moment to the door, expecting to see her sweet face coming in; but George never lifted his eyes from his book, or seemed to notice that her place was empty. Thus the whole service went by, and my thoughts wandered continually from the words of the preacher. As soon as the last blessing was spoken, and we were fairly across the threshold, I turned to George, and asked if Leah was ill?

'No,' said he, gloomily. 'She's not ill.'

'Then why wasn't she –?'

'I'll tell you why,' he interrupted, impatiently. 'Because you've seen her face here for the last time. She's never coming to chapel again.'

'Never coming to chapel again?' I faltered, laying my hand on his sleeve in the earnestness of my surprise. 'Why, George, what is the matter?'

But he shook my hand off, and stamped with his iron heel till the pavement rang again.

'Don't ask me,' said he, roughly. 'Let me alone. You'll know soon enough.'

And with this he turned off down a by-lane leading towards the hills, and left me without another word.

I had had plenty of hard treatment in my time; but never, until that moment, an angry look or syllable from George. I did not know how to bear it. That day my dinner seemed as if it would choke me; and in the afternoon I went out and wandered restlessly about the fields till the hour for evening prayers came round. I then returned to the chapel, and sat down on a tomb outside, waiting for George. I saw the congregation go in by twos and threes; I heard the first psalm-tune echo solemnly through the evening stillness; but no George came. Then the service began, and I knew that, punctual as his habits were, it was of no use to expect him any longer. Where could he be? What could have happened? Why should Leah Payne never come to chapel again? Had she gone over to some other sect, and was that why George seemed so unhappy?

Sitting there in the little dreary churchyard with the darkness fast gathering around me, I asked myself these questions over and over again, till my brain ached; for I was not much used to thinking about anything in those times. At last, I could bear to sit quiet no longer. The sudden thought struck me that I would go to Leah, and learn what the matter was, from her own lips. I sprang to my feet, and set off at once towards her home.

It was quite dark, and a light rain was beginning to fall. I found the garden-gate open, and a quick hope flashed across me that George might be there. I drew back for a moment, hesitating whether to knock or ring, when a sound of voices in the passage, and the sudden gleaming of a bright line of light under the door, warned me that someone was coming out. Taken by surprise, and quite unprepared for the moment with anything to say, I shrank back behind the porch, and waited until those within should have passed out. The door opened, and the light streamed suddenly upon the roses and the wet gravel.

'It rains,' said Leah, bending forward and shading the candle with her hand.

'And is as cold as Siberia,' added another voice, which was not George's, and yet sounded strangely familiar. 'Ugh! what a climate for such a flower to bloom in!'

'Is it so much finer in France?' asked Leah softly.

'As much finer as blue skies and sunshine can make it. Why, my angel, even your bright eyes will be ten times brighter, and your rosy cheeks ten times rosier, when they are transplanted to Paris. Ah! I can give you no idea of the wonders of Paris – the broad streets planted with trees, the palaces, the shops, the gardens! – it is a city of enchantment.'

'It must be, indeed!' said Leah. 'And you will really take me to see all those beautiful shops?'

'Every Sunday, my darling – Bah! don't look so shocked. The shops in Paris are always open on Sunday, and everybody makes holiday. You will soon get over these prejudices.'

'I fear it is very wrong to take so much pleasure in the things of this world,' sighed Leah.

The Frenchman laughed, and answered her with a kiss.

'Good night, my sweet little saint!' and he ran lightly down the path, and disappeared in the darkness. Leah sighed again, lingered a moment, and then closed the door.

Stupefied and bewildered, I stood for some seconds like a stone statue, unable to move; scarcely able to think. At length, I roused myself, as it were mechanically, and went towards the gate. At that instant a heavy hand was laid upon my shoulder, and a hoarse voice close beside my ear, said:

'Who are you? What are you doing here?'

It was George. I knew him at once, in spite of the darkness, and stammered his name. He took his hand quickly from my shoulder.

'How long have you been here?' said he fiercely. 'What right have you to lurk about, like a spy in the dark? God help me, Ben – I'm half mad. I don't mean to be harsh to you.'

'I'm sure you don't,' I cried, earnestly.

'It's that cursed Frenchman,' he went on, in a voice that sounded like the groan of one in pain. 'He's a villain. I know he's a villain; and I've had a warning against him ever since the first moment he came among us. He'll make her miserable, and break her heart some day – my pretty Leah – and I loved her so! But I'll be revenged – as sure as there's a sun in heaven, I'll be revenged!'

His vehemence terrified me. I tried to persuade him to go home; but he would not listen to me.

'No, no,' he said. 'Go home yourself, boy, and let me be. My blood is on fire: this rain is good for me, and I am better alone.'

'If I could only do something to help you –'

'You can't,' interrupted he. 'Nobody can help me. I'm a ruined man, and I don't care what becomes of me. The Lord forgive me! my heart is full of wickedness, and my thoughts are the promptings of Satan. There go – for Heaven's sake, go. I don't know what I say, or what I do!'

I went, for I did not dare refuse any longer; but I lingered a while at the corner of the street, and watched him pacing to and fro, to and fro in the driving rain. At length I turned reluctantly away, and went home.

I lay awake that night for hours, thinking over the events of the day, and hating the Frenchman from my very soul. I could not hate Leah. I had worshipped her too long and too faithfully for that; but I looked upon her as a creature given over to destruction. I fell asleep towards morning, and woke again shortly after daybreak. When I reached the pottery, I found George there before me, looking very pale, but quite himself, and setting the men to their work the same as usual. I said nothing about what had happened that day before. Something in his face silenced me; but seeing him so steady and composed, I took heart, and began to hope he had fought through the worst of his trouble. By-and-by the Frenchman came through the yard, gay and off-hand, with his cigar in his mouth, and his hands in his pockets. George turned sharply away into one of the workshops, and shut the door. I drew a deep breath of relief. My dread was to see them come to an open quarrel; and I felt that as long as they kept clear of that, all would be well.

Thus the Monday went by, and the Tuesday; and still George kept aloof from me. I had sense enough not to be hurt by this. I felt he had a good right to be silent, if silence helped him to bear his trial better; and I made up my mind never to breathe another syllable on the subject, unless he began.

Wednesday came. I had overslept myself that morning, and came to work a quarter after the hour, expecting to be fined; for George was very strict as foreman of the yard, and treated friends and enemies just the same. Instead of blaming me, however, he called me up, and said:

'Ben, whose turn is it this week to sit up?'

'Mine, sir,' I replied. (I always called him 'Sir' in working hours.)

'Well, then, you may go home today, and the same on Thursday and Friday; for there's a large batch of work for the ovens tonight, and there'll be the same tomorrow night and the night after.'

'All right, sir,' said I. 'Then I'll be here by seven this evening.'

'No, half-past nine will be soon enough. I've some accounts to make up, and I shall be here myself till then. Mind you are true to time, though.'

'I'll be as true as the clock, sir,' I replied, and was turning away when he called me back again.

'You're a good lad, Ben,' said he. 'Shake hands.'

I seized his hand, and pressed it warmly.

'If I'm good for anything, George,' I answered with all my heart, 'it's you who have made me so. God bless you for it!'

'Amen!' said he, in a troubled voice, putting his hand to his hat.

And so we parted.

In general, I went to bed by day when I was attending to the firing

238

by night; but this morning I had already slept longer than usual, and wanted exercise more than rest. So I ran home; put a bit of bread and meat in my pocket; snatched up my big thorn stick; and started off for a long day in the country. When I came home it was quite dark and beginning to rain, just as it had begun to rain at about the same time that wretched Sunday evening: so I changed my wet boots, had an early supper and a nap in the chimney-corner, and went down to the works at a few minutes before half-past nine. Arriving at the factory-gate, I found it ajar, and so walked in and closed it after me. I remember thinking at the time that it was unlike George's usual caution to leave it so; but it passed from my mind next moment. Having slipped in the bolt, I then went straight over to George's little counting-house, where the gas was shining cheerfully in the window. Here also, somewhat to my surprise, I found the door open, and the room empty. I went in. The threshold and part of the floor was wetted by the driving rain. The wages-book was open on the desk, George's pen stood in the ink, and his hat hung on its usual peg in the corner. I concluded, of course, that he had gone round to the ovens; so, following him, I took down his hat and carried it with me, for it was now raining fast.

The baking-houses lay just opposite, on the other side of the yard. There were three of them, opening one out of the other; and in each, the great furnace filled all the middle of the room. These furnaces are, in fact, large kilns built of brick, with an oven closed in by an iron door in the centre of each, and a chimney going up through the roof. The pottery, enclosed in seggars, stands round inside on shelves, and has to be turned from time to time while the firing is going on. To turn these seggars, test the heat, and keep the fires up, was my work at the period of which I am now telling you, Major.

Well! I went through the baking-houses one after the other, and found all empty alike. Then a strange, vague, uneasy feeling came over me, and I began to wonder what could have become of George. It was possible that he might be in one of the workshops; so I ran over to the counting-house, lighted a lantern, and made a thorough survey of the yards. I tried the doors; they were all locked as usual. I peeped into the open sheds; they were all vacant. I called 'George! George!' in every part of the outer premises; but the wind and the rain drove back my voice, and no other voice replied to it. Forced at last to believe that he was really gone, I took his hat back to the counting-house, put away the wages-book, extinguished the gas, and prepared for my solitary watch.

The night was mild, and the heat in the baking-rooms intense. I knew, by experience, that the ovens had been overheated, and that none of the porcelain must go in at least for the next two hours; so I

239

carried my stool to the door, settled myself in a sheltered corner where the air could reach me, but not the rain, and fell to wondering where George could have gone, and why he should not have waited till the time appointed. That he had left in haste was clear – not because his hat remained behind, for he might have had a cap with him – but because he had left the book open, and the gas lighted. Perhaps one of the workmen had met with some accident, and he had been summoned away so urgently that he had no time to think of anything; perhaps he would even now come back presently to see that all was right before he went home to his lodgings. Turning these things over in my mind, I grew drowsy, my thoughts wandered, and I fell asleep.

I cannot tell how long my nap lasted. I had walked a great distance that day, and I slept heavily; but I awoke all in a moment, with a sort of terror upon me, and, looking up, saw George Barnard sitting on a stool before the oven door, with the firelight full upon his face.

Ashamed to be found sleeping, I started to my feet. At the same instant, he rose, turned away without even looking towards me, and went out into the next room.

'Don't be angry, George!' I cried, following him. 'None of the seggars are in. I knew the fires were too strong, and –'

The words died on my lips. I had followed him from the first room to the second, from the second to the third, and in the third – I lost him!

I could not believe my eyes. I opened the end door leading into the yard, and looked out; but he was nowhere in sight. I went round to the back of the baking-houses, looked behind the furnaces, ran over to the counting-house, called him by his name over and over again; but all was dark, silent, lonely, as ever.

Then I remembered how I had bolted the outer gate, and how impossible it was that he should have come in without ringing. Then, too, I began again to doubt the evidence of my own senses, and to think I must have been dreaming.

I went back to my old post by the door of the first baking-house, and sat down for a moment to collect my thoughts.

'In the first place,' said I to myself, 'there is but one outer gate. That outer gate I bolted on the inside, and it is bolted still. In the next place, I searched the premises, and found all the sheds empty, and the workshop-doors padlocked as usual on the outside. I proved that George was nowhere about, when I came, and I know he could not have come in since, without my knowledge. Therefore it is a dream. It is certainly a dream, and there's an end of it.'

And with this I trimmed my lantern and proceeded to test the temperature of the furnaces. We used to do this, I should tell you, by the introduction of little roughly-moulded lumps of common fire-clay.

240

If the heat is too great, they crack; if too little, they remain damp and moist; if just right, they become firm and smooth all over, and pass into the biscuit stage. Well! I took my three little lumps of clay, put one in each oven, waited while I counted five hundred, and then went round again to see the results. The two first were in capital condition, the third had flown into a dozen pieces. This proved that the seggars might at once go into ovens One and Two, but that number Three had been overheated, and must be allowed to go on cooling for an hour or two longer.

I therefore stocked One and Two with nine rows of seggars, three deep on each shelf; left the rest waiting till number Three was in a condition to be trusted; and, fearful of falling asleep again, now that the firing was in progress, walked up and down the rooms to keep myself awake. This was hot work, however, and I could not stand it very long; so I went back presently to my stool by the door, and fell to thinking about my dream. The more I thought of it, the more strangely real it seemed, and the more I felt convinced that I was actually on my feet, when I saw George get up and walk into the adjoining room. I was also certain that I had still continued to see him as he passed out of the second room into the third, and that at that time I was even following his very footsteps. Was it possible, I asked myself, that I could have been up and moving, and yet not quite awake? I had heard of people walking in their sleep. Could it be that I was walking in mine, and never waked till I reached the cool air of the yard? All this seemed likely enough, so I dismissed the matter from my mind, and passed the rest of the night in attending to the seggars, adding fresh fuel from time to time to the furnaces of the first and second ovens, and now and then taking a turn through the yards. As for number Three, it kept up its heat to such a degree that it was almost day before I dared trust the seggars to go in it.

Thus the hours went by; and at half-past seven on Thursday morning, the men came to their work. It was now my turn to go off duty, but I wanted to see George before I left, and so waited for him in the counting-house, while a lad named Steve Storr took my place at the ovens. But the clock went on from half-past seven to quarter to eight; then to eight o'clock; then to a quarter-past eight – and still George never made his appearance. At length, when the hand got round to half-past eight, I grew weary of waiting, took up my hat, ran home, went to bed, and slept profoundly until past four in the afternoon.

That evening I went down to the factory quite early; for I had a restlessness upon me, and I wanted to see George before he left for the night. This time, I found the gate bolted, and I rang for admittance.

'How early you are, Ben!' said Steve Storr, as he let me in.

'Mr Barnard's not gone?' I asked quickly; for I saw at the first glance that the gas was out in the counting-house.

'He's not gone,' said Steve, 'because he's never been.'

'Never been?'

'No: and what's stranger still, he's not been home either, since dinner yesterday.'

'But he was here last night.'

'Oh yes, he was here last night, making up the books. John Parker was with him till past six; and you found him here, didn't you, at half-past nine?'

I shook my head.

'Well, he's gone now, anyhow. Good night.'

'Good night!'

I took the lantern from his hand, bolted him out mechanically, and made my way to the baking-houses like one in a stupor. George gone? Gone without a word of warning to his employer, or of farewell to his fellow-workmen? I could not understand it. I could not believe it. I sat down bewildered, incredulous, stunned. Then came hot tears, doubts, terrifying suspicions. I remembered the wild words he had spoken a few nights back; the strange calm by which they were followed; my dream of the evening before. I had heard of men who drowned themselves for love; and the turbid Severn ran close by – so close, that one might pitch a stone into it from some of the workshop windows.

These thoughts were too horrible. I dared not dwell upon them. I turned to work, to free myself from them, if I could; and began by examining the ovens. The temperature of all was much higher than on the previous night, the heat having been gradually increased during the last twelve hours. It was now my business to keep the heat on the increase for twelve more; after which it would be allowed, as gradually, to subside, until the pottery was cool enough for removal. To turn the seggars, and add fuel to the two first furnaces, was my first work. As before, I found number Three in advance of the others, and so left it for half an hour, or an hour. I then went round the yard; tried the doors; let the dog loose; and brought him back with me to the baking-houses, for company. After that, I set my lantern on a shelf beside the door, took a book from my pocket, and began to read.

I remember the title of the book as well as possible. It was called *Bowlker's Art of Angling*, and contained little rude cuts of all kinds of artificial flies, hooks, and other tackle. But I could not keep my mind to it for two minutes together; and at last I gave up in despair, covered my face with my hands, and fell into a long, absorbing, painful train of thought. A considerable time had gone by thus – maybe an hour – when I was roused by a low whimpering howl from Captain, who was lying at my feet. I looked up with a start, just as I had started from sleep the night before, and with the same vague terror; and saw, exactly in the same place and in the same attitude, with the firelight full upon him – George Barnard!

At this sight, a fear heavier than the fear of death fell upon me, and my tongue seemed paralysed in my mouth. Then, just as last night, he rose, or seemed to rise, and went slowly out into the next room. A power stronger than myself appeared to compel me, reluctantly, to follow him. I saw him pass through the second room – cross the threshold of the third room – walk straight up to the oven – and there pause. He then turned, for the first time, with the glare of the red firelight pouring out upon him from the open door of the furnace, and looked at me, face to face. In the same instant, his whole frame and countenance seemed to glow and become transparent, as if the fire were all within him and around him – and in that glow he became, as it were, absorbed into the furnace, and disappeared!

I uttered a wild cry, tried to stagger from the room, and fell insensible before I reached the door.

When I next opened my eyes, the grey dawn was in the sky; the furnace-doors were all closed as I had left them when I last went round; the dog was quietly sleeping not far from my side; and the men were ringing at the gate, to be let in.

I told my tale from beginning to end, and was laughed at, as a matter of course, by all who heard it. When it was found, however, that my statements never varied, and, above all, that George Barnard continued absent, some few began to talk it over seriously, and among those few, the master of the works. He forbade the furnace to be cleared out, called in the aid of a celebrated naturalist, and had the ashes submitted to a scientific examination. The result was as follows:

The ashes were found to have been largely saturated with some kind of fatty animal matter. A considerable portion of these ashes consisted of charred bone. A semi-circular piece of iron, which evidently had once been the heel of a workman's heavy boot, was found, half fused, at one corner of the furnace. Near it, a tibia bone, which still retained sufficient of its original form and texture to render identification possible. This bone, however, was so much charred, that it fell into powder on being handled.

After this, not many doubted that George Barnard had been foully murdered, and that his body had been thrust into the furnace. Suspicion fell upon Louis Laroche. He was arrested, a coroner's inquest was held, and every circumstance connected with the night of the murder was as thoroughly sifted and investigated as possible. All the sifting in the world, however, failed either to clear or to condemn Louis Laroche. On the very night of his release, he left the place by the mail-train, and was never seen or heard of there again. As for

243

Leah, I know not what became of her. I went away myself before many weeks were over, and never have set foot among the Potteries from that hour to this.

The Invisible Man

G. K. CHESTERTON

IN THE COOL BLUE TWILIGHT of the two steep streets in Camden Town, the shop at the corner, a confectioner's, glowed like the butt of a cigar. One should rather say, perhaps, like the butt of a firework, for the light was of many colours and some complexity, broken up by many mirrors and dancing on many gilt and gaily coloured cakes and sweetmeats. Against this one fiery glass were glued the noses of many guttersnipes, for the chocolates were all wrapped in those red and gold and green metallic colours which are almost better than chocolate itself; and the huge white wedding-cake in the window was somehow at once remote and satisfying, just as if the whole North Pole were good to eat. Such rainbow provocations could naturally collect the youth of the neighbourhood up to the ages of ten or twelve. But this corner was also attractive to youth at a later stage; and a young man, not less than twenty-four, was staring into the same shop window. To him also the shop was of fiery charm, but this attraction was not wholly to be explained by chocolates; which, however, he was far from despising.

He was a tall, burly, red-haired young man with a resolute face but a listless manner. He carried under his arm a flat grey portfolio of black-and-white sketches which he had sold with more or less success to publishers ever since his uncle (who was an admiral) had disinherited him for Socialism, because of a lecture which he had delivered against that economic theory. His name was John Turnbull Angus.

Entering at last, he walked through the confectioner's shop into the back room, which was a sort of pastrycook restaurant, merely raising his hat to the young lady who was serving there. She was a dark, elegant, alert girl in black, with a high colour and very quick, dark eyes; and after the ordinary interval she followed him into the inner room to take his order.

His order was evidently a usual one. 'I want, please,' he said with precision, 'one halfpenny bun and a small cup of black coffee.' An instant before the girl could turn away he added, 'Also, I want you to marry me.'

The young lady of the shop stiffened suddenly and said: 'Those are jokes I don't allow.'

The red-haired young man lifted grey eyes of an unexpected gravity.

'Really and truly,' he said, 'it's as serious – as serious as the halfpenny bun. It is expensive, like the bun. One pays for it. It is indigestible, like the bun. It hurts.'

The dark young lady had never taken her eyes off him, but seemed to be studying him with almost tragic exactitude. At the end of her scrutiny she had something like the shadow of a smile, and she sat down in a chair.

'Don't you think,' observed Angus absently, 'that it's rather cruel to eat these halfpenny buns? They might grow up into penny buns. I shall give up these brutal sports when we are married.'

The dark young lady rose from her chair and walked to the window, evidently in a state of strong but not unsympathetic cogitation. When at last she swung round again with an air of resolution she was bewildered to observe that the young man was carefully laying out on the table various objects from the shop window. They included a pyramid of highly coloured sweets, several plates of sandwiches and the two decanters containing that mysterious port and sherry which are peculiar to pastrycooks. In the middle of this neat arrangement he had carefully let down the enormous load of white sugared cake which had been the huge ornament of the window.

'What on earth are you doing?' she asked.

'Duty, my dear Laura,' he began.

'Oh, for the Lord's sake stop a minute,' she cried, 'and don't talk to me in that way. I mean what is all that?'

'A ceremonial meal, Miss Hope.'

'And what is *that*?' she asked impatiently, pointing to the mountain of sugar.

'The wedding-cake, Mrs Angus,' he said.

The girl marched to that article, removed it with some clatter and put it back in the shop window; she then turned and, putting her elegant elbows on the table, regarded the young man not unfavourably, but with considerable exasperation.

You don't give me any time to think,' she said.

'I'm not such a fool,' he answered; 'that's my Christian humility.'

She was still looking at him; but she had grown considerably graver behind the smile.

'Mr Angus,' she said steadily, 'before there is a minute more of this nonsense I must tell you something about myself as shortly as I can.'

'Delighted,' replied Angus gravely. 'You might tell me something about myself too, while you are about it.'

246

'Oh, do hold your tongue and listen,' she said. 'It's nothing that I'm ashamed of, and it isn't even anything that I'm specially sorry about. But what would you say if there were something that is no business of mine and yet is my nightmare?'

'In that case,' said the man seriously, 'I should suggest that you bring back the cake.'

'Well, you must listen to the story first,' said Laura, persistently. 'To begin with, I must tell you that my father owned the inn called the Red Fish at Ludbury, and I used to serve people in the bar.'

'I have often wondered,' he said, 'why there was a kind of a Christian air about this one confectioner's shop.'

'Ludbury is a sleepy, grassy little hole in the eastern counties, and the only kind of people who ever came to the Red Fish were occasional commercial travellers and, for the rest, the most awful people you can see, only you've never seen them. I mean little loungy men, who had just enough to live on, and had nothing to do but lean about in bar-rooms and bet on horses, in bad clothes that were just too good for them. Even these wretched young rotters were not very common at our house; but there were two of them that were a lot too common – common in every sort of way. They both lived on money of their own, and were very wearisomely idle and overdressed. But yet I was a bit sorry for them, because I half believe they slunk into our little empty bar because each of them had a slight deformity; the sort of thing that some yokels laugh at. It wasn't exactly a deformity either; it was more an oddity. One of them was a surprisingly small man, something like a dwarf, or at least like a jockey. He was not at all jockeyish to look at though; he had a round black head and a well-trimmed beard, and bright eyes like a bird's; he jingled money in his pockets; he jangled a great gold watch-chain; and he never turned up except dressed just too much like a gentleman to be one. He was no fool though, though a futile idler; he was curiously clever at all kinds of things that couldn't be the slightest use; a sort of impromptu conjuring; making fifteen matches set fire to each other like a regular firework; or cutting a banana or some such thing into a dancing doll. His name was Isidore Smythe; and I can see him still, with his little dark face, just coming up to the counter, making a jumping kangaroo out of five cigars.

'The other fellow was more silent and more ordinary; but somehow he alarmed me much more than poor little Smythe. He was very tall and slight and light-haired; his nose had a high bridge, and he might almost have been handsome in a spectral sort of way; but he had one of the most appalling squints I have ever seen or heard of. When he looked straight at you you didn't know where you were yourself, let alone what he was looking at. I fancy this sort of disfiguremnt embittered the poor chap a little; for while Smythe was

247

ready to show off his monkey tricks anywhere, James Welkin (that was the squinting man's name) never did anything except soak in our bar parlour, and go for great walks by himself in the flat grey country all round. All the same, I think Smythe too was a little sensitive about being so small, though he carried it off more smartly. And so it was that I was really puzzled, as well as startled, and very sorry, when they both offered to marry me in the same week.

'Well, I did what I've since thought was perhaps a silly thing. But, after all, these freaks were my friends in a way; and I had a horror of their thinking I refused them for the real reason, which was that they were so impossibly ugly. So I made up some gas of another sort, about never meaning to marry anyone who hadn't carved his way in the world. I said it was just a point of principle with me not to live on money that was just inherited like theirs. Two days after I had talked in this well-meaning sort of way the whole trouble began. The first thing I heard was that both of them had gone off to seek their fortunes, as if they were in some silly fairy-tale.

'Well, I've never seen either of them from that day to this. But I've had two letters from the little man called Smythe, and really they were rather exciting.'

'Ever heard of the other man?' asked Angus.

'No, he never wrote,' said the girl after an instant's hesitation.

'Smythe's first letter was simply to say that he had started out walking with Welkin to London; but Welkin was such a good walker that the little man dropped out of it, and took a rest by the roadside. He happened to be picked up by some travelling show and, partly because he was nearly a dwarf, and partly because he was really a clever little wretch, he got on quite well in the show business, and was soon sent up to the Aquarium, to do some tricks that I forget. That was his first letter. His second was much more of a startler, and I only got it last week.'

The man called Angus emptied his coffee-cup and regarded her with mild and patient eyes. Her own mouth took a slight twist of laughter as she resumed: 'I suppose you've seen on the hoardings all about this "Smythe's Silent Servant"? Or you must be the only person that hasn't. Oh, I don't know much about it; it's some clockwork invention for doing all the housework by machinery. You know the sort of thing: "Press a button – A Butler Who Never Drinks." "Turn a handle – Ten Housemaids Who Never Flirt." You must have seen the advertisements. Well, whatever these machines are, they are making pots of money; and they are making it all for that little imp whom I knew down in Ludbury. I can't help feeling pleased the poor little chap has fallen on his feet; but the plain fact is, I'm in terror of his turning up any minute and telling me he's carved his way in the world

248

– as he certainly has.'

'And the other man?' repeated Angus with a sort of obstinate quietude.

Laura Hope got to her feet suddenly. 'My friend,' she said, 'I think you are a witch. Yes, you are quite right. I have not seen a line of the other man's writing; and I have no more notion than the dead of what or where he is. But it is of him that I am frightened. It is he who is all about my path. It is he who has half driven me mad. Indeed I think he *has* driven me mad; for I have felt him where he could not have been, and I have heard his voice when he could not have spoken.'

'Well, my dear,' said the young man cheerfully, 'if he were Satan himself, he is done for now you have told somebody. One goes mad all alone, old girl. But when was it you fancied you felt and heard our squinting friend?'

'I heard James Welkin laugh as plainly as I hear you speak,' said the girl steadily. 'There was nobody there, for I stood just outside the shop at the corner and could see down both streets at once. I had forgotten how he laughed, though his laugh was as odd as his squint. I had not thought of him for nearly a year. But it's a solemn truth that a few seconds later the first letter came from his rival.'

'Did you ever make the spectre speak or squeak or anything?' asked Angus with some interest.

Laura suddenly shuddered, and then said with an unshaken voice: 'Yes. Just when I had finished reading the second letter from Isidore Smythe announcing his success, just then, I heard Welkin say, "He shan't have you though." It was quite plain, as if he were in the room. It is awful; I think I must be mad.'

'If you really were mad,' said the young man, 'you would think you must be sane. But certainly there seems to me to be something a little rum about this unseen gentleman. Two heads are better than one – I spare you allusions to any other organs – and really, if you would allow me, as a sturdy, practical man, to bring back the wedding-cake out of the window——'

Even as he spoke, there was a sort of steely shriek in the street outside, and a small motor, driven at devilish speed, shot up to the door of the shop and stuck there. In the same flash of time a small man in a shiny top hat stood stamping in the outer room.

Angus, who had hitherto maintained hilarious ease from motives of mental hygiene, revealed the strain of his soul by striding abruptly out of the inner room and confronting the newcomer. A glance at him was quite sufficient to confirm the savage guesswork of a man in love. This very dapper but dwarfish figure, with the spike of a black beard carried insolently forward, the clever unrestful eyes, the neat but very nervous fingers, could be none other than the man just described to him: Isidore Smythe, who made dolls out of banana skins and matchboxes: Isidore Smythe, who made millions out of undrinking butlers and unflirting housemaids of metal. For a moment the two men, instinctively understanding each other's air of possession, looked at each other with that curious cold generosity which is the soul of rivalry.

Mr Smythe, however, made no allusion to the ultimate ground of their antagonism, but said simply and explosively: 'Has Miss Hope seen that thing on the window?'

'On the window?' repeated the staring Angus.

'There's no time to explain other things,' said the small millionaire shortly. 'There's some tomfoolery going on here that has to be investigated.'

He pointed his polished walking-stick at the window, recently depleted by the bridal preparations of Mr Angus; and that gentleman was astonished to see along the front of the glass a long strip of paper pasted, which had certainly not been on the window when he had looked through it some time before. Following the energetic Smythe outside into the street, he found that some yard and a half of stamp paper had been carefully gummed along the glass outside, and on this was written in straggly characters: 'If you marry Smythe, he will die.'

'Laura,' said Angus, putting his big red head into the shop, 'you're not mad.'

'It's the writing of that fellow Welkin,' said Smythe gruffly. 'I haven't seen him for years, but he's always bothering me. Five times in the last fortnight he's had threatening letters left at my flat, and I can't even find out who leaves them, let alone if it is Welkin himself. The porter of the flats swears that no suspicious characters have been seen, and here he has pasted up a sort of dado on a public shop window, while the people in the shop——'

'Quite so,' said Angus modestly, 'while the people in the shop were having tea. Well, sir, I can assure you I appreciate your common sense in dealing so directly with the matter. We can talk about other things afterwards. The fellow cannot be very far off yet, for I swear there was no paper there when I went last to the window, ten or fifteen minutes ago. On the other hand he's too far off to be chased, as we don't even know the direction. If you'll take my advice, Mr Smythe, you'll put this at once in the hands of some energetic inquiry man, private rather than public. I know an extremely clever fellow who has set up in business five minutes from here in your car. His name's Flambeau, and though his youth was a bit stormy, he's a strictly honest man now, and his brains are worth money. He lives in Lucknow Mansions, Hampstead.'

'That is odd,' said the little man, arching his black eyebrows. 'I live myself in Himalaya Mansions round the corner. Perhaps you might care to come with me; I can go to my rooms and sort out these queer Welkin documents while you run round and get your friend the detective.'

'You are very good,' said Angus politely. 'Well, the sooner we act the better.'

Both men, with a queer kind of impromptu fairness, took the same sort of formal farewell of the lady, and both jumped into the brisk little car. As Smythe took the wheel and they turned the great corner of the street, Angus was amused to see a gigantic poster of 'Smythe's Silent Service,' with a picture of a huge headless iron doll carrying a saucepan with the legend, 'A Cook Who Is Never Cross'.

'I use them in my own flat,' said the little black-bearded man, laughing, 'partly for advertisement and partly for real convenience. Honestly, and all above board, those big clockwork dolls of mine do bring you coals or claret or a time-table quicker than any live servants I've ever known, if you know which knob to press. But I'll never deny, between ourselves, that such servants have their disadvantages too.'

'Indeed?' said Angus. 'Is there something they can't do?'

'Yes,' replied Smythe coolly; 'they can't tell me who left those threatening letters at my flat.'

The man's motor was small and swift like himself; in fact, like his domestic service, it was of his own invention. If he was an advertising quack he was one who believed in his own wares. The senses of something tiny and flying was accentuated as they swept up long white curves of road in the dead but open daylight of evening. Soon the white curves came sharper and dizzier; they were upon ascending spirals, as they say in the modern religions. For, indeed, they were cresting a corner of London which is almost as precipitous as Edinburgh, if not quite so picturesque. Terrace rose above terrace, and the special tower of flats they sought rose above them all to almost Egyptian height, gilt by the level sunset. The change, as they turned the corner and entered the crescent known as Himalaya Mansions, was as abrupt as the opening of a window; for they found that pile of flats sitting above London as above a green sea of slate. Opposite to the mansions, on the other side of the gravel crescent, was a bushy enclosure more like a steep hedge or dike than a garden, and some way below that ran a strip of artificial water, a sort of canal, like the moat of that embowered fortress. As the car swept round the crescent it passed, at one corner, the stray stall of a man selling chestnuts; and right away at the other end of the curve Angus could see a dim blue policeman walking slowly. These were the only human shapes in that high suburban solitude; but he had an irrational sense that they expressed the speechless poetry of London. He felt as if they were

251

figures in a story.

The little car shot up to the right house like a bullet and shot out its owner like a bombshell. He was immediately inquiring of a tall commissionaire in shining braid, and a short porter in shirt sleeves, whether anybody or anything had been seeking his apartments. He was assured that nobody and nothing had passed these officials since his last inquiries; whereupon he and the slightly bewildered Angus were shot up in the lift like a rocket, till they reached the top floor.

'Just come in for a minute,' said the breathless Smythe. 'I want to show you those Welkin letters. Then you might run round the corner and fetch your friend.'

He pressed a button concealed in the wall, and the door opened of itself. It opened on a long, commodious ante-room, of which the only arresting features, ordinarily speaking, were the rows of tall half-human mechanical figures that stood up on both sides like tailors' dummies. Like tailors' dummies they were headless; and like tailors' dummies they had a handsome unnecessary humpiness in the shoulders, and a pigeon-breasted protuberance of chest; but, barring this, they were not much more like a human figure than any automatic machine at a station that is about the human height. They had two great hooks, like arms, for carrying trays; and they were painted pea-green or vermilion or black for convenience of distinction; in every other way they were only automatic machines and nobody would have looked twice at them. On this occasion, at least, nobody did. For between the two rows of these domestic dummies lay something more interesting than most of the mechanics of the world. It was a white, tattered scrap of paper scrawled with red ink, and the agile inventor had snatched it up almost as soon as the door flew open. He handed it to Angus without a word. The red ink on it actually was not dry, and the message ran: 'If you have been to see her today I shall kill you.'

There was a short silence, and then Isidore Smythe said quietly: 'Would you like a little whisky? I rather feel as if I should.'

'Thank you; I should like a little Flambeau,' said Angus gloomily. 'This business seems to me to be getting rather grave. I'm going round at once to fetch him.'

'Right you are,' said the other with admirable cheerfulness. 'Bring him round here as quick as you can.'

But as Angus closed the front door behind him he saw Smythe push back a button, and one of the clockwork images glided from its place and slid along a groove in the floor carrying a tray with syphon and decanter. There did seem something a trifle weird about leaving the little man alone among those dead servants, who were coming to life as the door closed.

Six steps down from Smythe's landing the man in shirt sleeves was doing something with a pail. Angus stopped to extract a promise, fortified with a prospective bribe, that he would remain in that place until the return with the detective, and would keep count of any kind of stranger coming up those stairs. Dashing down to the front hall he then laid similar charges of vigilance on the commissionaire at the front door, from whom he learned the simplifying circumstance that there was no back door. Not content with this, he captured the floating policeman and induced him to stand opposite the entrance and watch it; and finally paused an instant for a pennyworth of chestnuts, and an inquiry as to the probable length of the merchant's stay in the neighbourhood.

The chestnut seller, turning up the collar of his coat, told him he should probably be moving shortly, as he thought it was going to snow. Indeed the evening was growing grey and bitter, but Angus, with all his eloquence, proceeded to nail the chestnut man to his post.

'Keep yourself warm on your own chestnuts,' he said earnestly. 'Eat up the whole stock; I'll make it worth your while. I'll give you a sovereign if you'll wait here till I come back, and then tell me whether any man, woman or child has gone into that house where the commissionaire is standing.'

He then walked away smartly, with a last look at the besieged tower.

'I've made a ring round that room, anyhow,' he said. 'They can't all four of them be Mr Welkin's accomplices.'

Lucknow Mansions were, so to speak, on a lower platform of that hill of houses of which Himalaya Mansions might be called the peak. Mr Flambeau's semi-official flat was on the ground floor, and presented in every way a marked contrast to the American machinery and cold hotel-like luxury of the flat of the Silent Service. Flambeau, who was a friend of Angus, received him in a rococo artistic den behind his office, of which the ornaments were sabres, harquebuses, Eastern curiosities, flasks of Italian wine, savage cooking-pots, a plumy Persian cat and a small, dusty-looking Roman Catholic priest who looked particularly out of place.

'This is my friend Father Brown,' said Flambeau. 'I've often wanted you to meet him. Splendid weather, this; a little cold for Southerners like me.'

'Yes, I think it will keep clear,' said Angus, sitting down on a violet-striped Eastern ottoman.

'No,' said the priest quietly; 'it has begun to snow.'

And indeed, as he spoke, the first few flakes, foreseen by the man of chestnuts, began to drift across the darkening window-pane.

'Well,' said Angus heavily. 'I'm afraid I've come on business, and rather jumpy business at that. The fact is, Flambeau, within a stone's throw of your house is a fellow who badly wants your help; he's perpetually being haunted and threatened by an invisible enemy – a scoundrel whom nobody has even seen.' As Angus proceeded to tell the whole tale of Smythe and Welkin, beginning with Laura's story and going on with his own, the supernatural laugh at the corner of two empty streets, the strange distinct words spoken in an empty room, Flambeau grew more and more vividly concerned, and the little priest seemed to be left out of it, like a piece of furniture. When it came to the scribbled stamp paper on the window, Flambeau rose, seeming to fill the room with his huge shoulders.

'If you don't mind,' he said, 'I think you had better tell me the rest on the nearest road to this man's house. It strikes me, somehow, that there is no time to be lost.'

'Delighted,' said Angus, rising also; 'though he's safe enough for the present, for I've set four men to watch the only hole to his burrow.'

They turned out into the street, the small priest trundling after them with the docility of a small dog. He merely said, in a cheerful way, like one making conversation: 'How quick the snow gets thick on the ground.'

As they threaded the steep side streets already powdered with silver Angus finished his story; and by the time they reached the crescent with the towering flats he had leisure to turn his attention to the four sentinels. The chestnut seller, both before and after receiving a sovereign, swore stubbornly that he had watched the door and seen no visitor enter. The policeman was even more emphatic. He said he had had experience of crooks of all kinds, in top hats and in rags; he wasn't so green as to expect suspicious characters to look suspicious; he looked out for anybody and, so help him, there had been nobody. And when all three men gathered round the gilded commissionaire, who still stood smiling astride of the porch, the verdict was more final still.

'I've got a right to ask any man, duke or dustman, what he wants in these flats,' said the genial and gold-laced giant, 'and I'll swear there's been nobody to ask since this gentleman went away.'

The unimportant Father Brown, who stood back looking modestly at the pavement, here ventured to say meekly: 'Has nobody been up or down stairs, then, since the snow began to fall? It began while we were all round at Flambeau's.'

'Nobody's been in here, sir, you can take it from me,' said the official with beaming authority.

'Then I wonder what that is?' said the priest, and stared at the ground blankly like a fish.

The others all looked down also; and Flambeau used a fierce

exclamation and a French gesture. For it was unquestionably true that down the middle of the entrance guarded by the man in gold lace, actually between the arrogant, stretched legs of that colossus, ran a stringy pattern of grey footprints stamped upon the white snow.

'God!' cried Angus involuntarily. 'The Invisible Man!'

Without another word he turned and dashed up the stairs, with Flambeau following; but Father Brown still stood looking about him in the snow-clad street as if he had lost interest in his query.

Flambeau was plainly in a mood to break down the door with his big shoulder; but the Scotsman, with more reason if less intuition, fumbled about the frame of the door till he found the invisible button; and the door swung slowly open.

It showed substantially the same serried interior; the hall had grown darker, though it was still struck here and there with the last crimson shafts of sunset, and one or two of the headless machines had been moved from their places for this or that purpose, and stood here and there about the twilit place. The green and red of their coats were all darkened in the dusk, and their likeness to human shapes slightly increased by their very shapelessness. But in the middle of them all, exactly where the paper with the red ink had lain, there lay something that looked very like red ink spilled out of its bottle. But it was not red ink.

With a French combination of reason and violence Flambeau simply said 'Murder!' and, plunging into the flat, had explored every corner and cupboard of it in five minutes. But if he expected to find a corpse he found none. Isidore Smythe simply was not in the place, either dead or alive. After the most tearing search the two men met each other in the outer hall with streaming faces and staring eyes. 'My friend,' said Flambeau, talking French in his excitement, 'not only is your murderer invisible, but he makes invisible also the murdered man.'

Angus looked round at the dim room full of dummies, and in some Celtic corner of his Scotch soul a shudder started. One of the life-size dolls stood immediately overshadowing the blood-stain, summoned, perhaps, by the slain man an instant before he fell. One of the high-shouldered hooks that served the thing for arms was a little lifted, and Angus had suddenly the horrid fancy that poor Smythe's own iron child had struck him down. Matter had rebelled, and these machines had killed their master. But even so, what had they done with him?

'Eaten him?' said the nightmare at his ear; and he sickened for an instant at the idea of rent human remains absorbed and crushed into all that acephalous clockwork.

He recovered his mental health by an emphatic effort and said to Flambeau: 'Well, there it is. The poor fellow has evaporated like a cloud and left a red streak on the floor. The tale does not belong to this world.'

'There is only one thing to be done,' said Flambeau, 'whether it belongs to this world or the other. I must go down and talk to my friend.'

They descended, passing the man with the pail, who again asseverated that he had let no intruder pass, down to the commission-aire and the hovering chestnut man, who rightly reasserted their own watchfulness. But when Angus looked round for his fourth confir-mation he could not see it, and called out with some nervousness: 'Where is the policeman?'

'I beg your pardon,' said Father Brown; 'that is my fault. I sent him down the road to investigate something – that I just thought worth investigating.'

'Well, we want him back pretty soon,' said Angus abruptly, 'for the wretched man upstairs has not only been murdered, but wiped out.'

'How?' asked the priest.

'Father,' said Flambeau after a pause, 'upon my soul I believe it is more in your department than mine. No friend or foe has entered the house, but Smythe is gone, as if stolen by the fairies. If that is not supernatural, I——'

As he spoke they were all checked by an unusual sight; the big blue policeman came round the corner of the crescent running. He came straight up to Brown.

'You're right, sir,' he panted, 'they've just found poor Mr Smythe's body in the canal down below.'

Angus put his hand wildly to his head. 'Did he run down and drown himself?' he asked.

'He never came down, I'll swear,' said the constable, 'and he wasn't drowned either, for he died of a great stab over the heart.'

'And yet you saw no one enter?' said Flambeau in a grave voice.

'Let us walk down the road a little,' said the priest.

As they reached the other end of the crescent he observed abruptly: 'Stupid of me! I forgot to ask the policeman something. I wonder if they found a light brown sack?'

'Why a light brown sack?' asked Angus, astonished.

'Because if it was any other colour sack the case must begin over again,' said Father Brown; 'but if it was a light brown sack, why, the case is finished.'

'I am pleased to hear it,' said Angus with hearty irony. 'It hasn't begun, so far as I am concerned.'

'You must tell us all about it,' said Flambeau with a strange heavy simplicity, like a child.

Unconsciously they were walking with quickening steps down the long sweep of road on the other side of the high crescent, Father Brown leading briskly, though in silence. At last he said, with an almost touching vagueness: 'Well, I'm afraid you'll think it so prosy. We always begin at the abstract end of things, and you can't begin this story anywhere else.

'Have you ever noticed this – that people never answer what you say? They answer what you mean – or what they think you mean. Suppose one lady says to another in a country house, "Is anybody staying with you?", the lady doesn't answer, "Yes; the butler, the three footmen, the parlourmaid and so on," though the parlourmaid may be in the room, or the butler behind her chair. She says, "There is *nobody* staying with us," meaning nobody of the sort you mean. But suppose a doctor inquiring into an epidemic asks, "Who is staying in the house?" then the lady will remember the butler, the parlourmaid and the rest. All language is used like that; you never get a question answered literally, even when you get it answered truly. When those four quite honest men said that no man had gone into the Mansions, they did not really mean that *no man* had gone into them. They meant no man whom they could suspect of being your man. A man did go into the house, and did come out of it, but they never noticed him.'

'An invisible man?' inquired Angus, raising his red eyebrows.

'A mentally invisible man,' said Father Brown.

A minute or two after he resumed in the same unassuming voice, like a man thinking his way, 'Of course, you can't think of such a man, until you do think of him. That's where his cleverness comes in. But I came to think of him through two or three little things in the tale Mr Angus told us. First, there was the fact that this Welkin went for long walks. And then there was the vast lot of stamp paper on the window. And then, most of all, there were the two things the young lady said – things that couldn't be true. Don't get annoyed,' he added hastily, noting a sudden movement of the Scotsman's head; 'she thought they were true all right, but they couldn't be true. A person *can't* be quite alone in a street a second before she receives a letter. She can't be quite alone in a street when she starts reading a letter just received. There must be somebody pretty near her; he must be mentally invisible.'

'Why must there be somebody near her?' asked Angus.

'Because,' said Father Brown: 'barring carrier-pigeons, somebody must have brought her the letters.'

'Do you really mean to say,' asked Flambeau with energy, 'that Welkin carried his rival's letters to his lady?'

'Yes,' said the priest. 'Welkin carried his rival's letters to his lady. You see, he *had* to.'

'Oh, I can't stand much more of this,' exploded Flambeau. 'Who is this fellow? What does he look like? What is the usual get-up of a mentally invisible man?'

'He is dressed rather handsomely in red, blue and gold,' replied the priest promptly with decision, 'and in this striking and even showy costume he entered Himalaya Mansions under eight human eyes; he killed Smythe in cold blood and came down into the street again carrying the dead body in his arms——'

'Reverend sir,' cried Angus, standing still, 'are you raving mad, or am I?'

'You are not mad,' said Brown; 'only a little unobservant. You have not noticed such a man as this, for example.'

He took three quick strides forward and put his hand on the shoulder of an ordinary postman who had bustled by them unnoticed under the shade of the trees.

'Nobody ever notices postmen, somehow,' he said thoughtfully; 'yet they have passions like other men, and even carry large bags where a small corpse can be stowed quite easily.'

The postman, instead of turning naturally, had ducked and tumbled against the garden fence. He was a lean, fair-bearded man of very ordinary appearance, but, as he turned an alarmed face over his shoulder, all three men were fixed with an almost fiendish squint.

Flambeau went back to his sabres, purple rugs and Persian cat, having many things to attend to. John Turnbull Angus went back to the lady at the shop, with whom that imprudent young man contrives to be extremely comfortable. But Father Brown walked those snow-covered hills under the stars for many hours with a murderer, and what they said to each other will never be known.

The Hound

WILLIAM FAULKNER

TO COTTON THE SHOT was the loudest thing he had ever heard in his life. It was too loud to be heard all at once. It continued to build up about the thicket, the dim, faint road, long after the hammer-like blow of the ten-gauge shotgun had shocked into his shoulder and long after the smoke of the black powder with which it was charged had dissolved, and after the maddened horse had whirled twice and then turned galloping, diminishing, the empty stirrups clashing against the empty saddle.

It made too much noise. It was outrageous, unbelievable – a gun which he had owned for twenty years. It stunned him with amazed outrage, seeming to press him down into the thicket, so that when he could make the second shot, it was too late and the hound, too, was gone.

Then he wanted to run. He had expected that. He had coached himself the night before. 'Right after it you'll want to run,' he told himself. 'But you can't run. You got to finish it. You got to clean it up. It will be hard, but you got to do it. You got to set there in the bushes and shut your eyes and count slow until you can make to finish it.'

He did that. He laid the gun down and sat where he had lain behind the log. His eyes were closed. He counted slowly, until he had stopped shaking and until the sound of the gun and the echo of the galloping horse had died out of his ears. He had chosen his place well. It was a quiet road, little used, marked not once in three months save by that departed horse; a short cut between the house where the owner of the horse lived and Varner's store; a quiet, fading, grass-grown trace along the edge of the river bottom empty save for the two of them, the one squatting in the bushes, the other lying on his face in the road.

Cotton was a bachelor. He lived in a chinked log cabin floored with clay on the edge of the bottom, four miles away. It was dusk when he reached home. In the well-house at the back he drew water and washed his shoes. They were not muddier than usual, and he did not wear them save in severe weather, but he washed them carefully.

259

Then he cleaned the shotgun and washed it too, barrel and stock; why he could not have said, since he had never heard of fingerprints, and immediately afterward he picked up the gun and carried it into the house and put it away. He kept firewood, a handful of charred pine knots, in the chimney corner. He built a fire on the clay hearth and cooked his supper and ate and went to bed. He slept on a quilt pallet on the floor; he went to bed by barring the door and removing his overalls and lying down. It was dark after the fire burned out; he lay in the darkness. He thought about nothing at all save that he did not expect to sleep. He felt no triumph, vindication, nothing. He just lay there, thinking about nothing at all, even when he began to hear the dog. Usually at night he would hear dogs, single dogs ranging alone in the bottom, or coon- or cat-hunting packs. Having nothing else to do, his life, his heredity, and his heritage centred within a five-mile radius of Varner's store. He knew almost any dog he would hear by its voice, as he knew almost any man he would hear by his voice. He knew his dog's voice. It and the galloping horse with the flapping stirrups and the owner of the horse had been inseparable: when he saw one of them, the other two would not be far away – a lean, rangy brute that charged savagely at anyone who approached its master's house, with something of the master's certitude and overbearance: and today was not the first time he had tried to kill it, though only now did he know why he had not gone through with it. 'I never knowed my own luck,' he said to himself, lying on the pallet. 'I never knowed. If I had went ahead and killed it, killed the dog . . .'

He was still not triumphant. It was too soon yet to be proud, vindicated. It was too soon. It had to do with death. He did not believe that a man could pick up and move that irrevocable distance at a moment's notice. He had completely forgotten about the body. So he lay with his gaunt, underfed body empty with waiting, thinking of nothing at all, listening to the dog. The cries came at measured intervals, timbrous, sourceless, with the sad, peacefully, abject quality of a single hound in the darkness, when suddenly he found himself sitting bolt upright on the pallet.

'Nigger talk,' he said. He had heard (he had never known a negro himself, because of the antipathy, the economic jealousy, between his kind and negroes) how negroes claimed that a dog would howl at the recent grave of its master. 'Hit's nigger talk,' he said, all the time he was putting on his overalls and his recently cleaned shoes. He opened the door. From the dark river bottom below the hill on which the cabin sat the howling of the dog came, bell-like and mournful. From a nail just inside the door he took down a coiled ploughline and descended the slope.

Against the dark wall of the jungle fireflies winked and drifted; from

260

beyond the black wall came the booming and grunting of frogs. When he entered the timber he could not see his own hand. The footing was treacherous with slime and creepers and bramble. They possessed the perversity of inanimate things, seeming to spring out of the darkness and clutch him with spiky tentacles. From the musing impenetrability ahead the voice of the hound came steadily. He followed the sound, muddy again; the air was chill, yet he was sweating. He was quite near the sound. The hound ceased. He plunged forward, his teeth drying under his dry lip, his hands clawed and blind, towards the ceased sound, the faint phosphorescent glare of the dog's eyes. The eyes vanished. He stopped, panting, stooped, the ploughline in his hand, looking for the eyes. He cursed the dog, his voice a dry whisper. He could hear silence but nothing else.

He crawled on hands and knees, telling where he was by the shape of the trees on the sky. After a time, the brambles raking and slashing at his face, he found a shallow ditch. It was rank with rotted leaves; he waded ankle-deep in the pitch darkness, in something not earth and not water, his elbow crooked before his face. He stumbled upon something, an object with a slack feel. When he touched it, something gave a choked, infantile cry, and he started back, hearing the creature scuttle away. 'Just a possum,' he said. 'Hit was just a possum.'

He wiped his hands on his flanks in order to pick up the shoulders. His flanks were foul with slime. He wiped his hands on his shirt, across his breast, then he picked up the shoulders. He walked backward, dragging it. From time to time he would stop and wipe his hands on his shirt. He stopped beside a tree, a rotting cypress shell, topless, about ten feet tall. He had put the coiled ploughline into his bosom. He knotted it about the body and climbed the stump. The top was open, rotted out. He was not a large man, not as large as the body, yet he hauled it up to him hand over hand, bumping and scraping it along the stump, until it lay across the lip like a half-filled meal sack. The knot in the rope had slipped tight. At last he took out his knife and cut the rope and tumbled the body into the hollow stump.

It didn't fall far. He shoved at it, feeling around it with his hands for the obstruction; he tied the rope about the stub of a limb and held the end of it in his hands and stood on the body and began to jump up and down upon it, whereupon it fled suddenly beneath him and left him dangling on the rope.

He tried to climb the rope, rasping off with his knuckles the rotten fibre, a faint powder of decay like snuff in his nostrils. He heard the stub about which the rope was tied crack and felt it begin to give. He leaped upward from nothing, scrabbling at the rotten wood, and got one hand over the edge. The wood crumbled beneath his fingers; he climbed perpetually without an inch of gain, his mouth cracked upon his teeth, his eyes glaring at the sky.

The wood stopped crumbling. He dangled by his hands, breathing. He drew himself up and straddled the edge. He sat there for a while. Then he climbed down and leaned against the hollow trunk.

When he reached his cabin he was tired, spent. He had never been so tired. He stopped at the door. Fireflies still blew along the dark band of timber, and owls hooted and the frogs still boomed and grunted. 'I ain't never been so tired,' he said, leaning against the house, the wall which he had built log by log. 'Like ever' thing had got outen hand. Climbing that stump, and the noise that shot made. Like I had got to be somebody else without knowing it, in a place where noise was louder, climbing harder to climb, without knowing it.' He went to bed. He took off the muddy shoes, the overalls, and lay down; it was late then. He could tell by a summer star that came into the square window at two o'clock and after.

Then, as if it had waited for him to get settled and comfortable, the hound began to howl again. Lying in the dark, he heard the first cry come up from the river bottom, mournful, timbrous, profound.

Five men in overalls squatted against the wall of Varner's store. Cotton made the sixth. He sat on the top step, his back against a gnawed post which supported the wooden awning of the veranda. The seventh man sat in the single splint chair; a fat, slow man in denim trousers and a collarless white shirt, smoking a cob pipe. He was past middle-age. He was sheriff of the county. The man about whom they were talking was named Houston.

'He hadn't no reason to run off,' one said. 'To disappear. To send his horse back home with an empty saddle. He hadn't no reason. Owning his own land, his house. Making a good crop every year. He was well-fixed as ere a man in the county. A bachelor too. He hadn't no reason to disappear. You can mark it. He never run. I don't know what; but Houston never run.'

'I don't know,' a second said. 'You can't tell what a man has got in his mind. Houston might a had a reason that we don't know, for making it look like something had happened to him. For clearing outen the county and leaving it to look like something had happened to him. It's been done before. Folks before him has had reason to light out for Texas with a changed name.'

Cotton sat a little below their eyes, his face lowered beneath his worn, stained, shabby hat. He was whittling at a stick, a piece of pine board.

'But a fellow can't disappear without leaving no trace,' a third said. 'Can he, Sheriff?'

'Well, I don't know,' the Sheriff said. He removed the cob pipe and spat neatly across the porch into the dust. 'You can't tell what a man will do when he's pinched. Except it will be something you never thought of. Never counted on. But if you can find just what pinched him you can pretty well tell what he done.'

'Houston was smart enough to do ere a thing he taken a notion to,' the second said. 'If he'd wanted to disappear, I reckon we'd a known about what we know now.'

'And what's that?' the third said.

'Nothing,' the second said.

'That's a fact,' the first said. 'Houston was a secret man.'

'He wasn't the only secret man around here,' a fourth said.

To Cotton it sounded sudden, since the fourth man had said no word before. He sat against the post, his hat slanted forward so that his face was invisible, believing that he could feel their eyes. He watched the sliver peel slow and smooth from the stick, ahead of his worn knife blade. 'I got to say something,' he told himself.

'He warn't no smarter than nobody else,' he said. Then he wished he had not spoken. He could see their feet beneath his hat brim. He trimmed the stick, watching the knife, the steady sliver. 'It's got to trim off smooth,' he told himself. 'It don't dast to break.' He was talking; he could hear his voice: 'Swelling around like he was the biggest man in the county. Setting that ere dog on folks' stock.' He believed that he could feel their eyes, watching their feet, watching the sliver trim smooth and thin and unhurried beneath the knife blade. Suddenly he thought about the gun, the loud crash, the jarring shock. 'Maybe I'll have to kill them all,' he said to himself – a mild man in worn overalls, with a gaunt face and lack-lustre eyes like a sick man, whittling a stick with a thin hand, thinking about killing them. 'Not them: just the words, the talk.' But the talk was familiar, the intonation, the gestures; but so was Houston. He had known Houston all his life: that prosperous and overbearing man. 'With a dog,' Cotton said, watching the knife return and bite into another sliver. 'A dog that et better than me. I work, and eat worse than his dog. If I had been his dog, I would not have . . . We're better off without him,' he said, blurted. He could feel their eyes, sober, intent.

'He always did rile Ernest,' the first said.

'He taken advantage of me,' Cotton said, watching the infallible knife. 'He taken advantage of ever man he could.'

'He was an overbearing man,' the Sheriff said.

Cotton believed that they were still watching him, hidden behind their detached voices.

'Smart, though,' the third said.

'He wasn't smart enough to win that suit against Ernest over that

263

hog.'

'That's so. How much did Ernest get outen that lawing? He ain't never told, has he?'

Cotton believed that they knew how much he had got from the suit. The hog had come into his lot one October. He penned it up; he tried by inquiry to find the owner. But none claimed it until he had wintered it on his corn. In the spring Houston claimed the hog. They went to court. Houston was awarded the hog, though he was assessed a sum for the wintering of it, and one dollar, a pound-fee for a stray. 'I reckon that's Ernest's business,' the Sheriff said, after a time.

Again Cotton heard himself talking, blurting. 'It was a dollar,' he said, watching his knuckles whiten about the knife handle. 'One dollar.' He was trying to make his mouth stop talking. 'After all I taken offen him . . .'

'Juries does queer things,' the Sheriff said, 'in little matters. But in big matters they're mostly right.'

Cotton whittled, steady and deliberate. 'At first you want to run,' he told himself. 'But you got to finish it. You got to count a hundred, if it needs, and finish it.'

'I heard that dog again last night,' the third said.

'You did?' the Sheriff said.

'It ain't been home since the day the horse come in with the saddle empty,' the first said.

'It's out hunting, I reckon,' the Sheriff said. 'It'll come in when it gets hungry.'

Cotton trimmed at the stick. He did not move.

'Niggers claim a hound'll howl till a dead body's found,' the second said.

'I've heard that,' the Sheriff said. After a time a car came up and the Sheriff got into it. The car was driven by a deputy. 'We'll be late for supper,' the Sheriff said. The car mounted the hill; the sound died away. It was getting towards sundown.

'He ain't much bothered,' the third said.

'Why should he be?' the first said. 'After all, a man can leave his house and go on a trip without telling everybody.'

'Looks like he'd unsaddled that mare, though,' the second said. 'And there's something the matter with that dog. It ain't been home since, and it ain't treed. I been hearing it ever night. It ain't treed. It's howling. It ain't been home since Tuesday. And that was the day Houston rid away from the store here on that mare.'

Cotton was the last one to leave the store. It was after dark when he reached home. He ate some cold bread and loaded the shotgun and sat beside the open door until the hound began to howl. Then he descended the hill and entered the bottom.

The dog's voice guided him; after a while it ceased, and he saw its eyes. They were not motionless; in the red glare of the explosion he saw the beast entire in sharp relief. He saw it in the act of leaping into the ensuing welter of darkness; he heard the thud of its body. But he couldn't find it. He looked carefully, quartering back and forth, stopping to listen. But he had seen the shot strike it and hurl it backward, and he turned aside for about a hundred yards in the pitch darkness and came to a slough. He flung the shotgun into it, hearing the sluggish splash, watching the vague water break and recover, until the last ripple fled. He went home and to bed.

He didn't go to sleep though, although he knew he would not hear the dog. 'It's dead,' he told himself, lying on his quilt pallet in the dark. 'I saw the bullets knock it down. I could count the shots. The dog is dead.' But still he did not sleep. He did not need to sleep; he did not feel tired or stale in the mornings, though he knew it was not the dog. So he took to spending the nights sitting up in a chair in the door, watching the fireflies and listening to the frogs and the owls.

He entered Varner's store. It was in mid-afternoon; the porch was empty, save for the clerk, whose name was Snopes. 'Been looking for you for two-three days,' Snopes said. 'Come inside.'

Cotton entered. The store smelled of cheese and leather and new earth. Snopes went behind the counter and reached from under the counter a shotgun. It was caked with mud. 'This is yourn' ain't it?' Snopes said. 'Vernon Tull said it was. A nigger squirl hunter found it in a slough.'

Cotton came to the counter and looked at the gun. He did not touch it; he just looked at it. 'It ain't mine,' he said.

'Ain't nobody around here got one of them old Hadley ten-gauges except you,' Snopes said. 'Tull says it's yourn.'

'It ain't none of mine,' Cotton said. 'I got one like it. But mine's to home.'

Snopes lifted the gun. He breeched it. 'It had one empty and one load in it,' he said. 'Who you reckon it belongs to?'

'I don't know,' Cotton said. 'Mine's to home.' He had come to purchase food. He bought it: crackers, cheese, a tin of sardines. It was not dark when he reached home, yet he opened the sardines and ate his supper. When he lay down he did not even remove his overalls. It was as though he waited for something, stayed dressed to move and go at once. He was still waiting for whatever it was when the window turned grey and then yellow and then blue; when, framed by the square window, he saw against the fresh morning a single soaring speck. By sunrise there were three of them, and then seven.

All that day he watched them gather, wheeling and wheeling,

265

drawing their concentric black circles, watching the lower ones wheel down and down and disappear below the trees. He thought it was the dog. 'They'll be through by noon,' he said. 'It wasn't a big dog.'

When noon came they had not gone away; there were still more of them, while still the lower ones dropped down and disappeared below the trees. He watched them until dark came, until they were away, flapping singly and sluggishly up from beyond the trees. 'I got to eat,' he said. 'With the work I got to do tonight.' He went to the hearth and knelt and took up a pine knot, and he was kneeling, nursing a match into flame, when he heard the hound again; the cry deep, timbrous, unmistakable, and sad. He cooked his supper and ate.

With his axe in his hand he descended through his meagre corn patch. The cries of the hound could have guided him, but he did not need it. He had not reached the bottom before he believed that his nose was guiding him. The dog still howled. He paid it no attention, until the beast sensed him and ceased, as it had done before; again he saw its eyes. He paid no attention to them. He went to the hollow cypress trunk and swung his axe into it, the axe sinking helve-deep into the rotten wood. While he was tugging at it something flowed silent and savage out of the darkness behind him and struck him a slashing blow. The axe had just come free; he fell with the axe in his hand, feeling the hot reek of the dog's breath on his face and hearing the click of its teeth as he struck it down with his free hand. It leaped again; he saw its eyes now. He was on his knees, the axe raised in both hands now. He swung it, hitting nothing, feeling nothing; he saw the dog's eyes, crouched. He rushed at the eyes; they vanished. He waited a moment, but heard nothing. He returned to the tree.

At the first stroke of the axe the dog sprang at him again. He was expecting it, so he whirled and struck with the axe at the two eyes and felt the axe strike something and whirl from his hands. He heard the dog whimper, he could hear it crawling away. On his hands and knees he hunted for the axe until he found it.

He began to chop at the base of the stump, stopping between blows to listen. But he heard nothing, saw nothing. Overhead the stars were swinging slowly past; he saw the one that looked into his window at two o'clock. He began to chop steadily at the base of the stump.

The wood was rotten; the axe sank helve-deep at each stroke, as into sand or mud; suddenly Cotton knew that it was not imagination he smelled. He dropped the axe and began to tear at the rotten wood with his hands. The hound was beside him, whimpering; he did not know it was there, not even when it thrust its head into the opening, crowding against him, howling.

'Git away,' he said, still without being conscious that it was the dog. He dragged at the body, feeling it slough upon its own bones, as though it were too large for itself; he turned his face away, his teeth glared, his breath furious and outraged and restrained. He could feel the dog surge against his legs, its head in the orifice, howling.

When the body came free, Cotton went over backwards. He lay on his back on the wet ground, looking up at a faint patch of starry sky. 'I ain't never been so tired,' he said. The dog was howling, with an abject steadiness. 'Shut up,' Cotton said. 'Hush. Hush.' The dog didn't hush. 'It'll be daylight soon,' Cotton said to himself. 'I got to get up.'

He got up and kicked at the dog. It moved away, but when he stooped and took hold of the legs and began to back away, the dog was there again, moaning to itself. When he would stop to rest, the dog would howl again; he kicked at it. Then it began to be dawn, the trees coming spectral and vast out of the miasmic darkness. He could see the dog plainly. It was gaunt, thin, with a long bloody gash across its face. 'I'll have to get shut of you,' he said. Watching the dog, he stooped and found a stick. It was rotten, foul with slime. He clutched it. When the hound lifted its muzzle to howl, he struck. The dog whirled; there was a long fresh scar running from shoulder to flank. It leaped at him, without a sound; he struck again. The stick took it fair between the eyes. He picked up the ankles and tried to run.

It was almost light. When he broke through the undergrowth upon the river bank the channel was invisible; a long bank of what looked like cotton batting, though he could hear the water beneath it somewhere. There was a freshness here; the edges of the mist licked into curling tongues. He stooped and lifted the body and hurled it into the bank of mist. At the instant of vanishing he saw it – a sluggish sprawl of three limbs instead of four, and he knew why it had been so hard to free from the stump. 'I'll have to make another trip,' he said; then he heard a pattering rush behind him. He didn't have time to turn when the hound struck him and knocked him down. It didn't pause. Lying on his back, he saw it in mid-air like a bird, vanish into the mist with a single short, choking cry.

He got to his feet and ran. He stumbled and caught himself and ran again. It was full light. He could see the stump and the black hole which he had chopped in it; behind him he could hear the swift, soft feet of the dog. As it sprang at him he stumbled and fell and saw it soar over him, its eyes like two cigar-coals; it whirled and leaped at him again before he could rise. He struck at its face with his bare hands and began to run. Together they reached the tree. It leaped at him again, slashing his arms as he ducked into the tree, seeking that member of the body which he did not know was missing until after he had released it into the mist, feeling the dog surging about his legs. Then the dog was gone. Then a voice said:

'We got him. You can come out, Ernest.'

The county seat was fourteen miles away. They drove to it in a battered Ford. On the back seat Cotton and the Sheriff sat, their inside wrists locked together by handcuffs. They had to drive for two miles before they reached the high road. It was hot, ten o'clock in the morning. 'You want to swap sides out of the sun?' the Sheriff said.

'I'm all right,' Cotton said.

At two o'clock they had a puncture. Cotton and the Sheriff sat under a tree while the driver and the second deputy went across a field and returned with a glass jar of buttermilk and some cold food. They ate, repaired the tyre, and went on.

When they were within three or four miles of town, they began to pass wagons and cars going home from market day in town, the wagon teams plodding homeward in their own inescapable dust. The Sheriff greeted them with a single gesture of his fat arm. 'Home for supper, anyway,' he said. 'What's the matter, Ernest? Feeling sick? Here, Joe; pull up a minute.'

'I'll hold my head out,' Cotton said. 'Never mind.' The car went on. Cotton thrust his head out the V strut of the top stanchion. The Sheriff shifted his arm, giving him play. 'Go on,' Cotton said, 'I'll be all right.' The car went on. Cotton slipped a little farther down in the seat. By moving his head a little he could wedge his throat into the apex of the iron V, the uprights gripping his jaws beneath the ears. He shifted again until his head was tight in the vise, then he swung his legs over the door, trying to bring the weight of his body sharply down against his imprisoned neck. He could hear his vertebrae; he felt a kind of rage at his own toughness; he was struggling then against the jerk on the manacle, the hands on him.

Then he was lying on his back beside the road, with water on his face and in his mouth, though he could not swallow. He couldn't speak, trying to curse, cursing in no voice. Then he was in the car again, on the smooth street where children played in the big, shady yards in small, bright garments, and men and women went home towards supper, to plates of food and cups of coffee in the long twilight of summer.

They had a doctor for him in his cell. When the doctor had gone he could smell supper cooking somewhere – ham and hot bread and coffee. He was lying on a cot; the last ray of copper sunlight slid through a narrow window, stippling the bars upon the wall above his head. His cell was near the common room, where the minor prisoners lived, the ones who were in jail for minor offences or for three meals a day; the stairway from below came up into that room. It was occupied for the time by a group of negroes from the chain-gang that worked the streets, in jail for vagrancy or for selling a little whisky or shooting craps for ten or fifteen cents. One of the negroes was at the window above the street, yelling down to someone. The others talked among themselves, their voices rich and murmurous, mellow and singsong. Cotton rose and went to the door of his cell and held to the bars, looking at the negroes.

'Hit,' he said. His voice made no sound. He put his hand to his throat; he produced a dry croaking sound, at which the negroes ceased talking and looked at him, their eyeballs rolling. 'It was all right,' Cotton said, 'until it started coming to pieces on me. I could a handled that dog.' He held his throat, his voice harsh, dry, and croaking. 'But it started coming to pieces on me . . .'

'Who him?' one of the negroes said. They whispered among themselves, watching him, their eyeballs white in the dusk.

'It would a been all right,' Cotton said, 'but it started coming to pieces . . .'

'Hush up, white man,' one of the negroes said. 'Don't you be telling us no truck like that.'

'Hit would a been all right,' Cotton said, his voice harsh, whispering. Then it failed him again altogether. He held to the bars with one hand, holding his throat with the other, while the negroes watched him, huddled, their eyeballs white and sober. Then with one accord they turned and rushed across the room, towards the staircase; he heard slow steps and then he smelled food, and he clung to the bars, trying to see the stairs. 'Are they going to feed them niggers before they feed a white man?' he said, smelling the coffee and the ham.

Three is a Lucky Number

MARGERY ALLINGHAM

AT FIVE O'CLOCK ON A September afternoon Ronald Frederick Torbay was making preparations for his third murder. He was being very wary, forcing himself to go slowly because he was perfectly sane and was well aware of the dangers of carelessness.

A career of homicide got more chancy as one went on. That piece of information had impressed him as being true as soon as he had read it in a magazine article way back before his first marriage. Also, he realized, success was liable to go to a man's head, so he kept a tight hold on himself. He was certain he was infinitely more clever than most human beings but he did not dwell on the fact and as soon as he felt the old thrill at the sense of his power welling up inside him, he quelled it firmly.

For an instant he paused, leaning on the rim of the wash-basin, and regarded himself thoughtfully in the shaving glass of the bathroom in the new villa he had hired so recently.

The face which looked at him was thin, middle-aged and pallid. Sparse dark hair receded from its high narrow forehead and the well-shaped eyes were blue and prominent. Only the mouth was really unusual. That narrow slit, quite straight, was almost lipless and, unconsciously, he persuaded it to relax into a half smile. Even Ronald Torbay did not like his own mouth.

A sound in the kitchen below disturbed him and he straightened his back hastily. If Edyth had finished her ironing she would be coming up to take her long discussed bubble-bath before he had prepared it for her and that would never do. He waited, holding his breath, but it was all right: she was going out of the back door. He reached the window just in time to see her disappearing round the side of the house into the small square yard which was so exactly like all the other square yards in the long suburban street. He knew that she was going to hang the newly pressed linen on the line to air and although the manœuvre gave him the time he needed, still it irritated him.

Of the three homely middle-aged women whom so far he had persuaded first to marry him and then to will him their modest possessions, Edyth was proving easily the most annoying. If he had told her once not to spend so much time in the yard he had done it a dozen times in their six weeks of marriage. He hated her being out of doors alone. She was shy and reserved but now that new people had moved in next door there was the danger of some over-friendly woman starting up an acquaintance with her and that was the last thing to be tolerated at this juncture.

Each of his former wives had been shy. He had been very careful to choose the right type and felt he owed much of his success to it. Mary, the first of them, had met her fatal 'accident' almost unnoticed in the bungalow on the housing estate very like the present one he had chosen but in the north instead of the south of England. At the time it had been a growing place, the coroner had been hurried, the police sympathetic but busy and the neighbours scarcely curious except that one of them, a junior reporter on a local paper, had written a flowery paragraph about the nearness of tragedy in the midst of joy, published a wedding day snapshot and had entitled the article with typical northern understatement 'Honeymoon Mishap'.

Dorothy's brief excursion into his life and abrupt exit from it and her own, had given him a little more bother but not much. She had deceived him when she had told him she was quite alone in the world and the interfering brother who had turned up after the funeral to ask awkward questions about her small fortune might have been a nuisance if Ronald had not been very firm with him. There had been a brief court case which Ronald had won handsomely and the insurance had paid up without a murmur.

All that was four years ago. Now, with a new name, a newly invented background and a fresh area in which to operate, he felt remarkably safe.

From the moment he had first seen Edyth, sitting alone at a little table under the window in a seaside hotel dining-room, he had known that she was to be his next subject. He always thought of his wives as 'subjects'. It lent his designs upon them a certain pseudo-scientific atmosphere which he found satisfying.

Edyth had sat there looking stiff and neat and a trifle severe but there had been a secret timidity in her face, an unsatisfied, half-frightened expression in her short-sighted eyes and once, when the waiter said something pleasant to her, she had flushed nervously and had been embarrassed by it. She was also wearing a genuine diamond brooch. Ronald had observed that from right across the room. He had an eye for stones.

That evening in the lounge he had spoken to her, had weathered the initial snub, tried again and, finally, had got her to talk. After that the acquaintance had progressed just as he had expected. His methods were old fashioned and heavily romantic and within a week she was hopelessly infatuated.

From Ronald's point of view her history was even better than he could have hoped. After teaching in a girls' boarding school for the whole of her twenties she had been summoned home to look after her recluse of a father whose long illness had monopolized her life. Now at forty-three she was alone, comparatively well off and as much at sea as a ship without a rudder.

Ronald was careful not to let her toes touch the ground. He devoted his entire attention to her and exactly five weeks from the day on which they first met, he married her at the registry office of the town where they were both strangers. The same afternoon they each made wills in the other's favour and moved into the villa which he had been able to hire cheaply because the holiday season was at an end.

It had been the pleasantest conquest he had ever made. Mary had been moody and hysterical, Dorothy grudging and suspicious but Edyth had revealed an unexpected streak of gaiety and, but for her stupidity in not realizing that a man would hardly fall romantically in love with her at first sight, was a sensible person. Any other man, Ronald reflected smugly, might have made the fatal mistake of feeling sorry for her, but he was 'above' all that, he told himself, and he began to make plans for what he described in his own mind rather grimly as 'her future'.

Two things signed her death warrant earlier than had been his original intention. One was her obstinate reticence over her monetary affairs and the other was her embarrassing interest in his job.

On the marriage certificate Ronald had described himself as a salesman and the story he was telling was that he was a junior partner in a firm of cosmetic manufacturers who were giving him a very generous leave of absence. Edyth accepted the statement without question, but almost at once she had begun to plan a visit to the office and the factory, and was always talking about the new clothes she must buy so as not to 'disgrace him'. At the same time she kept all her business papers locked in an old writing-case and steadfastly refused to discuss them however cautiously he raised the subject. Ronald had given up feeling angry with her and decided to act.

He turned from the window, carefully removed his jacket and began to run the bath. His heart was pounding, he noticed, frowning. He wished it would not. He needed to keep very calm.

The bathroom was the one room they had repainted. Ronald had done it himself soon after they had arrived and had put up the little shelf over the bath to hold a jar of bathsalts he had bought and a small electric heater of the old-fashioned two-element type, which was cheap but white like the walls and not too noticeable. He lent forward now and switched it on and stood looking at it until the two bars of glowing warmth appeared. Then he turned away and went out on to the landing, leaving it alight.

The fuse box which controlled all the electricity in the house was concealed in the bottom of the linen cupboard at the top of the stairs. Ronald opened the door carefully and using his handkerchief so that his fingerprints should leave no trace pulled up the main switch. Back in the bathroom the heater's glow died away; the bars were almost black again by the time he returned. He eyed the slender cabinet approvingly and then, still using the handkerchief, he lifted it bodily from the shelf and lowered it carefully into the water, arranging it so that it lay at an angle over the waste plug, close to the foot where it took up practically no room at all. The white flex ran up over the porcelain side of the bath, along the skirting board, under the door and into a wall socket, just outside on the landing.

When he had first installed the heater Edyth had demurred at this somewhat slipshod arrangement, but when he had explained that the local Council was stupid and fussy about fitting wall sockets in bathrooms since water was said to be a conductor she had compromised by letting him run the flex under the lino where it was not so noticeable.

At the moment the heater was perfectly visible in the bath. It certainly looked as if it had fallen into its odd position accidentally but no one in his senses could have stepped into the water without seeing it. Ronald paused, his eyes dark, his ugly mouth narrower than ever. The beautiful simplicity of the main plan, so certain, so swiftly fatal and above all, so safe as far as he himself was concerned gave him a thrill of pleasure as it always did. He turned off the bath and waited, listening. Edyth was coming back. He could hear her moving something on the concrete way outside the back door below and he leant over to where his jacket hung and took a plastic sachet from its inside breast pocket. He was re-reading the directions on the back of it when a slight sound made him turn his head and he saw, to his horror, the woman herself not five feet away. Her neat head had appeared suddenly just above the flat roof of the scullery, outside the bathroom window. She was clearing the dead leaves from the guttering and must, he guessed, be standing on the tall flight of steps which were kept just inside the back door.

It was typical of the man that he did not panic. Still holding the sachet lightly he stepped between her and the bath and spoke mildly.

'What on earth are you doing there, darling?'

Edyth started so violently at the sound of his voice that she almost fell off the steps and a flush of apprehension appeared on her thin cheeks.

'Oh, how you startled me! I thought I'd just do this little job before I came up to change. If it rains the gutter floods all over the back step.'

'Very thoughtful of you, my dear.' He spoke with that slightly acid amusement with which he had found he could best destroy her slender vein of self assurance. 'But not terribly clever when you knew I'd come up to prepare your beauty bath for you. Or was it?'

The slight intonation on the word 'beauty' was not lost on her. He saw her swallow.

'Perhaps it wasn't,' she said without looking at him. 'It's very good of you to take all this trouble, Ronald.'

'Not at all,' he said with a just amount of masculine, off-hand insensitivity. 'I'm taking you out tonight and I want you to look as nice as – er – possible. Hurry up, there's a good girl. The foam doesn't last indefinitely and like all these very high-class beauty treatments the ingredients are expensive. Undress in the bedroom, put on your gown and come straight along.'

'Very well, dear.' She began to descend at once while he turned to the bath and shook the contents of the sachet into the water. The crystals, which were peach coloured and smelled strongly of roses, floated on the tide and then, as he suddenly turned the pressure of water full on, began to dissolve into thousands of irridescent bubbles. A momentary fear that their camouflage would not prove to be sufficient assailed him, and he stooped to beat the water with his hand, but he need not have worried. The cloud grew and grew into a fragrant feathery mass which not only obscured the bottom of the bath and all it contained, but mounted the porcelain sides, smothering the white flex and overflowing on to the wall panels and the bath-mat. It was perfect.

He pulled on his jacket and opened the door.

'Edyth! Hurry, dearest!' The words were on the tip of his tongue but her arrival forestalled them. She came shrinking in, her blue dressing-gown strained round her thin body, her hair thrust into an unbecoming bathing cap.

'Oh, Ronald!' she said, staring at the display aghast. 'Won't it make an awful mess? Goodness! All over the floor!'

Her hesitation infuriated him.

'That won't matter,' he said savagely. 'You get in while the virtue of the foam is still there. Hurry. Meanwhile I'll go and change, myself. I'll give you ten minutes. Get straight in and lie down. It'll take some of the sallowness out of that skin of yours.'

He went out and paused, listening. She locked the door as he had known she would. The habit of a lifetime does not suddenly change with marriage. He heard the bolt slide home and forced himself to

274

walk slowly down the passage. He gave her sixty seconds. Thirty to take off her things and thirty to hesitate on the brink of the rosy mass.

'How is it?' he shouted from the linen cupboard doorway.

She did not answer at once and the sweat broke out on his forehead. Then he heard her.

'I don't know yet. I'm only just in. It smells lovely.'

He did not wait for the final word, his hand wrapped in his handkerchief had found the main switch again.

'One, two . . . three,' he said with horrible prosaicness and pulled it down.

From the wall socket behind him there was a single spluttering flare as the fuse went and then silence.

All round Ronald it was so quiet that he could hear the pulses in his own body, the faraway tick of a clock at the bottom of the stairs, the dreary buzzing of a fly imprisoned against the window glass and, from the garden next door, the drone of a mower as the heavy, fresh-faced man who had moved there, performed his weekly chore shaving the little green lawn. But from the bathroom there was no sound at all.

After a while he crept back along the passage and tapped at the door.

'Edyth?'

No. There was no response, no sound, nothing.

'Edyth?' he said again.

The silence was complete and, after a minute he straightened his back and let out a deep sighing breath.

Almost at once he was keyed up again in preparing for the second phase. As he knew well, this next was the tricky period. The discovery of the body had got to be made but not too soon. He had made that mistake about Dorothy's 'accident' and had actually been asked by the local inspector why he had taken alarm so soon, but he had kept his head and the dangerous moment had flickered past. This time he had made up his mind to make it half an hour before he began to hammer loudly at the door, then to shout for a neighbour and finally to force the lock. He had planned to stroll out to buy an evening paper in the interim, shouting his intention to do so to Edyth from the front step for any passer-by to hear, but as he walked back along the landing he knew there was something else he was going to do first.

Edyth's leather writing-case in which she kept all her private papers was in the bottom of her soft-topped canvas hatbox. She had really believed he had not known of its existence, he reflected bitterly. It was locked, as he had discovered when he had at last located it, and he had not prised the catch for fear of putting her on her guard, but now there was nothing to stop him.

He went softly into the bedroom and opened the wardrobe door.

275

The case was exactly where he had last seen it, plump and promising, and his hands closed over it gratefully. The catch was a little more difficult than he had expected but he got it open at last and the orderly contents of the leather box came into view. At first sight it was all most satisfactory, far better than he had anticipated. There were bundles of savings certificates, one or two thick envelopes whose red seals suggested the offices of lawyers and, on top, ready for the taking, one of those familiar blue books which the Post Office issues to its savings bank clients.

He opened it with shaking fingers and fluttered through the pages. Two thousand. The sum made him whistle. Two thousand eight hundred and fifty. She must have paid in a decent dividend there. Two thousand nine hundred. Then a drop as she had drawn out a hundred pounds for her trousseau. Two thousand eight hundred. He thought that was the final entry but on turning the page saw that there was yet one other recorded transaction. It was less than a week old. He remembered the book coming back through the mail and how clever she had thought she had been in smuggling the envelope out of sight. He glanced at the written words and figures idly at first but then as his heart jolted in sudden panic stared at them, his eyes prominent and glazed. She had taken almost all of it out. There it was in black and white: *September 4th Withdrawal Two thousand seven hundred and ninety-eight pounds.*

His first thought was that the money must still be there, in hundred-pound notes perhaps in one of the envelopes. He tore through them hastily, forgetting all caution in his anxiety. Papers, letters, certificates fell on the floor in confusion.

The envelope, addressed to himself, pulled him up short. It was new and freshly blotted, the name inscribed in Edyth's own unexpectedly firm hand, Ronald Torbay, Esqre.

He wrenched it open and smoothed the single sheet of bond paper within. The date, he noted in amazement, was only two days old.

'Dear Ronald,
   If you ever get this I am afraid it will prove a dreadful shock to you. For a long time I have been hoping that it might not be necessary to write it but now your behaviour has forced me to face some very unpleasant possibilities.
   I am afraid, Ronald, that in some ways you are very old-fashioned. Had it not occurred to you that any homely middle-aged woman who has been swept into hasty marriage to a stranger must, unless she is a perfect idiot, be just a little suspicious and touchy on the subject of *baths*?
   Your predecessor James Joseph Smith and his Brides are not

entirely forgotten, you know.

Frankly, I did not want to suspect you. For a long time I thought I was in love with you, but when you persuaded me to make my will on our wedding day I could not help wondering, and then as soon as you started fussing about the bathroom in this house I thought I had better do something about it rather quickly. I am old-fashioned too, so I went to the police.

Have you noticed that the people who have moved into the house next door have never tried to speak to you? We thought it best that I should merely talk to the woman over the garden wall, and it is she who has shown me the two cuttings from old provincial newspapers each about women who met with fatal accidents in bubble-baths soon after their marriages. In each case there was a press snapshot of the husband taken at the funeral. They are not very clear but as soon as I saw them I realized that it was my duty to agree to the course suggested to me by the inspector who has been looking for a man answering to that description for three years, ever since the two photographs were brought to his notice by your poor second wife's brother.

What I am trying to say is this: if you should ever lose me, Ronald, out of the bathroom I mean, you will find that I have gone out over the roof and am sitting in my dressing-gown in the kitchen next door. I was a fool to marry you but not quite such a fool as you assumed. Women may be silly but they are not so stupid as they used to be. We are picking up the idea, Ronald.

Yours, Edyth

PS. On re-reading this note I see that in my nervousness I have forgotten to mention that the new people next door are not a married couple but Detective Constable Batsford of the CID and his assistant, Policewoman Richards. The police assure me that there cannot be sufficient evidence to convict you if you are not permitted to attempt the crime again. That is why I am forcing myself to be brave and to play my part, for I am very sorry for those other poor wives of yours, Ronald. They must have found you as fascinating as I did.'

With his slit mouth twisted into an abominable 'O', Ronald Torbay raised haggard eyes from the letter.

The house was still quiet and even the whine of the mower in the next door garden had ceased. In the hush he heard a sudden clatter as the back door burst open and heavy footsteps raced through the hall and up the stairs towards him.

First Hate
ALGERNON BLACKWOOD

THEY HAD BEEN SHOOTING all day; the weather had been perfect and the powder straight, so that when they assembled in the smoking-room after dinner they were well-pleased with themselves. From discussing the day's sport and the weather outlook, the conversation drifted to other, though still cognate, fields. Lawson, the crack shot of the party, mentioned the instinctive recognition all animals feel for their natural enemies, and gave several instances in which he had tested it – tame rats with a ferret, birds with a snake, and so forth.

'Even after being domesticated for generations,' he said, 'they recognize their natural enemy at once by instinct, an enemy they can never even have seen before. It's infallible. They know instantly.'

'Undoubtedly,' said a voice from the corner chair; 'and so do we.'

The speaker was Ericssen, their host, a great hunter before the Lord, generally uncommunicative but a good listener, leaving the talk to others. For this latter reason, as well as for a certain note of challenge in his voice, his abrupt statement gained attention.

'What do you mean exactly by "so do we"?' asked three men together, after waiting some seconds to see whether he meant to elaborate, which he evidently did not.

'We belong to the animal kingdom, of course,' put in a fourth, for behind the challenge there obviously lay a story, though a story that might be difficult to drag out of him. It was.

Ericssen, who had leaned forward a moment so that his strong, humorous face was in clear light, now sank back again into his chair, his expression concealed by the red lampshade at his side. The light played tricks, obliterating the humorous, almost tender, lines, while emphasizing the strength of the jaw and nose. The red glare lent to the whole a rather grim expression.

Lawson, man of authority among them, broke the little pause.

'You're dead right,' he observed; 'but how do you know it?' – for John Ericssen never made a positive statement without a good reason for it. That good reason, he felt sure, involved a personal proof, but a story Ericssen would never tell before a general audience. He would tell it later, however, when the others had left. 'There's such a thing as

278

instinctive antipathy, of course,' he added, with a laugh, looking round him. 'That's what you mean, probably.'

'I meant exactly what I said,' replied the host bluntly. 'There's first love. There's first hate, too.'

'Hate's a strong word,' remarked Lawson.

'So is love,' put in another.

'Hate's strongest,' said Ericssen grimly. 'In the animal kingdom, at least,' he added suggestively, and then kept his lips closed, except to sip his liquor, for the rest of the evening – until the party at length broke up, leaving Lawson and one other man, both old trusted friends of many years' standing.

'It's not a tale I'd tell to everybody,' he began, when they were alone. 'It's true, for one thing; for another, you see, some of those good fellows' – he indicated the empty chairs with an expressive nod of his great head – 'some of 'em knew him. You both knew him too, probably.'

'The man you hated,' said the understanding Lawson.

'And who hated me,' came the quiet confirmation. 'My other reason,' he went on, 'for keeping quiet was that the tale involves my wife.'

The two listeners said nothing, but each remembered the curiously long courtship that had been the prelude to his marriage. No engagement had been announced, the pair were devoted to one another, there was no known rival on either side, yet the courtship continued without coming to its expected conclusion. Many stories were afloat in consequence. It was a social mystery that intrigued the gossips.

'I may tell you two,' Ericssen continued, 'the reason my wife refused for so long to marry me. It is hard to believe, perhaps, but it is true. Another man wished to make her his wife, and she would not consent to marry me until that other man was dead. Quixotic, absurd, unreasonable? If you like. I'll tell you what she said.' He looked up with a significant expression in his face which proved that he, at least, did not now judge her reason foolish. ' "Because it would be murder," she told me. "Another man who wants to marry me would kill you." '

'She had some proof for the assertion, no doubt?' suggested Lawson.

'None whatever,' was the reply. 'Merely her woman's instinct. Moreover, *I* did not know who the other man was, nor would she ever tell me.'

'Otherwise you might have murdered him instead?' said Baynes, the second listener.

'I did,' said Ericssen grimly. 'But without knowing he was the man.' He sipped his whisky and relit his pipe. The others waited.

279

'Our marriage took place two months later – just after Hazel's disappearance.'

'Hazel?' exclaimed Lawson and Baynes in a single breath. 'Hazel! Member of the Hunters!' His mysterious disappearance had been a nine days' wonder some ten years ago. It had never been explained. They had all been membrs of the Hunters' Club together.

'That's the chap,' Ericssen said. 'Now I'll tell you the tale, if you care to hear it.' They settled back in their chairs to listen, and Ericssen, who had evidently never told the affair to another living soul except his own wife, doubtless, seemed glad this time to tell it to two men.

'It began some dozen years ago when my brother Jack and I came home from a shooting trip in China. I've often told you about our adventures there, and you see the heads hanging up here in the smoking-room – some of 'em'. He glanced round proudly at the walls. 'We were glad to be in town again after two years' roughing it, and we looked forward to our first good dinner at the Club, to make up for the rotten cooking we had endured so long. We had ordered that dinner in anticipatory detail many a time together. Well, we had it and enjoyed it up to a point – the point of the *entrée*, to be exact.

'Up to that point it was delicious, and we let ourselves go, I can tell you. We had ordered the very wine we had planned months before when we were snow-bound and half starving in the mountains.' He smacked his lips as he mentioned it. 'I was just starting on a beautifully cooked grouse,' he went on, 'when a figure went by our table, and Jack looked up and nodded. The two exchanged a brief word of greeting and explanation, and the other man passed on. Evidently they knew each other just enough to make a word or two necessary, but enough.

' "Who's that?" I asked.

' "A new member, named Hazel," Jack told me. "A great shot." He knew him slightly, he explained; he had once been a client of his – Jack was a barrister, you remember – and had defended him in some financial case or other. Rather an unpleasant case, he added. Jack did not "care about" the fellow, he told me, as he went on with his tender wing of grouse.'

Ericssen paused to relight his pipe a moment.

'Not care about him!' he continued. 'It didn't surprise me, for my own feeling, the instant I set eyes on the fellow, was one of violent, instinctive dislike that amounted to loathing. Loathing! No. I'll give it the right word – hatred. I simply couldn't help myself; I hated the man from the very first go off. A wave of repulsion swept over me as I followed him down the room a moment with my eyes, till he took his seat at a distant table and was out of sight. Ugh! He was a big, fat-faced man, with an eyeglass glued into one of his pale-blue cod-like eyes – out of condition, ugly as a toad, with a smug expression of intense self-satisfaction on his jowl that made me long to——

'I leave it to you to guess what I would have liked to do to him. But the instinctive loathing he inspired in me had another aspect, too. Jack had not introduced us during the momentary pause beside our table, but as I looked up I caught the fellow's eye on mine – he was glaring at me instead of at Jack, to whom he was talking – with an expression of malignant dislike, as keen evidently as my own. That's the other aspect I meant. He hated me as violently as I hated him. We were instinctive enemies, just as the rat and ferret are instinctive enemies. Each recognized a mortal foe. It was a case – I swear it – of whoever got first chance.'

'Bad as that!' exclaimed Baynes. 'I knew him by sight. He wasn't pretty, I'll admit.'

'I knew him to nod to,' Lawson mentioned. 'I never heard anything particular against him.' He shrugged his shoulders.

Ericssen went on. 'It was not his character or qualities I hated,' he said. 'I didn't even know them. That's the whole point. There's no reason you fellows should have disliked him. My hatred – our mutual hatred – was instinctive, as instinctive as first love. A man knows his natural mate; also he knows his natural enemy. I did, at any rate, both with him and with my wife. Given the chance, Hazel would have done me in; just as surely, given the chance, I would have done him in. No blame to either of us, what's more, in my opinion.'

'I've felt dislike, but never hatred like that,' Baynes mentioned. 'I came across it in a book once, though. The writer did not mention the instinctive fear of the human animal for its natural enemy, or anything of that sort. He thought it was a continuance of a bitter feud begun in an earlier existence. He called it memory.'

'Possibly,' said Ericssen briefly. 'My mind is not speculative. But I'm glad you spoke of fear. I left that out. The truth is, I feared the fellow, too, in a way; and had we ever met face to face in some wild country without witnesses I should have felt justified in drawing on him at sight, and he would have felt the same. Murder? If you like. I should call it self-defence. Anyhow, the fellow polluted the room for me. He spoilt the enjoyment of that dinner we had ordered months before in China.'

'But you saw him again, of course, later?'

'Lots of times. Not that night, because we went on to a theatre. But in the Club we were always running across one another – in the houses of friends at lunch or dinner; at race meetings; all over the place; in fact, I even had some trouble to avoid being introduced to him. And every time we met, our eyes betrayed us. He felt in his heart what I felt in mine. Ugh! He was as loathsome to me as leprosy, and as dangerous. Odd, isn't it? The most intense feeling, except love, I've ever known. I remember' – he laughed gruffly – 'I used to feel quite sorry for him. If he felt what I felt, and I'm convinced he did, he must have suffered. His one object – to get me out of the way for good – was so impossible. Then Fate played a hand in the game. I'll tell you how.

'My brother died a year or two later, and I went abroad to try and forget it. I went salmon fishing in Canada. But, though the sport was good, it was not like the old times with Jack. The camp never felt the same without him. I missed him badly. But I forgot Hazel for the time; hating did not seem worth while, somehow.

'When the best of the fishing was over on the Atlantic side I took a run back to Vancouver and fished there for a bit. I went up to the Campbell River, which was not so crowded then as it is now, and had some rattling sport. Then I grew tired of the rod and decided to go after wapiti for a change. I came back to Victoria and learned what I could about the best places, and decided finally to go up the west coast of the island. By luck I happened to pick up a good guide, who was in the town at the moment on business, and we started off together in one of the little Canadian Pacific Railway boats that ply along that coast.

'Outfitting two days later at a small place the steamer stopped at, the guide said we needed another man to help pack our kit over portages, and so forth, but the only fellow available was a Siwash of whom he disapproved. My guide would not have him at any price; he was lazy, a drunkard, a liar, and even worse, for on one occasion he came back without the sportsman he had taken up country on a shooting trio, and his story was not convincing, to say the least. These disappearances are always awkward, of course, as you both know. We preferred, anyhow, to go without the Siwash, and off we started.

'At first our luck was bad. I saw many wapiti, but no good heads; only after a fortnight's hunting did I manage to get a decent head, though even that was not so good as I should have liked.

'We were then near the head waters of a little river that ran down into the Inlet; heavy rains had made the river rise; running downstream was a risky job, what with old log-jams shifting and new ones forming; and, after many narrow escapes, we upset one afternoon and had the misfortune to lose a lot of our kit, amongst it most of our cartridges. We could only muster a few between us. The guide had a dozen; I had two – just enough, we considered, to take us out all right. Still, it was an infernal nuisance. We camped at once to dry out our soaked things in front of a big fire, and while this laundry work was going on the guide suggested my filling in the time by taking a look at the next little valley, which ran parallel to ours. He had seen some

282

good heads over there a few weeks ago. Possibly I might come upon the herd. I started at once, taking my two cartridges with me.

'It was the devil of a job getting over the divide, for it was a badly bushed-up place; and where there were no bushes there were boulders and fallen trees, and the going was slow and tiring. But I got across at last and came out upon another stream at the bottom of the new valley. Signs of wapiti were plentiful, though I never came up with a single beast all the afternoon. Blacktail deer were everywhere, but the wapiti remained invisible. Providence, or whatever you like to call that fate which there is no escaping in our lives, made me save my two cartridges.'

Ericssen stopped a minute then. It was not to light his pipe or sip his whisky. Nor was it because the remainder of his story failed in the recollection of any vivid detail. He paused a moment to think.

'Tell us the lot,' pleaded Lawson. 'Don't leave out anything.'

Ericssen looked up. His friend's remark had helped him to make up his mind apparently. He *had* hesitated about something or other, but the hesitation passed. He glanced at both his listeners.

'Right,' he said. 'I'll tell you everything. I'm not imaginative, as you know, and my amount of superstition, I should judge, is microscopic.' He took a longer breath, then lowered his voice a trifle. 'Anyhow,' he went on, 'it's true, so I don't see why I should feel shy about admitting it – but as I stood there, in that lonely valley, where only the noises of wind and water were audible, and no human being, except my guide, some miles away, was within reach, a curious feeling came over me I find difficult to describe. I felt' – obviously he made an effort to get the word out – 'I felt creepy.'

'You,' murmured Lawson, with an incredulous smile – 'you creepy?' he repeated under his breath.

'I felt creepy and afraid,' continued the other, with conviction. 'I had the sensation of being seen by someone – as if someone, I mean, was watching me. It was so unlikely that anyone was near me in that God-forsaken bit of wilderness that I simply couldn't believe it at first. But the feeling persisted. I felt absolutely positive somebody was not far away among the red maples, behind a boulder, across the little stream, perhaps – somewhere, at any rate, so near that I was plainly visible to him. It was not an animal. It was human. Also, it was hostile.

'I was in danger.

'You may laugh, both of you, but I assure you the feeling was so positive that I crouched down instinctively to hide myself behind a rock. My first thought, that the guide had followed me for some reason or other, I at once discarded. It was not the guide. It was an enemy.

'No, no, I thought of no one in particular. No name, no face occurred to me. Merely that an enemy was on my trail, that he saw me, and I did not see him, and that he was near enough to me to – well, to take instant action. This deep instinctive feeling of danger, of fear, of anything you like to call it, was simply overwhelming.

'Another curious detail I must also mention. About half an hour before, having given up all hope of seeing wapiti, I had decided to kill a blacktail deer for meat. A good shot offered itself, not thirty yards away. I aimed. But just as I was going to pull the trigger a queer emotion touched me, and I lowered the rifle. It was exactly as though a voice said, "Don't!" I heard no voice, mind you; it was an emotion only, a feeling, a sudden inexplicable change of mind – a warning, if you like. I didn't fire, anyhow.

'But now, as I crouched behind that rock, I remembered this curious little incident, and was glad I had not used up my last two cartridges. More than that I cannot tell you. Things of that kind are new to me. They're difficult enough to tell let alone to explain. But they were *real*.

'I crouched there, wondering what on earth was happening to me, and feeling a bit of a fool, if you want to know, when suddenly, over the top of the boulder, I saw something moving. It was a man's hat. I peered cautiously. Some sixty yards away the bushes parted, and two men came out on the river's bank, and I knew them both. One was the Siwash I had seen at the store. The other was Hazel. Before I had time to think I cocked my rifle.'

'Hazel. Good Lord!' exclaimed the listeners.

'For a moment I was too surprised to do anything but cock that rifle. I waited, for what puzzled me was that, after all, Hazel had *not* seen me. It was only the feeling of his beastly proximity that had made me feel I was seen and watched by him. There was something else, too, that made me pause before – er – doing anything. Two other things, in fact. One was that I was intensely interested in watching the fellow's actions. Obviously he had the same uneasy sensation that I had. He shared with me the nasty feeling that danger was about. His rifle, I saw, was cocked and ready; he kept looking behind him, over his shoulder, peering this way and that, and sometimes addressing a remark to the Siwash at his side. I caught the laughter of the latter. The Siwash evidently did not think there was danger anywhere. It was, of course, unlikely enough————'

'And the other thing that stopped you?' urged Lawson, impatiently interrupting.

Ericssen turned with a look of grim humour on his face.

'Some confounded or perverted sense of chivalry in me, I suppose,' he said, 'that made it impossible to shoot him down in cold blood, or, rather, without letting him have a chance. For my blood, as a matter of fact, was far from cold at the moment. Perhaps, too, I wanted the added satisfaction of letting him know who fired the shot that was to end his vile existence.'

He laughed again. 'It was rat and ferret in the human kingdom,' he went on, 'but I wanted my rat to have a chance, I suppose. Anyhow, though I had a perfect shot in front of me at easy distance, I did not fire. Instead I got up, holding my cocked rifle ready, finger on trigger, and came out of my hiding-place. I called to him. "Hazel, you beast! So there you are – at last!"

'He turned, but turned away from me, offering his horrid back. The direction of the voice he misjudged. He pointed down-stream, and the Siwash turned to look. Neither of them had seen me yet. There was a big log-jam below them. The roar of the water in their ears concealed my footsteps. I was, perhaps, twenty paces from them when Hazel, with a jerk of his whole body, abruptly turned clean round and faced me. We stared into each other's eyes.

'The amazement on his face changed instantly to hatred and resolve. He acted with incredible rapidity. I think the unexpected suddenness of his turn made me lose a precious second or two. Anyhow he was ahead of me. He flung his rifle to his shoulder. "You devil!" I heard his voice. "I've got you at last!" His rifle cracked, for he let drive the same instant. The hair stirred just above my ear.

'He had missed!

'Before he could draw back his bolt for another shot I had acted.

' "You're not fit to live!" I shouted, as my bullet crashed into his temple. I had the satisfaction, too, of knowing that he heard my words. I saw the swift expression of frustrated loathing in his eyes.

'He fell like an ox, his face splashing in the stream. I shoved the body out. I saw it sucked beneath the log-jam instantly. It disappeared. There could be no inquest on him, I reflected comfortably. Hazel was gone – gone from this earth, from my life, our mutual hatred over at last.'

The speaker paused a moment. 'Odd,' he continued presently – 'very odd indeed.' He turned to the others. 'I felt quite sorry for him suddenly. I suppose,' he added, 'the philosophers are right when they gas about hate being very close to love.'

His friends contributed no remark.

'Then I came away,' he resumed shortly. 'My wife – well, you know the rest, don't you? I told her the whole thing. She – said nothing. But she married me, you see.'

There was a moment's silence. Baynes was the first to break it. 'But – the Siwash?' he asked. 'The witness?'

Lawson turned upon him with something of contemptuous

'He told you he had *two* cartridges.'
Ericssen, smiling grimly, said nothing at all.

The Victim

P. D. JAMES

YOU KNOW PRINCESS ILSA MANCELLI, of course. I mean by that that you must have seen her on the cinema screen; on television; pictured in newspapers arriving at airports with her latest husband; relaxing on their yacht; bejewelled at first nights, gala nights, at any night and in any place where it is obligatory for the rich and successful to show themselves. Even if, like me, you have nothing but bored contempt for what I believe is called the international jet-set, you can hardly live in a modern world and not know Ilsa Mancelli. And you can't fail to have picked up some scraps about her past. The brief and not particularly successful screen career, when even her heart-stopping beauty couldn't quite compensate for the paucity of talent; the succession of marriages, first to the producer who made her first film and who broke a twenty-year-old marriage to get her; then to a Texan millionaire; lastly to a prince. About two months ago I saw a nauseatingly sentimental picture of her with her two-day-old son in a Rome nursing home. So it looks as if this marriage, sanctified as it is by wealth, a title and maternity may be intended as her final adventure.

The husband before the film producer is, I notice, no longer mentioned. Perhaps her publicity agent fears that a violent death in the family, particularly an unsolved violent death, might tarnish her bright image. Blood and beauty. In the early stages of her career they hadn't been able to resist that cheap, vicarious thrill. But not now. Nowadays her early history, before she married the film producer, has become a little obscure, although there is a suggestion of poor but decent parentage and early struggles suitably rewarded. I am the most obscure part of that obscurity. Whatever you know, or think you know of Ilsa Mancelli, you won't have heard about me. The publicity machine has decreed that I be nameless, faceless, unremembered, that I no longer exist. Ironically, the machine is right; in any real sense, I don't.

I married her when she was Elsie Bowman aged seventeen. I was assistant librarian at our local branch library and fifteen years older, a

287

thirty-two-year-old virgin, a scholar manqué, thin-faced, a little
stooping, my meagre hair already thinning. She worked on the
cosmetic counter of our High Street store. She was beautiful then, but
with a delicate, tentative, unsophisticated loveliness which gave little
promise of the mature beauty which is hers today. Our story was very
ordinary. She returned a book to the library one evening when I was
on counter duty. We chatted. She asked my advice about novels for
her mother. I spent as long as I dared finding suitable romances for
her on the shelves. I tried to interest her in the books I liked. I asked
her about herself, her life, her ambitions. She was the only woman I
had been able to talk to. I was enchanted by her, totally and
completely besotted.

I used to take my lunch early and make surreptitious visits to the
store, watching her from the shadow of a neighbouring pillar. There is
one picture which even now seems to stop my heart. She had dabbed
her wrist with scent and was holding out a bare arm over the counter
so that a prospective customer could smell the perfume. She was
totally absorbed, her young face gravely preoccupied. I watched her,
silently, and felt the tears smarting my eyes.

It was a miracle when she agreed to marry me. Her mother (she
had no father) was reconciled if not enthusiastic about the match. She
didn't, as she made it abundantly plain, consider me much of a catch.
But I had a good job with prospects; I was educated; I was steady and
reliable; I spoke with a grammar school accent which, while she
affected to deride it, raised my status in her eyes. Besides, any
marriage for Elsie was better than none. I was dimly aware when I
bothered to think about Elsie in relation to anyone but myself that she
and her mother didn't get on.

Mrs Bowman made, as she described it, a splash. There was a full
choir and a peal of bells. The church hall was hired and a sit-down
meal, ostentatiously unsuitable and badly cooked, was served to
eighty guests. Between the pangs of nervousness and indigestion I was
conscious of smirking waiters in short white jackets, a couple of
giggling bridesmaids from the store, their freckled arms bulging from
pink taffeta sleeves, hearty male relatives, red faced and with
buttonholes of carnation and waving fern, who made indelicate jokes
and clapped me painfully between the shoulders. There were speeches
and warm champagne. And, in the middle of it all, Elsie my Elsie, like
a white rose.

I suppose that it was stupid of me to imagine that I could hold her.
The mere sight of our morning faces, smiling at each other's reflection
in the bedroom mirror, should have warned me that it couldn't last.
But, poor, deluded fool, I never dreamed that I might lose her except
by death. Her death I dared not contemplate, and I was afraid for the

first time of my own. Happiness had made a coward of me. We moved into a new bungalow, chosen by Elsie, sat in new chairs chosen by Elsie, slept in a befrilled bed chosen by Elsie. I was so happy that it was like passing into a new phase of existence, breathing a different air, seeing the most ordinary things as if they were newly created. One isn't necessarily humble when greatly in love. Is it so unreasonable to recognize the value of a love like mine, to believe that the beloved is equally sustained and transformed by it?

She said that she wasn't ready to start a baby and, without her job, she was easily bored. She took a brief training in shorthand and typing at our local Technical College and found herself a position as shorthand typist at the firm of Collingford and Major. That, at least, was how the job started. Shorthand typist, then secretary to Mr Rodney Collingford, then personal secretary, then confidential personal secretary; in my bemused state of uxorious bliss I only half registered her progress from occasionally taking his dictation when his then secretary was absent to flaunting his gifts of jewellery and sharing his bed.

He was everything I wasn't. Rich (his father had made a fortune from plastics shortly after the war and had left the factory to his only son), coarsely handsome in a swarthy fashion, big muscled, confident, attractive to women. He prided himself on taking what he wanted. Elsie must have been one of his easiest pickings.

Why, I still wonder, did he want to marry her? I thought at the time that he couldn't resist depriving a pathetic, under-privileged, un-attractive husband of a prize which neither looks nor talent had qualified him to deserve. I've noticed that about the rich and successful. They can't bear to see the undeserving prosper. I thought that half the satisfaction for him was in taking her away from me. That was partly why I knew that I had to kill him. But now I'm not so sure. I may have done him an injustice. It may have been both simpler and more complicated than that. She was, you see – she still is – so very beautiful.

I understand her better now. She was capable of kindness, good humour, generosity even, provided she was getting what she wanted. At the time we married, and perhaps eighteen months afterwards, she wanted me. Neither her egoism nor her curiosity had been able to resist such a flattering, overwhelming love. But for her, marriage wasn't permanency. It was the first and necessary step towards the kind of life she wanted and meant to have. She was kind to me, in bed and out, while I was what she wanted. But when she wanted someone else, then my need of her, my jealousy, my bitterness, she saw as a cruel and wilful denial of her basic right, the right to have what she wanted. After all, I'd had her for nearly three years. It was two years more than I had any right to expect. She thought so. Her darling Rodney thought so. When my acquaintances at the library learnt of the divorce I could see in their eyes that they thought so too. And she couldn't see what I was so bitter about. Rodney was perfectly happy to be the guilty party; they weren't, she pointed out caustically, expecting me to behave like a gentleman. I wouldn't have to pay for the divorce. Rodney would see to that. I wasn't being asked to provide her with alimony. Rodney had more than enough. At one point she came close to bribing me with Rodney's money to let her go without fuss. And yet – was it really as simple as that? She had loved me, or at least needed me, for a time. Had she perhaps seen in me that father that she had lost at five years old?

During the divorce, through which I was, as it were, gently processed by highly paid legal experts as if I were an embarrassing but expendable nuisance to be got rid of with decent speed, I was only able to keep sane by the knowledge that I was going to kill Collingford. I knew that I couldn't go on living in a world where he breathed the same air. My mind fed voraciously on the thought of his death, savoured it, began systematically and with dreadful pleasure to plan it.

A successful murder depends on knowing your victim, his character, his daily routine, his weaknesses, those unalterable and betraying habits which make up the core of the personality. I knew quite a lot about Rodney Collingford. I knew facts which Elsie had let fall in her first few weeks with the firm, typing pool gossip. I knew the fuller and rather more intimate facts which she had disclosed in those early days of her enchantment with him, when neither prudence nor kindness had been able to conceal her obsessive preoccupation with her new boss. I should have been warned then. I knew, none better, the need to talk about the absent lover.

What did I know about him? I knew the facts that were common knowledge, of course. That he was wealthy; aged thirty; a notable golfer; that he lived in an ostentatious mock Georgian house on the banks of the Thames looked after by over-paid but non-resident staff; that he owned a cabin cruiser; that he was just over six feet tall; that he was a good business man but reputedly close-fisted; that he was methodical in his habits. I knew a miscellaneous and unrelated set of facts about him, some of which would be useful, some important, some of which I couldn't use. I knew – and this was rather surprising – that he was good with his hands and liked making things in metal and wood. He had built an expensively-equipped and large workroom in the grounds of his house and spent every Thursday evening working there alone. He was a man addicted to routine. This creativity, however mundane and trivial, I found intriguing, but I didn't let myself dwell on it. I was interested in him only so far as his personality and habits were relevant to his death. I never thought of him as a human being. He had no existence for me apart from my hate. He was Rodney Collingford, my victim.

First I decided on the weapon. A gun would have been the most certain, I supposed, but I didn't know how to get one and was only too well aware that I wouldn't know how to load or use it if I did. Besides, I was reading a number of books about murder at the time and I realized that guns, however cunningly obtained, were easy to trace. And there was another thing. A gun was too impersonal, too remote. I wanted to make physical contact at the moment of death. I wanted to get close enough to see that final look of incredulity and horror as he recognized, simultaneously, me and his death. I wanted to drive a knife into his throat.

I bought it two days after the divorce. I was in no hurry to kill Collingford. I knew that I must take my time, must be patient if I were to act in safety. One day, perhaps when we were old, I might tell Elsie. But I didn't intend to be found out. This was to be the perfect murder. And that meant taking my time. He would be allowed to live for a full year. But I knew that the earlier I bought the knife the more difficult it would be, twelve months later to trace the purchase. I didn't buy it locally. I went one Saturday morning by train and bus to a north-east suburb and found a busy ironmongers and general store just off the High Street. There was a variety of knives on display. The blade of the one I selected was about six inches long and was made of strong steel screwed into a plain wooden handle. I think it was probably meant for cutting lino. In the shop its razor edge was protected by a strong cardboard sheath. It felt good and right in my hand. I stood in a small queue at the pay desk and the cashier didn't even glance up as he took my notes and pushed the change towards me.

But the most satisfying part of my planning was the second stage. I wanted Collingford to suffer. I wanted him to know that he was going to die. It wasn't enough that he should realize it in a last second before I drove in the knife or in that final second before he ceased to know anything for ever. Two seconds of agony, however horrible, weren't an adequate return for what he had done to me. I wanted him to know that he was a condemned man, to know it with increasing certainty, to wonder every morning whether this might be his last day. What if this knowledge did make him cautious, put him on his guard? In this country, he couldn't go armed. He couldn't carry on his business with a hired protector always at his side. He couldn't bribe the police to watch him every second of the day. Besides, he wouldn't want to be thought a coward. I guessed that he would carry on, ostentatiously

291

normal, as if the threats were unreal or derisory, something to laugh about with his drinking cronies. He was the sort to laugh at danger. But he would never be sure. And by the end, his nerve and confidence would be broken. Elsie wouldn't know him for the man she had married.

I would have liked to have telephoned him but that, I knew, was impracticable. Calls could be traced; he might refuse to talk to me; I wasn't confident that I could disguise my voice. So the sentence of death would have to be sent by post. Obviously, I couldn't write the notes or the envelopes myself. My studies in murder had shown me how difficult it was to disguise handwriting and the method of cutting out and sticking together letters from a newspaper seemed messy, very time consuming and difficult to manage wearing gloves. I knew, too, that it would be fatal to use my own small portable typewriter or one of the machines in the library. The forensic experts could identify a machine.

And then I hit on my plan. I began to spend my Saturdays and occasional half days journeying round London and visiting shops where they sold secondhand typewriters. I expect you know the kind of shop; a variety of machines of different ages, some practically obsolete, others hardly used, arranged on tables where the prospective purchaser may try them out. There were new machines too, and the proprietor was usually employed in demonstrating their merits or discussing hire-purchase terms. The customers wandered desultorily around, inspecting the machines, stopping occasionally to type out an exploratory passage. There were little pads of rough paper stacked ready for use. I didn't, of course, use the scrap paper provided. I came supplied with my own writing materials, a well-known brand sold in every stationers and on every railway bookstall. I bought a small supply of paper and envelopes once every two months and never from the same shop. Always, when handling them, I wore a thin pair of gloves, slipping them on as soon as my typing was complete. If someone were near, I would tap out the usual drivel about the sharp brown fox or all good men coming to the aid of the party. But if I were quite alone I would type something very different.

'This is the first comunication, Collingford. You'll be getting them regularly from now on. They're just to let you know that I'm going to kill you.'

'You can't escape me, Collingford. Don't bother to inform the police. They can't help you.'

'I'm getting nearer, Collingford. Have you made your will?'

'Not long now, Collingford. What does it feel like to be under sentence of death?'

The warnings weren't particularly elegant. As a librarian I could think of a number of apt quotations which would have added a touch of individuality or style, perhaps even of sardonic humour, to the bald sentence of death. But I dared not risk originality. The notes had to be ordinary, the kind of threat which anyone of his enemies, a worker, a competitor, a cuckolded husband, might have sent.

Sometimes I had a lucky day. The shop would be large, well supplied, nearly empty. I would be able to move from typewriter to typewriter and leave with perhaps a dozen or so notes and addressed envelopes ready to send. I always carried a folded newspaper in which I could conceal my writing pad and envelopes and into which I could quickly slip my little stock of typed messages.

It was quite a job to keep myself supplied with notes and I discovered interesting parts of London and fascinating shops. I particularly enjoyed this part of my plan. I wanted Collingford to get two notes a week, one posted on Sunday and one on Thursday. I wanted him to come to dread Friday and Monday mornings when the familiar typed envelope would drop on his mat. I wanted him to believe the threat was real. And why should he not believe it? How could the force of my hate and resolution not transmit itself through paper and typescript to his gradually comprehending brain?

I wanted to keep an eye on my victim. It shouldn't have been difficult; we lived in the same town. But our lives were worlds apart. He was a hard and sociable drinker. I never went inside a public house, and would have been particularly ill at ease in the kind of public house he frequented. But, from time to time, I would see him in the town. Usually he would be parking his Jaguar, and I would watch his quick, almost furtive, look to left and right before he turned to lock the door. Was it my imagination that he looked older, that some sort of confidence had drained out of him?

Once, when walking by the river on a Sunday in early Spring, I saw him manoeuvring his boat through Teddington Lock. Ilsa – she had, I knew, changed her name after her marriage – was with him. She was wearing a white trouser suit, her flowing hair was bound by a red scarf. There was a party, I could see two more men and a couple of girls and hear high female squeals of laughter. I turned quickly and slouched away as if I were the guilty one. But not before I had seen Collingford's face. This time I couldn't be mistaken. It wasn't, surely, the tedious job of getting his boat unscratched through the lock that made his face look so grey and strained.

The third phase of my planning meant moving house. I wasn't sorry to go. The bungalow, feminine, chintzy, smelling of fresh paint and the new shoddy furniture which she had chosen, was Elsie's home not mine. Her scent still lingered in cupboards and on pillows. In these inappropriate surroundings I had known greater happiness than

293

I was ever to know again. But now I paced restlessly from room to empty room fretting to be gone.

It took me four months to find the house I wanted. It had to be on or very near a river within two or three miles upstream of Collingford's house. It had to be small and reasonably cheap. Money wasn't too much of a difficulty. It was a time of rising house prices and the modern bungalow sold at three hundred pounds more than I had paid for it. I could get another mortgage without difficulty if I didn't ask for too much, but I thought it likely that, for what I wanted, I should have to pay cash.

The house agents perfectly understood that a man on his own found a three bedroom bungalow too large for him and, even if they found me rather vague about my new requirements and irritatingly imprecise about the reasons for rejecting their offerings, they still sent me orders to view. And then, suddenly on an afternoon in April, I found exactly what I was looking for. It actually stood on the river, separated from it only by a narrow tow path. It was a one-bedroom shack-like wooden bungalow with a tiled roof, set in a small neglected plot of sodden grass and overgrown flower beds. There had once been a wooden landing stage but now the two remaining planks, festooned with weeds and tags of rotted rope, were half-submerged beneath the slime of the river. The paint on the small veranda had long ago flaked away. The wallpaper of twined roses in the sitting-room was blotched and faded. The previous owner had left two old cane chairs and a ramshackle table. The kitchen was pokey and ill-equipped. Everywhere there hung a damp miasma of depression and decay. In summer, when the neighbouring shacks and bungalows were occupied by holiday makers and week-enders it would, no doubt, be cheerful enough. But in October, when I planned to kill Collingford, it would be as deserted and isolated as a disused morgue. I bought it and paid cash. I was even able to knock two hundred pounds off the asking price.

My life that summer was almost happy. I did my job at the library adequately. I lived alone in the shack, looking after myself as I had before my marriage. I spent my evenings watching television. The images flickered in front of my eyes almost unregarded, a monochrome background to my bloody and obsessive thoughts.

I practised with the knife until it was as familiar in my hand as an eating utensil. Collingford was taller than I by six inches. The thrust then would have to be upward. It made a difference to the way I held the knife and I experimented to find the most comfortable and effective grip. I hung a bolster on a hook in the bedroom door and lunged at a marked spot for hours at a time. Of course, I didn't actually insert the knife; nothing must dull the sharpness of its blade.

Once a week, a special treat, I sharpened it to an even keener edge.

Two days after moving into the bungalow I bought a dark blue untrimmed track suit and a pair of light running shoes. Throughout the summer I spent an occasional evening running on the tow path. The people who owned the neighbouring chalets, when they were there which was infrequently, got used to the sound of my television through the closed curtains and the sight of my figure jogging past their windows. I kept apart from them and from everyone and summer passed into autumn. The shutters were put up on all the chalets except mine. The tow path became mushy with falling leaves. Dusk fell early, and the summer sights and sounds died on the river. And it was October.

He was due to die on Thursday 17 October, the anniversary of the final decree of divorce. It had to be a Thursday, the evening which he spent by custom alone in his workshop, but it was a particularly happy augury that the anniversary should fall on a Thursday. I knew that he would be there. Every Thursday for nearly a year I had padded along the two and a half miles of the footpath in the evening dusk and had stood briefly watching the squares of light from his windows and the dark bulk of the house behind.

It was a warm evening. There had been a light drizzle for most of the day but, by dusk, the skies had cleared. There was a thin white sliver of moon and it cast a trembling ribbon of light across the river. I left the library at my usual time, said my usual good-nights. I knew that I had been my normal self during the day, solitary, occasionally a little sarcastic, conscientious, betraying no hint of the inner tumult.

I wasn't hungry when I got home but I made myself eat an omelette and drink two cups of coffee. I put on my swimming trunks and hung around my neck a plastic toilet bag containing the knife. Over the trunks I put on my track suit, slipping a pair of thin rubber gloves into the pocket. Then, at about a quarter past seven, I left the shack and began my customary gentle trot along the tow path.

When I got to the chosen spot opposite to Collingford's house I could see at once that all was well. The house was in darkness but there were the customary lighted windows of his workshop. I saw that the cabin cruiser was moored against the boathouse. I stood very still and listened. There was no sound. Even the light breeze had died and the yellowing leaves on the riverside elms hung motionless. The tow path was completely deserted. I slipped into the shadow of the hedge where the trees grew thickest and found the place I had already selected. I put on the rubber gloves, slipped out of the track suit, and left it folded around my running shoes in the shadow of the hedge. Then, still watching carefully to left and right, I made my way to the river.

I knew just where I must enter and leave the water. I had selected a place where the bank curved gently, where the water was shallow and the bottom firm and comparatively free of mud. The water struck very cold, but I expected that. Every night during that autumn I had bathed in cold water to accustom my body to the shock. I swam across the river with my methodical but quiet breast stroke, hardly disturbing the surface of the water. I tried to keep out of the path of moonlight but, from time to time, I swam into its silver gleam and saw my red gloved hands parting in front of me as if they were already stained with blood.

I used Collingford's landing stage to clamber out the other side. Again I stood still and listened. There was no sound except for the constant moaning of the river and the solitary cry of a night bird. I made my way silently over the grass. Outside the door of his workroom, I paused again. I could hear the noise of some kind of machinery. I wondered whether the door would be locked, but it opened easily when I turned the handle. I moved into a blaze of light.

I knew exactly what I had to do. I was perfectly calm. It was over in about four seconds. I don't think he really had a chance. He was absorbed in what he had been doing, bending over a lathe, and the sight of an almost naked man, walking purposefully towards him, left him literally impotent with surprise. But, after that first paralysing second, he knew me. Oh yes, he knew me! Then I drew my right hand from behind my back and struck. The knife went in as sweetly as if the flesh had been butter. He staggered and fell. I had expected that and I left myself go loose and fell on top of him. His eyes were glazed, his mouth opened and there was a gush of dark red blood. I twisted the knife viciously in the wound, relishing the sound of tearing sinews. Then I waited. I counted five deliberately, then raised myself from his prone figure and crouched behind him before withdrawing the knife. When I withdrew it there was a fountain of sweet smelling blood which curved from his throat like an arch. There is one thing I shall never forget. The blood must have been red, what other colour could it have been? But, at the same time and for every day afterwards, I saw it as a golden stream.

I checked my body for blood stains before I left the workshop and rinsed my arms under the cold tap at his sink. My bare feet made no marks on the wooden block flooring. I closed the door quietly after me and, once again, stood listening. Still no sound. The house was dark and empty.

The return journey was more exhausting than I had thought possible. The river seemed to have widened and I thought that I should never reach my home shore. I was glad I had chosen a shallow part of the stream and that the bank was firm. I doubt whether I could have drawn myself up through a welter of mud and slime. I was shivering violently as I zipped up my track suit and it took me precious seconds to get on my running shoes. After I had run about a mile down the tow path I weighted the toilet bag containing the knife with stones from the path and hurled it into the middle of the river. I guessed that they would drag part of the Thames for the weapon but they could hardly search the whole stream. And, even if they did, the toilet bag was one sold at the local chain store which anyone might have bought, and I was confident that the knife could never be traced to me. Half an hour later I was back in my shack. I had left the television on and the news was just ending. I made myself a cup of hot cocoa and sat to watch it. I felt drained of thought and energy as if I had just made love. I was conscious of nothing but my tiredness, my body's coldness gradually returning to life in the warmth of the electric fire, and a great peace.

He must have had a lot of enemies. It was nearly a fortnight before the police got round to interviewing me. Two officers came, a Detective Inspector and a Sergeant, both in plain clothes. The Sergeant did most of the talking; the other just sat, looking round at the sitting room, glancing out at the river, looking at the two of us from time to time from cold grey eyes as if the whole investigation were a necessary bore. The Sergeant said the usual reassuring platitudes about just a few questions. I was nervous, but that didn't worry me. They would expect me to be nervous. I told myself that, whatever I did, I mustn't try to be clever. I mustn't talk too much. I had decided to tell them that I spent the whole evening watching television, confident that no one would be able to refute this. I knew that no friends would have called on me. I doubted whether my colleagues at the library even knew where I lived. And I had no telephone so I need not fear that a caller's ring had gone unanswered during that crucial hour and a half.

On the whole it was easier than I had expected. Only once did I feel myself at risk. That was when the Inspector suddenly intervened. He said in a harsh voice:

'He married your wife didn't he? Took her away from you some people might say. Nice piece of goods, too, by the look of her. Didn't you feel any grievance? Or was it all nice and friendly? You take her, old chap. No ill feelings. That kind of thing?'

It was hard to accept the contempt in his voice but if he hoped to provoke me he didn't succeed. I had been expecting this question. I was prepared. I looked down at my hands and waited a few seconds before I spoke. I knew exactly what I would say.

'I could have killed Collingford myself when she first told me about him. But I had to come to terms with it. She went for the money you see. And if that's the kind of wife you have, well she's going to leave you sooner or later. Better sooner than when you have a family. You tell yourself "good riddance". I don't mean I felt that at first, of course. But I did feel it in the end. Sooner than I expected, really.'

That was all I said about Elsie then or ever. They came back three times. They asked me if they could look round my shack. They looked round it. They took away two of my suits and the track suit for examination. Two weeks later they returned them without comment. I never knew what they suspected, or even if they did suspect. Each time they came I said less, not more. I never varied my story. I never allowed them to provoke me into discussing my marriage or speculating about the crime. I just sat there, telling them the same thing over and over again. I never felt in any real danger. I knew that they had dragged some lengths of the river but that they hadn't found the weapon. In the end they gave up. I always had the feeling that I was pretty low on their list of suspects and that, by the end, their visits were merely a matter of form.

It was three months before Elsie came to me. I was glad that it wasn't earlier. It might have looked suspicious if she had arrived at the shack when the police were with me. After Collingford's death I hadn't seen her. There were pictures of her in the national and local newspapers, fragile in sombre furs and black hat at the inquest, bravely controlled at the crematorium, sitting in her drawing room in afternoon dress and pearls with her husband's dog at her feet, the personification of loneliness and grief.

'I can't think who could have done it. He must have been a madman. Rodney hadn't an enemy in the world.'

That statement caused some ribald comment at the library. One of the assistants said:

'He's left her a fortune I hear. Lucky for her she had an alibi. She was at a London theatre all the evening, watching *Macbeth*. Otherwise, from what I've heard of our Rodney Collingford, people might have started to get ideas about his fetching little widow.'

Then he gave me a sudden embarrassed glance, remembering who the widow was.

And so one Friday evening, she came. She drove herself and was alone. The dark green Saab drove up at my ramshackle gate. She came into the dining room and looked around in a kind of puzzled contempt. After a moment, still not speaking, she sat down in one of the fireside chairs and crossed her legs, moving one caressingly against the other. I hadn't seen her sitting like that before. She looked up at me. I was standing stiffly in front of her chair, my lips dry. When I spoke I didn't recognize my own voice.

'So you've come back?' I said.

298

She glared at me, incredulous, and then she laughed:
'To you? Back for keeps? Don't be silly, darling! I've just come to pay a visit. Besides, I wouldn't dare to come back would I? I might be frightened you'd stick a knife into my throat.'

I couldn't speak. I stared at her, feeling the blood drain from my face. Then I heard her high, rather childish voice. It sounded almost kind.

'Don't worry, I shan't tell. You were right about him, darling, you really were. He wasn't at all nice really. And mean! I didn't care so much about your meanness. After all, you don't earn so very much do you? But he had half a million! Think of it, darling. I've been left half a million! And he was so mean that he expected me to go on working as his secretary even after we were married. I typed all his letters! I really did! All that he sent from home, anyway. And I had to open his post every morning, unless the envelopes had a secret little sign on them he'd told his friends about to show that they were private.'

I said through bloodless lips.

'So all my notes –'

'He never saw them darling. Well, I didn't want to worry him did I? And I knew they were from you. I knew when the first one arrived. You never could spell communication, could you? I noticed that when you used to write to the house agents and the solicitor before we were married. It made me laugh considering that you're an educated librarian and I was only a shop assistant.'

'So you knew all the time. You knew that it was going to happen.'

'Well, I thought that it might. But he really was horrible, darling. You can't imagine. And now I've got half a million! Isn't it lucky that I have an alibi? I thought you might come on that Thursday. And Rodney never did enjoy a serious play.'

After that brief visit I never saw or spoke to her again. I stayed in the shack, but life became pointless after Collingford's death. Planning his murder had been an interest, after all. Without Elsie and without my victim there seemed little point in living. And, about a year after his death, I began to dream. I still dream, always on a Monday and Friday. I live through it all again; the noiseless run along the tow path over the mush of damp leaves, the quiet swim across the river; the silent opening of his door; the upward thrust of the knife; the vicious turn in the wound; the animal sound of tearing tissues; the curving stream of golden blood. Only the homeward swim is different. In my dream the river is no longer a cleansing stream, luminous under the sickle moon, but a cloying, impenetrable, slow moving bog of viscous blood through which I struggle in impotent panic towards a steadily receding shore.

299

I knew about the significance of the dream. I've read all about the psychology of guilt. Since I lost Elsie I've done all my living through books. But it doesn't help. And I no longer know who I am. I know who I used to be, our local Assistant Librarian, gentle, scholarly, timid, Elsie's husband. But then I killed Collingford. The man I was couldn't have done that. He wasn't that kind of person. So who am I? It isn't really surprising, I suppose, that the Library Committee suggested so tactfully that I ought to look for a less exacting job. A less exacting job than the post of Assistant Librarian? But you can't blame them. No one can be efficient and keep his mind on the job when he doesn't know who he is.

Sometimes, when I'm in a public house – and I seem to spend most of my time there nowadays since I've been out of work – I'll look over someone's shoulder at a newspaper photograph of Elsie and say:

'That's the beautiful Ilsa Mancelli. I was her first husband.'

I've got used to the way people sidle away from me, the ubiquitous pub bore, their eyes averted, their voices suddenly hearty. But sometimes, perhaps because they've been lucky with the horses and feel a spasm of pity for a poor deluded sod, they push a few coins over the counter to the barman before making their way to the door, and buy me a drink.

The Mystery of the Sleeping-Car Express
FREEMAN WILLS CROFTS

NO ONE WHO WAS IN ENGLAND in the autumn of 1909 can fail to remember the terrible tragedy which took place in a North-Western express between Preston and Carlisle. The affair attracted enormous attention at the time, not only because of the arresting nature of the events themselves, but even more for the absolute mystery in which they were shrouded.

Quite lately a singular chance has revealed to me the true explanation of the terrible drama, and it is at the express desire of its chief actor that I now take upon myself to make the facts known. As it is a long time since 1909, I may, perhaps, be pardoned if I first recall the events which came to light at the time.

One Thursday, then, early in November of the year in question, the 10.30 pm sleeping-car train left Euston as usual for Edinburgh, Glasgow, and the North. It was generally a heavy train, being popular with business men who liked to complete their day's work in London, sleep while travelling, and arrive at their northern destination with time for a leisurely bath and breakfast before office hours. The night in question was no exception to the rule, and two engines hauled behind them eight large sleeping-cars, two firsts, two thirds, and two vans, half of which went to Glasgow, and the remainder to Edinburgh.

It is essential to the understanding of what follows that the composition of the rear portion of the train should be remembered. At the extreme end came the Glasgow van, a long, eight-wheeled, bogie vehicle, with Guard Jones in charge. Next to the van was one of the third-class coaches, and immediately in front of it came a first-class, both labelled for the same city. These coaches were fairly well filled, particularly the third class. In front of the first-class came the last of the four Glasgow sleepers. The train was corridor throughout, and the officials could, and did, pass through it several times during the journey.

It is with the first-class coach that we are principally concerned, and it will be understood from the above that it was placed in between the sleeping-car in front and the third-class behind, the van following immediately behind the third. It had a lavatory at each end and six compartments, the last two, next the third-class, being smokers, the next three non-smoking, and the first, immediately beside the sleeping car, a 'Ladies Only.' The corridors in both it and the third-class coach were on the left-hand side in the direction of travel – that is, the compartments were on the side of the double line.

The night was dark as the train drew out of Euston, for there was no moon and the sky was overcast. As was remembered and commented on afterwards, there had been an unusually long spell of dry weather, and, though it looked like rain earlier in the evening, none fell till the next day, when, about six in the morning, there was a torrential downpour.

As the detectives pointed out later, no weather could have been more unfortunate from their point of view, as, had footmarks been made during the night, the ground would have been too hard to take good impressions, while even such traces as remained would more than likely have been blurred by the rain.

The train ran to time, stopping at Rugby, Crewe and Preston. After leaving the latter station Guard Jones found he had occasion to go forward and speak to a ticket-collector in the Edinburgh portion. He accordingly left his van in the rear and passed along the corridor of the third-class carriage adjoining.

At the end of this corridor, beside the vestibule joining it to the first class, were a lady and gentleman, evidently husband and wife, the lady endeavouring to soothe the cries of a baby she was carrying. Guard Jones addressed some civil remark to the man, who explained that their child had been taken ill, and they had brought it out of their compartment as it was disturbing the other passengers.

With an expression of sympathy, Jones unlocked the two doors across the corridor at the vestibule between the carriages, and, passing on into the first-class coach, re-closed them behind him. They were fitted with spring locks, which became fast on the door shutting.

The corridor of the first-class coach was empty, and as Jones walked down it he observed that the blinds of all the compartments were lowered, with one exception – that of the 'Ladies Only.' In this compartment, which contained three ladies, the light was fully on, and the guard noticed that two out of the three were reading.

Continuing his journey, Jones found that the two doors at the vestibule between the first-class coach and the sleeper were also locked, and he opened them and passed through, shutting them behind him. At the sleeping-car attendant's box, just inside the last of these doors, two car attendants were talking together. One was actually inside the box, the other standing in the corridor. The latter moved aside to let the guard pass, taking up his former position as, after exchanging a few words, Jones moved on.

His business with the ticket-collector finished, Guard Jones returned to his van. On this journey he found the same conditions obtaining as on the previous – the two attendants were at the rear end of the sleeping-car, the lady and gentleman with the baby in the front end of the third-class coach, the first-class corridor deserted, and both doors at each end of the latter coach locked. These details, casually remarked at the time, became afterwards of the utmost importance, adding as they did to the mystery in which the tragedy was enveloped.

About an hour before the train was due at Carlisle, while it was passing through the wild moorland country of the Westmorland highlands, the brakes were applied – at first gently, and then with considerable power. Guard Jones, who was examining parcel waybills in the rear end of his van, supposed it to be a signal check, but as such was unusual at this place, he left his work and, walking down the van, lowered the window at the left-hand side and looked out along the train.

The line happened to be in a cutting, and the railway bank for some distance ahead was dimly illuminated by the light from the corridors of the first and third-class coaches immediately in front of his van. As I have said, the night was dark, and, except for this bit of bank, Jones could see nothing ahead. The railway curved away to the right, so, thinking he might see better from the other side, he crossed the van and looked out of the opposite window, next the up line.

There were no signal lights in view, nor anything to suggest the cause of the slack, but as he ran his eye along the train he saw that something was amiss in the first-class coach. From the window at its rear end figures were leaning, gesticulating wildly, as if to attract attention to some grave and pressing danger. The guard at once ran through the third-class to this coach, and there he found a strange and puzzling state of affairs.

The corridor was still empty, but the centre blind of the rear compartment – that is, the first reached by the guard – had been raised. Through the glass Jones could see that the compartment contained four men. Two were leaning out of the window on the opposite side, and two were fumbling at the latch of the corridor door, as if trying to open it. Jones caught hold of the outside handle to assist, but they pointed in the direction of the adjoining compartment, and the guard, obeying their signs, moved on to the second door.

The centre blind of this compartment had also been pulled up, though here, again, the door had not been opened. As the guard peered in through the glass he saw that he was in the presence of a tragedy.

Tugging desperately at the handle of the corridor door stood a lady,

303

her face blanched, her eyes starting from her head, and her features frozen into an expression of deadly fear and horror. As she pulled she kept glancing over her shoulder, as if some dreadful apparition lurked in the shadows behind. As Jones sprang forward to open the door his eyes followed the direction of her gaze, and he drew in his breath sharply.

At the far side of the compartment, facing the engine and huddled down in the corner, was the body of a woman. She lay limp and inert, with head tilted back at an unnatural angle into the cushions and a hand hanging helplessly down over the edge of the seat. She might have been thirty years of age, and was dressed in a reddish-brown fur coat with toque to match. But these details the guard hardly glanced at, his attention being riveted to her forehead. There, above the left eyebrow, was a sinister little hole, from which the blood had oozed down the coat and formed a tiny pool on the seat. That she was dead was obvious.

But this was not all. On the seat opposite her lay a man, and, as far as Guard Jones could see, he also was dead.

He apparently had been sitting in the corner seat, and had fallen forward so that his chest lay across the knees of the woman and his head hung down towards the floor. He was all bunched and twisted up – just a shapeless mass in a grey frieze overcoat, with dark hair at the back of what could be seen of his head. But under the head the guard caught the glint of falling drops, while a dark, ominous stain grew on the floor beneath.

Jones flung himself on the door, but it would not move. It stood fixed, an inch open, jammed in some mysterious way, imprisoning the lady with her terrible companions.

As she and the guard strove to force it open, the train came to a standstill. At once it occurred to Jones that he could now enter the compartment from the opposite side.

Shouting to reassure the now almost frantic lady, he turned back to the end compartment, intending to pass through it on to the line and so back to that containing the bodies. But here he was again baffled, for the two men had not succeeded in sliding back their door. He seized the handle to help them, and then he noticed their companions had opened the opposite door and were climbing out on to the permanent way.

It flashed through his mind that an up-train passed about this time, and, fearing an accident, he ran down the corridor to the sleeping-car, where he felt sure he would find a door that would open. That at the near end was free, and he leaped out on to the track. As he passed he shouted to one of the attendants to follow him, and to the other to remain where he was and let no one pass. Then he joined the men who had already alighted, warned them about the up-train, and the four opened the outside door of the compartment in which the tragedy had taken place.

Their first concern was to get the uninjured lady out, and here a difficult and ghastly task awaited them. The door was blocked by the bodies, and its narrowness prevented more than one man from working. Sending the car attendant to search the train for a doctor, Jones clambered up, and, after warning the lady not to look at what he was doing, he raised the man's body and propped it back in the corner seat.

The face was a strong one with clean-shaven but rather coarse features, a large nose, and a heavy jaw. In the neck, just below the right ear, was a bullet hole which, owing to the position of the head, had bled freely. As far as the guard could see, the man was dead. Not without a certain shrinking, Jones raised the feet, first of the man, and then of the woman, and placed them on the seats, thus leaving the floor clear except for its dark, creeping pool. Then, placing his handkerchief over the dead woman's face, he rolled back the end of the carpet to hide its sinister stain.

'Now, ma'am, if you please,' he said; and keeping the lady with her back to the more gruesome object on the opposite seat, he helped her to the open door, from where willing hands assisted her to the ground.

By this time the attendant had found a doctor in the third-class coach, and a brief examination enabled him to pronounce both victims dead. The blinds in the compartment having been drawn down and the outside door locked, the guard called to those passengers who had alighted to resume their seats, with a view to continuing their journey.

The fireman had meantime come back along the train to ascertain what was wrong, and to say the driver was unable completely to release the brake. An examination was therefore made, and the tell-tale disc at the end of the first-class coach was found to be turned, showing that someone in that carriage had pulled the communication chain. This, as is perhaps not generally known, allows air to pass between the train pipe and the atmosphere, thereby gently applying the brake and preventing its complete release. Further investigation showed that the slack of the chain was hanging in the end smoking-compartment, indicating that the alarm must have been operated by one of the four men who travelled there. The disc was then turned back to normal, the passengers reseated, and the train started, after a delay of about fifteen minutes.

Before reaching Carlisle, Guard Jones took the name and address of everyone travelling in the first and third-class coaches, together with the numbers of their tickets. These coaches, as well as the van, were thoroughly searched, and it was established beyond any doubt that no one was concealed under the seats, in the lavatories, behind luggage, or, in fact, anywhere about them.

One of the sleeping-car attendants having been in the corridor in the rear of the last sleeper from the Preston stop till the completion of this search, and being positive no one except the guard had passed during that time, it was not considered necessary to take the names of the passengers in the sleeping-cars, but the numbers of their tickets were noted.

On arrival at Carlisle the matter was put into the hands of the police. The first-class carriage was shunted off, the doors being locked and sealed, and the passengers who had travelled in it were detained to make their statements. Then began a most careful and searching investigation, as a result of which several additional facts became known.

The first step taken by the authorities was to make an examination of the country surrounding the point at which the train had stopped, in the hope of finding traces of some stranger on the line. The tentative theory was that a murder had been committed and that the murderer had escaped from the train when it stopped, struck across the country, and, gaining some road, had made good his escape.

Accordingly, as soon as it was light, a special train brought a force of detectives to the place, and the railway, as well as a tract of ground on each side of it, were subjected to a prolonged and exhaustive search. But no traces were found. Nothing that a stranger might have dropped was picked up, no footsteps were seen, no mark discovered. As has already been stated, the weather was against the searchers. The drought of the previous days had left the ground hard and unyielding, so that clear impressions were scarcely to be expected, while even such as might have been made were not likely to remain after the downpour of the early morning.

Baffled at this point, the detectives turned their attention to the stations in the vicinity. There were only two within walking distance of the point of the tragedy, and at neither had any stranger been seen. Further, no trains had stopped at either of these stations; indeed, not a single train, either passenger or goods, had stopped anywhere in the neighbourhood since the sleeping-car express went through. If the murderer had left the express, it was, therefore, out of the question that he could have escaped by rail.

The investigators then turned their attention to the country roads and adjoining towns, trying to find the trail – if there was a trail – while it was hot. But here, again, no luck attended their efforts. If there were a murderer, and if he had left the train when it stopped, he had vanished into thin air. No traces of him could anywhere be discovered.

Nor were their researches in other directions much more fruitful. The dead couple were identified as a Mr and Mrs Horatio Llewelyn, of Gordon Villa, Broad Road, Halifax. Mr Llewelyn was the junior partner of a large firm of Yorkshire ironfounders. A man of five-and-thirty, he moved in good society and had some claim to wealth. He was of kindly though somewhat passionate disposition, and, so far as could be learnt, had not an enemy in the world. His firm was able to show that he had business appointments in London on the Thursday and in Carlisle on the Friday, so that his travelling by the train in question was quite in accordance with his known plans.

His wife was the daughter of a neighbouring merchant, a pretty girl of some seven-and-twenty. They had been married only a little over a month, and had, in fact, only a week earlier returned from their honeymoon. Whether Mrs Llewelyn had any definite reason for accompanying her husband on the fatal journey could not be ascertained. She also, so far as was known, had no enemy, nor could any motive for the tragedy be suggested.

The extraction of the bullets proved that the same weapon had been used in each case – a revolver of small bore and modern design. But as many thousands of similar revolvers existed, this discovery led to nothing.

Miss Blair-Booth, the lady who had travelled with the Llewelyns, stated she had joined the train at Euston, and occupied one of the seats next to the corridor. A couple of minutes before starting the deceased had arrived, and they sat in the two opposite corners. No other passengers had entered the compartment during the journey, nor had any of the three left it; in fact, except for the single visit of the ticket-collector shortly after leaving Euston, the door into the corridor had not been even opened.

Mr Llewelyn was very attentive to his young wife, and they had conversed for some time after starting, then, after consulting Miss Blair-Booth, he had pulled down the blinds and shaded the light, and they had settled down for the night. Miss Blair-Booth had slept at intervals, but each time she wakened she had looked round the compartment, and everything was as before. Then she was suddenly aroused from a doze by a loud explosion close by.

She sprang up, and as she did so a flash came from somewhere near her knee, and a second explosion sounded. Startled and trembling, she pulled the shade off the lamp, and then she noticed a little cloud of smoke just inside the corridor door, which had been opened about an inch, and smelled the characteristic odour of burnt powder. Swinging round, she was in time to see Mr Llewelyn dropping heavily forward across his wife's knees, and then she observed the mark on the latter's forehead and realized they had both been shot.

Terrified, she raised the blind of the corridor door which covered the handle and tried to get out to call assistance. But she could not move the door, and her horror was not diminished when she found herself locked in with what she rightly believed were two dead bodies. In despair she pulled the communication chain, but the train did not appear to stop, and she continued struggling with the door till, after what seemed to her hours, the guard appeared, and she was eventually released.

In answer to a question, she further stated that when her blind went up the corridor was empty; and she saw no one till the guard came.

The four men in the end compartment were members of one party travelling from London to Glasgow. For some time after leaving they had played cards, but, about midnight, they, too, had pulled down their blinds, shaded their lamp, and composed themselves to sleep. In this case also, no person other than the ticket-collector had entered the compartment during the journey. But after leaving Preston the door had been opened. Aroused by the stop, one of the men had eaten some fruit, and having thereby soiled his fingers, had washed them in the lavatory. The door then opened as usual. This man saw no one in the corridor, nor did he notice anything out of the common.

Some time after this all four were startled by the sound of two shots. At first they thought of fog signals, then, realizing they were too far from the engine to hear such, they, like Miss Blair-Booth, unshaded their lamp, raised the blind over their corridor door, and endeavoured to leave the compartment. Like her they found themselves unable to open their door, and, like her also, they saw that there was no one in the corridor. Believing something serious had happened, they pulled the communication chain, at the same time lowering the outside window and waving from it in the hope of attracting attention. The chain came down easily as if slack, and this explained the apparent contradiction between Miss Blair-Booth's statement that she had pulled it, and the fact that the slack was found hanging in the end compartment. Evidently the lady had pulled it first, applying the brake, and the second pull had simply transferred the slack from one compartment to the next.

The two compartments in front of that of the tragedy were found to be empty when the train stopped, but in the last of the non-smoking compartments were two gentlemen, and in the 'Ladies Only,' three ladies. All these had heard the shots, but so faintly above the noise of the train that the attention of none of them was specially arrested, nor had they attempted any investigation. The gentlemen had not left their compartment or pulled up their blinds between the time the train left Preston and the emergency stop, and could throw no light whatever on the matter.

The three ladies in the end compartment were a mother and two daughters, and had got in at Preston. As they were alighting at Carlisle they had not wished to sleep, so they had left their blinds up and their light unshaded. Two of them were reading, but the third was seated at the corridor side, and this lady stated positively that no one except the guard had passed while they were in the train.

She described his movements – first, towards the engine, secondly, back towards the van, and a third time, running, towards the engine after the train had stopped – so accurately in accord with the other evidence that considerable reliance was placed on her testimony. The stoppage and the guard's haste had aroused her interest, and all three ladies had immediately come out into the corridor, and had remained there till the train proceeded, and all three were satisfied that no one else had passed during that time.

An examination of the doors which had jammed so mysteriously revealed the fact that a small wooden wedge, evidently designed for the purpose, had been driven in between the floor and the bottom of the framing of the door, holding the latter rigid. It was evident therefore that the crime was premeditated, and the details had been carefully worked out beforehand. The most careful search of the carriage failed to reveal any other suspicious object or mark.

On comparing the tickets issued with those held by the passengers, a discrepancy was discovered. All were accounted for except one. A first single for Glasgow had been issued at Euston for the train in question, which had not been collected. The purchaser had therefore either not travelled at all, or had got out at some intermediate station. In either case no demand for a refund had been made.

The collector who had checked the tickets after the train left London believed, though he could not speak positively, that two men had then occupied the non-smoking compartment next to that in which the tragedy had occurred, one of whom held a Glasgow ticket, and the other a ticket for an intermediate station. He could not recollect which station nor could he describe either of the men, if indeed they were there at all.

But the ticket collector's recollection was not at fault, for the police succeeded in tracing one of these passengers, a Dr Hill, who had got out at Crewe. He was able, partially at all events, to account for the missing Glasgow ticket. It appeared that when he joined the train at Euston, a man of about five-and-thirty was already in the compartment. This man had fair hair, blue eyes, and a full moustache, and was dressed in dark, well-cut clothes. He had no luggage, but only a waterproof and a paper-covered novel. The two travellers had got into conversation, and on the stranger learning that the doctor lived at

Crewe, said he was alighting there also, and asked to be recommended to an hotel. He then explained that he had intended to go on to Glasgow and had taken a ticket to that city, but had since decided to break his journey to visit a friend in Chester next day. He asked the doctor if he thought his ticket would be available to complete the journey the following night, and if not, whether he could get a refund.

When they reached Crewe, both these travellers had alighted, and the doctor offered to show his acquaintance the entrance to the Crewe Arms, but the stranger, thanking him, declined, saying he wished to see to his luggage. Dr Hill saw him walking towards the van as he left the platform.

Upon interrogating the staff on duty at Crewe at the time, no one could recall seeing such a man at the van, nor had any inquiries about luggage been made. But as these facts did not come to light until several days after the tragedy, confirmation was hardly to be expected.

A visit to all the hotels in Crewe and Chester revealed the fact that no one in any way resembling the stranger had stayed there, nor could any trace whatever be found of him.

Such were the principal facts made known at the adjourned inquest on the bodies of Mr and Mrs Llewelyn. It was confidently believed that a solution to the mystery would speedily be found, but as day after day passed away without bringing to light any fresh information, public interest began to wane, and became directed into other channels.

But for a time controversy over the affair waxed keen. At first it was argued that it was a case of suicide, some holding that Mr Llewelyn had shot first his wife and then himself; others that both had died by the wife's hand. But this theory had only to be stated to be disproved.

Several persons hastened to point out that not only had the revolver disappeared, but on neither body was there powder blackening, and it was admitted that such a wound could not be self-inflicted without leaving marks from this source. That murder had been committed was therefore clear.

Rebutted on this point, the theorists then argued that Miss Blair-Booth was the assassin. But here again the suggestion was quickly negatived. The absence of motive, her known character and the truth of such of her statements as could be checked were against the idea. The disappearance of the revolver was also in her favour. As it was not in the compartment nor concealed about her person, she could only have rid herself of it out of the window. But the position of the bodies prevented access to the window, and, as her clothes were free from any stain of blood, it was impossible to believe that she had moved these grim relics, even had she been physically able.

But the point that finally demonstrated her innocence was the wedging of the corridor door. It was obvious she could not have wedged the door on the outside and then passed through it. The belief was universal that whoever wedged the door fired the shots, and the fact that the former was wedged an inch open strengthened that view, as the motive was clearly to leave a slot through which to shoot.

Lastly, the medical evidence showed that if the Llewelyns were sitting where Miss Blair-Booth stated, and the shots were fired from where she said, the bullets would have entered the bodies from the direction they were actually found to have done.

But Miss Blair-Booth's detractors were loath to recede from the position they had taken up. They stated that of the objections to their theory only one – the wedging of the doors – was overwhelming. And they advanced an ingenious theory to meet it. They suggested that before reaching Preston Miss Blair-Booth had left the compartment, closing the door after her, that she had then wedged it, and that, on stopping at the station, had passed out through some other compartment, re-entering her own through the outside door.

In answer to this it was pointed out that the gentleman who had eaten the fruit had opened the door *after* the Preston stop, and if Miss Blair-Booth was then shut into her compartment she could not have wedged the other door. That two people should be concerned in the wedging was unthinkable. It was therefore clear that Miss Blair-Booth was innocent, and that some other person had wedged both doors, in order to prevent his operations in the corridor being interfered with by those who would hear the shots.

It was recognized that similar arguments applied to the four men in the end compartment – the wedging of the doors cleared them also.

Defeated on these points the theorists retired from the field. No further suggestions were put forward by the public or the daily press. Even to those behind the scenes the case seemed to become more and more difficult the longer it was pondered.

Each person known to have been present came in turn under the microscopic eye of New Scotland Yard, but each in turn had to be eliminated from suspicion, till it almost seemed proved that no murder could have been committed at all. The prevailing mystification was well summed up by the chief at the Yard in conversation with the inspector in charge of the case.

'A troublesome business, certainly,' said the great man, 'and I admit that your conclusions seem sound. But let us go over it again. There *must* be a flaw somewhere.'

'There must, sir. But I've gone over it and over it till I'm stupid and every time I get the same result.'

'We'll try once more. We begin, then, with a murder in a railway carriage. We're sure it was a murder, of course?'

'Certain, sir. The absence of the revolver and of powder blackening and the wedging of the doors prove it.'

'Quite. The murder must therefore have been committed by some person who was either in the carriage when it was searched, or had left before that. Let us take these two possibilities in turn. And first, with regard to the searching. Was that efficiently done?'

'Absolutely, sir. I have gone into it with the guard and attendants. No one could have been overlooked.'

'Very good. Taking first, then, those who were in the carriage. There were six compartments. In the first were the four men, and in the second Miss Blair-Booth. Are you satisfied these were innocent?'

'Perfectly, sir. The wedging of the doors eliminated them.'

'So I think. The third and fourth compartments were empty, but in the fifth there were two gentlemen. What about them?'

'Well sir, you know who they were. Sir Gordon M'Clean, the great engineer, and Mr Silas Hemphill, the professor of Aberdeen University. Both utterly beyond suspicion.'

'But, as you know, inspector, *no one* is beyond suspicion in a case of this kind.'

'I admit it, sir, and therefore I made careful inquiries about them. But I only confirmed my opinion.'

'From inquiries I also have made I feel sure you are right. That brings us to the last compartment, the "Ladies Only." What about those three ladies?'

'The same remarks apply. Their characters are also beyond suspicion, and, as well as that, the mother is elderly and timid, and couldn't brazen out a lie. I question if the daughters could either. I made inquiries all the same, and found not the slightest ground for suspicion.'

'The corridors and lavatories were empty?'

'Yes, sir.'

'Then everyone found in the coach when the train stopped may be definitely eliminated?'

'Yes. It is quite impossible it could have been any that we have mentioned.'

'Then the murderer must have left the coach?'

'He must; and that's where the difficulty comes in.'

'I know, but let us proceed. Our problem then really becomes – *how* did he leave the coach?'

'That's so, sir, and I have never been against anything stiffer.'

The chief paused in thought, as he absently selected and lit another cigar. At last he continued:

'Well, at any rate, it is clear he did not go through the roof or the floor, or any part of the fixed framing or sides. Therefore he must have gone in the usual way – through a door. Of these, there is one at each end and six at each side. He therefore went through one of these fourteen doors. Are you agreed, inspector?'

'Certainly, sir.'

'Very good. Take the ends first. The vestibule doors were locked?'

'Yes, sir, at both ends of the coach. But I don't count that much. An ordinary carriage key opened them and the murderer would have had one.'

'Quite. Now, just go over again our reasons for thinking he did not escape to the sleeper.'

'Before the train stopped, sir, Miss Bintley, one of the three in the "Ladies Only," was looking out into the corridor, and the two sleeper attendants were at the near end of their coach. After the train stopped, all three ladies were in the corridor, and one attendant was at the sleeper vestibule. All these persons swear most positively that no one but the guard passed between Preston and the searching of the carriage.'

'What about these attendants? Are they reliable?'

'Wilcox has seventeen years' service, and Jeffries six, and both bear excellent characters. Both, naturally, came under suspicion of the murder, and I made the usual investigation. But there is not a scrap of evidence against them, and I am satisfied they are all right.'

'It certainly looks as if the murderer did not escape towards the sleeper.'

'I am positive of it. You see, sir, we have the testimony of two separate lots of witnesses, the ladies and the attendants. It is out of the question that these parties would agree to deceive the police. Conceivably one or other might, but not both.'

'Yes, that seems sound. What, then, about the other end – the third-class end?'

'At the end,' replied the inspector 'were Mr and Mrs Smith with their sick child. They were in the corridor close by the vestibule door, and no one could have passed without their knowledge. I had the child examined, and its illness was genuine. The parents are quiet persons, of exemplary character, and again quite beyond suspicion. When they said no one but the guard had passed I believed them. However, I was not satisfied with that, and I examined every person that travelled in the third-class coach, and established two things: first, that no one was in at the time it was searched who had not travelled in it from Preston; and secondly, that no one except the Smiths had left any of the compartments during the run between Preston and the emergency stop. That proves beyond question that no one left the first-class coach for the third after the tragedy.'

313

'What about the guard himself?'

'The guard is also a man of good character, but he is out of it, because he was seen by several passengers as well as the Smiths running through the third-class after the brakes were applied.'

'It is clear, then, the murderer must have got out through one of the twelve side doors. Take those on the compartment side first. The first, second, fifth and sixth compartments were occupied, therefore he could not have passed through them. That leaves the third and fourth doors. Could he have left by either of these?'

The inspector shook his head.

'No, sir,' he answered, 'that is equally out of the question. You will recollect that two of the four men in the end compartment were looking out along the train from a few seconds after the murder until the stop. It would not have been possible to open a door and climb out on to the footboard without being seen by them. Guard Jones also looked out at that side of the van and saw no one. After the stop these same two men, as well as others, were on the ground, and all agree that none of these doors were opened at any time.'

'H'm,' mused the chief, 'that also seems conclusive, and it brings us definitely to the doors on the corridor side. As the guard arrived on the scene comparatively early, the murderer must have got out while the train was running at a fair speed. He must therefore have been clinging on to the outside of the coach while the guard was in the corridor working at the sliding doors. When the train stopped all attention was concentrated on the opposite, or compartment, side, and he could easily have dropped down and made off. What do you think of that theory, inspector?'

'We went into that pretty thoroughly, sir. It was first objected that the blinds of the first and second compartments were raised too soon to give him time to get out without being seen. But I found this was not valid. At least fifteen seconds must have elapsed before Miss Blair-Booth and the men in the end compartment raised their blinds, and that would easily have allowed him to lower the window, open the door, pass out, raise the window, shut the door, and crouch down on the footboard out of sight. I estimate also that nearly thirty seconds passed before Guard Jones looked out of the van at that side. As far as time goes he could have done what you suggest. But another thing shows he didn't. It appears that when Jones ran through the third-class coach, while the train was stopping, Mr Smith, the man with the sick child, wondering what was wrong, attempted to follow him into the first-class. But the door slammed after the guard before the other could reach it, and, of course, the spring lock held it fast. Mr Smith therefore lowered the end corridor window and looked out ahead, and he states positively no one was on the footboard of the first-class. To see how far Mr Smith could be sure of this, on a dark night we ran the same carriage, lighted in the same way, over the same part of the line, and we found a figure crouching on the footboard was clearly visible from the window. It showed a dark mass against the lighted side of the cutting. When we remember that Mr Smith was specially looking out for something abnormal, I think we may accept his evidence.'

'You are right. It is convincing. And, of course, it is supported by the guard's own testimony. He also saw no one when he looked out of his van.'

'That is so, sir. And we found a crouching figure was visible from the van also, owing to the same cause – the lighted bank.'

'And the murderer could not have got out while the guard was passing through the third-class?'

'No, because the corridor blinds were raised before the guard looked out.'

The chief frowned.

'It is certainly puzzling,' he mused. There was silence for some moments, and then he spoke again.

'Could the murderer, immediately after firing the shots, have concealed himself in a lavatory and then, during the excitement of the stop have slipped out unperceived through one of the corridor doors and, dropping on the line, moved quietly away?'

'No, sir, we went into that also. If he had hidden in a lavatory he could not have gone out again. If he had gone towards the third-class the Smiths would have seen him, and the first-class corridor was under observation during the entire time from the arrival of the guard till the search. We have proved the ladies entered the corridor *immediately* the guard passed their compartment, and two of the four men in the end smoker were watching through their door till considerably after the ladies had come out.'

Again silence reigned while the chief smoked thoughtfully.

'The coroner had some theory, you say?' he said at last.

'Yes sir. He suggested the murderer might have, immediately after firing, got out by one of the doors on the corridor side – probably the end one – and from there climbed on the outside of the coach to some place from which he could not be seen from a window, dropping to the ground when the train stopped. He suggested the roof, the buffers, or the lower step. This seemed likely at first sight, and I tried therefore the experiment. But it was no good. The roof was out of the question. It was one of those high curved roofs – not a flat clerestory – and there was no handhold at the edge above the doors. The buffers were equally inaccessible. From the handle and guard of the end door to that above the buffer on the corner of the coach was seven feet two inches. That is to say, a man could not reach from one to the other, and there was nothing he could hold on to while passing along the step. The lower step was not possible either. In the first place it was divided – there was only a short step beneath each door – not a continuous board like the upper one – so that no one could pass along the lower while holding on to the upper, and secondly, I couldn't imagine anyone climbing down there, and knowing that the first platform they came to would sweep him off.'

'That is to say, inspector, you have proved the murderer was in the coach at the time of the crime, that he was not in it when it was searched, and that he did not leave it in the interval. I don't know that that is a very creditable conclusion.'

'I know, sir. I regret it extremely, but that's the difficulty I have been up against from the start.'

The chief laid his hand on his subordinate's shoulder.

'It won't do,' he said kindly. 'It really won't do. You try again. Smoke over it, and I'll do the same, and come in and see me again tomorrow.'

But the conversation had really summed up the case justly. My Lady Nicotine brought no inspiration, and, as time passed without bringing to light any further facts, interest gradually waned till at last the affair took its place among the long list of unexplained crimes in the annals of New Scotland Yard.

And now I come to the singular coincidence referred to earlier whereby I, an obscure medical practitioner, came to learn the solution of this extraordinary mystery. With the case itself I had no connection, the details just given being taken from the official reports made at the time, to which I was allowed access in return for the information I brought. The affair happened in this way.

One evening just four weeks ago, as I lit my pipe after a long and tiring day, I received an urgent summons to the principal inn of the little village near which I practised. A motor-cyclist had collided with a car at a cross-roads and had been picked up terribly injured. I saw almost at a glance that nothing could be done for him; in fact, his life was a matter of a few hours. He asked coolly how it was with him, and, in accordance with my custom in such cases, I told him, inquiring was there anyone he would like sent for. He looked me straight in the eyes and replied:

'Doctor, I want to make a statement. If I tell it you will you keep it to yourself while I live and then inform the proper authorities and the public?'

'Why, yes,' I answered; 'but shall I not send for some of your friends or a clergyman?'

'No,' he said, 'I have no friends, and I have no use for parsons. You look a white man; I would rather tell you.'

I bowed and fixed him up as comfortably as possible, and he began, speaking slowly in a voice hardly above a whisper.

'I shall be brief for I feel my time is short. You remember some few years ago a Mr Horatio Llewelyn and his wife were murdered in a train on the North-Western some fifty miles south of Carlisle?'

I dimly remembered the case.

' "The sleeping-car express mystery," the papers called it?' I asked.

'That's it,' he replied. 'They never solved the mystery and they never got the murderer. But he's going to pay now. I am he.'

I was horrified at the cool, deliberate way he spoke. Then I remembered that he was fighting death to make his confession and that, whatever my feelings, it was my business to hear and record it while yet there was time. I therefore sat down and said as gently as I could:

'Whatever you tell me I shall note carefully, and at the proper time shall inform the police.'

His eyes, which had watched me anxiously, showed relief.

'Thank you. I shall hurry. My name is Hubert Black, and I live at 24, Westbury Gardens, Hove. Until ten years and two months ago I lived at Bradford, and there I made the acquaintance of what I thought was the best and most wonderful girl on God's earth – Miss Gladys Wentworth. I was poor, but she was well off. I was diffident about approaching her, but she encouraged me till at last I took my courage in both hands and proposed. She agreed to marry me, but made it a condition our engagement was to be kept secret for a few days. I was so mad about her I would have agreed to anything she wanted, so I said nothing, though I could hardly behave like a sane man from joy.

'Some time before this I had come across Llewelyn, and he had been very friendly, and had seemed to like my company. One day we met Gladys, and I introduced him. I did not know till later that he had followed up the acquaintanceship.

'A week after my acceptance there was a big dance at Halifax. I was to have met Gladys there, but at the last moment I had a wire that my mother was seriously ill, and I had to go. On my return I got a cool little note from Gladys saying she was sorry, but our engagement had been a mistake, and I must consider it at an end. I made a few inquiries, and then I learnt what had been done. Give me some stuff, doctor; I'm going down.'

I poured out some brandy and held it to his lips.

'That's better,' he said, continuing with gasps and many pauses: 'Llewelyn, I found out, had been struck by Gladys for some time. He knew I was friends with her, and so he made up to me. He wanted the introduction I was fool enough to give him, as well as the chances of meeting her he would get with me. Then he met her when he knew I was at my work, and made hay while the sun shone. Gladys spotted what he was after, but she didn't know if he was serious. Then I proposed, and she thought she would hold me for fear the bigger fish would get off. Llewelyn was wealthy, you understand. She waited till the ball, then she hooked him, and I went overboard. Nice, wasn't it?'

I did not reply, and the man went on:

'Well, after that I just went mad. I lost my head and went to Llewelyn, but he laughed in my face. I felt I wanted to knock his head off, but the butler happened by, so I couldn't go on and finish him then. I needn't try to describe the hell I went through – I couldn't, anyway. But I was blind mad, and lived only for revenge. And then I got it. I followed them till I got a chance, and then I killed them. I shot them in that train. I shot her first and then, as he woke and sprang up, I got him too.'

The man paused.

'Tell me the details,' I asked; and after a time he went on in a weaker voice:

'I had worked out a plan to get them in a train, and had followed them all through their honeymoon, but I never got a chance till then. This time the circumstances fell out to suit. I was behind him at Euston and heard him book to Carlisle, so I booked to Glasgow. I got into the next compartment. There was a talkative man there, and I tried to make a sort of alibi for myself by letting him think I would get out at Crewe. I did get out, but I got in again, and travelled on in the same compartment with the blinds down. No one knew I was there. I waited till we got to the top of Shap, for I thought I could get away easier in a thinly populated country. Then, when the time came, I fixed the compartment doors with wedges, and shot them both. I left the train and got clear of the railway, crossing the country till I came on a road. I hid during the day and walked at night till after dark on the second evening I came to Carlisle. From there I went by rail quite openly. I was never suspected.'

He paused, exhausted, while the dread visitor hovered closer.

'Tell me,' I said, 'just a word. How did you get out of the train?'

He smiled faintly.

'Some more of your stuff,' he whispered; and when I had given him a second dose of brandy he went on feebly and with long pauses which I am not attempting to reproduce:

'I had worked the thing out beforehand. I thought if I could get out on the buffers while the train was running and before the alarm was raised, I should be safe. No one looking out of the windows could see me, and when the train stopped, as I knew it soon would, I could drop down and make off. The difficulty was to get from the corridor to the buffers. I did it like this:

'I had brought about sixteen feet of fine, brown silk cord, and the same length of thin silk rope. When I got out at Crewe I moved to the corner of the coach and stood close to it by way of getting shelter to light a cigarette. Without anyone seeing what I was up to I slipped the end of the cord through the bracket handle above the buffers. Then I strolled to the nearest door, paying out the cord, but holding on to its two ends. I pretended to fumble at the door as if it was stiff to open, but all the time I was passing the cord through the handle-guard, and knotting the ends together. If you've followed me you'll understand this gave me a loop of fine silk connecting the handles at the corner and the door. It was the colour of the carriage, and was nearly invisible. Then I took my seat again.

'When the time came to do the job, I first wedged the corridor doors. Then I opened the outside window and drew in the end of the cord loop and tied the end of the rope to it. I pulled one side of the cord loop and so got the rope pulled through the corner bracket handle and back again to the window. Its being silk made it run easily, and without marking the bracket. Then I put an end of the rope through the handle-guard, and after pulling it tight, knotted the ends together. This gave me a loop of rope tightly stretched from the door to the corner.

'I opened the door and then pulled up the window. I let the door close up against a bit of wood I had brought. The wind kept it to, and the wood prevented it from shutting.

'Then I fired. As soon as I saw that both were hit I got outside. I kicked away the wood and shut the door. Then with the rope for a handrail I stepped along the footboard to the buffers. I cut both the cord and the rope and drew them after me, and shoved them in my pocket. This removed all traces.

'When the train stopped I slipped down on the ground. The people were getting out at the other side so I had only to creep along close to the coaches till I got out of their light, then I climbed up the bank and escaped.'

The man had evidently made a desperate effort to finish, for as he ceased speaking his eyes closed, and in a few minutes he fell into a state of coma which shortly preceded his death.

After communicating with the police I set myself to carry out his second injunction, and this statement is the result.

Moxon's Master

AMBROSE BIERCE

'ARE YOU SERIOUS? – DO you really believe that a machine thinks?'
I got no immediate reply. Moxon was apparently intent upon the
coals in the grate, touching them deftly here and there with the fire-
poker till they signified a sense of his attention by a brighter glow. For
several weeks I had been observing in him a growing habit of delay in
answering even the most trivial of commonplace questions. His air,
however, was that of preoccupation rather than deliberation. One
might have said that he had something on his mind.

Presently he said:

'What is a "machine"?' The word has been variously defined. Here
is one definition from a popular dictionary: "Any instrument or
organization by which power is applied and made effective, or a
desired effect produced." Well, then, is not a man a machine? And
you will admit that he thinks – or thinks he thinks.'

'If you do not wish to answer my question,' I said, rather testily,
'why not say so? All that you say is mere evasion. You know well
enough that when I say "machine" I do not mean a man, but
something that man has made and controls.'

'When it does not control him,' he said, rising abruptly and looking
out of a window, whence nothing was visible in the blackness of a
stormy night. A moment later he turned about and with a smile said,
'I beg your pardon; I had no thought of evasion. I considered the
dictionary man's unconscious testimony suggestive and worth something in the discussion. I can give your question a direct answer easily
enough: I do believe that a machine thinks about the work that it is
doing.'

That was direct enough, certainly. It was not altogether pleasing,
for it tended to confirm a sad suspicion that Moxon's devotion to
study and work in his machine shop had not been good for him. I
knew, for one thing, that he suffered from insomnia, and that is no
light affliction. Had it affected his mind? His reply to my question
seemed to me then evidence that it had; perhaps I should think
differently about it now. I was younger then, and among the blessings
that are not denied to youth is ignorance. Incited by that great

320

stimulant to controversy, I said:

'And what, pray, does it think with – in the absence of a brain?'

The reply, coming with less than his customary delay, took his favourite form of counterinterrogation:

'With what does a plant think – in the absence of a brain?'

'Ah, plants also belong to the philosopher class! I should be pleased to know some of their conclusions; you may omit the premises.'

'Perhaps,' he replied, apparently unaffected by my foolish irony, 'you may be able to infer their convictions from their acts. I will spare you the familiar examples of the sensitive mimosa, the several insectivorous flowers and those whose stamens bend down and shake their pollen upon the entering bee in order that he may fertilize their distant mates. But observe this. In an open spot in my garden I planted a climbing vine. When it was barely above the surface I set a stake into the soil a yard away. The vine at once made for it, but as it was about to reach it after several days I removed it a few feet. The vine at once altered its course, making an acute angle, and again made for the stake. This maneuver was repeated several times, but finally, as if discouraged, the vine abandoned the pursuit and ignoring further attempts to divert it traveled to a small tree, farther away, which it climbed.

'Roots of the eucalyptus will prolong themselves incredibly in search of moisture. A well-known horticulturist relates that one entered an old drain pipe and followed it until it came to a break, where a section of the pipe had been removed to make way for a stone wall that had been built across its course. The root left the drain and followed the wall until it found an opening where a stone had fallen out. It crept through and, following the other side of the wall back to the drain, entered the unexplored part and resumed its journey.'

'And all this?'

'Can you miss the significance of it? It shows the consciousness of plants. It proves that they think.'

'Even if it did – what then? We were speaking, not of plants, but of machines. They may be composed partly of wood – wood that no longer has vitality – or wholly of metal. Is thought an attribute also of the mineral kingdom?'

'How else do you explain the phenomena, for example, of crystallization?'

'I do not explain them.'

'Because you cannot without affirming what you wish to deny, namely, intelligent cooperation among the constituent elements of the crystals. When soldiers form lines, or hollow squares, you call it reason. When wild geese in flight take the form of a letter V you say instinct. When the homogeneous atoms of a mineral, moving freely in

321

solution, arrange themselves into shapes mathematically perfect, or particles of frozen moisture into the symmetrical and beautiful forms of snowflakes, you have nothing to say. You have not even invented a name to conceal your heroic unreason.'

Moxon was speaking with unusual animation and earnestness. As he paused I heard in an adjoining room known to me as his machine shop, which no one but himself was permitted to enter, a singular thumping sound, as of someone pounding upon a table with an open hand. Moxon heard it at the same moment and, visibly agitated, rose and hurriedly passed into the room whence it came. I thought it odd that anyone else should be in there, and my interest in my friend – with doubtless a touch of unwarrantable curiosity – led me to listen intently, though, I am happy to say, not at the keyhole. There were confused sounds, as of a struggle or scuffle; the floor shook. I distinctly heard hard breathing and a hoarse whisper which said, 'Damn you!' Then all was silent, and presently Moxon reappeared and said, with a rather sorry smile:

'Pardon me for leaving you so abruptly. I have a machine in there that lost its temper and cut up rough.'

Fixing my eyes steadily upon his left cheek, which was traversed by four parallel excoriations showing blood, I said:

'How would it do to trim its nails?'

I could have spared myself the jest; he gave it no attention, but seated himself in the chair that he had left and resumed the interrupted monologue as if nothing had occurred.

'Doubtless you do not hold with those (I need not name them to a man of your reading) who have taught that all matter is sentient, that every atom is a living, feeling, conscious being. *I* do. There is no such thing as dead, inert matter. It is all alive; all instinct with force, actual and potential; all sensitive to the same forces in its environment and susceptible to the contagion of higher and subtler ones residing in such superior organisms as it may be brought into relation with, as those of man when he is fashioning it into an instrument of his will. It absorbs something of his intelligence and purpose – more of them in proportion to the complexity of the resulting machine and that of its work.

'Do you happen to recall Herbert Spencer's definition of life? I read it thirty years ago. He may have altered it afterward, for anything I know, but in all that time I have been unable to think of a single word that could profitably be changed or added or removed. It seems to me not only the best definition, but the only possible one.

' "Life," he says, "is a definite combination of heterogeneous changes, both simultaneous and successive, in correspondence with external coexistences and sequences." '

322

'That defines the phenomenon,' I said, 'but gives no hint of its cause.'

'That,' he replied, 'is all that any definition can do. As Mill points out, we know nothing of cause except as an antecedent – nothing of effect except as a consequent. Of certain phenomena, one never occurs without another, which is dissimilar: the first in point of time we call cause, the second, effect. One who had many times seen a rabbit pursued by a dog, and had never seen rabbits and dogs otherwise, would think the rabbit the cause of the dog.

'But I fear', he added, laughing naturally enough, 'that my rabbit is leading me a long way from the track of my legitimate quarry. I'm indulging in the pleasure of the chase for its own sake. What I want you to observe is that in Herbert Spencer's definition of life the activity of a machine is included – there is nothing in the definition that is not applicable to it. According to this sharpest of observers and deepest of thinkers, if a man during his period of activity is alive, so is a machine when in operation. As an inventor and constructor of machines I know that to be true.'

Moxon was silent for a long time, gazing absently into the fire. It was growing late and I thought it time to be going, but somehow I did not like the notion of leaving him in that isolated house, all alone except for the presence of some person of whose nature my conjectures could go no further than that it was unfriendly, perhaps malign. Leaning toward him and looking earnestly into his eyes while making a motion with my hand through the door of his workshop, I said:

'Moxon, whom have you in there?'

Somewhat to my surprise he laughed lightly and answered without hesitation:

'Nobody. The incident that you have in mind was caused by my folly in leaving a machine in action with nothing to act upon, while I undertook the interminable task of enlightening your understanding. Do you happen to know that Consciousness is the creature of Rhythm?'

'Oh bother them both!' I replied, rising and laying hold of my overcoat. 'I'm going to wish you good night. And I'll add the hope that the machine which you inadvertently left in action will have her gloves on the next time you think it needful to stop her.'

Without waiting to observe the effect of my shot I left the house.

Rain was falling, and the darkness was intense. In the sky beyond the crest of a hill toward which I groped my way along precarious plank sidewalks and across miry, unpaved streets I could see the faint glow of the city's lights, but behind me nothing was visible but a single window of Moxon's house. It glowed with what seemed to me a mysterious and fateful meaning. I knew it was an uncurtained

323

aperture in my friend's machine shop, and I had little doubt that he had resumed the studies interrupted by his duties as my instructor in mechanical consciousness and the fatherhood of Rhythm. Odd, and in some degree humorous, as his convictions seemed to me at that time, I could not wholly divest myself of the feeling that they had some tragic relation to his life and character – perhaps to his destiny – although I no longer entertained the notion that they were the vagaries of a disordered mind. Whatever might be thought of his views, his exposition of them was too logical for that. Over and over, his last words came back to me: 'Consciousness is the creature of Rhythm.' Bald and terse as the statement was, I now found it infinitely alluring. At each recurrence it broadened in meaning and deepened in suggestion. Why, here (I thought) is something upon which to found a philosophy. If consciousness is the product of rhythm, all things *are* conscious, for all have motion, and all motion is rhythmic. I wondered if Moxon knew the significance and breadth of his thought – the scope of this momentous generalization; or had he arrived at his philosophic faith by the tortuous and uncertain road of observation?

That faith was then new to me, and all Moxon's expounding had failed to make me a convert; but now it seemed as if a great light shone about me, like that which fell upon Saul of Tarsus; and out there in the storm and darkness and solitude I experienced what Lewes calls 'the endless variety and excitement of philosophic thought.' I exulted in a new sense of knowledge, a new pride of reason. My feet seemed hardly to touch the earth; it was as if I were uplifted and borne through the air by invisible wings.

Yielding to an impulse to seek further light from him whom I now recognized as my master and guide, I had unconsciously turned about, and almost before I was aware of having done so found myself again at Moxon's door. I was drenched with rain, but felt no discomfort. Unable in my excitement to find the doorbell I instinctively tried the knob. It turned and, entering, I mounted the stairs to the room that I had so recently left. All was dark and silent; Moxon, as I had supposed, was in the adjoining room – the machine shop. Groping along the wall until I found the communicating door I knocked loudly several times but got no response, which I attributed to the uproar outside, for the wind was blowing a gale and dashing the rain against the thin walls in sheets. The drumming upon the shingle roof spanning the unceiled room was loud and incessant.

I had never been invited into the machine shop – had, indeed, been denied admittance, as had all others, with one exception, a skilled metalworker, of whom no one knew anything except that his name was Haley and his habit silence. But in my spiritual exaltation, discretion and civility were alike forgotten and I opened the door.

What I saw took all philosophical speculation out of me in short order.

Moxon sat facing me at the farther side of a small table upon which a single candle made all the light that was in the room. Opposite him, his back toward me, sat another person. On the table between the two was a chessboard; the men were playing. I knew little of chess, but as only a few pieces were on the board it was obvious that the game was near its close. Moxon was intensely interested – not so much, it seemed to me, in the game as in his antagonist, upon whom he had fixed so intent a look that standing though I did directly in the line of his vision, I was altogether unobserved. His face was ghastly white, and his eyes glittered like diamonds. Of his antagonist I had only a back view, but that was sufficient; I should not have cared to see his face.

He was apparently not more than five feet in height, with proportions suggesting those of a gorilla – a tremendous breadth of shoulders, thick, short neck and broad, squat head, which had a tangled growth of black hair and was topped with a crimson fez. A tunic of the same color, belted tightly to the waist, reached the seat – apparently a box – upon which he sat; his legs and feet were not seen. His left forearm appeared to rest in his lap; he moved his pieces with his right hand, which seemed disproportionately long.

I had shrunk back and now stood a little to one side of the doorway and in shadow. If Moxon had looked farther than the face of his opponent he could have observed nothing now, except that the door was open. Something forbade me either to enter or to retire, a feeling – I know not how it came – that I was in the presence of an imminent tragedy and might serve my friend by remaining. With a scarcely conscious rebellion against the indelicacy of the act, I remained.

The play was rapid. Moxon hardly glanced at the board before making his moves, and to my unskilled eye seemed to move the piece most convenient to his hand, his motions in doing so being quick, nervous and lacking in precision. The response of his antagonist, while equally prompt in the inception, was made with a slow, uniform, mechanical and, I thought, somewhat theatrical movement of the arm that was a sore trial to my patience. There was something unearthly about it all, and I caught myself shuddering. But I was wet and cold.

Two or three times after moving a piece the stranger slightly inclined his head, and each time I observed that Moxon shifted his king. All at once the thought came to me that the man was dumb. And then that he was a machine – an automaton chessplayer! Then I remembered that Moxon had once spoken to me of having invented such a piece of mechanism, though I did not understand that it had actually been constructed. Was all his talk about the consciousness and intelligence of machines merely a prelude to eventual exhibition

325

of this device – only a trick to intensify the effect of its mechanical action upon me in my ignorance of its secret?

A fine end, this, of all my intellectual transports – my 'endless variety and excitement of philosophic thought'! I was about to retire in disgust when something occurred to hold my curiosity. I observed a shrug of the thing's great shoulders, as if it were irritated, and so natural was this – so entirely human – that in my new view of the matter it startled me. Nor was that all, for a moment later it struck the table sharply with its clenched hand. At that gesture Moxon seemed even more startled than I. He pushed his chair a little backward, as in alarm.

Presently Moxon, whose play it was, raised his hand high above the board, pounced upon one of his pieces like a sparrow hawk and with the exclamation 'Checkmate!' rose quickly to his feet and stepped behind his chair. The automaton sat motionless.

The wind had now gone down, but I heard, at lessening intervals and progressively louder, the rumble and roll of thunder. In the pauses between I now became conscious of a low humming or buzzing which, like the thunder, grew momentarily louder and more distinct. It seemed to come from the body of the automaton, and was unmistakably a whirring of wheels. It gave me the impression of a disordered mechanism which had escaped the repressive and regulating action of some controlling part – an effect such as might be expected if a pawl should be jostled from the teeth of a ratchet wheel. But before I had time for much conjecture as to its nature my attention was taken by the strange motions of the automaton itself. A slight but continuous convulsion appeared to have possession of it. In body and head it shook like a man with palsy or an ague chill, and the motion augmented every moment until the entire figure was in violent agitation. Suddenly it sprang to its feet and with a movement almost too quick for the eye to follow shot forward across table and chair, with both arms thrust forth to their full length – the posture and lunge of a diver. Moxon tried to throw himself backward out of reach, but he was too late: I saw the horrible thing's hands close upon his throat, his own clutch its wrists. Then the table was overturned, the candle thrown to the floor and extinguished, and all was black dark. But the noise of the struggle was dreadfully distinct, and most terrible of all were the raucous, squawking sounds made by the strangled man's efforts to breathe. Guided by the infernal hubbub, I sprang to the rescue of my friend, but had hardly taken a stride in the darkness when the whole room blazed with a blinding white light that burned into my brain and heart and memory a vivid picture of the combatants on the floor, Moxon underneath, his throat still in the clutch of those iron hands, his head forced backward, his eyes protruding, his mouth wide open and his tongue thrust out; and – horrible contrast! – upon the painted face of his assassin an expression of tranquil and profound thought, as in the solution of a problem in chess! This I observed, then all was blackness and silence.

Three days later I recovered consciousness in a hospital. As the memory of that tragic night slowly evolved in my ailing brain I recognized in my attendant Moxon's confidential workman, Haley. Responding to a look he approached, smiling.

'Tell me about it,' I managed to say, faintly – 'all about it.'

'Certainly,' he said. 'You were carried unconscious from a burning house – Moxon's. Nobody knows how you came to be there. You may have to do a little explaining. The origin of the fire is a bit mysterious, too. My own notion is that the house was struck by lightning.'

'And Moxon?'

'Buried yesterday – what was left of him.'

Apparently this reticent person could unfold himself on occasion. When imparting shocking intelligence to the sick he was affable enough. After some moments of the keenest mental suffering I ventured to ask another question:

'Who rescued me?'

'Well, if that interests you – I did.'

'Thank you, Mr Haley, and may God bless you for it. Did you rescue, also, that charming product of your skill, the automaton chess-player that murdered its inventor?'

The man was silent for a long time, looking away from me. Presently he turned and gravely said:

'Do you know that?'

'I do,' I replied. 'I saw it done.'

That was many years ago. If asked today I should answer less confidently.

The Basket Chair

WINSTON GRAHAM

I

WHITELEAF HAD HIS FIRST coronary when he was staying with his niece Agnes and her husband Roy Paynter. He came through it, as of course he fully expected he would. When a healthy man is struck down with a near fatal blow it is as if he has walked into a brick wall in the dark; he is brought up starkly against the realization of his own mortality, and there is nothing to cushion the psychological shock. But Julian Whiteleaf had lived so closely with his own mortality for so long that a heart attack was just another obstacle to be carefully surmounted and added to his list of battle scars. No doubt this attitude of mind had helped him to stay alive when probability was not on his side.

But this was a nasty business, so painful and so disabling. It was hospital for three weeks and then it would be another four at least in Agnes's house before he was well enough to go home. The doctor had been a little reluctant to let him out of hospital, but Whiteleaf badly wanted to leave and Agnes had had some training as a nurse and said she could manage, as Roy was out all day. She was a highly efficient woman.

Although she was his only surviving relative Whiteleaf had never really cared for Agnes. She was a childless, stocky, formidable woman of forty, who made ends meet on Roy's inadequate salary and found time and money for endless good works. Yet whether it was the Red Cross or the Women's Institute or the Homebound Club, every good deed was performed with the same grim patient efficiency so that joy was noticeably lacking from the occasion. Far better, Whiteleaf thought – and had sometimes said – if she took a paid job of her own to supplement the family income; but this advice was not appreciated.

So in some ways he would have been happy enough to stay another week or so in hospital; but as he had opted out of the Health Service some time ago it saved a great deal of money to leave, and anyway he rather thought Agnes liked making the effort to prove her devotion.

Another four weeks with Agnes, mainly in bed, was a daunting prospect. But the time would pass. Whiteleaf was a great reader, and Agnes brought a portable radio up to his bedroom. He would have

328

time to ruminate, time to rest. At sixty-five one becomes philosophical.

He had had an interesting life, and it bore looking back on. Born above a small bookshop in Bloomsbury, he had been vaguely literary from an early age but his talents had lain in the unprofitable fields for which Bloomsbury in the thirties offered so much scope. Apart from helping in his father's bookshop, he had worked on two Fabian magazines, then had been assistant editor on a Theosophist newspaper which shortly folded up; he had reviewed and done freelance work, had dabbled in Spiritualism and then become secretary to the Society for Psychoneural Research. Here he met Mrs Melanie Buxton who financed the society, and had become her lover.

At this stage the war had come and he had found himself a reluctant soldier entering a world which had almost no physical or psychological resemblance to the ingrown, rather intense, fringe-intellectual world he had inhabited before. For a while the fresh air and the hard life did him good. He strengthened and broadened and mellowed under it. But in 1943 he was invalided out, having been twice seriously wounded in the desert and having contracted asthma and a kidney complaint from which he would suffer for the rest of his life.

To his surprise he found himself a rich man. Mrs Melanie Buxton, who was twenty years older than he was, had just died, and she left the bulk of her personal fortune – about £200,000 – to Julian Whiteleaf, 'to help him continue in the paths of research to which we are both devoted'.

Whiteleaf sold the bookshop, which he had also just inherited, and at forty years of age settled down to the existence of a quiet, ailing, dilettante. He never went back to live in Bloomsbury but bought himself a pleasant service flat in Hurlingham and never moved again. There was no one to oversee his interpretation of Mrs Buxton's will, but to fulfil the spirit of the bequest he kept the society in being with a tiny office and a secretary and continued to review books and write articles on paranormal phenomena. So, gradually, he had become something of an authority. Once or twice he helped to conduct inquiries into so-called haunted houses. He continued to dabble in Theosophy. He was known as a fair-minded commentator on the spiritualist scene. He was neither a committed believer nor a scoffing sceptic. Editors of national newspapers, confronted with an unusual book which did not quite fit into any of the recognized slots, would say: 'Oh, send it to Whiteleaf; see what he makes of it.'

He never married. His experiences with Mrs Buxton had satisfied him, and his ill-health after the war was a sufficient disincentive to extreme physical effort.

He joined a good London club and had many friendly acquaintances there among those with interests like his own; but he had no real friends. He did not feel the lack of them. He looked at life through books. He was a precise, quiet man, sandy and rather small, who spoke without moving his lips. He lived very much within his income and never gave money away, except £20 to his niece each Christmas.

His visits to her were annual and largely a duty. She was the daughter of his sister who had died in the fifties, and blood, he supposed, etc . . . but it was really rather an effort. He would, he knew, have made an excuse to stop the visits before this, had it not been for her husband Roy, who had a responsible but dead-end and underpaid job on the railways, and who, apart from being a nice inoffensive chap for whom Whiteleaf felt some sympathy at having married Agnes, also appealed to the other interest in Whiteleaf's life, which was the steam-engine.

This was the topic of conversation four nights out of the seven that Whiteleaf usually came to spend with them, especially when Agnes was out on some charitable mission; and sometimes at the week-end the two men would go to the railway museum, which was only a few miles away, and study the old locomotives and compare notes. It was a bond. And when he was dangerously ill two years ago after a gall-bladder operation, Roy had come up to London each week-end to see him and had brought up old catalogues and lists of engines from the days of steam, which he had been able to borrow from the local files.

Now that Whiteleaf was convalescing in their house and for a lengthy period, he felt he should pay them something for his keep, and he offered them £5 a week which Agnes accepted – grudgingly, he thought. But it would be a considerable help to them, he well knew, and not to be sniffed at, his weekly cheque. Agnes spent no more time on him than she would have done on her unpaid good works. The doctor called daily and Agnes took his blood pressure night and morning when she gave him his pills. And a starvation diet. His £5 was all profit.

Convalescence is a strange experience. Whiteleaf was used to it, but 'every time', he wrote in his diary a couple of days after he came back from hospital, 'it presents a new face. It is as if the mind during serious illness concentrates all its energies on survival; but once the crisis is past it relaxes. It even relaxes its normal vigilance and controls – so that strange fancies, wayward concepts, take a hold that in normal times of health they would never begin to do. Nerves are on edge, imagination gets loose, temper frays as if one were a child again. Why snap at Agnes over the fire in my room? She so obviously is doing her best. Why allow oneself to think so much about the basket chair?'

Whiteleaf's diary was the one thing he had kept to all his life. Very often he wrote in it thoughts which later were useful to him when reviewing books or writing articles. He had been glad to get back to it when the doctor's prohibition was removed, and to fill in the empty days. He had always done this after his operations, even calling on the nurses to help him. This time happily there had been no unconsciousness, only great pain and then forced immobility.

'Of course,' he wrote two days after that, 'one wonders how far all paranormal phenomena is explained in this way. And in this context, what does "explained" mean? "Imagination gets loose", I see I wrote overleaf. But how do we separate illusion from reality? We define reality as something which because it is apprehended by the majority of men is therefore assumed to exist. But does consensus of opinion necessarily prove the *positive* of any theory of reality? Still less therefore can it disprove the negative. Galileo believed that the earth moved round the sun. His was the scientific eye, perceiving what others could not see. May not the psychic eye perceive another area of truth at present hidden from the rest of us?'

'Is something worrying you, Uncle?' Roy asked that evening when he was sitting with him after supper.

'No. Why?'

'You kept staring at the fireplace as if something didn't please you.'

'Not at all. Nothing is worrying me. But in fact I was looking at that chair on the other side beside the lamp.'

'That one? What about it?'

'It's new, isn't it? I mean new to you? Since my last visit.'

'We've had it about a year. Agnes bought it at a sale. It's a bit of a rickety old thing but it's very comfortable. You'll be able to try it in another week or so.'

'It looks seventy or eighty years old to me.'

'Maybe. But it's *strong*. The frame's strong. Like iron. It's quite heavy to lift. I think Agnes paid a pound for it. About this film . . .'

They returned to discussing *La Bête Humaine*, which Whiteleaf had seen thirty years ago and considered the best film about railways ever made. Roy had never seen it and wanted to. There were copies in France, and being in railways he might be able to pull a string or two. He also knew the proprietor of the local cinema who, between alternate bingo nights, was always willing to risk a bit of something way-out. He preferred sex or horror films, but if the French film were offered to him to show for a couple of nights without rental charge he would certainly agree to show it.

But it would cost money to bring it over and to put it on. It was no good Roy trying to do anything unless he knew Uncle Julian would bear the cost. Uncle Julian was doubtful, discouraging: he'd want to know a lot more about what he was letting himself in for before he

331

even considered it. They discussed it for a long time and came as near an argument as they ever got, Roy pressing and Whiteleaf hedging away.

After Roy had gone Agnes came in and settled him down for the night. It was diuretic pills in the morning and potassium pills at night, and she gave him these now and saw his inhaler was within reach, threw some slack coal on the fire, which kept it in most of the night but almost extinguished it as a provider of heat, and then stood by the bed, square and uncompromising, and asked him if he wanted anything more.

He said no and she kissed his forehead perfunctorily and left. It was eleven o'clock. He read for a few minutes and then put out the light and composed himself for sleep. The room and the house were very quiet. Roy and Agnes were separated from him by the bathroom and the box room and their movements could not be heard. In the distance a diesel train hooted. It was a lonely sound.

Then the basket chair creaked as if someone had just sat down in it.

II

'I think,' said Dr Abrahams, 'you might have stayed in another week. Are you moving about too much?'

'No. Only once or twice a day, with my niece's help, just as you advised.'

'He never has need to stir a finger otherwise,' said Agnes uncompromisingly.

'Well, the electrocardiograms are satisfactory. But why aren't you sleeping?'

'I do well enough when I get off, but it takes an hour or two to – compose myself.'

'He sleeps in the afternoon,' Agnes said. 'I expect that takes the edge off. I can *never* sleep at night if I have a nap after lunch.'

'The breathing all right?'

'No worse than usual. I always need the inhaler a few times.'

After the doctor had gone, Agnes came back and found Whiteleaf writing in his diary.

'You shouldn't do that,' she said. 'It tires you. Dr Abrahams was asking me if you were worried about something. I said not so far as I know.'

'Not so far as I know either. Tell me, Agnes, about that basket chair. Roy says you bought it in a sale.'

Agnes looked rather peculiar. 'Yes. Why? What's wrong with it?'

'Nothing at all. But what sale?'

'Oh, it was that big house about a mile out of Swindon. D'you remember it? No, you won't, I don't expect.'

'D'you mean Furze Hall?'

'No. Beyond that. There was a Miss Covent lived there, all by herself with only one servant. It had thirty-four rooms. Fantastic. She was eighty when she died.'

'What made you go?'

'Oh, it was advertised. Carol Elliot wanted a few things – you know, from down the road – so I went with her. It was an awful old place; she'd let it go to ruin, this Miss Covent: all the roofs leaked, I should think; it's being pulled down. Most of the furniture was junk but it went very cheap. I paid a pound for the chair and ten bob for that bookcase in the hall and two pounds for four kitchen mats and –'

Agnes went on about her bargains and then switched to some other subject, which Whiteleaf ignored.

'Did you know anything about it?' he asked presently. 'About the house where you bought those things?'

'The Covents' place? Well, of course, I'd never been in before. Hardly anyone had. It was like something out of Boris Karloff, I can tell you. The old lady must have been bats living there alone. There was some story Carol Elliot was telling me about it but I didn't pay much attention.'

'Ask her sometime.'

'Carol? Yes, I'll ask her. But why?'

'I'm interested in old places. You know my interests.'

'Well, I never heard it was *haunted*, if that's what you mean. Don't you like the chair? I can take it out.'

'No, leave it where it is. I like old things.'

'Well, it's comfy, I can tell you that. I always enjoy sitting in it when I come to see you last thing.'

When she had gone Whiteleaf continued in his diary: 'Recorded and authenticated "possession" of small items of furniture is relatively rare and has no reliable weight of testimony behind it such as the "possession" of houses has. The poltergeist one accepts, because one has to accept it. Beyond that there is only reasonable cause to believe and reasonable cause to doubt. In the case of a chair . . .' He wrote no more that evening.

The following day he began a new entry. 'Is this the hallucination of illness or the clearer perception of convalescence? It is certainly a very peculiar shape. That high rounded back. It is a half-way style, reminiscent of one of the old hooded hall chairs of the 18th century. Why does someone or something appear to sit in it every night when I am trying to go to sleep? And am I right in supposing sometimes that I can hear breathing and footsteps? Odd that in all these years of interest and study this should be the first possibly psychic event that has ever happened to me . . .'

The next evening Agnes said: 'I saw Carol today. It is a funny story about the Covents. Of course, she's lived here all her life and we've only been here ten years. She says it was before her time but her mother often spoke of it.'

'Spoke of what?' Whiteleaf asked.

'Well, it's not a very nice story, Uncle. It won't upset you to talk about it?'

'I'm not made of cotton wool,' he said impatiently. 'In any case, how can something that presumably happened years ago have any effect? I'm allowed to read the daily papers, aren't I?'

'Yes, well, yes . . .' Agnes plucked at her lip. 'Well, Carol says they were a young married couple, the Covents, during World War One. He was in the Battle of the Somme and was blown up and hideously disfigured. Apparently spent a couple of years in hospital and then they let him out. I suppose plastic surgery wasn't much help in those days . . .'

'No, it was in an experimental stage.'

'So they hadn't done him any good. He was still terrible to look at, and when he came home he never went out of the house but used to sit by the fire all day reading and thinking. His wife used to go and do all the shopping, etc., Carol's mother says, and that way she met another man and had an affair with him. Somehow or other Captain Covent discovered this and it must have turned his brain because she suddenly stopped going shopping and everyone thought they had gone away . . .'

Whiteleaf felt his heart give a slight excited lurch. 'Interesting.'

'After a few weeks someone got suspicious and they broke into the house and there they were, both dead, one on either side of the empty fireplace. Apparently he'd tied her to a chair and then sat down opposite her and watched her starve to death. Then he cut his own throat. That's what the doctors said. It was a big sensation in the twenties.'

'Very interesting,' said Whiteleaf.

'Well, horrible I say. They hadn't any children so the property came to his eldest sister and she took it over and lived there until last year. I tell you the house would have given me the creeps without any funny stories.'

Silence fell and the door downstairs banged.

'That's Roy,' said Agnes. 'I'll get him to shift that chair tonight, just so that it won't worry you.'

'Not at all,' said Whiteleaf. 'Leave it just where it is.'

Agnes shivered. 'Don't tell Roy. He's superstitious about these things.'

Whiteleaf shifted himself up the bed. 'D'you realize I remember the First World War?'

'Do you, Uncle? Yes, I suppose you do. But you'd be very young.'

'I well remember celebrating the Armistice. I was thirteen at the time. It never occurred to me than that I should have to fight in another war myself.'

When she had gone downstairs to get Roy his tea, Whiteleaf wrote just one sentence in his diary. 'I wonder if this chair, this basket chair, was the one Captain Covent sat in? Or was it hers?'

III

That night, although he was still not sure about the breathing, he was quite certain about the footsteps. The creaking of the chair as someone sat in it began about ten minutes or so after he was left alone and went on for a little while with faint furtive creaks. They were very faint but very distinct as someone stirred in the chair. Then also quite distinctly there was the soft pad of footsteps, about six or seven, moving away from the chair towards the door. They did not reach the door. They stopped half-way and were heard no more. Presently the creaking died away.

It is surprising what tension is generated by the supernatural. One can write about it. One can attend spiritualist séances. One can even visit haunted houses and still remain detached, scientific, aloof. But in a silent bedroom, entirely alone, with only this wayward wandering spirit for company, Julian Whiteleaf felt himself screwing up to meet some crisis that he greatly feared but could not imagine. It was clearly not doing his health much good or aiding his recovery. The whole thing was strikingly interesting; but he would have to take care, to take great care, to find some means of rationalizing this experience so that he could regain his detachment. Only his diary helped.

'Supposing,' he wrote, 'that I am *not* the victim of a sick man's hallucination and that for some reason I have become clairaudient. (The "some reason" could well be the rare combination of my hypersensitive perceptions during convalescence and the presence of a chair with such an evil aura, amounting to "possession".) Supposing that, then is there any resolution or solution of the situation in which I find myself? Is there any *progress* in this nightly occurrence? Is there a likelihood that I may become clairvoyant too? (And in the circumstances would I wish to be? Hardly!) Why are there only six or seven steps, and why do they always move towards the door?'

That night there were exactly the same number of steps but they were quite audible now, a soft firm foot-fall, measured but fading at the usual spot.

Whiteleaf never kept his light on, but Agnes had lent him her electric clock, which had an illuminated face, so that when one's eyes were accustomed to the dark one could just see about the room. And tonight a pale blue flame was flickering in the fire, so this helped. But sitting up in bed, Whiteleaf wished there had been no such fire, for the flame conjured up movements about the old chair. He thought: insanity is not evil, yet it so often wears the same guise. Covent must have been insane, driven insane by his own mutilated face rather than by jealousy of his wife. Only an insane man could tie a woman to a chair and watch her starve to death. I must examine that chair more closely. There may even be signs of where the rope has frayed the frame.

It was four o'clock in the morning before he fell asleep.

IV

Dr Abrahams said to Agnes: 'Your uncle is not making the progress that I'd hoped for. His blood pressure is up a little and his breathing is not too satisfactory. If this goes on we'll get him back in hospital.'

'It's just as you like,' said Agnes. 'I always help him when he gets out of bed, and we're careful he doesn't overdo it. I keep the fire going all day and night to help his asthma.'

'Of course he uses that inhaler too much: I've told him to go easy on it, but it would be unwise to take it away; he has come to depend on it. One is between the devil and the deep sea.'

'I'll watch him,' said Agnes. 'But he *is* difficult. Strong minded. He'd fight before he went back to hospital.'

'That's what I'm afraid of,' said Abrahams.

While they were downstairs talking, Whiteleaf was up and examining the chair, as he had done once before when left to himself. As Roy had said, it was a strangely heavy chair for one made principally of cane. The framework was of a thin rounded wood like bamboo but enormously hard. You couldn't make any indentation in it with a fruit knife. There were a number of stains on the seat under the cushion: they could have been bloodstains: impossible without forensic equipment to tell. Whiteleaf had never sat in the chair and did not want to do so now. He felt he might have been sitting on something that should not be there. Only Agnes sat on it, in the evenings, and he had been tempted more than once to ask her not to.

He hastily climbed back into bed as he heard her feet on the stairs.

Later he wrote: 'I get the feeling that someone or something is trying to escape. To escape from the bondage of the chair. (Not surprising, perhaps, in view of its history!) But something more than just that – otherwise why the steps? It's as if the body rotted away long ago but the spirit is still attached to the scene of its suffering and still striving to get away. The footsteps always move towards the door. If they ever reached the door, would Something go out? This I could accept more readily were this the actual room in which the tragedy took place. Yet perhaps in the room in which this *did* happen, there *were* only eight steps from chair to door. Perhaps after the tragedy the chair was not moved for years and this "possession", this spirit, became bound for ever to a routine of "escape" each night. Even so it does *not* escape: it repeats for ever the ghastly ritual. Could it now in this new situation really escape for ever if the footsteps could reach *this* door? How to encourage them?'

It was the following day that he had the idea. Agnes, with her passion for cleanliness, was scouring his room as she did every day, and when she moved the basket chair to vacuum under it he suddenly called to her not to put it back.

Frowning she switched off the vacuum and listened.

'Don't put the chair back there. Put it – put it just by the dressing-table, just to the left of the dressing-table. I think I fancy it over there.'

She did not move. 'What's the matter, Uncle? Doesn't the furniture suit you? I do my best, you know.'

'You do very well,' he said. 'I'm not complaining, but if you move the chair by the dressing-table it will give me a better view of the fire.'

She stared. 'I don't see how it can. The fire . . .' She stopped and shrugged. 'Oh, well, it makes no difference to me. If that's your fancy. *Where* d'you want it?'

'Over there. A bit further. That's a good place for it there, I think.'

'D'you want me to move this other chair over? Make more room for the commode.'

'Er – no. Just leave that. Thank you, Agnes.' He began to say something more but she had switched on the vacuum again.

He didn't really mind because he was counting the steps. At the most the chair was not seven from the door.

'An experiment,' he wrote in his diary. 'Possibly nothing will come of it. Possibly shall have interfered with the "possession" altogether. Or possibly the footsteps will reach the door and something will *go out*.'

He spent the rest of the day quietly reading an old book on the Great Western Railway which Roy had brought him. This, he thought, was one of the sagas of our time. The wonderful Castle locomotives that set up records seventy years ago which have never been broken. The 4-4-0's that preceded them. The Cities and the Kings . . . He wished he could concentrate. He wished, perhaps, that he had agreed to pay the expense of having that old film over, even though it dealt with French railways and French engines. They were indeed majestic

337

in their own right. The great snorting locomotives of the Train Bleu, of the Orient Express, with their strange pulsating beat even when they are at rest . . . He wished he could concentrate.

Roy was out that evening at a social affair, Masonic or Rotary or something, so he did not see him. Agnes came up as usual, and, in spite of its uncustomary position, she sat in the basket chair. It was on the tip of his tongue to ask her not to; but again he refrained, partly because he was afraid of her uncomprehending stare, with its half implication that Uncle must be going a bit peculiar, and partly because her having been in the chair had not affected the manifestation on earlier nights.

She stayed longer than normal, talking about some work she was doing for refugees, and he listened impatiently, longing for her to be gone. She stayed in fact until Roy came in, by which time it was nearly midnight; then she gave the fire an unsympathetic poke, thumped his pillow, saw that he had enough water for the night, gave him her perfunctory kiss and was gone.

Roy had come straight upstairs, and the house soon settled. Whiteleaf's heart was thumping. To try to ease it, he began to compose the article he would write for one of the psychic papers on his experiences with a basket chair. One of the psychic papers? But possibly *The Guardian* would print it, or even *The Times*. It all depended upon the end, upon the resolution. It all depended on what happened tonight. In a way it was a triumph, that a man so involved as he had been all his life in paranormal phenomena, should at this late stage *experience* it in the most personal way. To steady himself, he tried to look on it as if it had already happened. He was recounting the most exciting moment of his life. The trouble was it wasn't over yet; he was in the middle of it; and the final experience, if there was one, was yet to come.

The fire was burning a little brighter tonight; Agnes had forgotten to bring up as much slack as usual, and this, with the help of the clock, gave adequate light – though dim. He could see all but the corners of the room. The chair in its new position was not so clearly outlined as it had been by the fire: it looked taller, still more hump-backed, like a man without a head. It cast a faint shadow on the wall behind that did not look quite its own.

The creaking was late coming tonight. He had thought it might not come at all. Always it began with a fairly definite over-all creaking such as would occur when Mrs Covent first sat in it. Then it would be silent, except for the faint creaks that broke out whenever she moved. There was no sign of her struggling, as she must have struggled before she became too weak. Perhaps it was her dying that one heard. And the footsteps were the release of her spirit, moving away.

Yet always towards the door. Now they would reach the door. Perhaps – who knew – he would see something go out.

They began. They were slower and heavier tonight. Every step was distinct, seemed to shake the room, measured itself with a thumping of his heart. He sat up sharply in bed, straining to the darker side of the room to see if he could see anything. A flickering flame from the fire, just like that other night, brought shadows to life in the silent room.

The footsteps reached five, reached six and appeared to hesitate. They were at the door. A seventh and then the fire did play tricks, for he saw the door quiver and begin to open. He screwed up his eyes, one hand pulling at the skinny flesh around his throat.

But there was no mistake. He *was* seeing something. The door was literally *opening* to allow something to go out. He could feel the difference in the air. The door was wide and something must be going out.

Then he twisted round in the bed, clutching at the rail behind him, trying to get up, to move away, to get out of bed and scream. Because round the door a hideous deformed face was appearing, with one eye, and the flesh drawn up and scarred, and a gash where the mouth should have been, and no recognizable nose.

It was clear then – quite clear – that moving the chair was not enabling Mrs Covent to go out. Captain Covent was coming in.

v

'It was always a possibility, of course,' said Dr Abrahams. 'The pulmonary oedema was an added complication. But I'm disappointed. He gave one the impression of great tenacity – great physical tenacity, I mean; such men can often endure more than ordinary people and yet recover and live to a great age.'

'Well, I can tell you it gave me the shock of my life,' said Agnes, drying her eyes. 'I came in at half past seven as usual and there he was half out of bed and clutching his throat. He seemed all right when I left him. We were a bit later than usual – about twelve it would be. I never heard a thing in the night. But he'd such an *expression* on his face.'

'He's been dead some hours. He probably died soon after you left him. I think the expression is due to the nature of the complaint: a sudden great pain, shortness of breath, no doubt he was trying to call you.'

'He had a bell there,' said Roy. 'It was on the table. Just there on the table. I'd have heard if he'd rung. I always sleep light.'

'Yes, well, there it is, there it is. His condition had been vaguely

339

unsatisfactory all this last week, without there being anything one could necessarily pick on. I take it you're his nearest relatives?'

'His only relatives,' said Agnes. 'But he was well known in his circle. I think there will be a fair number of people at the funeral.'

VI

There were a fair number of people at the funeral. Representatives of societies with long names and short membership lists, club friends who had known Whiteleaf for a long time, one or two newspaper men, nominees from charities which had benefited in the past, some of Agnes's friends. It was a fine day, and the ceremony passed off well. After it, after a discreet interval, after a quiet period of mourning, Agnes and Roy burned the diary which had first put the idea into their heads. By discreetly opening it each afternoon while Uncle Julian was asleep, Agnes had been able to keep in touch with the progression of his thoughts.

At the same time they burned a rubber mask of humorously unpleasant appearance which Roy had bought in the toy department of a big store and painted and altered to look more hideous. There seemed no particular reason to burn the mop with which Agnes had bumped nightly on the ceiling beneath Uncle Julian's bedroom. Nor did they bother to burn the basket chair which Agnes had bought in a jumble sale and whose cane had the peculiarity of reacting with creaks and clicks about fifteen minutes after a person had been sitting in it, a peculiarity they had not noticed until Uncle Julian had drawn attention to it in his diary. It seemed a pity, Agnes said, to destroy a useful chair.

That spring they had their first real holiday for ten years. They went to the South of France for two weeks. Roy had considered giving up the railway job, but for the moment he was keeping it to see how much Uncle Julian's invested income brought in. On the way back from the South of France they spent two days in Paris, and Roy made inquiries about the film he was interested in. Later that year in Swindon he intended to give a private showing to his interested friends of *La Bête Humaine*.

The Drop of Blood

MOR JOKAI

A CELEBRATED MEDICAL practitioner of Pesth, Dr K——, was early one morning urged to receive a new client. The man, who was waiting in the ante-room, sent word by the servant that delay would be dangerous; he had, therefore, to be received at once.

The doctor quickly wrapped a dressing-gown about himself, and ordered that the patient should be admitted.

He found himself in the presence of a man who was a stranger to him, but who appeared to belong to the best society, to judge by his manners. On his pale face could have been observed traces of great physical and spiritual suffering. His right hand was in a sling, and, though he tried to control himself, he now and then could not restrain sighs of unhappiness.

'Dr K——?' His voice was low. 'I live in the country, and have not the honour of knowing you, except by reputation. But I cannot say I am delighted to make your acquaintance, because my visit is not an agreeable one.'

Seeing that the sufferer's legs were hardly able to sustain him, the doctor invited him to be seated.

'I am fatigued. It is a week since I had any proper sleep. Something is the matter with my right hand; I don't know what it is – whether it is a carbuncle, or cancer. At first the pain was slight, but now it is a continuous horrible burning, increasing from day to day. I could bear it no longer so threw myself into my carriage and came to you, to beg you to cut out the affected spot. An hour more of this torture will drive me mad.'

The doctor tried to reassure him, by saying that he might be able to cure the pain with dissolvents and ointments, without resorting to the use of the bistoury.

'No, no, sir!' cried the patient; 'no plasters or ointments can give me any relief. I must have the knife. I have come to you to cut out the place which causes me so much trouble.'

The doctor asked to see the hand, which the patient held out to him, grinding his teeth, so insufferable appeared to be the pain he was enduring and with all imaginable precaution he unwound the

341

bandages in which it was enveloped.

'Above all, Doctor, I beg of you not to hesitate on account of anything you may see. My disorder is so strange, that you will be surprised; but do not let that weigh with you.'

Doctor K—— reassured the stranger. As a doctor he was used to seeing everything, and there was nothing that could surprise him.

What he saw when the hand was freed from its bandages stupefied him nevertheless. Nothing abnormal was to be seen on it – neither wound nor graze; it was a hand like any other. Bewildered, he let it fall from his own.

A cry of pain escaped from the stranger, who raised the afflicted member with his left hand, showing the doctor that he had not come with the intention of mystifying him.

'Where is the sensitive spot?'

'Here, sir,' said the stranger, indicating on the back of his hand a point where two large veins crossed, his whole frame trembling when the doctor lightly touched it with the tip of his finger.

'Is it here that the burning pain makes itself felt?'

'Abominably!'

'Do you feel the pressure when I place my finger on it?'

The man made no reply, but his eyes filled with tears of agony.

'It is surprising! I can see nothing at that place.'

'Nor can I; yet what I feel there is so terrible that at times I am almost driven to dash my head again the wall.'

The doctor examined the spot with a magnifying-glass, then shook his head.

'The skin is full of life; the blood within it circulates, there is neither inflammation nor growth under it; it is as healthy at that spot as elsewhere.'

'Yet I think it is a little redder there.'

'Where?'

The stranger took a pencil from his pocket-book and traced on his hand a ring about the size of a sixpenny-piece and said:

'It is there.'

The doctor looked in his face; he was beginning to believe that his patient's mind was unhinged.

'Remain here,' he said, 'and in a few days I'll cure you.'

'I cannot wait. Don't think that I am a maniac; it is not in that way you would cure me. The little circle which I have marked with my pencil causes me infernal tortures and I have come to you to cut it away.'

'That I cannot do,' said the doctor.

'Why?'

'Because your hand exhibits no pathological disorder. I see at the spot you have indicated nothing more amiss than on my own hand.'

'You really seem to think that I have gone out of my senses, or that I have come here to mock you,' said the stranger, taking from his pocket-book a bank-note for a thousand florins, and laying it on the table. 'Now, sir, you see that I am not playing off any childish jest, and that the service I seek of you is as urgent as it is important. I beg you to remove this part of my hand.'

'I repeat, sir, that for all the treasures in the world you cannot make me regard as unsound a member that is perfectly sound and still less induce me to cut it with my instruments.'

'And why not?'

'Because such an act would cast a doubt upon my medical knowledge and compromise my reputation. Everybody would say that you were mad; that I was dishonest in taking advantage of your condition, or ignorant in not perceiving it.'

'Very well. I will only ask a small service of you, then. I am myself capable of making the incision. I shall do it rather clumsily with my left hand; but that does not matter. Be good enough only to bind up the wound after the operation.'

It was with astonishment that the doctor saw that this strange man was speaking seriously. He stripped off his coat, turned up the wristbands of his shirt, and took a bistoury in his left hand.

A second later, and the steel had made a deep incision in the skin.

'Stay!' cried the doctor, who feared that his patient might through his awkwardness, sever some important vein. 'Since you have determined on the operation, let me perform it.'

He took the bistoury and placing in his left hand the right hand of the patient, begged him to turn away his face, the sight of blood being insupportable to many persons.

'Quite needless. On the contrary, it is I who must direct you where to cut.'

In fact he watched the operation to the end with the greatest coolness, indicating the limits of the incisions. The open hand did not even quiver in that of the doctor, and when the circular piece was removed, he sighed profoundly, like a man experiencing an enormous relief.

'Nothing burns you now?'

'All has ceased,' said the stranger, smiling. 'The pain has completely disappeared, as if it had been carried away with the part excised. The little discomfort, compared with the other pain, is like a fresh breeze after a blast from the infernal regions. It does me good to see my blood flowing.'

The stranger watched the blood pouring from the wound, and the doctor was obliged to insist on binding up the hand.

During the bandaging the aspect of his face completely changed. It no longer bore a dolorous expression, but a look full of good humour was turned upon the doctor. No more contraction of the features, no more despair. A taste for life had returned; the brow was once again calmed; the colour found its way back to the cheeks. The entire man exhibited a complete transformation.

As soon as his hand was laid in the sling he warmly wrung the doctor's hand, and said cordially;

'Accept my sincere thanks. You have positively cured me. The trifling remuneration I offer you is not at all proportioned to the service you have rendered me: for the rest of my life I shall search for the means of repaying my debt to you.'

The doctor would not listen to anything of the kind, and refused to accept the thousand florins placed on the table. On his side the stranger refused to take them back, and, observing that the doctor was losing his temper, begged him to make a present of the money to some hospital and took his departure.

K—— remained for several days at his town house until the wound in his patient's hand should be cicatrized, which it was without the least accident. During this time the doctor was able to satisfy himself that he had to do with a man of extensive knowledge, reflective and having very positive opinions in regard to the affair of life. Besides being rich, he occupied an important official position. Since the taking away of his invisible pain, no trace of moral or physical malady was discoverable in him.

The cure completed, the man returned tranquilly to his residence in the country.

About three weeks had passed when one morning, at an hour as unduly as before, the servant again announced the strange patient.

The stranger whom K—— hastened to receive entered the room with his right hand in a sling, his features convulsed and hardly recognizable from suffering. Without waiting to be invited to sit down, he sank into a chair, and being unable to master the torture he was enduring, groaned, and without uttering a word, held out his hand to the doctor.

'What has happened?' asked K——.

'We have not cut deep enough,' replied the stranger sadly, and in a fainting voice. 'It burns me more cruelly than before. I am worn out by it; my arm is stiffened by it. I did not wish to trouble you a second time, and have borne it, hoping that by degrees the invisible inflammation would either mount to my head or descend to my heart and put an end to my miserable existence; but it has not done so. The pain never goes beyond the spot, but it is indescribable! Look at my face, and you will be able to imagine what it must be!'

344

The colour of the man's skin was that of wax. The doctor unbound the bandaged hand. The point operated on was well healed; a new skin had formed, and nothing extraordinary was to be seen. The sufferer's pulse beat quickly without feverishness, while yet he trembled in every limb.

'This really smacks of the marvellous!' exclaimed the doctor, more and more astonished. 'I have never before seen such a case.'

'It is a fantasy, a horrible fantasy, doctor. Do not try to find a cause for it, but deliver me from this torment. Take your knife and cut deeper and wider: only that can relieve me.'

The doctor was obliged to give in to the prayers of his patient. He performed the operation once again, cutting into the flesh more deeply; and, once more, he saw in the sufferer's face the expression of astonishing relief, the curiosity at seeing the blood flow from the wound, which he had observed on the first occasion.

When the hand was dressed, the deadly pallor passed from the face, the colour returned to the cheeks; but the patient no more smiled. This time he thanked the doctor sadly.

'I thank you, doctor,' he said. 'The pain has once more left me. The wound will soon heal. Do not be astonished, however, to see me return before a month has passed.'

'Oh, my dear sir, drive this idea from your mind.'

The doctor mentioned this strange case to several of his colleagues, who each held a different opinion in regard to it, without any of them being able to furnish a plausible explanation of its nature.

As the end of the month approached, K—— awaited with anxiety the reappearance of this enigmatic personage. But the month passed and he did not reappear.

Several weeks more went by. At length the doctor received a letter from the sufferer's residence. It was very closely written, and by the signature he saw that it had been penned by his patient's own hand; from which he concluded that the pain had not returned, for otherwise it would have been very difficult for him to have held a pen.

These are the contents of the letter:

Dear Doctor, I cannot leave either you or science in doubt in regard to the mystery of the strange malady which will shortly carry me to the grave.

I will here tell you the origin of this malady. For the past week it has returned the third time, and I will no longer struggle with it. At this moment I am only able to write by placing upon the sensitive spot a piece of burning tinder in the form of a poultice. While the tinder is burning I do not feel the other pain; and what distress it causes me is a mere trifle by comparison.

Six months ago I was still a happy man. I lived on my income without a care. I was on good terms with everybody and enjoyed all that is of interest to a man of five-and-thirty. I had married a year before – married for love – a young lady, handsome, with a cultivated mind, and a heart as good as any heart could be, who had been a governess in the house of a countess, a neighbour of mine. She was fortuneless, and attached herself to me, not only from gratitude, but still more from real childish affection. Six months passed, during which every day appeared to be happier than the one which had gone before. If, at times, I was obliged to go to Pesth and quit my own land for a day, my wife had not a moment's rest. She would come two leagues on the way to meet me. If I was detained late, she passed a sleepless night waiting for me; and if by prayers I succeeded in inducing her to go and visit her former mistress who had not ceased to be extremely fond of her, no power could keep her away from her home for more than half a day; and by her regrets for my absence, she invariably spoiled the good-humour of others. Her tenderness for me went so far as to make her renounce dancing, so as not to be obliged to give her hand to strangers, and nothing more displeased her than gallantries addressed to her. In a word I had for my wife an innocent girl, who thought of nothing but me, and who confessed to me her dreams as enormous crimes, if they were not of me.

I know not what demon one day whispered in my ear: Suppose that all this were dissimulation? Men are mad enough to seek torments in the midst of the greatest happiness.

My wife had a work-table, the drawer of which she carefully locked. I had noticed this several times. She never forgot the key, and never left the drawer open.

That question haunted my mind. What could she be hiding there? I had become mad. I no longer believed either in the innocence of her face or the purity of her looks, nor in her caresses, or in her kisses. What if all that were hypocrisy?

One morning the countess came anew to invite her to her house, and, after much pressing, succeeded in inducing her to go and spend the day with her. Our estates were some leagues from each other, and I promised to join my wife in the course of a few hours.

As soon as the carriage had quitted the courtyard I collected all the keys in the house and tried them on the lock of the little drawer. One of them opened it. I felt like a man committing his first crime. I was a thief about to surprise the secrets of my poor wife. My hands trembled as I carefully pulled out the drawer, and, one by one, turned over the objects within it, so that no derangement of them might betray the fact of a strange hand having disturbed them. Suddenly – under some lace – I put my hand upon a packet of letters. It was as if a flash of lightning had passed through me from my head to my heart. They were the sort of letters one recognizes at a glance – love letters!

The packet was tied with a rose-coloured ribbon, edged with silver. As I touched that ribbon this thought came into my mind: Is it conceivable? – is this the work of an honest man? To steal the secrets of his wife – secrets belonging to the time when she was a young girl. Have I any right to exact from her a reckoning for thoughts she may have had before she belonged to me? Have I any right to be jealous of a time when I was unknown to her? Who could suspect her of a fault? Who? I am guilty for having suspected her. The demon again whispered in my ears: 'But what if these letters date from a time when you already had a right to know all her thoughts, when you might already be jealous of her dreams, when she was already yours?' I unfastened the ribbon. Nobody saw me. I opened one letter, then another, and I read them to the end.

What was there in these letters? The vilest treason of which a man has ever been the victim. The writer of these letters was one of my intimate friends! And the tone in which they were written – what passion, what love, certain of being returned! How he spoke of 'keeping the secret!' And all these letters dated at a time when I was married and so happy! How can I tell you what I felt? Imagine the intoxication caused by a mortal poison. I read all those letters – every one. Then I put them up again in a packet, retied them with the ribbon, and, replacing them under the lace, relocked the drawer.

I knew that if she did not see me by noon she would return in the evening from her visit to the countess – as she did. She descended from the *calèche* hurriedly, to rush towards me as I stood awaiting her on the steps. She kissed me with excessive tenderness and appeared extremely happy to be once again with me. I allowed nothing of what was passing within me to appear in my face. We conversed, we supped together, and retired to our bedrooms. I did not close an eye. Broad awake, I counted all the hours. When the clock struck the first quarter after midnight, I rose and entered her room. The beautiful fair head was there, resting on the white pillows.

I was resolved with the headlong wilfulness of a madman, haunted by a fixed idea. The poison had completely corroded my soul. I resolved to kill her as she lay.

I pass over the details of the crime. She died without offering the least resistance, as tranquilly as one goes to sleep. One single drop of blood fell on the back of my hand – you know where. I did not perceive it until the next day, when it was dry.

We buried her without anybody suspecting the truth. I lived in solitude. Who could have controlled my action? She had neither

347

parent nor guardian who could have addressed to me any questions on the subject and I designedly put off sending the customary invitations to the funeral, so that my friends could not arrive in time.

On returning from the vault I felt not the least weight upon my conscience. I had been cruel, but she had deserved it. I would not hate her – I would forget her. I scarcely thought of her. Never did a man commit an assassination with less remorse than I.

The countess, so often mentioned, was at the *château* when I returned there. My measures had been so well taken that she also had arrived too late for the interment. On seeing me she appeared greatly agitated. Terror, sympathy, sorrow, or I know not what, had put so much into her words that I could not understand what she was saying to console me.

Was I even listening to her? Had I any need of consolation? I was not sad. At last she took me familiarly by the hand, and, dropping her voice, said that she was obliged to confide a secret to me, and that she relied on my honour as a gentleman not to abuse it. She had given my wife a packet of letters to mind, not having been able to keep them in her own house; and these letters she now requested me to return to her. While she was speaking, I several times felt a shudder run through my frame. With seeming coolness, however, I questioned her as to the content of the letters. At this interrogation the lady started, and replied angrily:

'Sir, your wife has been more generous than you! When she took charge of *my* letters, she did not demand to know what they contained. She even gave me her promise that she would never set eyes on them, and I am convinced that she never read a line of any one of them. She had a noble heart, and would have been ashamed to forfeit the pledge she had given.'

'Very well,' I replied. 'How shall I recognize this packet.'

'It was tied with a rose-coloured ribbon edged with silver.'

'I will go and search for it.'

I took my wife's keys, knowing perfectly well where I should find the packet; but I pretended to find it with much difficulty.

'Is this it?' I asked the countess handing it to her.

'Yes, yes – that is it! See – the knot I myself made has never been touched.'

I dare not raise my eyes to hers; I feared lest she should read in them that I had untied the knot of the packet and something more.

I took leave of her abruptly; she went to her carriage and drove off.

The drop of blood had disappeared, the pain was not manifested by any external symptom; and yet the spot marked by the drop burned me as if it had been bitten by a corrosive poison. This pain grows from hour to hour. I sleep sometimes, but I never cease to be conscious of my suffering. I do not complain to anybody; nobody, indeed, would believe my story. You have seen the violence of my torment, and you know how much the two operations have relieved me; but concurrently with the healing of the wound, the pain returns. It has now attacked me for the third time, and I have no longer strength to resist it. In an hour I shall be dead. One thought consoles me; it is that she has avenged herself here below. She will perhaps forgive me above. I thank you for all you have done for me.

A few days later one might have read in the newspapers that S——, one of the richest landowners, had blown out his brains. Some attributed his suicide to sorrow caused by the death of his wife; others better informed, to an incurable wound. Those who best knew him said that his incurable wound existed only in his imagination.

Acknowledgments

The Publishers gratefully acknowledge permission granted by the following to reprint the copyright material included in this volume:

The Fruit at the Bottom of the Bowl by Ray Bradbury. Reprinted by permission of Don Congdon Associates, Inc. Copyright © 1948 by Ray Bradbury, renewed in 1976 by Ray Bradbury.

'We Know You're Busy Writing . . .' by Edmund Crispin. From *The Fen Country*. Used by permission of Ann Montgomery, Victor Gollancz Ltd, Walker & Company. Copyright 1979 by Barbara Montgomery.

Back for Christmas by John Collier. From *The Touch of Nutmeg*, published by Readers Club. Reprinted by permission of A. D. Peters & Co. Ltd.

Before the Party by W. Somerset Maugham. From *The Casuarina Tree*. Reprinted by permission of the Executors of the Estate of W. Somerset Maugham, William Heinemann Ltd and Doubleday & Co. Inc. Copyright 1922 by W. Somerset Maugham.

The Evidence of the Altar-Boy by Georges Simenon. Published by Hamish Hamilton Ltd. Reprinted by permission of the author, the publishers and the Secrétariat de Georges Simenon.

Tickled to Death by Simon Brett. Reprinted from *Winter's Crimes 14* by permission of the author and the publishers Macmillan, London Ltd. © 1982 Simon Brett.

Miss Marple Tells a Story by Agatha Christie. Reprinted from *The Regatta Mystery* by permission of Dodd, Mead & Company, Inc. and the author's agents. Copyright 1931, 1934, 1935, 1936, 1937, 1939 by Agatha Christie Mallowan. Copyright renewed 1959, 1962, 1963, 1964, 1965, 1967 by Agatha Christie Mallowan.